MW01125254

The Pleasure of Pain 4
-Written By-
Shameek Speight

Copyright © 2019 by True Glory Publications
Published by True Glory Publications
Join our Mailing List by texting True Glory to
77453 or click here http://eepurl.com/dtX4UL

Facebook: Author Shameek Speight
Instagram: Shameek_speight_

Cover Design: Tina Louise
Editor: Tamyra L. Griffin

Table of Contents

Chapter One

Snow fell from the sky, covering the building and streets of Sound View Projects in the Bronx. The temperature had dropped to -25 degrees, making it one of the coldest winters in New York; too cold for people to be outside. The wind blowing the snow made it even worse.

"Come on, run faster!" Oldrick shouted at his ten-year-old daughter gripping his hand tightly, feeling as if she would fall any second into the lobby floor. Sabrina had on a dark blue snorkel jacket with the hood over her head, knowing it would keep her warm, wishing her father would have let her grab her gloves before rushing her and her sister out of their apartment. She looked up to see her father holding onto her younger sister for dear life. *'Why is he holding Haley so tight, especially, when he normally makes her walk?'* Sabrina thought to herself as she tried to figure out what was going on. Oldrick saw that his daughter was moving slower, as if she was daydreaming.

He tugged on her hand. "Come on Sabrina, this isn't a game!" he shouted.

Oldrick was twenty-nine-years-old, 6'1" and 150 pounds with a cinnamon skin tone; causing him to appear African American. The only way you could tell he was Dominican was if you knew him or heard him speak, revealing his deep Spanish accent. Pushing open the double lobby doors, he ran outside. The snow now came up to his calf, soaking his jeans and making it hard for him to walk; and the extra weight from carrying his daughter Haley really slowed him down. "Daddy where are we going?" Sabrina asked. Not knowing why her father had her running in the snow.

"We have to make it to daddy's truck and get far away from here!" Oldrick shouted while pulling Sabrina along.

The lobby door busts open and a beautiful dark brown skinned woman with black hair steps out of it into the snow holding a short small barrel shotgun, no bigger than someone's forearm. She wore a cream full-length fur coat with matching fur boats, looking like an expensive diva.

"Oldrick, stop fucking running!" Catalina shouts as two of her henchmen came out and stood by her side dressed in all black, with the hoods of their snorkel coats covering their faces. Both were holding AR-15 submachine guns. The snow began to fall even harder, making it almost impossible to see.

"Oldrick! I said stop mutherfucking running!" Catalina shouts in a thick Spanish accent. She looks on at Oldrick trying hard to make it through the thick snow to get away with his kids. "Hijo de puta!" Catalina cursing in Spanish, calling him a mutherfucker as she raised the shotgun and squeezed the trigger.

The shotgun roared. Bright red and orange light came from the muzzle of the gun. More than 49 tiny melt balls flew out the gun with incredible speed and slammed into Oldrick's left leg, blowing it off. His leg detached from his knee cap and flew sideways.

"Ahhh!" Oldrick screams. as the new-found pain traveled through his body. He tries to continue to run or hop but fell face forward into the snow with Haley still in his arms. His daughters both start to cry uncontrollably.

"Daddy, daddy!" Haley cried, crawling out from under him.

Sabrina looks around not knowing what to do. She grabs his hand and pulled. "Daddy get up! Get up!" she shouted.

Oldrick tried to move but couldn't. "Take your sister and run baby. Run." Oldrick said in a weak voice. Blood was gushing from his leg fast, soaking the white snow, causing it to resemble a cherry Italian icy.

Sabrina looked up and could see the lady and her two men coming closer. She stared at her father while crying, feeling as if her tears would freeze on her face. She hugged her father, grabbed her sister's hand and ran. Doing her best not to stumble or trip, she picked up

Haley, even though her sister was only two years younger than her and ran faster.

"Shhh! Stop crying Haley," Sabrina said, running as fast as she could.

"Go fucking get them now!" Catalina said looking at her henchman on the right of her before he took off running in the snow.

Catalina looked like a model walking up to Oldrick. He moaned and groaned in pain as he tried to crawl away until Catalina stepped on his back.

"Now where in the world do you think you're going asshole? Turn your bitch ass around!" Catalina shouted.

Oldrick felt the pressure of her foot leave his back and he slowly turned around. He was now looking up at Catalina and one of her henchmen as they stared down at him.

"You've been loyal to me for five years. Five fucking years; and out the blue you just decide to steal from me. Maybe you been doing it the whole time and just now got caught, huh? It was your job to run this area and keep the fools in this project in check. I never thought you'd cross me. Shit, we grew up together." Catalina spat.

"Fuck you! Pinche puta!" Oldrick screamed, calling her a fucking bitch in Spanish.

"Now is that any way to talk to your baby cousin? Where's my fucking money and the information I need? Where are you hiding it? Catalina asked.

"I won't tell you shit! I'm the oldest, it should be me running Santiago cartel, not you. I'm next in line you bougie bitch." Oldrick shouted.

"That's true, you are older and next in line to head the family business; but you forget two things. One is I have no weaknesses, but you do, those little girls of yours; and two, I have bigger balls then you. If I want something, I take it." Catalina said, aiming and squeezing the trigger, blowing off his right foot.

"Ahhh!" Oldrick screamed at the top of his lungs. "Hijo de puta! Hijo de puta!" he cried out in agonizing pain as he sat up and held his ankle, praying if he squeezed it hard enough the pain would stop. "God please just let me bleed out. I can't take no more." Oldrick mumbled to himself.

Sabrina continued to run with her sister and did her best not to slip in the thick snow. She looked back and could see the tall man chasing them and getting closer.

"Daddy! I want daddy!" Haley cried.

"Shhhh! Daddy will find us, but we can't let the bad men get us." Sabrina said as she turned the corner then ran into the street, knowing it would be easier to walk there than the sidewalk because the city workers come by in trucks every hour in a snow storm and plows the snow to the side of the road.

Feeling herself slipping a few times in the black ice, Sabrina said to herself, *'I'm not going be able to out run him. Think. Think Sabrina.'*. Looking behind them, she saw the henchmen hadn't caught up yet and made it around the corner to the block. Seeing the solution to their problem, Sabrina smiled, ran across the street and put down her sister. Both of them crawled under a truck and laid low.

"Sabrina I'm cold on the ground like this. It's wet, and I'm hungry. I want daddy." Haley whined as tears filled her eyes.

"No, we have to stay here. Think of it as a game of Hide and Go Seek. We can't let no one find us until daddy calls for us." Sabrina replied, whispering for Haley to be quiet.

She could hear the snow making a crushing sound, letting her know someone heavy was walking nearby. She looked and could see the man's giant black boot. He was walking in the street looking down as if he was trying to follow her foot prints, before a loud boom could be heard echoing through the neighborhood followed by a man's piercing screams. Sabrina and Haley recognized the voice instantly.

"That's papi. He needs us. Daddy! Daddy," Haley said and crawled from up under the truck.

"No wait! No Haley. No!" Sabrina yelled, but it was too late. Haley stood up from up under the truck and was now in the middle of the street.

"Got you!" the henchmen said as he ran up and grabbed Haley by the legs. Picked her up, he hung her upside down, dangling her in the air like a rag doll.

"Daddy help me! Help me Sabrina!" Haley screamed.

'Why couldn't she just listen to me? Daddy's going to kill me.' Sabrina said to herself and looked around under the truck for anything she could use as a weapon. She noticed four pieces of long thick icicles, so she reached and grabbed the longest and thickest one. Sabrina pulled it until it snapped free from the truck then touched the point of it.

"Ouch." she mumbled.

Crawling from underneath the truck, the tall man grabbed her right of way. "It's too damn cold for me to be chasing y'all." he said as he dangled both girls in the air as if they weighed nothing at all.

"Put me down! Put us down! Daddy! Daddy!" Sabrina shouted while trying to breathe as he held her by the neck choking her.

"Your daddy ain't going to do shit." the henchmen seethed.

"Help us! Daddy, Sabrina help me!" Haley cried out.

Sabrina's facial expression tightened in anger knowing what she has to do. She gripped the cold icicle as the man brought her closer to his face and prepared to swing.

"Aghhh!" she screamed as her world went black when the tall man head butted her. Her head throbbed, and a speed not popped up on her forehead. It felt as if it had split open.

"Y'all stop squirming around." he said as he held them tight and stomped through the snow.

Catalina smiled at the sight of her henchman approaching with Oldrick's daughters before looking down at him. "Now cousin, are you going to talk so I can get out the cold, or do I have to hurt your daughters? I really don't want to, they're family; but you know I would." Catalina stated.

Oldrick turned his head around and could see Haley moving around trying to break free, but Catalina's henchman had her tucked under his arm.

"No, don't hurt them. I'll tell you everything," Oldrick said.

"Good cousin. Start talking already. I got things to do, people to kill, and a spa appointment to keep. If I like what you tell me, I'll let your children live." Catalina said through clenched teeth.

Oldrick took a deep breath as he held on to life and looked at his daughters once more. Sabrina looked to be knocked out. Lowering his head, he began to speak.

"When the Teflon Divas killed Anador and his family, is when the title of boss passed to you; but the story was the Teflon Divas started to kill each other afterwards and only one lived. I was paying people to find out which one, because I was going to pay her to kill your bougie ass. Why would I want to be ruled by a woman? Y'all think life's a fucking fashion show. It should be a man that runs the Santiago Family." Oldrick said.

"And look what happened with the men running the business; almost wiped is out." Catalina replied as she processed what she just hard. *If a Teflon Diva is still alive and made it out of the Dominican Republic, this could be a huge problem. They pretty much killed my whole family line and if it's Tess or Iris, I'll have a big issue. I need more info. I need to know which one survived and kill them,'* Catalina thought to herself.

"Oldrick what else you know?" Catalina asked.

Oldrick coughed up blood. "I don't know anything else; just that she'll be on a flight to New York today." Oldrick said as he reached in his jack pocket and grabbed the handle to his 9mm Taurus. "You should never threaten a man's family." he said as he pulled the 9mm Taurus out his pocket, aimed and squeezed the trigger twice. Two hollow point bullets flew out the gun and slammed into Catalina's chest.

"Ugh! Ahh!" she screamed in pain as it felt as if someone hit her with a sledge hammer, lifting her up in the air as she flew backwards from the impact.

Aiming for Oldy's head, she squeezed the trigger and the shotgun roared once more, exploding his head like a watermelon being thrown to the ground. His brain matter, along with pieces of his face and skull splattered everywhere. Sabrina started squirming around with the sound of the loud gunshot waking her. She slowly opened her eyes and her head began to spin. Looking around and finally focusing on what was left of her father, she began to scream.

"Papi! Papi!"

Her heart felt as if it broke in half. Looking at her hand to see if she still had the icicle, she used all her strength to pull her body up until she reached the tall man's face and swung with all her might.

"Ahhhh!" The tall man hollered in excruciating pain as the sharp icicle ripped through the flesh of his ear and punctured his eardrum. "Ahhh! Ahh fuck! Fuck!" he continued to screamed before tossing Sabrina into the building's brick wall.

"Ughhh!" Sabrina groaned in pain as it felt like every bone in her back broke and the oxygen left her lungs from the impact of hitting the wall. She laid in the snow and looked up in time to see her sister flying through the air. Haley hit the wall twice as hard as she did, maybe because she was lighter, or the fact the tall henchmen was angry. Sabrina didn't know.

"No." Sabrina cried out while trying to move and sit up but couldn't. She crawled to her sister and shook her, but Haley wasn't crying or moving.

"Get up Haley. Get up." Sabrina said while shaking her, noticing for the first time her head was split wide open.

The impact had broken her ribs, causing them to pierced her lungs. She was breathing funny, and Sabrina knew something was completely wrong with her. It was the first time she wasn't crying. Sabrina crawled closer and could see the blood leaking out the back of her sister's head. he quickly lifted her sister's head and held the wound with her pink mitten, which was now red from Haley's blood.

"Help! Help us!" Sabrina shouted then looked down at her sister. "You're going be okay. You're going be okay." Sabrina said while crying.

She stared into her sister's eyes and could see blood where it should've been white. Haley looked at her sister and begged for help with her body language and facial expression. Haley's breath became shorter by the second. She looked like a fish out of the water, fighting for their life. Sabrina looked at her sister's chest, not understanding what was going on. Her breathing sounds like hiccups and continued to slow down. Haley looked into her sister's eyes and the tears that ran down the side of her little cheeks was the color of blood. She took one last breath and stopped moving altogether.

"Haley! Haley wake up! Haley wake up!" Sabrina cried hysterically while rocking her sister back and forth, waiting for her to open her eyes; but she didn't, causing Sabrina to cry even harder. "Wake up! Please wake up. I'll let you play with my toys. You can even play with my phone and I promise I won't get mad. I promise. Just wake up, please." Sabrina cried as she sat in the snow, soaked in her little sister's blood.

The tall henchman finally manged to pull the icicle from his ear and could her a ringing sound that wouldn't stop. He unzipped his jacket, pulled out a Smith and Wesson 49 caliber hand gun, aimed it at Sabrina and squeeze the trigger. The bullet slammed into Sabrina's stomach and ripped out her back. To his surprise, she didn't scream out in pain or die. She looked up at him with tears in her eyes.

"Look what you did to my sister." she said while pointing to Haley before leaning back over to her. "Get up Haley. Get up please. l love you." Sabrina said in a weak voice as her eye lids got heavy and she turned to look at the tall henchmen aiming at her face.

Boom! The sound of a loud gunshot echoed through the block and the tall henchman's stomach exploded, sending his guts and flying into Sabrina.

"Ughhh! What the fuck! Why?" the tall henchman said as he flew face forward, dead.

Catalina walked over to him and aimed for the back of his head, "I didn't give you the order to kill them." she mumbled and squeezed the trigger, blowing his head into tiny pieces. "Damnit, his blood got on my fur coat. Blood don't come out easy. Shit." Catalina said. "Felipe, I'm going to need you to send some men to the airport and find out which Teflon Divas is alive and kill her." Catalina stated.

"Yes." Felipe replied.

"Please wake up. Haley, please wake up." Catalina and Felipe heard a little voice say. They turned their heads to see it was Sabrina laying across her sister's lap, still shaking her dead stiff body.

"Grab the girl and call the doctor before she bleeds to death or make me cry." ordered Catalina.

"Yes boss." Felipe replied

Chapter Two

Tears flowed continuously from Layla's eyes. "I can't believe it, I'm the only one left. Tess, Vanessa, Ebony, and even that bitch Iris was all the family I ever knew or had in this world." Layla mumbled to herself while trying to hold back her tears, knowing it was only matter of time before she fully broke down mentally.

"Please return to your seats and fasten your seat belts. We will be landing in ten minutes. Thank you for flying with Delta Airlines." a voice said over the loud speaker.

"Are you okay?" Layla heard a voice ask. She turned her head to see a beautiful dark chocolate flight attendant.

"No, but I will be." she replied.

Layla stepped off the plane and felt a sense of belonging. "Damn. It feels like a lifetime ago since I been home to New York. I swear you can live everywhere in the world, but nothing like being home." Layla said to herself as she watched how busy the airport was, and how everyone rushing but going nowhere fast.

From the airport window she could see her plane and the workers unloading the two small coffins holding Iris and Ebony, that would head to the cemetery in east new your Brooklyn. Layla turned her head to pay attention to her environment at the airport. She missed the woman climbing out the cargo hold of the plane where the coffins were kept.

"Hey you, stop! What are you doing here?" a tall, slim Caucasian man with dark brown hair wearing an orange vest and hat asked with a confused look on his face. He grabbed his walkie-talkie to report the strange, beautiful woman who looked as if she caught a free flight; but before he could, Iris punched him in the throat.

"Ugghh!" The man gagged for air, holding his chest.

Iris moved in closer, and in one swift move she used one hand to grab his chin and the other at the top of his head as she twisted. A loud cracking sound was heard, sounding like the breaking of a thick twig off a tree. The man's eyes rolled to the back of his head as soon as his neck snapped, and his body fell limp to the hard ground. Iris quickly looked around to make sure she wasn't seen then grabbed his legs.

"Ugh! Fuck! Fuck!" she screamed in pain while dragging him back into the cargo hold on the plane. The stitches in her chest and back ripped slowly, and she could feel them pop one by one. "God damn!" she screamed.

Using only one arm to remove his vest and hat, Iris grabbed his security ID card and exited the plane with the hat low over her forehead.

'I'm gonna need time to heal before I kill Layla. In this condition I'm no match for her. There's no telling how long Tess been secretly training her to be fucking mini version of herself.' Iris said to herself sarcastically while rolling her eyes, feeling blood starting to drip from the wound. *'I've got to find a doctor and just wait. Then I'll finish this once and for all.'* She continued thinking as she blended in with the crowd at the airport, made her way to the front door and hopped into a cab.

"Where to miss?" a brown skin man asked in a deep Indian accent.

"Home!" Iris replied.

"Where's home?" the cab driver asked, looking in the review mirror as if she was dumb or on crack. "How the hell am I supposed to know where home is?"

"Take me to east New York. Brooklyn." Iris said while squinting her eyes.

'I'm going kill his curry eating ass as soon as we reach Brooklyn.' she thought as she felt around and found a black pen jammed between the backseat

cushions and grabbed it. Twenty minutes later, they'd arrived in Brooklyn.

"That will be $80." the cab driver said as he pulled up on a side block on Blake ave.

Iris dug in her pocket and grab a few twenty-dollar bills as she fussed. "Fucking $80 from Queens to Brooklyn? That why everybody using Uber now and you'll fuckers are going out of business."

"Just giving my money you stupid Spanish bitch and get out my car before I call the cops; and I hope one of those Uber drivers rape you!" the cab driver shouted in his deep accent and was about to say something else until Iris jammed the pen into his right eye. "Ahhhh! Ahhh!" he yelled out in excruciating pain while holding his face. "You bitch! I'm calling the cops!"

Iris smirked. "See, that's why you in the position you're in now; your fucking attitude and that mouth. You don't know how to speak to a woman; and wishing rape on me. I've been raped. You never wish that on any one!" Iris shouted and stood frozen for a second as she had flashbacks of her father rapping her every night as a child. Then it all stopped once she met Bless.

Iris took a deep breath as she thought of him, then snap back into reality from the screaMs. of the cab driver.

"I was going to kill you fast, but you fucked that up now." Iris spat then grabbed the cabdriver by the neck.

He gagged for air as thick blood dripped from his eye and he slowly lost consciousness. Iris looked around then dragged him out the cab and into a small stash house.

A tingling feeling, as if butterflies were flying around in her stomach mixed with nausea overcame her. Tess always said listen to your gut.

"Something's fucking wrong." Layla mumble to herself, then began to scan looking around the airport to see if anyone was out of place.

As she walked at a slow pace, she noticed a young couple that looked to be twenty-five years old, kissing on each other but watching her from the corner of their eyes.

"Fucking rookies. Ain't no one that damn happy in a relationship. I ain't believe that shit." Layla mumble to herself and continued to look around.

Years as an assassin had taught her a lot. She spotted four more men watching her, a bald-headed man acting like he was reading a newspaper, and three following. *'Damn! What the hell is this? They're not cops and all look to be Latino. We killed all the heads from the*

Santiago Cartel, and no one knows I'm alive. As far as the world knows, The Teflon Divas died in the Dominican Republic.' Layla thought to herself as she spotted a sign for the women's bathroom. She quickly dashed in, unzipped her duffle bag to grab her Kevlar Bullet-proof custom body suit and quickly undressed to put it on before sliding back on her Fashion Nova jeans and black blouse.

"They said this bitch was supposed to be a big deal. The boss said we need twenty soldiers or more to stop her; but this going be a piece of cake, she trapped herself in the bathroom. I hope we get a bonus for killing the last Teflon Diva. To think the world thought they was some dangerous bitches." the young man pretending to be coupled with a dirty blonde hair woman said.

"Benjamin, shut the fuck up. You know nothing about the Teflon Divas. I looked up to them. They represent strong women; and that we don't have to be victims. That we can be assassins and more." the woman replied.

"Rosa, you sound like a groupie bitch." Benjamin replied, causing Rosa to raise her right eyebrow.

"You know what, you go in there by yourself stupid." she spat with an attitude."

"No, I'll go in with him." the 6'2 tall bald head henchmen said in a deep voice.

He looked to weight about 280 pounds. Rosa's facial expressions twisted up just looking at him. He looked like a killer or a wrestler, one.

"Come on, let do this. You play look out and make sure no one else is in the bathroom; with your groupie ass." Benjamin stated as him and the bald henchman pulled out Smith and Weston handguns from, they waists.

Screwing silencers on their guns, they entered the bathroom. The woman's bathroom was very clean, with bright white walls and smelled of lavender Fabulous mixed with White Diamonds perfume. Right away the two men scanned the bathroom, spotting Layla's black duffle bag in the third bathroom stall under the closed bathroom door. Benjamin smirked and looked at his giant partner and nodded his head, suggesting their next move. Taking aim and squeezing the trigger, Smith and Wesson 9mm and bullets whistled from the silencer and slammed into the closed stall door, turning the door into Swiss cheese. Stopping after a few seconds, they looked down on the ground under the stall to see if there was any blood, but there wasn't. The giant bald-headed henchman kicked open the stall door, and both men stood there wearing a look of shock on their faces.

"Where is she?! Where that bitch at?! She couldn't have gotten past us, we seen here go in. Check the other stalls!" Benjamin shouted at bald head, frustration evident in his voice, who just stared at him.

'Who the hell this lil muthafucka talking to? I'll snap his fuckin' neck.' Bald head thought but didn't say a word. Kicking in the second stall door, there was no one there.

Layla smiled while looking down at the two men. *'Fucking amateurs.'* she said to herself before activating the spike in her Kelver cat body suit. Six hard, sharp plastic spears came from each side of the body suit's forearm. *'Shit! I wish I had my good suit with the metal spikes and blades; but I had to ship that one through Ups to a p.o. box because I couldn't get it through the airport. This suit should do for now though. The plastic spikes as strong as they come.'* Layla through to herself while continuing to smirk while looking at the two stupid men. She had used the spike a few seconds ago the help her climb the wall and was now spread out gripping the ceiling while looking down at them both. She released her grip and let herself fall. Benjamin heard something and looked up, but it was too late to react.

"Oh shitttt!" he managed to say before Layla's body weight crashed down on top of him. "Ughh!" he groaned in pain and was unable to move.

"Got you, you little fucker!" Layla said, prepared to stab him with the forearm spikes in her suit as he lay there on the floor with her on top of him.

She quickly realized she moved too slow when she felt a giant hand back slap her, sending her 5'4 and 150 pounds body flying up in the air backwards.

"Fuckkk!" she hollered as she hit the wall so hard pieces of tile cracked and fell, leaving an imprint of her body.

'Shake it off Layla and fight! Fight for your life with every breath, because it could be your last.' Layla could hear Tess' voice echoed in her mind, and flashbacks of when they would train together flashed before her eyes. How Tess would beat her ass but would still make her get up and fight until she couldn't no more; until she got good enough that she no longer was getting her ass whipped, but instead put up a good fight that match her mother figure.

Layla smirked as she quickly rose from the ground, raising her arms. and crossed them into an X, using her forearms. to block her face just as Bald Head aimed at her and squeezed the trigger rapidly; sending seven bullets whistling out the silencer towards her. The first two slammed into her stomach area but bounce right off impenetrable Kevlar catsuit she had on. The next slammed into her legs but did little to stop her from now charging full speed toward the henchmen. Bald Head looked on with fear in his eyes, not knowing whether to run or scream as he witnessed this little woman not even half his size running toward him without stopping, with the bullets doing little to slow her down. He back pedaled but had nowhere to go. The women's bathroom was only so big.

The last two shots hit her forearms., which were still crossed into an X to protect her face. Bald Head continued to back up until he hit the wall, and fire two more shots before screaming.

"Ahhh! Ahhh!" he yelled loudly, hoping to draw attention and stop her from killing him.

"Oh, don't scream now you big pussy!" Layla shouted as she dropped down to her knees, sliding across the smooth bathroom floor and sending an upper cut to his balls before raising her forearm. The hard-plastic spikes tore through his jeans shredding his ball sack and splitting his penis in half.

"Ahhhhh! Ahhhhhh!" the giant henchman hollered in excruciating pain as he looked down to see one of his balls landed on Layla's lap and the other torn to pieces. "Ahhh! Ahhh you little bitch! You fucking little bitch!" he screamed, holding his groin area as blood rushed from it.

Hopping to her feet, the ball that landed on her lap hit the floor. Looking down at it she stomped it, squishing it like a large cockroach. "Who you calling a bitch? You were screaming before I even reached your big ass. Now tell me who sent you!" Layla shouted, and before she could attack again the giant henchmen grabbed her, locking both arms. around her and began to squeeze the air out her with a bear hug.

"I will break every bone in your body before I bleed out, you tiny bitch!" Bald Head said in a deep voice.

"Ughh!"

Layla gasped for air and was barely able to breath. Every time she exhaled, he squeezed tighter, making it almost impossible to inhale and get her lungs filled with air. *'No! I can't go out like this! I'm a Teflon Diva. The last; and was taught by the best. What would she do?'* Layla thought to herself as training from Tess began to replay in her mind.

Tess was trapped by Layla in a leather whip, wrap up like a helpless pig.

"I finally got you. You have no more weapons, and soon you'll pass out from lack of oxygen." Layla stated as she stepped closer to Tess while pulling the end of the whip and wrapping it around her arm.

"See, that's where you're wrong." Tess replied while trying to breath and Layla stepped even closer. "We're Warriors. We don't need weapons. We are the weapon!" Tess shouted before popping up, head butting Layla in the face and unwrapping herself before flipping her to the ground. "Remember, you're the weapon. Everything else is a tool we use. A woman is the deadliest, most fearless weapon in this world." Tess said while looking down at her.

"Ugh!" Layla grunted in pain, snapping back into reality as the giant henchmen squeezed tighter.

Noticing a smile on Layla's pretty face, he grunted, "Why are you smiling? You're about to die."

"That where your wrong!" Layla shouted, sending her forehead flying into his nose then sent it into his mouth twice, breaking a tooth.

The lose tooth fell loose and into his mouth before he began choking on it. Blood gushed from his nose, running like a faucet. His eyes watered up, making him to be unable to see. Loosening the bear hug, Layla quickly climbed up out of his arms. as if she was climbing a tall thick tree, then leap up in the air and wrapped her legs around his neck; twisting and turning while leaning backwards. Using her weight, she flips him to the ground. She then sat on his chest grabbing his shirt and head butt him repeatedly in the face.

"I am the weapon! I am the weapon! I am the weapon!" she shouted over and over as she slammed her head into his nose breaking it then his jaw.

A cracking sound echoed throughout the bathroom. The henchman tried to raise his arms. to protect his face, but she smacked them down and continued her assault. Blood shot everywhere as the bones in his face cracked and his cheek bone shattered.

Rose knew that Benjamin and the big stupid looking bald-headed   giant were no match for the Teflon Diva. The longer it took for them to emerge from the bathroom, the greater the chances were that they'd met their demise. *'Damn. Should I really even care if she killed them?'* Rose thought to herself before deciding to enter the bathroom.

She pulled out her 9 mm Taurus with a silencer attached and headed into the bathroom. Her eyes shot wide open in shock and disgust when she saw Benjamin knocked out on the floor a few inches from her, and not further down a pretty light brown skin woman on top of what looked to be left of the Bald Head. Her face and chest area were soaked in blood as she continue to headbutt the giant henchmen as if he stole her lunch money or hurt a family member or something.

"I'm the weapon! I'm the weapon!" Layla shouted.

"Uhmm, I thought you Teflon Divas were some type of discipline paid assassins that barely lose their cool." Rose said with her face twisted up.

The sound of her voice made Layla jump back into attack mode, rolling forward in a tumble and grabbing the gun the bald head henchmen dropped when she smashed his balls, aiming it at Rose.

"Wow! Whoa, slow down! I didn't come in here for all that." Rose stated and lowered her gun.

"Oh yeah? It doesn't look like that. You have a gun and I have the drop on you. What's stopping me from killing you right now?" Layla asked with blood dripping from her chin.

"Well, for one, I want to join you. I want to be a Teflon Diva. I want you to teach me." Rose replied.

Layla studied the woman and could tell she was in her early twenties. She was Dominican and Haitian, but the Haitian side dominate more according to her complexion. She had dark brown skin, 5'6, and had to weight close to 180 pounds. Solid, thick shape, and in head about four bundles of weave that hung down her back. She also noticed a long scar on her forehead. She was a beautiful woman with lost eyes.

"I'm not looking for anyone to join me. Besides, you have a boss. Who sent y'all?" Layla asked while aiming for her left eye.

"I don't have a boss anymore. I want out and want to run with you, but I was part of the Santiago Cartel. There are about seventeen more soldiers around this airport and outside of it with orders to kill you. I can help you. I have a car, and I know where most of the men are posted at. I'm tired of being treated like I'm weak. Speaking of weak, I thought y'all were better killers. What the fuck was that?" Rose asked while pointing at what was left the giant henchmen laying in a pool of his own blood.

"Uhmm, I lost it for a second, but you try not to. After the only people you know as family are killed by someone, we called family… Give me your car keys;

that's how you can help." Layla said while scratching at her hand to get the keys.

Rose dig in her pocket, then out of nowhere raised her gun. Layla hesitated. *'Damnit! You're never supposed to hesitate. I didn't get a bad vibe with her and don't want to kill her; but shit, Iris was a sneak and we didn't get a bad vibe from her for years, until it was too late. Is this that moment? Will my weakness cost me my life?'* Layla thought to herself, knowing she moved too slow and Rose had gotten off one shot. Layla squeezed the trigger and sent a bullet slamming into Rose's shoulder, causing her to stumble backwards and drop her gun.

"Ahh! Bitch, you shot me! You really shot me, you fucking traitor!" Layla heard a man's voice boom from behind her.

She swiftly spun around to see Benjamin clenching his chest and then drop on to his knees. While Layla and Rose were talking, he regained consciousness and tried to seize the perfect opportunity. Layla was distracted, and Benjamin could tell she was off her game today. Any other day he might've already been dead. He knew that after the brief encounter he had with her; but with Rose distracting her, he raised his gun to shoot her in the back of the head, only to have a bullet rip through his chest and out his back.

"You bitch." he groaned once more.

It took Layla only a second to realize what had taken place. "You saved me." Layla stated.

"Yeah, duh; and you fucking shot me." Rose replied while holding her shoulder.

"Stop crying. I don't miss, and I mean never. So, if I wanted you dead, you'd be dead. Quit bitching, I shot you in your arm. Now let's go; and don't try nothing funny. We been in this bathroom far too long and security will notice." Layla said while grabbing her duffle off the floor before lifting Rose up.

She washed her face in the sink then passed Rose a jacket before both exited the airport and made their way to the parking lot. Layla pulled the car keys she'd gotten from Rose out her pocket then hit the alarm. "Really? How cliché can you get; a fucking Honda? I thought you work for the cartel, and you driving a Honda? That's what they say all Latinos drive." Layla stated.

"Shit, it's all I can afford; and it's a Honda Accord. That shit fast and good on gas; and I already told you I get treated like shit in the Santiago Cartel. Rose said in pain. Her shoulder was throbbing and leaking.

"This should be fun." Layla said shaking her head.

"We only got two guns, and once we pull out of this airport the other soldiers will attack. What the hell are we going do?" Rose asked.

"What you mean we?!" Layla perked.

"I just crossed the cartel. No one ever crosses a cartel and lives to talk about it. Shit, that guy I shot, we were kind of seeing each; but he was an asshole anyway and kept belittling me." Rose stated.

"So, you crossed the cartel and shot your boyfriend? Damn Rose, you making so easy to trust you; but I got this. Just be ready to shoot." Layla replied.

Chapter Three

New Friends and Old Enemy

"Ahhhh! This shit hurt. I need a doctor!" Rose shouted while crying and leaning back in the passenger seat, applying pressure to the hole in her shoulder. "You couldn't have just killed me and got it over with? Ugh!" Rose moaned.

"Shut up with the crying. Pain is a part of life, especially a woman's life; and you say you want to be a Teflon Diva. You're going to get shot, stabbed or hurt." Layla spat.

"How y'all always got the suit on; and I'll never get a chance, because where going die as soon as we leave. We're as good as dead. We're outnumbered." Rose stated.

"You're a real downer, ugh. That blows my mind, but I told you we got this. I have some friends." Layla stated, picking up the phone and placed a call. "Hello. Yeah, it's Layla. I can't make it there, I'm going be too hot. Try the borderline between Queens and Brooklyn." Layla said.

"Me and brother got you." Rose heard a male voice reply before hanging up.

"Who was that? I didn't know Teflon Divas have friends." Rose said.

"You sound stupid. I'm starting to reconsider why I didn't just shoot you in the head; but yes, we have friends, and I wasn't always an assassin. I used to run these streets with Tess; but I've said too much. Let's do this." Layla said before starting up the car and driving off.

Once she left JFK Airport, Layla immediately knew she made a mistake and there was no way she was going to make it to the borderline between Brooklyn and Queens. There were three black Cadillac Escalades, one black Chrysler 300, and a black Porsche following the car.

'There's no way in hell we're gonna outrun a damn Porsche in this fuckin' Honda.' Layla texted quickly and then stomped on the gas.

"I told you we're dead. At least we won't go out like punks." Rose said as she sat up, turned around and pulled down the back seats to reveal a chrome short barrel pump shotgun and one black automatic Shotgun with a hundred round drum. She passed the short barrel shotgun to Layla and grabbed the automatic shotgun for herself, attaching the magazine to it.

"What the fuck up with all these shotguns?" Layla asked and laugh.

"Laugh if you want. I love shotguns. I can never miss, and the damage they do is amazing." Rose replied just as one of the Escalades picked up speed and pulled next to them on the passenger side. The windows rolled down and the barrel of an AK-47 stuck out the driver's window and the rear driver side window.

"Lean back!" Layla shouted, stretching her arm out across Rose and aimed out the passenger side window.

Gripping the 9mm Smith Weston, she squeezed the trigger once and a bullet slammed into the back tire; causing it to pop and the truck to swerve. Before the driver could regain control, Layla squeezed the trigger twice. The first bullet slammed into the front tire, ripping it to shreds. The second billet slammed into the driver's temple, killing him instantly. His dead body slouched, and his foot mashed down on the gas. The Escalade twisted and swerved, while the shooter in the passenger seat tried to grab the steering wheel; but it was too late. The truck flipped and rolled four times before landing upside down and sliding. Layla sent another bullet slamming into the gas tank for good measure. Gas began to pour out the hole with rapid speed and hit the spark on the road cause by the truck sliding. The remaining four henchmen trapped inside screamed as the Escalade exploded. The ones that didn't die from the explosion burnt alive in the matter of seconds.

"Damn, your fucking good." Rose said with her eyes wide open, not believing what she just seen.

"See, you can never miss with small bullets too. Maybe I'll teach you one day." Layla said with a smirk on her face, turning a hard left as the other two Escalades tailed closely behind her. "Who's in the 911 Porsche; because he could have been caught up with us and blocked us in by now." Layla asked while looking through the review window a little confused.

"That will be Flacco, he's Catalina's lieutenant. Very ruthless, but intelligent. He gets off of cutting people with razors and killing. He's not going move in on you yet. I always thought he was kind of pussy. One of those dudes that need twenty niggas with him before he popped off, or so he can show off, but the repetition of the Teflon Divas are well known. He'll wait until your badly hurt or cornered than attack, so he can go back taking credit for killing you." Rose stated.

"Hmmm. Well he's not that smart." Layla replied then turned onto Main Street and made a right turn down a dead-end block.

The first house's garage door was open, so Layla drove in fast and press a button and shut the garage door.

"Come on, move! Move fast or we're dead! Layla shouted as they exited the car and entered the house.

Rose move a little slow as she try to bear the pain, she was in. They ran to the living room, where Rose saw an AR- 15 assault rifle with a scope resting by a window with a few magazines resting on the floor.

"How's Flacco stupid when you just trapped us in a house? We're dead." Rose stated.

"You have a lot to learn." Layla replied with a laugh. "Make sure no one gets through that front door." She added while dropping to one knee and aiming out the window as she watched the two Cadillac Escalades pull up on the dead-end block. Five men arm with AK-47's hopped out of each truck. They'd already seen what house Layla and Rose went in. There were six homes on each side on the Cul de sac styled block. The henchmen scanned the block as the Chrysler 300 pulled up and a few more men jumped out. Flacco watched his men and drove up slowly, but still kept his distance at the same time.

"This gonna be too easy; but why did she run here? Hmm. It's really not gonna matter. I'll bring the Teflon Diva's dead body to Catalina along with that trader bitch Rose's body. It's a win situation. Flacco said out loud to himself in a smooth Spanish accent, then felt something was wrong. His heart race as he looked around trying to figure out what it could be.

"Get down!" Layla shouted to Rose as the cartel henchmen opened fire, sending bullets tearing through the house just as Rose dove to the floor.

"I told you we're dead. It's been an honor to meet you and actually ride with a Teflon Diva." Rose said as tears fell down her face.

"Don't give up yet. The fun is just about to start." Layla said while smiling. For the life of her, Rose couldn't understand why Layla was so relaxed.

"Please tell me already." Rose said with a confused look on her face as she laid on the floor and bullets flew pass her head.

"It's easy. The cartel soldiers didn't pay attention to their environment and allowed us to bring them to a dead-end block." was Layla's response.

"And how does that help us? It just gives us nowhere to run." Rose replied.

"You're wrong. The fish only sees the worm, not the hook when they get trapped; so those henchmen and yourself, only saw the bait, not the trap"

As soon as the worlds left her mouth, an eighteen-wheel truck came speeding down the block and turned sideways, blocking the only way out the dead-end street. Flacco's heart raced, feeling as if it would beat out his chest. Men and women, some with blue bandannas wrapped around their mouth to conceal their face and some with red bandannas doing the same, hung out the windows and some on the roof of the truck. "East side Blood! East side Crip!" the group shouted and opened fire. The henchmen were caught in a crossfire. Bullets were slamming into them from the left and right side. Four ran towards the house Layla and Rose were in. Layla squeezed the trigger and send a bullet flying. It tore through one of the henchmen and exited out the back of his head, leaving a huge hole. Before he could register what had happened, she sent another bullet through his heart, killing him before hitting the ground. She squeezed the trigger once more and a bullet crash into another henchman's stomach, which came out his side.

"Ahhhhh! Ahhhh!" he hollered in pain but was quickly silenced by a bullet entering his open mouth and exited out the back of his throat. He twisted sideways, fell to the ground and began to shake as if he was having a seizure before he stopped moving all together.

"Ahhh!!" Rose screamed as the front door was shot open and two of the cartel's henchmen ran in.

"I told you to guard the door!" Layla shouted, not knowing if she should turn her gun on Rose or the henchmen as thoughts of her setting her up played out in her mind.

Rose popped up off the floor from watching the action outside. For the second time that day, couldn't believe her eyes. The cartel soldiers were being gunned down like trapped animal with nowhere to go by a street gang. Rose snap back to reality and squeezed the trigger to her automatic shotgun five times, and the shotgun roared life. Pellets from the bullet blasted a hole in the first henchman's chest, then the second shot blew off his arms. and some finger on his left hand. The third bullet slammed into the henchmen's face, causing it to explode as if someone dropped a watermelon off a roof. Pieces of his skull, bone matter and brain tissue flew onto Rose face and into her mouth. Spitting it out, she continued firing. Her last shot didn't do much damage, due to the bulletproof vest the henchman wore. He aimed for Rose's head and she fire. A loud explosion sounded off as the pellets slammed into the henchman's AK-47, blowing it to pieces along with both his hands.

"Ahhhh… you bitch! Stupid hoe!" He stood there cursing in Spanish with raw meat and blood hanging where his arms. should be.

Rose aimed and fired twice, sending pellets ripping through his left leg, blowing it off at the knee cap. She fired again, doing the same to his other leg.

"Ahhh! Ahhh!" the henchmen cried out in Spanish at the excruciating pain from the floor as Rose aimed for his head, blowing it to pieces. \

"I guess you are good with that thing. Very messy I see, but I can work with it and teach you some things." Layla said while wiping a pieces raw, bloody flesh from her chest area that flew on her.

"Death to all!" another henchman shouted while running towards the doorway. He didn't make it fully into the house.

Rose aim and fired. The shotgun roared, and the powerful blast sliced him in half while pushing him backwards out the door. While the last of the henchmen was being gun down, Flacco drove forward while shooting out the window of his 911 Porsche, sending a bullet in to the check bone of a guy wearing a Blue bandanna. Flacco made a swift U-turn and stepped on the gas, taking off at full speed.

"I refuse to die out here!" he shouted while ducking low and dodging bullets as they rip through his car.

The Porsche was so low to the ground it was able to go up under the eighteen-wheel truck with no issue. Flaco busted a hard right and speed down the stip.

"I'm gonna get those bitches, I swear. Thinking they out smarted me and got me running; but I'd rather run now and live to fight another day. No one can stop the Santiago Cartel." Flacco said through clenched teeth while checking his review mirror.

Rose sat on the floor breathing hard. "I need a doctor." she mumbled in pain.

"Just hold on a little longer. I'll take care of you, I promise." Layla said as two men entered what used to be the front door.

One was a brown complexion with braids, with an all red bandanna around his face that he removed and wore as a scarf. You could tell he was mixed but was more Spanish, and very handsome. When he smiled you could see the dimple showing off in his cheek. The second one was a dark, smooth chocolate complexion with a blue New York fitted hat and blue bandanna around his face that he removed. Smiling, he showed off a set of perfect white teeth.

"Damn." Rose mumbled as her pussy throbbed from looking at him.

"I thought we'd never see you again." the brown skin one said as he lifted Layla off her feet, hugging her tightly before the dark one did the same.

"Ughhmm." Rose cleared her throat as if saying are you going to introduce me.

"Oh yeah. Rose, these are the two of the realest gangsters I know. This is Red banger and Blue banger; the famous Banger Brothers."

"Oh snap! I've heard of them. They brought the Crips and Bloods together; but damn, I didn't know Blue would be so damn handsome." Rose said while smiling.

"Thank you beautiful." Blue replied.

"Now isn't the time for chit chat. We can get caught up in a more comfortable environment." Red banger stated.

"You're absolutely right." Layla agreed as she and Rose went through the kitchen, into the garage and hopped into the Honda Accord.

"I'll text you the address. Send the doctor." Layla said as she started up the car and opened the garage door.

"What the fuck!" Rose exclaimed.

To her surprise, all the dead bodies from the Santiago Cartel were gone but two. Fours Bloods and Crips could be see dragging the last two bodies and tossing them into the back of the eighteen-wheeler truck. Even the bullet's shells on the ground was gone, and the cartel vehicles.

"What the fuck! H... How?" Rose stuttered.

"Their good at what they do. Ten minutes from now no one will be able to tell what happened here. They've got most of the police on payroll, and they own all the homes on this block. Layla said as they drove past two Crip soldiers pressure washing the street, and some blood soldiers throwing bleach onto the ground as the eighteen-wheeler truck pulled off with all the dead bodies locked in the back of the trailer.

"I've always heard stories of the Banger Brothers, and to be honest, I didn't think they were real. Two brothers from different gangs actually getting along together? How do you know them?" Rose asked.

Layla sat quiet for a second as her heart raced. "My mother Tess or the woman who became my mother, we weren't always assassins, but drug dealers. That's how we got into some of the drama with the Santiago Cartel. They were one of our suppliers. Iris killed them off slowly one by one and made it look like another member of our team did it. Between being on the run from the Cartel and FBI, we got tired of running and learned a new trade, the art of killing. and got good at it. Long story short, I used to sell weight to the banger brothers. Me and my ex Damou ran Crown Heights for Tess." Layla replied and looked over to Rose, realizing she was talking to herself as she jumped onto the highway.

Chapter Four

Death to The Weak

"Ahhh! Please stop! Just stop, please!" the Indian cab driver screamed out in agonizing pain.

He found himself in a basement with two large sharp hooks dug into his back and two in his legs, that held him dangling from the ceiling by a black rope. The more he squirmed and moved, the more pain he felt as they tore his skin.

"See what happens when you have a smart mouth." Iris said while holding him still from swinging then pushed him with all her might; causing him to twist and spin fast like one of those old metal swings on the playground kids stand on.

"Ahhhh! Please stop! Just stop! I'm sorry! I'm sorry!" he shouted.

"Shhh! Stop talking so much. Do you think I'm wrong for wanting to kill Layla?" Iris asked.

"Who?! I don't know who you're talking about." the Indian cab driver replied in pain.

"We've been talking all these days and you haven't been taking notes. At least act like your listening or hear the main part of the conversation like most men do." Iris said, then pulled out her knife and slice him on the arm slowly. She watched the sharp knife rip open his skin until you could see the white meat then turn red from blood rushing to it.

"I'll listen! I'll listen! Please no more!" the cab driver shouted.

"If we're going to be friends you need a nick name. I'll call you Habib. Yes, I like that…. You're Habib. Now follow along Habib. I was wondering if I was going crazy. Like I pretty much killed all the Teflon Divas, but Layla, she really doesn't count. She was the youngest out all of us. I'm really the last one left; but the question was should I kill her?" Iris asked while looking at Habib dangling from the ceiling dripping blood from the new wound that she'd made.

"Uhmm… Uhmm Habib said nervously in an Indian accent, not knowing how to answer the question. *'If I don't answer she'll cut me, or maybe she'll kill me, and I can be with God; but what if she just keeps cutting me slowly and I live for a long time? I gotta say something.'*

Habib thought to himself as his body throbbed in excruciating pain. "I think you should kill her and me." he answered through his pain. *'Please, kill me. I can't take this no more. God help me. Please help me.'* Habib prayed in his head over and over again, but his prayers went unanswered.

"You know what, your right Habib. I've got to finish this. What I look like letting her get away after I done killed my daughter and niece all over this situation; and the love of my life not picking me first? I need to come before anyone else! Just me! I need the love for once; and with everyone gone, maybe I can find love. The attention will finally be on me, like it's supposed to be." Iris said out loud.

'Wow, this bitch is completely insane. She killed her daughter? Yep, I'm going die.' Habib thought to himself.

"Don't worry Habib, I'm not going kill you fast. I like you. We have great girl talk, and you love me. That's what I needed; but I do need to kill someone. It's like an itching sensation that I can't scratch. I should be healing, but I have a better idea." Iris said as she walked up the stairs, into the kitchen, and opened up the top cabinet over the stove. Removing a panel from the back of it revealed what looked like a digital safe that only could open by a fingerprint.

Placing her thumb on the black scanner, a green beam moved up a down, verifying her print. A creaking sound could be heard, and dust traveled up into the air as the large, ugly white refrigerator slid out to reveal a secret room. Iris fanned her nose at the smell and dust that lingered.

"Damn it's been a long time since we been here; one of our first safe houses. Damn how I miss them." Iris said out loud as tears began to pour down her checks while thinking of her only friends and old team. "Was I right to kill them? Now I'm all alone I really have no one to care for me or love. I was right, wasn't I? Yeah, I was right. It's only room to love me only. My love shouldn't be shared. People need to pay attention to me and me only; and with them gone, that will happen." Iris said to herself while wiping her tears away.

In the secret room were guns of different kinds and sizes hang up on the wall along with knives and swords. Teflon Diva custom bullet proof cat suits hung in front of a table. Opening up a drawer, she found an air tight ounce of weed and bamboo paper next to it.

"Hmmm. Not what I want, but it will do for now." she said out loud as she opened the bag and rolled a blunt. Finding a lighter in the drawer, she lit the blunt, inhaled deeply and exhaled. "Damn that's some good shit." she said as the weed started to take effect.

Grabbing one of the body suits, a pair of thigh high boots, two black uzis and a Glock 26, she left out with everything in her arms. and could hear the secret door shut behind her. Making her way upstairs to the bathroom, she dropped everything on the floor but the blunt. Continuing to take small pulls, letting it relax her mind and body, she ran a hot bath and hopped in.

"I'll soak for a few then it's off to find Layla. As along as she doesn't see me coming, I can kill her easy." Iris though to herself while sinking down in the hot water.

"Ahhh! Ahhh!" Habib screamed while wiggling from side to side like a tire swing in a tree. The hooks in his back began to stretch his skin. "Ahhh! Ahhh!" he hollered in excruciating pain but continued to swing his body from side to side.

The more he did that, the more his skin stretched. He rocked his body one last time and the hooks ripped through his flesh, causing him to hit the floor with a loud thump.

"Lord why?! Why?!" he cried out.

Wiggling his hands free of the rope, he rolled around on the floor in pain. Flesh from his back hung loosely from his back, making it look like he had wings made of skin. Habib ease up onto his feet and try to stand but his legs buckled.

"Come on! I gotta get the hell out of here and away from that crazy bitch." Habib said to himself before trying to stand again, and this time his legs didn't give out on him.

Looking around he found a dusty old sheet, ripped it then tied it around his back and chest, trying his best to replace the ripped skin and stop the bleeding. Spotting his clothes in a corner, he moved towards them and slowly put on his jeans and sneakers, groaning in pain every time he bent or moved. Habib took another look around then made his way up the basement stairs. The strong smell of dust and weed linger the air. It looked as if no one lived there in years. The couches were covered in sheets, and the TV was outdated.

Habib moved as fast as he could to the front door and shook the door knob, quickly realizing you needed a key to get out the steel security door.

"Fuck! fuck!" he said in frustration as he kicked the door.

Moving over to the window by the door, he pulled back the curtain. 'Okay. I can just break the glass and jump out. That's how I'll escape.' Habib said to himself then ran to the kitchen to grab one of the wooded chairs that was at a small round table, and limped back into the living room, where he tossed the chair with all his might at the window.

"Ahh." he grunted with a huge smile on his face, as he could taste his freedom and the thought of being back with his wife and two children. "I quit being a cab driver, this is it. Mo more for me." he said to himself; but than his face twisted in confusion and disbelief as the chair bounced back like a basketball.

"Oh Lord. What the fuck!" he said in his deep accent before picking up the chair again. "Maybe I'm too weak. I've got to try harder before the psycho lady comes back." he said to himself. not knowing Iris was upstairs in the tub, smoking another blunt she rolled while listening to the new Beyoncé and Jay-Z album.

Habib balled his face up in rage, raised the chair and hit the window with all his might. Boom! A loud thumping noise echoed through the first floor as it hit the window. This time the chair broke into pieces before it bounced back.

"Oh Lord! What the fuck! What the fuck?!" Habib said, worried and confused. "I know that should have broken the window."

Habib slowly walked toward the window as if he was expecting someone to jump out and say he'd been punk or part of a prank that'd be on YouTube. He got to the window and touched it. His eyes grew wide as he realized that the window was thick, like the ones in banks, hood check cashing spots and Chinese restaurants. He then realized people couldn't hear or see through the glass, but he could see out. His heart raced, pounding hard in his chest. He quickly made his way to all the windows in the living room then the kitchen. Everyone was the same.

"No! No! No!" he said as he checked more windows. "Maybe the windows upstairs are different, and I can jump out. Yes, that's it. That's what I can do." he said out loud to himself to get his heart to stop racing.

Walking up the stairs slowly, each step he took, the stair made a creaking sound. Having made his way up the stairs, he could hear music playing and what sounded like the woman weakly singing. Habib tip-toed down the hall, peeked around a corner, and could see the tub in a beautiful bathroom; and the psycho woman in the tub smoking while singing. Clouds of weed smoke danced in the air and made different shapes. A few inches from the tub Habib could see two guns resting on top on some clothes.

"Fuck that." Habib spat quietly and crept past the bathroom.

There was three bedrooms. down the hall, so he checked each room one by one and got the same results. All the windows were bullet proof, unbreakable, sound proof, and no one could see him. He held his head and began to cry.

"I'm trapped here. I'm really trapped here. This is where I'm going die. Why God, why? I was just trying to making a living for my family." Habib said with snot dripping from his nostrils and tears streaming down his cheeks. "No, I won't die here. I've got to see my little girls again." he told himself as he thought of his daughters, using the back of his hands to whip away his tears. "She must have a key for me to get out of here. I'll kill her or die trying." Habib said to himself then crept out the room he was in and tip-toed back down the hall; blood from his back soaking the dusty sheet he had wrapped around it.

Pain traveled through his entire body, but he fought the urge to groan out in pain. He reached the bathroom, peeked his head in and could see iris with her eyes closed; still signing and casually taking pulls of the blunt she was smoking. Habib stared at the two uzis laying on top of some clothes. He looked at them than look at her repeatedly.

"Just do it." he mumbled to himself, trying to build his courage." "Fuck it." he said, power walked right into the bathroom, scooped up one of the black uzis and grabbed it with both hands.

Hesitating at squeezing the trigger, Habib noticed a huge smile on Iris' face then her opening her eyes and turning the music down from her phone before she put it on the floor and took another pull of her blunt.

"It took you long enough. I heard since you finally got yourself free in the basement, then you start doing all that damn banging. Honestly I was waiting for you just start screaming for help like a little girl; then I would've sliced your neck like a do with a screaming horny cat for make too much nose outside my windows." Iris said while still smiling.

"Your got damn evil! You're an evil psycho bitch!" Habib shouted, then flinched when Iris balled up her face and she looked like she was about jump out the tub and snap his neck.

"You're really pushing it. I've been trying not to kill you fast." Iris warned.

"You don't want to kill me. I studied you. You're lonely and have no damn friends; and I can see why! You need me to talk to!" Habib shouted, spit flying from his mouth as he became more frustrated about the situation, he was in.

Iris stare at him as if he'd stolen something, then Boom! A loud sound went off. Habib looked on in confusion as a large hole appeared on the side of the bathtub and water began to pour out. He then felt a sharp pain in his left hand. Looking down at it, he screamed while dropping the uzi to the floor.

"Ahhhh! Ahhh! Oh Lord! What the fuck!" he hollered while trying to cover up the large hole in his left hand.

Iris slowly stepped out of the tub holding the Glock 26, 9mm pistol. "I bet you didn't know Glocks are one of the only guns that can shoot in water. Shit, they'll shoot in the sand or snow. You can drop them a thousand fucking times and they'll still work." she said as she grabbed a blue towel and wrap it around her.

Walking quickly up to Habib she swung, hitting him hard on the side of the head with the gun. He stumbled backwards and fell to the ground. "What the fuck you know about me?!" Iris shouted and swung again, hitting him in the face with the gun.

"Ahhh!" Habib shouted in pain as he tried to use his forearms. to block the blow.

"What the fuck you know about my life?! How you know if I'm lonely or not bitch?! You don't know me! You don't know shit about me!"

The more Iris screamed, the harder the blows came down on to Habib. She moved his arms. to the side as if slapping down the hands of a five-year-old, then beat his ass effortlessly. The rage in her eyes and anger on her face let Habib know he done and said the wrong thing. They say the truth hurts and when you speak it people that don't want to hear it, they react with anger. Well today Habib found out it was true.

'If I don't stop her, she'll kill me. She'll fucking kill me! I'll never get home to my family.' Habib thought to himself while fighting to stay consciousness. Iris had a lock on the sheet he was using as a shirt with one hand, and with the other she continued to pistol whip him. He was too weak to fight back or even use his arms. to block and try to protect his face.

"You don't know shit about me or my life!" Iris cried as she began to hit him so hard blood began to leak from his forehead. The white bathroom floor was now soaked red with his blood.

"Stop, I love you! I love you. Only you. Don't hurt me." Habib said weakly, causing Iris stop mid swing.

"What did you say?" she asked with a puzzled look on her face.

"Aghh! Ugh!" Habib coughed then spit up blood that landed on his face and slowly slide down to the floor. "I love you." he repeated weakly.

"You love me?" Iris asked with her eyes growing wide and a huge Kool-Aid smile on her face.

She dropped to her knees, unclasped with his belt, pulled his pants down, grabbed his dick and began jerking it. Habib laid there with pain throbbing through his whole body. All he wanted to do was scream. Iris put the gun down, moved her left hand around while still jerking his dick, grabbed a bottle of Percocet and took two pills out before popping them into her mouth. Inch up his body, she leaned forward, and tongue kissed him, pushing one of the pills down his throat.

"That will make you feel better in no time.' Iris moaned.

'This bitch is truly crazy; but if I didn't say I loved her she would've killed me. I have to feed her impulse. Feed what drives her, or I'm good as fucking dead; but she didn't lie, the pill has me feeling numb and the pain is going away. I just have to stay alive to get to my

family.' Habib thought to himself as the pain in his body fade away.

He could feel Iris' warm, wet lips wrap around his dick as she began to suck it; slurping up and down, then using the extra saliva to jerk his dick off all while moaning.

"Hmmm. You like that? You like that?! Huh baby?" she asked then began to suck the tip of the head of his dick.

"Fuck! Fuck!" Habib groaned. The sensation was too much for him. His body shook as he ejaculated; shooting cum all into her mouth. Iris greedily sucked it up and continued to deep throat his dick.

"Oh, you don't get off that easy baby." Iris said as she sucked his dick, making it even harder, then climb up and sat on it. She began to grind her hips, rocking it back and forth while holding his chest. "Say it again! Say it again!" she moaned while starting to bounce up and down on his dick.

'What the fuck is going on?' Habib thought to himself, but the wetness of her sweet pussy was feeling more than good on his dick. "I love you! I love you!" he shouted as Iris bounced harder and faster. "Yes! Yes!" he screamed as she became wetter and began to climax, splashing cum all over his chest and face.

"I love you too." she said then collapsed on his chest out of breath. "You know what we have to do now." iris said while breathing hard.

"What?" Habib asked weakly.

"You'll see." Iris said with a wicked smile on her face.

Two more nuts and a few hours later, Habib was more confused than ever. Iris had stitched up his back, wrapped his head and give him a black eye pack to cover the eye she stuck a pen in. He had been on Percocet, so his body was numb to pain. He now sat in the passenger side of a Nissan 370 coupe, watching houses and cars speed by. 'This can't be rea. It feels like a dream. It must be a damn dream.' Habib said to himself while looking at the street lights, fighting the urge to vomiting. It felt like he was on a roller coaster as Iris drove the stick shift in the night, speeding, switching gears and cutting through traffic. Then she suddenly stopped.

"We're here." she said with the sick smirk still on her face.

'We're' here.' Habib repeated to himself with his eyes closed, not knowing if it was the drugs that had his head spinning, the fact he had taken so many without eating, or the fast driving; but didn't care which one it was.

"Come, I'll show you." Iris said before hopping out the car and going to Habib's door to open it.

He took her hand and she led him up a flight of steps. He could hear keys jiggling in her hands and a door opening.

"Honey is that you?! You're late. We were starting dinner without you." a woman said in an Indian accent.

The sound of her voice made Habib open his one good eye right away. The feeling of being high and dizziness disappeared as adrenaline mixed with fear made his heart race.

"No! No! Please no!" Habib then screamed, "Run!" at the top of his lungs.

Iris pulled out a chrome 45 caliber Taurus hand gun with a chrome matching silencer attached and smacked Habib in the face with it. He stumbled sideways and hit the ground. The woman walked towards the front room, not hearing Habib scream.

"Baby what's wrong?" she asked before she stood in shock as she came face to face with Iris and saw her husband on the floor.

"Helen… I said run." Habib said while slobbering and crying.

"So, you're the other woman, huh Helen? Let's go."
Iris said while pointing the gun at her, pushing her
towards the kitchen. "You have a lovely home." she
added while walking pass the living and taking in
everything. Get up Habib and come on."
"This can't be happening. This can't be my life. God
please help us. Save us from this mad woman. Please
Lord don't let this be happening." Habib prayed out
loud.
"Baby, shut up and come here!" Iris shouted.
Habib slowly walked through the living room and to
the kitchen where he could see his two daughters, Esha
who was 10 and Chahna was 8, and Helen's parents
sitting at the table.
The smell of Curry Chicken lingered in the air. Iris
looked down at their plates as the everyone looked at
her in fear while she pointed the gun and looked at
Habib in confusion, pleading for help with their eyes.
"Go fix me a plate." Iris said and pointed the gun at
Helen's head.
"Y…yes." Helen replied nervously before slowly
making her way over to the stove to grab a plate and
spoon to fix her a plate of before she tried to pass it to
Iris.

"No, sit it at the table." Iris said, and Helen did as she was ordered.

"Daddy! Daddy!" Chahna, the youngest daughter said before getting up and running to him. Habib embraced her in his arms. "Who is this crazy woman, and why is she here in our home?" the little girls asked.

"Shhh baby." Habib hushed her, praying she'd be quiet.

"Get out of out our house!" Helen's father shouted while standing up from the table.

Iris twisted her head to the side and look at the older Indian man with grey hair and a grey goatee in a tan short shelve button up shirt. Iris smirked, raised the gun and squeezed the trigger. A strange sound was heard, as if someone was whistling or birds chirping as the bullet traveled out the gun and slammed in the older man's forehead. His forehead split wide open like a cracked egg right in front of his family eyes. He leaned forward and fell dead on top the table with his brains oozing out and pieces of his skull on the floor.

"Noooo! Not my husband my. Ahhh!" the older woman screamed, and Iris sent a bullet slamming in to her chest, ripping through the fat of her breast and coming out her back. The impact of the bullet lifted the small older woman off her feet and slammed her back into the stove where she slid down slowly and died with her eyes open.

"Ahhh! Ahhh!" the little girls began screaming at the top of their lungs.

"Mommy! Mommy! She hurt grandpa and grandma!" Chana said as she jumped out her chair and ran into her mother's arms.

"Who is this woman you brought into our home?! You brought death into our home!" Helen shouted in her thick Indian accent.

"Yeah Habib, tell her who I am! Tell her you only love me now. That you don't love or need them no more. That I'm all the family you need." Iris ordered with a smile on her face, full of joy.

"You lost grip of reality! This my family! Are you fucking crazy?!" Habib shouted.

The smile on Iris' face quickly disappeared and you could now see the rage as her face turn red. "You said you love me! Tell her you love me." Iris said through gritted teeth.

"I don't love you, I love my family! Leave us alone. Go! Just go and find what you looking for!" Habib shouted back while holding Esha tight.

"Say that you love me." Iris said and look at Habib, but he didn't say anything. Iris aimed and pulled the trigger, sending a bullet crashing into Helen's leg, shattering her kneecap.

"Ahhhh!" Helen yelled at the top of her lungs as her right leg buckled and she collapsed to the floor.

"Mommy! Mommy!" Chana cried while still holding onto her.

"Say you love me!" Iris said while staring dead into Habib eyes.

Habib's facial expression tighten up as he contemplated rushing her but thought about how fast she had taken his eye.

"Say you love me!" Iris shouted then squeezed the trigger again, sending a bullet into Helen's foot, blowing off four toes at once.

"Ohhh God! Ahhhhhh!" Helen screamed in excruciating pain.

"Say it! Say it!" Iris ordered while squeezing the trigger twice, blowing a larger hole into Helen's shoulder while she lay in the floor and a hole in to her left thigh.

"Run! Girls run!" Habib shouted then ran full speed at Iris.

To Iris it was as if he was moving in slow motion. All the years of martial arts training made a normal person seem beyond weak and much slower then she. She raised her left eyebrow as if to say like really, sidestepped and bent low sweep kicking his legs from up under him.

"Ughh!" Habib grunted as he went flying face first into the floor.

Chana and Esha took off running for the front door. Iris hesitated for as second as she had a flashback of her daughter Isis playing Tag on the beach with her sister Ayoyna. "Hmmm." she said to herself then squeezed the trigger twice. A bullet slammed into Chana's eight-year-old back, leaving a golf ball sized hole through to her chest. Before she could fall to the ground a bullet slammed into the back of her head, exploding her little head like someone squishing a tiny green bean with their fingers. Ten-year-old Esha stood there in shock looking at her sister, or what was left of her.

"Get up! Sister get up! Chanha please get up. I promise I won't be mad at you when you play with my toys. I promise I won't get mad when you jump in my bed at night. Get up. Please sister get up." Esha begged while on her knees in front of her sister's body, her yellow dress now soaked in blood.

Iris turned to Habib and looked into his eyes. "Say that you love me!" she said, aiming at his wife who was squirming around on the floor in pain.

"My babies! No! You bought the devil into our house. Why husband, why?!" Helen screamed.

"Habib, I said say that you love me." Iris said with her head tilted to the side.

"I love you! I love you! Just please stop. No more. I love you." Habib said while snot ran from his noise as he cried uncontrollably.

"Good. I'm happy she knows before she dies." Iris said with a smile on her face.

"Huh? No, wait…"

Habib's words were cut short as Iris squeezed the trigger and send a 45-caliber bullet slamming into Helen's neck. The larger bullet blew off a huge chunk of the left side of her neck. Iris fired another bullet and it blew off the right side of her neck, decapitating her, completely severing her head from her body. Habib's eyes opened wide in shock and horror as he looked at his wife. Her lips were still moving, but no words come out. Habib just read her lips.

"How can you do this to us? How can you do this to us?" she mouthed repeatedly.

"I told you, you can only love me. There's no room for anyone else! I am the priority! Not your wife, not you your old family, just me; and I refuse to share!" Iris stated and pointed the gun at Esha.

"Noooo!" Habib screamed.

Chapter Five

Building My Own Legacy

"I'm so sorry for your loss. I can't even imagine the pain you're in mami." Red Banger said while laying naked next to Layla.

"It hurts a lot that I'm all alone. The people I called my family are gone; but can I tell you something?" Layla asked.

"Sure. You know we're people's and you can trust me." Red Banger replied.

Layla look at him and thought, *'Damn. Why didn't I ever try to make him my man? He's fine, strong and take charge of things; but no, it's Domau who had my heart, and Red is just someone to take care of this pussy for a second just to get this monkey off my back.'*

"I feel free for once. I love Tess. She was the mother that I never had, but I always felt I was under her foot, like living her life; and I know that's not true at all. She really just wanted what was best for us, protect from different crime syndicates and the FBI; but deep down I was tired of being on the run, and kind of jealous Of Bless and Tess." Layla stated.

"How can you be jealous of those two? They been through hell and back, and still showed love to the streets. Shit, from what you told me, to have Iris, a close friend, try to kill them repeatedly and finally kill their daughter. If you ask me, it's nothing to be jealous of. It's more of a sad story." Red Banger replied.

"You're absolutely right, but it wasn't my story. I was jealous of their love. I want to have love like that. I had love like that but had to leave it when the FBI came after us." Layla said sadly.

"You want the truth or a lie?" Red Banger asked.

Layla raised her left eyebrow and looked at him funny. "Why wouldn't I want the truth?"

"Because people never want to hear the truth. The truth hurts and lies feel good. The truth of the matter is, you would be nothing without Tess; just another girl lost in these New York streets. No telling how you would've turned out. Tess saved you from a foster home where you were being beat and raped, taught you how to survive, became a Lieutenant Drug boss with Crown Heights Brooklyn on lock. Then when shit went to hell, she taught you a new skill on how to survive. Taught her whole team how to be assassins, made you the best snipper in the world and made you super rich. I don't even want to ask how much you're really worth, but I'm pretty sure it's in the millions. Money some will never see in this life time. So, I think your ungrateful; and that's the truth." Red Banger stated while getting up from the bed.

"Ungrateful?! Ungrateful how? How am I ungrateful? It sounds like you wanted my mother or some shit." Layla said sucking her teeth.

"Not at all mami. I loved my mother. She was the best woman I know and would give my lung and kidney to bring her back to me in this world after my uncle gunned her down; but I have this feeling you wouldn't do the same for the woman that you called your mother. You need to ask yourself would you give your lung to have her back, and you need to ask yourself if you really had that great love you talked about. Would you have been fuckin' me back in the day when you were with him before you left; and if you loved him so much you wouldn't be fuckin' me now, as soon as you came back in town." Red Banger said with a smile on his face as he got dress.

"You do know I can kill you without breaking a sweat right?" Layla said, anger written on her face.

"I'm pretty sure it won't be that easy; but I told you, the truth hurts. If you want yes friends, you'll have no problem finding them; but if you want real, you deal with people like me mami." he said while smiling, showing off a perfect set of white teeth.

Layla looked at him, not knowing if she wanted to stab him in the neck or sit back on his face. "You're lucky you're so damn handsome; but I respect your honesty, because it's coming from you. I still feel the way I feel, like I'm free; and it's finally my time to shine my time to do what I like."

Red Banger shrugged his shoulders as Layla grabbed a pink robe, slid it on and both of them walked out the room, down the stars to the second floor. Blue Banger was laying out on a coach, and next to him was a short beautiful dark skin woman with her hair cut in one of those short Halle Berry styles, but it fit her. Layla studied her for a second then went to the kitchen where Rose was sitting at the table eating a grilled cheese sandwich.

"Really? That's all you going to eat?" Layla asked.

"Well shit bitch, that's all I got from the store. There's no food in this nice ass place, and um, I'm broke. My cartel wasn't paying me." Rose stated.

Layla shook her head. "Here, call this number and order groceries. They'll deliver to the house. Tell them to put it on the diva's account." Layla replied and passed Rose the cell phone from her robe pocket.

"The diva's account? I can get used to this type of living." Rose replied.

"You have to earn this type of living. Now go to the first floor and order us some food." Layla said while shaking her head.

Rose hopped up happily, heading to the first floor while studying every inch of the town house. "I've never been in nothing this fly and nice." Rose said to herself as she rode the elevator to the first floor.

"This is a very nice place. Are you safe here? The Santiago Cartel will keep coming, and me and Blue can only do so much. We have our own wars we're fighting, but we'll help the best we can." Red stated.

"Yeah, I'm safe here. No one knows about this place. It was one of the secrets Tess only told me about. It may look luxurious, but it's full of security and defense systems." Layla replied.

"Hmmm. Sounds like more blessings from that mother you didn't appreciate." Red Banger said sarcastically.

"Psst." Layla suck her teeth and roll her eyes. "Okay, y'all can get out now." she said rudely.

"Hold up shorty. Before we leave, I want you to meet Harmony B. I know you need soldiers and she's as loyal as they come." Blue Banger said, getting off the white coach in the living room.

Harmony B stood up, and Layla really look at her for the first time. She was short 5'1 and thick. She had to be 160 pounds solid, but it was all in her thighs and hips. The short haircut she wore Layla found strange, when in today's society most women wear long weaves. She was beautiful in the face and dressed in all blue dress with a blue bandanna tied around her left wrist. Her skin complexion was the color of smooth Hershey's chocolate.

"Hi, I'm Harmony B." she said with a smile, showing off a pretty set of white teeth, and reached her hand out. Layla took her hand and shook it.

"Why do y'all think I need soldiers? I'm an army by myself; and no offense, but Harmony looks more like a thick pretty chocolate Instagram model." Layla stated and laughed but was the only one laughing in the room.

"Damn, you really forgot where you came from fam." Blue Banger replied.

"Yeah, she did; been overseas and out of New York too long, forgetting the lessons from Bless and Tess. You judging Harmony by the way she looks, but that's what weak mean do, think with their dicks. Red Banger replied and smirk as Harmony raised up her blue baby doll dress and pulled two 38 revolvers from her thigh holster and pointed them at Layla.

Before she could get a good aim, Layla bent and punch Harmony in the stomach, knocking the wind out of her then grab both her wrists, twisting them outside while leaping up in the air and jump kicking her in the chest with both her feet. She went flying backwards, knocking both guns out her hands. Layla grabbed both guns and popped back up on her feet without using her hands, aiming one gun at Red Banger and the other at Bluer Banger.

"I don't know what kind of games y'all playing, but I'm not the one it with the bullshit!" Layla shouted.

"Hold up little mami." Blue Banger said while laughing.

"Yeah, hold up. You know we don't know all that Kung Fu shit; but we were making a point. You were judging shorty off her looks like motherfuckers never did that to you, not knowing you're a weapon. Well Harmony is a Rolling 60's Crip Lieutenant and lays down more bodies for me then I can count; and she was there today when you needed helping. You gonna need some soldiers sis. You're not going be able to survive out here all alone. Someone has to have your back; and like my brother Red said, we can't do it, not now. We have our own issues, and to be honest, not too many people want to join the drama you into; but Harmony begged to meet you and to help you." Blue Banger said while fixing his fitted hat.

Layla lowered the guns, popped the barrel chambers open, emptied the bullets onto the floor and tossed them back to Harmony B who was still on the floor gasping for air.

"Y'all right. She can stay; and I need a favor. I need some of those uranium blue bullets I heard some much about on the street. I'll wire money to your count."

"Aight cool, but we can only send two boxes of those. We running low on them ourselves. I'll have someone bring them over. Later love, take care of yourself; and I'm sorry for your loss." Blue Banger said then kissed Layla on the forehead.

"Stay safe; and think about what we talked about." Red Banger said, kissing her softly on her lips before following his brother to the elevator.

Layla raised her left eyebrow. "Damn that's one fine man." she mumbled to herself and then look down at Harmony B, still holding her chest. "Girl, if you can't handle that little old kick how you going handle me training you? Layla asked.

"Train me? What you mean?" Harmony B asked with a confused look on her face.

"Yes, training. If you gonna be with me, you must learn the Teflon Diva way." Layla replied.

"I've heard a lot about the famous Teflon Divas and their skills. To be real, I always thought it was all fairytales. Strong women assassins that were beautiful and deadly?! To be real, every woman wanted to be a Teflon Diva." Harmony stated.

"Well let's get to it." Layla said as Rose stepped out the elevator with bags of groceries in her arms. and on the elevator floor.

"I love this lifestyle. I got the good ice cream." Rose said with a huge smile on her face.

"Well let's put up the food and see how much you still love this lifestyle." Layla said.

They put up the groceries and Layla led both them to the elevator, pressing two and three at the same time. *'Basement level activated.'* a computerized voice in the elevator said.

"We have a basement. Shit, we already in a four-story townhouse. I've never seen nothing this luxurious; and we in Spanish Harlem across the street from Central Park. This is where all the rich white people live. Shit, we're only a block away from Park Ave. I didn't know people of color can live this good." Rose stated.

"We are women, we can live how we choose. We're stronger than men. Always remember, you're smart and stronger than any man. I'll teach you how to make money, and it won't be easy. You must first train hard or you'll die out there; or I'll die with y'all watching my back, and we can't have that shit." Layla said as they reached the basement and the door opened.

"What the fuck is this, the bat cave? I feel like a secret spy." Rose said as they exited the elevator and white lights automatically turned on. The first thing you saw was six Ducati street bikes.

"This place is huge. What the hell? Why the ceilings so damn tall?" Rose asked while walking around.

Rose and Harmony B studied everything. There was suits on the wall, and the wall to the right that was full of different types of guns. They walked down further into the basement and could see big glass doors. Rose and Harmony peeked in and could see blue pathed matte floors, swords and knives on the wall, and two of those punching dummies you see people kicking all the time on T.V.

"What is this?" Harmony asked.

"Teflon Divas have stash houses all over the world. Each house has a place to train and two secret exits in every house or apartment. This townhouse was one of many owned by my mother and mentor Tess. I'm going to teach you what I know the best I can." Layla stated. "Let's start with this first."

Layla led them into a shooting range with more guns on the wall and a cabinet full of bullets. "Grab a gun and show me what you got. Harmony show me what you can do with a rifle. Grab the M-16 and the vest."

"Why the vest?" Harmony B asked while taking off her heels.

"If one of the practice targets shoots you, you'll feel it. Get past the obstacle course without getting shot."

"Not a problem." Harmony said with a smirk on her face as she grabbed two magazines for the rifle that was about half her size.

Harmony walked onto the obstacle course, and right away a male target wearing a mask popped up began shooting at her. Harmony raised the riffle and squeezed the trigger, blowing off its head before she ducked and rolled. Hopping up, she shot two more targets before they could even aim at her. Peeking around, she began shooting again, taking out four more targets.

"Bitch how you get so good at shooting?" Layla asked with a confused look on her face.

"I'm from Florida; the gun laws are different there. I've been shooting since I was ten years old. My father taught me up until the age of sixteen years old when he died; but I continued to go the range and took my little brothers with me. I taught them until I decide to move to New York at twenty-one, became Crip under Blue Banger's set, and moved up fast in ranking." Harmony stated.

"Yeah, your very good, but shooting isn't everything. You must learn hand to hand combat; and I'm not talking about no street fighting bulkshit." Layla stated.

"Why we got to learn that when I can just shoot a muthafucker; and don't you want me to go through the obstacle course to show you my skills?" Rose asked.

"Hell no! I already know you can't aim for shit; that's why you use shotguns most of the time. You can't miss a target with them, but the only issue is shotguns are only good close up. As far as why you need to learn how to fight, bullets run out, but a blade can cut forever. The main thing about being a Teflon Diva is to remember all the tools aren't the weapons, they're just tools; but you are the weapon. The woman using the gun and knife or fist. It's you." Layla replied as she led them in to the fight training room.

The first and deadliest style is the science of the eight limbs. It's called Muythai. It's violent, and similar to kick boxing." Layla stated.

"Why is it called the science of the eight limbs if it's pretty much like kickboxing?" Rose asked while shrugging her shoulders.

"Because you will also be using your knees and elbows with this style. Let's start."

They'd been training for a week straight, and Harmony and Rose were learning fast. Layla stood sweetly in black tights and tank top watching Rose and Harmony B spar against each other. Rose sweep kicked and Harmony flip backwards then forward trying to take Rose's head off with a round house kick but was too slow. Rose moved her head in time and sent an elbow crashing in to Harmony's jaw. "Ughh! Ahh!" Harmony grunted in pain and stumbled backwards as Rose sent two punches to her stomach and rib. Rose swung again and Harmony caught her right hand in mid-swing, twisting it and flipping Rose to the ground hard; knocking the air out of her and applying pressure to her elbow as if she was going to break it. Rose tapped the blue mat.

"Okay! Okay, I gave! You win! You win!" Rose cried out. Harmony released her grip and smiled, wiping blood from her mouth.

"Don't gloat." Layla said.

"Why not? I won." Harmony B replied.

"Barely. You have to know your own weaknesses before an enemy does, and you don't know yours." Layla replied.

"I'll have no weaknesses, once I learn more styles. I'll be unstoppable." Harmony retorted cockily.

"Rose, what's Harmony weakness?" Layla asked as she got up off the floor rubbing her shoulder and elbow.

"She's short, and small." Rose stated.

"What?! We're all short. You bitches only an inch or two taller than me. I'm 5'1, Rose you like 5'7, and Layla maybe 5'5; almost the same as me. Short and cute. Okuur." Harmony said, sounding like the rapper Cardi B.

"Yeah, we all a little short, but you're shorter and your arms. are a little shorter." Rose replied.

"What you trying to say hoe, that I'm shaped like a midget; because I'm not shaped like a small person. My arms. are perfectly normal for my body." Harmony spat.

"Shhh! Just shut up and listen." Layla hissed. "Rose, continue; and state your weakness as well." Layla said.

"Your arms. are normal and fit your body; but they're still short, so you have no reach. So, fighting a person like me that has reach or a real tall person, they just got to keep jabbing you and keeping you back. You from the hood, so I know you've seen a tall nigga fight a real stocky dude built like a football player. Yeah, the dude's big, but he loses to the tall nigga because he has reach; but if that big dude grabs him it's over for that tall dude. He's getting body slammed or put in ahead lock. That's what happened here. I allowed myself to get too close. My weakness is my impatience. If I kept you back and waited for the right hit, you would've gone down, but I rushed in and you grabbed me." Rose stated.

"Hmmm, that made sense." Harmony replied. "So how do I fix it?" she asked looking at Layla.

"If you can't reach someone with your hands, use your feet. Your legs are longer, and they are already the strongest thing on your body. Girl, all your weight is in your legs and butt, so you must become a master at leg work. Kicking getting your legs strong enough to break a man's leg and shattering every bone in them. That will be my goal for you. I want you to side kick the training bag a thousand times with your right leg before you leave the training room today."

"What?! A thousand times?! I won the match." Harmony said.

"Yes, but you lost the fight. Now go; and tomorrow you'll do it with your left leg." Rose started to laugh. "What's so funny Rose? You're going to punch the punching bag a thousand times until you learn to concentrate on your attack."

"Yeah yeah; but where you going? You got that look on your face again like you about to go out." Rose said.

"It's dark and I need fresh air. No one will recognize or notice me. I can't be cooped up in the house, I feel like a trapped bird. I'm finally free to live my own life and back in New York but stuck inside. Layla replied shaking her head.

"I understand sis, but if the any one from the Santiago Cartel recognizes you, you'll be in danger. You been going out every week, just walking like you have a lot on your mind." Rose said.

"I'm good. Let me worry about that. Besides, y'all both got your watches on, so we're connected. If there's any sign of danger, I'll press the silent alarm. You'll be able to track me and come help me kick ass." Layla said with a smile on her face as she entered the elevator, leaving the basement.

Chapter Six

The Search is on. Death to all Teflon Divas!

"It's been a fucking month! A whole month and none of y'all have seen or found that Teflon Diva bitch! I have a five hundred-thousand-dollar bounty for anyone that can tell me her whereabouts, and million dollars for her head, but still nothing!" Catalina shouted at the ten soldiers standing in front of her in her massive penthouse office with white marble floors and black walls.

Sitting in the chair behind her desk, she spun it around to look at the view. Behind her was floor to ceiling windows that give her an incredible view of the Bronx. She watched the snow come down slowly and began to speed up.

"Boss, with it being winter and all, we think it's easier to hide." Flacco said.

"Yeah boss. Why we even worried about one bitch and one we should be thinking of taking out the

Russians in Coney Island; and that damn Damou and his team in Brownsville that owe us four hundred thousand for the keys of cocaine they took on consignment!" one of the solider, Antonio, shouted.

Catalina squinted her eyes, and the other solider in the room took a step back. "What you say?" she asked while cocking her head to the side. She stood up from her chair dressed in her royal blue blouse, a black skirt that stopped at her knees with matching blue stocking and Louboutin's.

"Nothing boss. I'm just saying where wasting time focusing on the wrong thing. We need to handle the real issues, like people owning us money and taking over new territory." Antonio replied.

"Hmmm. Like I thought." Catalina said while hiking up her shirt just a little to her thighs and took off running at top speed before sending a round house kick to his face that sent Antonio stumbling sideways.

Rage cover Antonio's face expression and he balled up his fist.

"It sounds like you giving me orders and telling me how to run my business motherfucker! Y'all keep asking why I'm worried about one woman. Well it's really two of them you idiots, and I hope they kill each other; but if one of them teams. up with our enemies, we're fucked. There's a difference between street war and   a military war and fighting, and those bitches are on that level. They were paid assassins that took out major crime bosses and their teams. They're more organized and powerful then mines right now, and it was only five or six of them. Can you imagine an army of them? Oh, and let's not forget we tried to kill one. If that's not enough reason for her to come after us, maybe the fact they have history with the Santiago Cartel because of my cousins is you fools!" Catalina shouted then noticed Antonio's fist still balled up. "You got something on your chest you need to say?" she asked sarcastically.

"Yeah I do! I don't even know why we follow a fucking woman. Women belong on their knees with a dick in their mouth!" Antonio yelled before reaching behind him under his black blazer, pulled a chrome 45 hand gun and squeezed the trigger.

Catalina moved to the side just before the bullet hit her, slid on a pair of brass knuckles with wide three inches blade that extended from it and punched him in the chest.

"What the fuck you mean why y'all work for a woman?! Women are smarter and stronger. You little pussies couldn't do have the shit women do!" Catalina shouted with each punch she sent to his rib and chest, before stabbing him with the blade, seeing thick red blood flying.

"Ugh! Fuck!" Antonio groaned in pain as he tried to step back so he could get a good aim at Cataline, but she stepped closer, now standing in his face.

"Oh, don't try to run now bitch ass nigga! You were talking all that shit a second ago. It's men like you that bring out the other side of me, and why people call me lady death! Weak ass me!"

Before Catalina could get another word out, Antonio reared his head back and sent it forwarded with incredible force, head butting her dead in the nose. The sound of it breaking could be heard echoing throughout the room. The blow was so hard it knocked her to the floor and tears welled up her eyes, making it almost impossible to see.

"Lady death my ass! People only scared of you because of your family name bitch. How rumors got started of you killing people and getting hit now I'll never know. You're nothing special. We all can squeeze the trigger hoe. Watch, let me show you." Antonio said as he raised his gun.

Catalina sat up off the floor and spit out the blood she's swallowed from her leaking nose as blood poured from it all over the floor. She burst out laughing and you could now see her pretty white teeth were also covered in blood. Flacco and the rest of the men stood still in confusion, looking from her to Antonio.

"What's so funny bitch?" Antonio asked as he was about to pull the trigger.

"The fact that y'all all are stupid. Men, I swear." Calanthe said with a snap of her finger. Her office door busts open and Benjamin along with his new giant friend Tito, who had survived Layla's attack a month again in the bathroom, stood there with AK-47s pointed at the remaining 9 high ranking soldiers.

"For one, I always have a backup plan; and two, Antonio you're right. I need to go back to being who I was. No more Catalina, the classy woman. It seems. y'all only respect and fear when a woman is a bitch, so I'll be who I always was, and that's Lady Death." Catalina replied while smiling.

"Yeah. That sounds good and all, but there's one problem." Antonio stated.

"Yeah, what's that?" Calanthe asked while standing up.

"I'm about to kill your ass hoe. I don't care if your two little goons kill me after." Antonio said and try to pull the trigger but couldn't. He continued to try, but it was as if his body wouldn't listen to his mind. "Why can't I move? What's going on?!" Antonio asked with fear written all over his face and his eye watering as if he was about to cry.

"For one, y'all all stupid. Once you talk shit to me the first time, a press of a button on my dress released a nerve toxin. It takes a little while to kick in, and you can't smell or see the gas. It paralyzes you unless you take an antitoxin pill, which I been took. The funny thing is, I wasn't going to release the gas until I didn't see the other four of my so call loyal lieutenants just stand by and let someone talk to me with disrespect and try to kill me. I realize y'all all feel the same way about a woman ruling over you and wanted poor Antonio to kill me so y'all won't have to get your hands dirty." Catalina said.

"No. Not me my queen." Flacoo said, unable to move. "I knew nothing about this. I just thought it better for you to show your power and authority then let me try or anyone else." Flacco pleaded.

"Hmmm, I'll think about that. Now back to you." Catalina said and turned back to face Antonio as he collapsed and began to shake uncontrollably.

"W... what's happening to me?" he asked, realizing his body was soaking wet. His clothes were drenched as if someone had poured a bucket of water on him.

"Dummy, I stabbed you in six arteries when we were fighting. To be completely honest, I'm shocked you're still alive. It must be because of your size. You been bleeding out profusely for five minutes now, your dumb ass just didn't notice. Each cut I made was precise. You never stood a chance." Catalina said while standing over him before raising her leg high up in the air and came down with force. The point of her heel pierced his right eye before it and bloody pus oozed out of his eye socket and the point of the heel dug into his brain, killing him instantly.

"Kill them all, except Flacco." Catalina ordered as she pulled her heel out of Antonio's face. "Now I got to get new heels. What a waste."

"No! Noo!" The sound of two of her lieutenants screaming simultaneously was cut short as a hail of bullets entered their backs and burst through there chest, dropping dead to the floor face first.

"Uhmm, why'd you leave that one alive?" Catalina asked, pointing to the third man, who was shaking with his eyes closed. he was a middle size man with long hair in a ponytail.

Benjamin smiled and replied, "My giant friend Tito wants him." he said.

"For what?" Catalina asked with a confused look on her face.

"Oh, he's gay and wants to have fun with him before that neurotoxin wears off, then kill him."

"Well tell him to take Flacco with him as well. He can have fun with him too, just don't kill him."

Tito's eyes lit up with joy as the thought of the two men turned him on instantly and could feel himself growing hard in his jeans. Catalina looked down at his hard on and her eyes opened wide.

"That thing looks like it's the size of a horse's dick. Y'all going have some good fun." she stated.

"No. No Boss, please don't do this!" Flacco cried out as Tito threw him over his shoulder, carrying him as if he was a bag of laundry.

Tito grabbed the next solider with long hair and scooped him up in his arms. as if he was carrying a small child and not a grown ass man.

"I'm not going to do anything to you, he is." Catalina replied while smiling.

"No Boss! Please, no Catalina!" Flacco screamed.

"Next time someone tries to harm me you move faster; and there's no more Catalina. To you it's Lady Death." Catalina stated.

"Noooooo!" Both men scream at the top of their lungs and tried to move their bodies to escape, but couldn't as the 6'5, three hundred-pound Tito took them out the penthouse office and to the fifth floor of the building to his apartment.

"We have some things to discuss Boss Lady." Benjamin said.

"Like what? I just started to like you, so don't ruin it. You've got to keep it mind it was your girlfriend that help that little Teflon diva bitch escape and double crossed you. I shouldn't even let you off that easy, but shit who be better to hunt down the Teflon Diva then someone who want to kill their girlfriend." Catalina said and smiled, knowing the anger and rage you feel from being betrayed by a loved one is a hell of a motivation for revenge.

The thought of Rose caused Benjamin to twist his face up in an angry expression. *'How could that bitch?! How could she shoot me? She was my woman.'* Benjamin thought to himself.

"Now I'm not about tell you how to run your business, but I have two files, one on each Teflon Diva that came to town. The crazy one we missed while we were busy chasing the little one. Iris is the real problem, and we haven't seen her since; but here…" Benjamin paused while removing two white folders from the inside of his black suit jacket and placed them on the table. "…is the issue at hand. I need you come with me in about two or three hours, after your lunch." Benjamin said

"Why? Where we going, and why three hours?" Catalina asked curiously.

"One of the reasons I almost died was because I under estimated Layla and the loyalty of my girlfriend; and the full bodysuit she had on. If you read the files, you'll see the Teflon Divas had new age body armor and technology, unlike anything anyone had seen before. The suit fits like normal clothes. Light weight but can take a bullet from a sniper rifle and any hand gun. That made it almost impossible to kill them, that mixed with their skills; but I had my ears to the street, and the first time in six years their suit Technology is being sold by the Asian Mafia. This stuff is not cheap at all boss lady, but it will put us on the same playing field as them the next time we encounter them. I won't be at a disadvantage. I'm not saying suit up the whole cartel, just me, yourself and Tito. They're only selling five suits, technology and weapons to outsiders. I won the bid for three." Benjamin said.

"What?! You bid on something without my ……." Catalina screamed.

"It's worth it, I'll show you." Benjamin replied.

Four hours later, Catalina sat in the back seat of a bulletproof Cadillac Escalade with Benjamin next to her in traffic, driving. She touched the tip of the handle of her gun in her shoulder holster under her light brown fox fur bomber jacket with a hood. *'I can't trust no one. Was it a bad idea listening to Benjamin? Could he be setting me up to be killed by the Asian mafia; but what if he's telling the truth. An opportunity like this never come around. It will help me kept my spot as queen of the underworld.'* Catalina thought to herself while looking out the window. The street was dark at six o'clock, but still busy as hell with people rushing to and from work, or just out and about. It snowed lightly and the street light made it look falling crystals. Catalina continued to look around and knew they were in Chinatown in lower Manhattan. Chinese restaurants and food markets were on every corner, all the business signs on the buildings were in Chinese. The truck came to a stop at a pet store. Cutie Huskie puppies could be seen playing in the front glass window.

"Where here." her driver Jova said.

Catalina waited for Benjamin to get out the truck and open the door for her. She flipped her hoodie overhead and quickly scanned her environment, looking for anything that looked out of place. *'Shit, everything looks out of place. I'm not supposed to be here.'* Catalina thought to herself. She had already noticed five Asian men dressed in plain clothes, acting as if they shopping but was really guarding the block. Under their jackets were sub- machine guns. Benjamin stood in front of her, leading the way while Tito stood behind her guarding her back as they entered the pet shop, where three customers shopped. Benjamin walk to the register and approved an old lady who looked to be eight years old but in great health, with short grey, curly hair. Benjamin looked at her and bowed.

"We came to enter the mouth of the Tiger." he said, speaking in code.

"Follow me. I've been expecting you." she said as she led them to the back of the shop and into what seemed to be a large kitchen filled with Chinese cooks and waiters. Catalina took everything in from the corner of her eyes. She could see a cage holding little brown puppies. A short man in a chef's shirt grabbed one of the puppies by its neck. The puppy whimpered and cried just as he placed in a giant pot of boiling water. Catalina's eyes open wide as she watched the man toss four more live puppies into the boiling water then carry the pot to the sink and pour it in. Hot, thick steam filled that area. The chef refilled the pot, put it back on the stove and went back to the sink where seven boiled dead puppies lay. He pulled on a black glove, grabbed one of the dead hot puppies and with one firm swipe of his hand peeled all the dog's hair off, like a woman using Nair in the shower. He then picked up a meat cleaver and chopped the puppy into little pieces, before repeating the process.

"What the fuck…" Catalina said.

"Oh, dear hush. You've been eating it for years and never knew the difference. Dog meat is cheap and easy to bread." Ms. Wung Shu said.

"Fuck that. I never ate no damn puppy. That's just some inhumane shit." Catalina responded.

"Have you ever eaten chicken and broccoli dear?" Ms. Wung Shu asked.

"Yes. I'm from the hood, born and raised in the Bronx. Who hasn't eaten chicken and broccoli?" Catalina replied.

"Well there you go sweetie. Puppy is an Asian secret you people been eating for generations without knowing. Shit, it's the General Tso Chicken you have to really worry about, that's rat meats. We don't even like eating that. Come, follow me." Ms. Wung Shu said.

Catalina could see the double swinging doors opening as the waiters went in and out. She could tell it was a Hibachi restaurant, as they followed the old lady through buildings and businesses. Catalina could see people sitting down with their families and wanted to throw up in her mouth but held he composure. As they walked through the kitchen, Ms. Wung Shu led them through a secret door and now they were now in a Chinese strip club. Heading to the basement, Ms. Wung walked to a brick wall, hit a secret panel and the wall slid to the side, leading to a large room. Lights automatically turned on as they entered, and the wall behind them slim shut.

"So, when do I get to speak to the designer and tech person behind the gear I'm paying for?" Catalina asked.

"Why dear, you've been speaking to her the whole time." The old woman replied as another wall slid open, exposing the weapons that hung from the wall.

She walked around to a table and pulled out three large armored suit cases. *'How the fuck did she lift that?*

Damn, those cases look to be the size of her and heavy; but these Chinese be eating healthy and shit.' Catalina thought to herself.

"It will be four million for the suits and weapons." Ms. Wung Shu said with a straight face.

Catalina look at the old woman as if she was crazy then at Benjamin. "You didn't say it would be that much." she said through her teeth. "Um, I didn't know it was that high. Can we negotiate?" Catalina asked.

"This isn't a used car lot, there's no negotiating. You're a crime Boss. Please don't disrespect me or my work again." Ms. Wung Shu said as her little round face began to turn red.

"We're sorry. We meant no disrespect." Benjamin said and bowed. *'Please don't fuck this up. I hope she relaxes. This is a once in a lifetime opportunity; and the only way I can get revenge on that bitch Rose and Layla is to be as strong as them.'* Benjamin thought to himself.

"Well, let me see what my money's paying for." Catalina said as she walked over to the desk and popped one of the briefcases open to review an all-black body suit.

"As you know, Teflon is a rare and strong metal. You'll be bullet proof with it, but there's more. Each suit is specially made for the person wearing it. Like your big bodyguard friend over there. I made an instructor chrome boots that he can kick through walls with; and if he stomps, enemies will get a nasty surprise. I also heard you like to put daggers, well blades on your brass knuckles, so I made you something better as a weapon. Ms. Wung Shu said while picking up two melt rings the size of a frisbee and handed them to Catalina. Right away she noticed they were razor sharp, and lighter than any metal she felt before.

"What am I supposed to do with these? I might cut my own hand off trying to stab someone with it." Catalina said.

Ms. Wung Shu raised her left eyebrow and smiled before placing two long chrome bracelets around Catalina's wrist. "Now throw the rings at that dummy over there."

"Ms. Wung Shu, as much as I'd like to, I need him alive." Catalina said looking at Tito.

"No, the practice doll over there." she said as she pointed to the far side of the room at the to practice dummies.

"Uhmm, okay." Catalina replied before aiming and tossing one ring then the next one. She felt a jerk at her arm as if from the recoil of shooting a big gun. The two rings cut through the air at top speed, slicing one of the dummies' head off and the second one in half from the torso.

"Hold your hand out." Ms. Wung Shu said.

Catalina couldn't believe her eyes. The spinning rings were not coming back. Catalina panicked and began to back pedal as the rings slowed down and went straight into her hands. "How? How didn't they cut me; and how come when I threw it, it had more strength? I know I'm strong, but not that strong."

"I told you my Technology is the best. Certain things I only sold to the Teflon Divas because the leader was close friends with my grandson; but now I just make weapons and feel empty and incomplete if they're not being used. To answer your question, the bracelets have special magnets in them that turn on the negative side, pushing your rings away from you with incredible force and speed; and when you raise your arms. it calls them back. The braces make it so only you can catch or use them. No one else. They do a lot more, but you have to train and find out for yourself. Now wire my money to my account, I have other business to conduct." Ms. Wung Shu said.

'This shit is worth four million, but she fucked up and gave me the rings. I can just kill her and make my way out of here with the weapons and keep my money.'

Catalina thought to herself then give Francis and Benjamin the eye, letting them know to attack. Benjamin shook his head no, bowed and got to his knees.

"Forgive my boss and friend for their disrespect…"

Before Benjamin could finish, Catalina tossed the rings and they cut through the air with rapid speed. Ms. Wung Shu shook her head in disbelief and did a back flip, dodging the first spinning ring.

"Huh?! How the hell does an old lady move that fast?"

Ms. Wung raised her arms. and the second ring stopped mid-air in front of her face, just spinning and floating like a drone. Catalina squinted her eyes and noticed that Ms. Wung Shu had the same bracelets on that she had given her. She quickly grabbed the gun form the hostler inside of her fox fur jacket and squeezed the trigger four times, sending two bullets into Ms. Wung Shu's chest and stomach. The impact knocked the older woman backwards to the floor.

"I swear I just seen this bitch do some Jackie Chain bullshit and block one of the bullets with the bracelet. Tito, go over there and stomp her face out for me for good measure; and you." Catalina turned her attention to Benjamin. "While you still on your knees. When I say go, you go; and when I say kill, you fucking do it you fuck boy. No wonder your girl crossed you, you've got no balls." Catalina said, but Benjamin kept his head bowed low while on his knees, rocking and repeating, "I'm sorry for the disrespect."

Catalina looked down at him with disgust. "Weak ass fuck boy." she said and rolled her eyes, then looked at Tito make his way over to the desk. Moving it to the side, he saw Ms. Wung Shu's small body lying there. He walked closer and raised his foot high as he prepared to step on her face but stopped when he noticed there wasn't any blood on the floor from Catalina shooting her. Ms. Wung Shu opened her eyes and hopped up from the floor before Tito could react. She grabbed his arm, twisted it and used his weight to flip him. Then with her index and pointer she poked him in his chest then his neck four times.

"I'll kill you." Tito groaned and tried to get up but couldn't move. It was as if he was frozen solid and couldn't move anything on his body but his eyes.

"No! No!" he began to cry as he thought of the things, he did to the men a few hours ago while they were poisoned by Catalina's nerve toxin.

"You big punk." Ms. Wung Shu said while looking at the tears streaming down the side of his face.

Catalina didn't know what to make of the situation. She aimed her gun and fired twice. Ms. Wung Shu turned her head and moved just as she fired, dodging both bullets.

"What the fuck! What kind of bullshit is this?!" Catalina yelled, unsure of where Ms. Wung Shu was.

Ms. Wung Shu tapped her on the wrist with her index and pointer fingers, then her on the shoulder and neck. Catalina tried to move, but her arm was locked and stuck straight in the air. She tried to get up off her knees but couldn't. The only thing she could move was her right arm, and she swung it like a helpless child trying to hit Ms. Wung Shu.

"What have you done to me?! Why can't I move?! You poisoned me!" Catalina shouted.

"No, I use a style called the heaven touch, where I hit the pressure points in your body. You don't need drugs to control the body. I might have taught you this one day, but you're a waste of life and show so much disrespect in my place of business. Even if you thought you could make it past me, you're in Chinatown and outnumbered. You would have died on the spot. It's not the suit that's the weapon, but the person; and you're no weapon. A fake boss that rules with fear and impulse." Ms. Wung Shu said then raised her hand and the spinning ring came to her. She placed the ring on Catalina's neck.

"Do you know how easy it would be for me to kill you? I could have done it a long time again with the ring, but I wanted to see if you were smart enough to keep using it. The ring would have eventually obeyed one master. I was hoping you'd give me a good fight. I needed to scratched these old legs, but you didn't. Now instead of four million, you have to wire transfer eight million to my account for the disrespect in my house." Ms. Wung Shu said.

"Eight million! What the fuck; can we negotiate?" Catalina asked.

"You really want to negotiate with your life? You're lucky I don't kill you, and you want to bargain. Stupid American. The only reason you're alive is because of this one." she said pointing to Benjamin, who was still on his knees looking like he was praying, saying, "Forgive us of our disrespect." in a chant over and over while bowing his head. "He's got Asian in him if you didn't know; and he's showing respect and begging for your forgiveness. That's a smart one, I like him. Now wire my damn money!" Ms. Wung Shu, her face showing she was losing her patience.

Using her left hand, Catalina dig in her pocket, pulled out her iPhone, logged into her bank account and wired the eight million to Ms. Wung Shu's account.

"See; it's done now. Can I go?" Catalina asked, mad that she was unable to move and was beaten by an old woman.

Ms. Wung Shu waited until the door opened and one of her henchmen dressed in a black suit with a white shirt nodded his head, confirming the money was in her account. Ms. Wung Shu poked Catalina quickly in her neck.

"Ahh!" Cataline let out a weak scream but could slowly feel her arm and body again. She could feel blood moving. "It's like you stopped the circulation of blood in certain parts of my body." she said as she eased off the floor, but her legs felt weak, as if she had sat on the toilet for hours and they fell asleep.

"Hmm, you're not as dump as you seen; and yes, I cut the circulation of blood to the limbs of your body. It feels like that part of your body would have to be cut off from being dead." Ms. Wung Shu said while walking over to Tito and pressing on his neck. "Get up you big baby, you're okay. Just big for nothing." Ms. Wung Shau said as Tito eased off the ground wiping the tears off his face, acting as if he wasn't just crying, and put in this tough guy face.

"As for you Benjamin, I put something special in your case and suit. You have a great battle a head of you, and I'll be watching. It should be entertaining." the old woman said with a smile on her face. "The two of you can never come back. If you damage your suit, that's on you. You can never do business with me again?" she added as Benjamin bowed one more time as Tito grabbed the suit case and followed him out with Catalina close behind.

"I'll kill that old bitch one day. Just watch." Cataline mumbled under her breathe.

Chapter Seven

Would You Die for Me?! Would You kill for Me?!

"Again motherfucker! Remember I killed your family, use that rage and attack!" Iris shouted.

Habib stood dressed in great sweat pants and grey shirt drenched in sweat. The eye he lost itched for some reason and made him dig up under his black pirate style eye cover to scratch the flesh that was there as he bounced back and forth in his fighting stance with two ice picks in his hand.

"Ahhh!" he shouted as he charged her, swing rapidly trying to poke her. Iris blocked his move with ease with her kombu crude knives. The sound of metal crashing together could be heard ringing throughout the air.

"Yes, the face! Aim for the spot I told you. If you stab someone there, they'll die instantly, and here they'll bleed out internally and die. Good, use that rage." Iris coached with a smile on her face as Habib spin kicked then jumped up in the air, kneeing her in the chin.

"Hmm." She spit up blood as Habib continued his attack with pure rage on his face, managing to jab her in the nose. "Wait, hold up." she said, but Habib continue his attack and swung, trying to put the ice pick in her face.

"Oh, you for real. I was taking it easy on your ass." Iris said then jumped in the air, looking like Van Damme as she kicked him in the face. Habib stumbled back and she toss her knifes to the floor, running up on him with incredible speed, punching him in the chest and stomach six times.

"Uughh!" Habib groaned in pain as he bent over and vomited everywhere.

"You nasty motherfucker!" Iris spat, cursing in Spanish before she spin-kicked him. The blow was so hard to the temple Habib hit the floor sideway.

"I'm getting better. I could've got you." he said as he lost consciousness.

"You got better, but nowhere near on my level. I'm being nice, but you got better." Iris said then spit the thick blood out of her mouth onto his face.

"My kids. My family." Habib cried out in his sleep as tears escaped the corner of his eye. Flashbacks of that terrible night played over in his mind, haunting his dreams. He opened his eyes and realize he wasn't there at the horrible event, but in the bedroom, Iris forced him to sleep in. For seven weeks she'd forced him to train and learn how to fight.

The bedroom door open and Habib sat up slowly. His body ached from the punches Iris had hit him with.

"Time to go." Iris said as she entered the room holding her hips.

"I need more rest, my head's still spinning; and go where?" Habib asked.

"We have some errands to run baby. Besides, you've been out for damn near eight hours. I had to keep checking on you to make sure I didn't kill your ass. Now we couldn't have that; then your daughter would have to take your place as my body guard." Iris said with a wicked smile on her face. "Come on, time to have fun."

Habib got up and followed Iris downstairs to the secret room behind the refrigerator that was full of weapons.

"Here, take this, and this." Iris said, passing him a small Mp5 Machine gun with a strap and two clips, and a Glock 17 with three 30 bullet magazines. Handing him a shoulder holster, then his two ice picks with the handles wrapped in black tape, she grabbed a few weapons began to place them on her.

"Where are we going? You never gave me this many weapon at once, not to train. I get one at a time." Habib said nervously.

Iris just looked at him and pass him gun silencers. "Remember, when screwing them on go clock wise. We don't need any mistakes like last time. Come on." Iris said and lead him to the garage.

They climbed in a matte black S550 Mercedes-Benz with dark tinted windows, making it impossible to see in. Habib sat in the passenger seat with his heart pounding, feeling as if it wanted to come out of his chest. 'I have to do what she tells me or Esha is as good as dead. I can't keep living like this, but if I get close enough, I can get my daughter and kill her.' Habib thought to himself as his mind replayed the worse night of his life. He laid on the floor crying, holding his wife and youngest daughter. He screamed, "Run!" as Iris aim at Esha, then everything went black.

Habib opened his eyes and took a deep breath. The streets were dark, but people were still moving about. Iris stopped at a light and saw a tall light skin man in a dark blue peacoat bending down kissing a short woman in a brown jacket. *'Is that what love is really like? Someone that truly cares for you and shows you affection in public?'* Iris thought to herself.

"Kiss me." Iris ordered.

Habib's face twisted up with disgust and he did his best to hide it as he turned from looking out the window and leaned over to kiss her softly, giving her flashbacks backs of the way Tess used to kiss her, deeply and passionate with so much love.

"You're doing it wrong." Iris said and pulled away while trying not to cry at the thought of Tess.

She quick pulled the car over and watched the couple turn down a quite block before hoping out the car.

"Come on fool!" she shouted while speed walking.

"Oh Lord, what now? Will dying be easier? How much more do I have to bare?" Habib asked himself as he got out the car and follow her lead.

Iris watched the couple closely, looking around to make sure no one was watching before she picked up speed. Like a cat or a tiger about to pounce on its prey, she pulled her kombu knife from the hostler on her lower back and in one swift move grabbed the woman, putting her in a head lock and placed the knife to her neck. The tall man she was with reacted quickly. Iris could tell right away he was a street dude, as he grabbed Iris' arm and try to pry the knife away from his woman, then punched Iris dead in the face.

"Get off my woman bitch! Get off her!" he shouted as he pulled back to punch her again, but Iris kicked him the in the shin.

"Ahhhhh!" he screamed out and bent over slightly before receiving a front kick the face, knocking him backward.

"You tall bastard. If you move or run up on me again, I promise you I'll slice this bitch's throat and let her bleed out all over you." Iris said, pressing the blade deeper into the woman's neck cutting her.

"Ouch! Please baby, chill." the woman said as she felt her warm blood run down her neck and onto her coat. The tall man looked at his woman then Iris as he rubbed his shin while thinking of his next move.

"Let's play a fast game. If y'all do it, I'll let y'all go. Okay." Iris said and squeezed her arm tighter around the woman's neck.

"Okay okay, we'll play. Don't hurt her." the tall man pleaded with his hands up, thinking of a way to get to the small 32 caliber handgun he kept inside the hole he cut in the pocket of his peacoat. *'I should've pulled it out when it first went down.'* he thought to himself.

"Okay, the game is called would you bleed for me." Iris said as Habib walk up and couldn't believe what was happening.

"Help us." the tall man said looking at Habib.

Habib stood there nervously. "I wish I could." he mumbled, stepping closer and put the man in a head lock.

"What are you doing?!" the man shouted.

"When I let you go, run. Go for that gun in your pocket. I'm going hit you and you run for your life. Grab your woman and run for your life. Run towards people." Habib whispered.

"It took you long enough to get over here. I thought for a second you'd stay on the corner and watch like a pussy." Iris said. "Now back to the game. Do you love her? Iris asked.

"Yes, I do." the tall man answered while fake struggling with Habib.

"Would you bleed for her?" Iris asked, knowing he would say no.

"Yes, I would." was his response.

Iris' face twisted up. "I don't believe you. Habib stab him. Make him bleed and don't hit the organs!" Iris shouted. Habib pulled out his ice pick with the taped handle. "Habib do it." she ordered again in frustration.

Habib held the ice pick nervously and hesitated at following her orders. "If you want to live don't pull the gun yet. You'll know when." Habib whispered then stabbed the man in the back with the ice pick.

"Ahhh! Ahhh!" he screamed as he squirmed, trying to break free of Habib's grip, feeling blood running down his back and soak into his jeans.

"Let's try this again." Iris said. "Would you bleed for her?" she asked.

"Yes!" the man screamed to Iris' surprise.

"Stab him again!" Iris shouted, and Habib stabbed the tall man in the shoulder blade.

"Ahhhh! Ahhh fuck! Fuck! Fuck y'all! Fuck; let my woman go!" he shouted.

"This is bullshit! No one loves someone else more than they love themselves! That love is fake! No one loved me like that. I don't believe it." Iris said then looked down at the woman crying in her arms. 'Did Tess love me like that? She would bleed for me and kill for me, but picked Bless over me; and did he love me? He saved me from my father, but again he picked someone else over me. Everyone always picks someone else over me. Am I not good enough?" Iris said, talking to herself out loud causing Habib, the tall man and the woman look at her as if she'd lost her mind.

"Okay, I got an idea! Would you bleed for him?" she asked the woman.

"I said yes!" the tall man shouted.

"I wasn't talking to you, I was talking to her. I bet she knows better, don't you? If you say yes, I'll stab you. If you say no, I'll let you go right now." Iris said to the woman.

Tears streamed down the woman's face as she looked at her man and mouthed, 'I love you.'

"Just say no." the tall man said with tears in his eyes.

"I asked you a question. Would you bleed for him?" Iris asked while smiling and releasing her grip from the head lock, knowing the answer. "See, love is fake. No one loves another person more then they love themselves."

"Yes, I'll bleed for him bitch; and die for him, you insane, jealous asshole! Lonely bitch; and you wonder why no one loves you. Do what you gonna do!" the woman shouted, catching all of them by surprise.

Iris' eyes open wide. She couldn't believe what she just had heard. They say the truth hurts, so what the woman said felt like a knife was jammed into her stomach and twisted. Iris' eyes trembled, not out of anger, but true pain.

"Oh shit." Habib said, knowing that it was no way in the world that woman was going live after that statement.

"Now! Do it now!" Habib whisper into the tall man's ear.

The man reached into the hole in his pocket, pulled out the 32-caliber handgun, aimed and squeezed the trigger. Just like Habib said, Iris snapped out of the psycho daze she was in and released her grip on the woman neck, but not before Shoving the woman in to the bullet path. The bullet slammed into the top left shoulder of the woman.

"Ahhh! she screams in pain as the bullet tore through her flesh, causing a burning sensation to come from her back where the bullet exited.

"No! You bitch!" the tall man shouted and fired two more times.

"Get your girl and run." Habib said, knocking the gun out his head and then stumbled in front of Iris as if was an accident, knocking her to the ground.

"What the fuck are you doing?! Get off me now and go kill those motherfuckers. You heard what that little bitch said to me!" Iris said with tears in their eyes.

The tall man had grabbed his woman by the hand and took off running in the opposite direction while screaming, "Help us!" He pulled his girl, yanking her arm as she slowed down from the pain in her shoulder and the loss of blood.

"Come on baby! Come on!" the tall man ordered. Neighbors on the block began to look out their windows and could see the young couple running and screaming for help before they began to call the cops.

"Get the fuck off me!" Iris shouted, pushing Habib off her. "You think you're slick. I know you did that shit on purpose. Ain't no way you been training close for two months and still this damn clumsy. Iris said as she ran around the corner and hopped back in the Mercedes-Benz and stomping on the gas.

The car did a burn out, tires spinning on the street as it pulled off with incredible speed. Iris whipped around the corner and pulled out a few feet away from the running couple as she grabbed a Mac 10 machine gun with a silencer on it. The good held fifty bullets, that she was eager to use.

"Come here! Hurry, hurry!" an old couple said as they opened the door to their home.

The older man held a double pump shot gun and aimed it at Iris while the young couple opened the front gate to the house and started to climb up the stairs.

"Mine your own fucking business! They're mine! They belong to me!" Iris shouted.

Boom! The sound of the double barrel shout gun roared. Pellets from the blast slammed into the right side of the front windshield of the Mercedes-Benz, and some hit Iris in the chest, knocking her off her feet.

"You old motherfucker you! Fucking senior citizen ass!" Iris shouted, feeling lucky she had the Kevlar bullet-proof body suit on. A few more inches and pellets would had blown off her face.

Everything was happening so fast, but in slow motion at the same time. The old man popped open his double barrel shotgun and the old shells few out. He dug into his pocket and pulled out two new fresh ones. The arthritis in his hand began to act up because of the cold air outside, and he could no long hold his hand steady as he tries to load the shotgun.

"Shit!" he groaned as his wife stretched out her arm to help the young couple up the stairs.

Iris popped up and squeezed the trigger while the old man looked at her then his gun, trying to load it in time, but he was too late. Bullets tore through his face like paper, making it look like someone took a meat hammer to it and pounded on it repeatedly. Another ten bullets ripped through his body, making it jerk and shake. His body collapsed hard on top the front step.

"Rufus no !!"

The old woman screamed, picked up the shotgun and took the shells out her dead husband hands to load it. She pointed without arming and squeezed the trigger.

'What fuck is up with these old people tonight? I shouldn't be going through so much trouble. I must really be out of practice, or my head must really be fuck up over Tess. I'm a trained assassin for crying out loud. I've killed drug lords and bosses, but Habib was able to kick and punch me earlier; and now I'm in a shootout with grandma.' Iris thought as the shotgun roared and she quickly ducked behind the open driver side door of the Mercedes Benz as the pellets made tiny holes in to it. The old woman quickly dug into her husband's pocket and grabbed two more shotgun shells, reloading her gun. Iris popped up and fired one shot. The bullet cut through the air at lightning speed and missed the old woman's forehead but skinned her scalp, knocking off her grey curly hair wig.

"Oh, you little young hoe! You got to die! You killed my husband, then shot my favorite wig! You shot Regina." the old lady said, talking about the name she gave her wig as she walked pass the young couple and made her way down the front stairs of her house to get a better shot at Iris. "If I could throw hot grits on you bitch, I would!" the old lady shouted, raised her shotgun, and a hail of bullets tore through her chest and stomach. Her body violently shook as if she was doing the Macarena before hitting the ground. Iris walked up to her and emptied the remaining ten bullets into her face, then looked up at the couple on the house stairs with a huge smile in her face showing off a set of perfect white teeth. She pressed a button on the side of the Mac 10 releasing the magazine, let it drop to the ground and grabbed a new one from the hostler on her thigh and loaded up into the gun. The man jumped in front of his woman, using himself as a shield as he waited for what was to come next. Police sirens could be heard come from both ends of the block.

"Fuck! Fuck!" Iris shouted. "Habib if I die or get caught your daughter dies as well. Fucking react now pussy!" Iris shouted, cursing at him in Spanish.

Habib thought about what she said and turned around to face the police car that was coming up behind Iris. He pulled out the Glock 17 with the 34-clip in it from his side hostler and squeeze the trigger. The modifications Iris did to the handgun made it work like an Uzi. It spit out bullets rapidly at a high speed, tearing into the windshield and into the first of the face and chest of the two officers and front hood. Hitting the engine, the car, it slowed down to a roll before stopping on the sidewalk.

Iris aim squeezed the trigger and sent a spray of bullets at the police car coming toward her. The bullets tore through the vehicle, hitting the front and back tires, causing them to explode. The officer driving the car tried to turn the car, but only caused it to flip and roll two times before finally landing upside down.

"Help! Help!" the Hispanic officer in the passenger side of the car screamed at the top of his lungs as he tried to crawl out the window, but the pain from his broken leg and shoulder was too much to bare.

He sniffed the air and could smell fresh gas. Listening, he could hear it pouring out the cracked gas tank. "Help! Help!" he screamed then grab his walkie talkie that was connected to his shirt. "Officer down! Officer down!" he shouted over and over, then could feel eyes on him.

He looked over to see Iris smiling next her Mercedes-Benzes, aiming to fire! "Holy shit!!!" He screamed as the bullet zoom through the air nowhere near him but hit the gas tank of the car. A larger explosion went off, blowing the car and two officers inside up, sending pieces of metal flying everywhere.

"Come on baby." the tall man said while grabbing his woman, pulling her past the dead old couple and entered their house.

Iris seen them from the corner of her eyes and turned around to fire aim at them, but the sound of sirens could be heard getting closer.

"I'll get y'all later!" Iris shouted as the couple looked at her and shut the front door. "Come on, we gotta go. We can't battle the whole NYPD and expect to live. Let's go!" Iris shouted.

Habib quickly hopped in the car and Iris took off in reverse at top speed. When she reached the corner, she turned and headed straight up the block and made another turn. A police car driving by saw the bullet holes in her car and the broken window shield and made a U-turn before turning on the siren.

"Fuck! Fuck!" This is all your fault!" Irish shouted while pounding on the dash board.

"How?! I didn't tell you to try and kill those innocent couple for no reason." Habib replied, causing Iris to look at him from the corner of her eye as if she wanted to chop his head off.

She stepped on the gas and the Mercedes-Benz accelerated, picking up faster speed than the cop car could handle.

"You're really pushing it buddy! I swear, you make one more mistake I'll put to a bullet in your head, then your daughters. You've just been pissing me off. I know you let that man go. Ain't no way he got out your grip, and I know you fell on me on purpose. So, you did this, and I'm going make you pay for your mistake. Not tonight, but you're going pay and learn not to cross me. People don't live long when they cross or upset me or hurt my feelings; and you're coming dangerously close to do all three my friend." Iris said while speeding and trying to lose the police.

She made a quick right, pressed a button and the garage door to a grey house opened. She quickly drove in and it closed behind her. A few seconds later the police car zoomed by looking for them. Habib noticed they were now on Merrick Boulevard in Queens.

"How many stash houses do you have?" Habib asked in confusion.

"Why? You trying figure out where I put your daughter? You never will find her. Now get the fuck out the car, we have to restock and switch vehicles because of you. Get the fuck out." Iris said as she got out the car. Habib noticed a grey Cadillac Escalade with dark tints right next to it in the garage.

"This house is bigger than the Brooklyn one, and smells dusty."

"Just shut up! That's because no one's used it in years." Iris said, pulled out her iPhone and pressed a few buttons. The power in the house came on as they entered the house through the door in the garage.

"How you turn on the power; some secret spy assassin code mess?" Habib asked curiously. Iris look at his as if he was stupid.

"No, you idiot, it's called pre-paid electricity. All the stash homes and apartments run on it. You pay as you go, so when I reach a stash house, I pay a bill to get everything cut on. So no, it's no secret spy shit, just paying a bill." Iris said while rolling her eyes.

'Hmmm, so that mean there's a record on her phone for the stash homes she recently activated. That could be the way I find my daughter. I just have to get her phone and keep her talking to learn more, then I will find away from her with my daughter.' Habib thought to himself.

Habib looked around the house, which was decorated it as if it belonged to an older woman but, very nice. Plastic was thrown over the couches and chairs. Iris went to a beautiful brown China cabinet that held white plates. She grabbed a plate and a panel dropped, revealing what looked like a tablet screen. Iris took off her gloves and placed a hand on the device. It scanned her hand and she stepped back as the china cabinet slid to the side and a steel door opened to a large room.

"Come on, grab more ammo. We got shit to do, the night's just getting started." Iris said, filling a black duffel bag with weapons before going to a tiny fridge and grabbed a few bottles of water. She tossed one to Habib, twisted one open and drink it fast as if she was dehydrated.

'You know, it was actually fun starting off like this. My chest and shoulder are feeling much better, but I've still got some healing to do. I'm not as fast as I used to be with my right arm.' Iris thought to herself.

"Come on, let's go." she said.

Habib looked around the room full of weapons. *'How do people live like this? I would've never thought a world like this existed right up on my nose. People live their everyday life not knowing there's a killer living next door to you. It's just crazy.'* Habib thought to himself, grabbing three more magazines for his Glock 17's, put them in his hostler and followed Iris out.

They hopped in the dark grey Cadillac Escalade and left the house.

"Because of what you did with that couple, police are everywhere. They'll be checking random cars half the night, so now what I had planned we have to do a little later. Lucky for you I have other things we can do for fun." Iris said.

Habib just lowered his head in shame and closed his eyes. *'Maybe death would be better. If I die, then my daughter dies. Anything must be better than being stuck with her. It explains why she has no friends and keeping me alive. All her friends probably ran from her fast, or she killed them. I put nothing pass her.'* Habib thought to himself and realized he could no longer hear police sirens or the loud noise that come with New York. Everything seemed quiet. He opened his eyes and looked around.

"Where are we?" Habib asked with a confused look on his face.

"Why you always got that stupid look on your face like you can't tell up or down? I hate that shit. Fix your face." Iris said. "Shit, having a man in your life is like having a damn child." she mumbled.

"Oh yeah, we're in New Jersey if you want to know."

Habib's heart started to race and sweat began to drop down his forehead. "Why are we in New Jersey? Iris, why are we in New Jersey?" Habib asked twice but didn't get an answer.

The truck came to a full stop in front of a large brown house. "You know why? To kill your bothering in-law's and whatever's left of your ex-wife's family." Iris said with a smile on her face while opening the door and hoping out the truck. "Come on." she said, grinning from ear to ear like the cat that swallowed the canary.

"No, I can't! I will not do this! No more killing! I refuse to do it! Kill me now! I won't be your puppet no more!" Habib shouted, meaning every word.

"I thought you would say that." Iris turned back on the Cadillac, sat back down in the driver's seat, leaned forward and pressed a button. "Siri show me live video of Esha." Iris said.

"Yes." the iPad replied.

For the first time, Habib noticed the iPad that was built into the dash board. The screen brightened and came to life, showing four different angles of Esha on a bed crying, and a tv a few feet away mounted on the wall playing cartoons. Daddy! Mommy help me!" the little girl cried out while holding her stomach.

"What have you done to her? What's wrong with her?!" Habib yelled, fighting the urge to pull the Glock 17 in the hostler on his waist. I did nothing, but that's the point. Every two weeks since I knocked you out and took your daughter, I go to the stash house where I keep her and live her with about 11 days' worth of food and snacks. TV dinners, peanut butter and jelly, even popcorn and juice. The thing is, I haven't been to the house in a while because you kept messing up in training. I was supposed to drop food off tonight, but you fucked up with that couple. Soooooo, your dear daughter hasn't eaten in three days. I give her two day or less and she'll be too weak to move or make it to the kitchen to get water; and I think the body can only go five days without water, then she'll die slowly." Iris said while smiling.

"No, you monster! No! Go give her food, please." Habib said with tears in his eyes and streaming down his face.

"Would you like to speak to her?" Iris asked while looking as if she was really enjoying his pain and it turned her on in way.

"Yes, please." Habib said while never looking away from the iPad.

"Siri, code little red riding hood." Iris said, speaking in code.

"Yes. Speakers activating now." Siri replied.

"Esha baby, be strong. Please stay strong." Habib said.

"Daddy daddy! Where are you? Help me daddy. I'm hungry daddy. The mean lady didn't bring me food daddy. My stomach hurts daddy. It hurts bad." Esha said while sitting her eight-year-old frame while holding her stomach and looking around to see where the voice was coming from, but it was coming from all around the room. "Daddy come get me please. I'm hungry." Esha said and started crying hysterically.

"Siri, speakers off." Iris said.

"No, wait. I wasn't done talking to her." Habib said while crying.

"If you don't start doing what I say, you won't be talking to her at all. To be honest, I thought she would be dead when I pulled up the live feed, but she's strong little one." Iris said.

"You bitch! You fucking evil hoe, treacherous spawn of Satan. I'll kill you, I swear!" Habib shouted with spit flying out of his mouth.

"Go head, do it and your daughter will die slow and painful; or you can shut the fuck up, do what I say, and she lives. Never in your life question my orders; and know if I die, she dies. Am I clear?" Iris asked, looking him straight in the eyes.

"Yes, your clear." Habib said trying to clam down.

"Now let's kill your ex-wife's family, it will be fun. Plus, I need another solider." Iris said while smiling from ear to ear.

"Yes Boss." Habib said while lowering his head down, knowing he had to comply for his child to eat.

He hopped out the truck and walked up to the large house, he'd visit so often on weekends to have cook outs, drink with his brother-in-law, and play with his son or talk mess with his wife's father.

"Kill the first person that answers the door." Iris said. "This is exciting, the fact we don't know who will answer the door." Iris perked as she tossed him a short barrel pump shotgun she had in a hostler on her back. "Here." she said and tossed it to Habib.

He caught the shotgun and wanted to aim at her but knew better. He rang the bell, knowing it was going be his brother in law Rashia's second to oldest son Jason who was 14 years old to come to the door. The door opened and the aroma of curry chicken, fresh roti bread, and mixed vegetable rice lingered in the air.

"Hey, it's uncle Habib." Jason said as he stood in the doorway with a huge smile on his face and stepped to the side. "Where's auntie and my cousins?" Jason asked, looking behind Habib to only see Iris. "Who's that …"

Before he could get the words out his mouth, Habib aimed the shotgun, turned his head and squeezed the trigger. The small shot gun roared loudly, and pellets slammed into Jason's chest, knocking him backwards; but he stood strong on his feet by holding on to the handle of the front door. He looked down at the gigantic hole where his chest used to be. He could know see through himself as blood dripped down his mouth.

"Uncle Habib." he said as his body hit the floor hard, making a thumping sound.

"Yayyy, that was beautiful. Do more. The nastier the kill, the more food I'll bring Esha. I'll even get new clothes and toys for her, so she can feel more relaxed; but you have to show me something. That you're committed to me and me only." Iris said while smiling.

"Sure." Habib replied with his head low then looked up as the sounds of screaming could be heard coming from inside of the house.

"Jason! Jason!" a slim, dark brown Indian woman with long jet-black hair that came down her back in a tan long dress that flowed as she ran, rushed toward her son's body at the front door.

Habib strapped the small pump shotgun to his back and pulled out his ice pick with the black tape wrap around it.

"Habib, what have you done? What have you done?!!" the woman screamed as she dropped to her knees, grabbing her son's head and pulling him close.

"I did it for Esha." Habib said before grabbing a handful of her hair, pushing her head towards the wall and stabbing her in the face repeatedly. The ice pick went through her skin like a needle through cloths, easily ripping through the meat on her cheek down to the bone. He then jammed it in her chin, tearing through it and getting stuck. Habib tried to pull it out, but the more he shook it, the more the woman head wobbled like a bobble head. He shook the ice pic so hard you could her jaw bone snap and crack coming out the socket.

"Oh fuck! Oh fuck!" Habib screamed while looking down at her. She looked possessed as her jaw hung down to her chest, and the side of her mouth ripped wide open.

"Ughhughh!" Henna groan in pain and tried to cry out but couldn't move her tongue to pronounce her words.

"Eww, what the fuck." Habib said, seeing enough and pulling out the second ice pick he had in a hostler on his right leg, jamming it in her eye. Her right eyeball popped like a grape being squeezed between two fingers.

Green puss oozed out her eye mixed with red blood and pieces of skin, killing her instantly as the needle from the ice pick pierced her brain. Habib pulled it out, jammed the ice pick in to the top of her skull then pulled it out once more and wiped it on her tan dress to clean it.

"My wife! You motherfucker!" Rashi shouted.

Holding a long nose 357 Revolver, he squeezed the trigger twice. Iris moved at the speed of light and stepped in front of Habib, hugging him. At the same time, Habib tossed his ice pick. It cut through the air, hitting his brother in law in his Adam's apple and two inches of the long pick poking out the back of his neck. The two 347 blasts slammed into her back and dented the Kevlar bullet proof bodysuit. Habib looked down at Iris clinching in pain and holding him tight as he looked at the bullet resting in her back.

"Why did you do that?" he asked, confused.

"Because you're all I have, and you know that." Iris groaned while trying to stand up fully.

"I thought you were bullet proof; but you look hurt and those bullets look like they almost went through your suit."

"This is the Kelvar suit. It's not as strong as the Teflon. The right bullet, or one with enough power will rip right through it and me; and getting shot with a 357 is like Mike Tyson Punching you straight in the face then stomping on you." Iris said, trying to shake the pain her back was now in.

"You mother skunk!" a man in his 60's with a head full of grey hair shouted. Habib knew it was Rashi's father.

Iris spun around and pulled out her Mac 10 Uzi from her side and squeezed the trigger. Bullets filled the old man's body in a matter of seconds. He fell face first to the ground, and his back could be seen going up and down as if he was gasping for air, fighting for his life. Iris aimed for the top of his head and squeezed, sending four bullets at rapid speed, piercing his skull and splitting it in half. The old man stopped breath as his brain matter and bones lay in front of him. Rashi tried to scream at witnessing the death of his father but couldn't. He wanted to pull the ice pick out his neck but knew better, being that he was an ER doctor going on eighteen years now. He gripped the 357 Revolver tightly but felt a pair of hands pry it from his. He looked up to see his older son Gunjan, who was nineteen, now gripping it.

"How could you uncle?! How fucking dare, you turn on your family?!" he shouted with tears streaming down his cheeks and spit flying out his mouth.

"I like him Habib. Don't kill him, just hurt him."

Habib's emotions seemed to leave his body as he started to become numb to the killing. *'Maybe this is life and I've been living in the dream world.'* he said to himself as he aimed and squeezed the trigger. The shotgun roared and orange sparks came out the barrel followed by pellets, blowing up the 357 and Gunjan's hands; crushing the bones in his knuckles and blowing all the fingers on his right hand off.

"Ahhhh! Ahhh!" he hollers. Habib aimed at his head.

"No, I need him alive I said!" Iris shouted.

"Sure, whatever you say." Habib said, numb as he walked over to Rashi laying on the floor holding his neck.

The sound of Gunjan's screams. echoed through the big house as he rolled around the floor in pain. Habib raised his foot high and held it in the air as he had flashbacks of all the good times, he and Rashi had over the years. The BBQ's, the children's birthday parties, the weekends they just relaxed, and drink while playing domino's all played in Habib's mind. Then the image of Esha on the iPad crying she was hungry popped up in his head and he came down hard with his foot. Rashi held his arms. up to block the blow, but it did little to no help to protect him as Habib's size nine Timberland boot came crashing down on his forearms. and face. Habib bent down and pulled the ice pick out of Rashi's neck.

Rashi eyes open up wide with fear as he panicked, and the blood flowed out of him like a water hose. He tried to hold the wound on his neck to stop the blood flow, but his hands did little to nothing to help. He flopped around and bucked on the floor like a fish out of water rolling in his own blood, then just suddenly stopped dead.

"Hmm." Habib said then walked off, heading upstairs to where he could hear a woman trying to whisper.

"Police, please hurry. I think the intruder is my son in law and he's killing my family. I can hear my grandson screaming. Please come." Habib heard the woman say before he kicked open the hallway bathroom door.

He looked around and didn't see anything, so he aimed at the shower curtain and fired the shotgun twice. The old woman hiding behind the shower curtain's body lifted up off its feet and slammed in to the wall as large holes opened up where her ribcage used to be. Habib walk deeper in to the bathroom. Somehow the old woman's hand had hit the knob and turned on the shower. Water poured down on her face as she lay in the tub, leaking out all the fluids in her body. Ultimately, Habib was surprise she was still alive. Habib looked down at her and aimed. "Nooo!" was her last words before her head exploded it like a pumpkin getting hit with sledgehammer. Leaving nothing left of her face, pieces of flesh and skin few onto Habib's face and in to his mouth. He spit it out and wiped his face. He knew there was one family member left, and that was Amit, Rashi's 9-year-old son.

Iris looked at Gunjan still screaming and crying. She could tell he was a strong young man and played sport with a middle built muscular body as she walked over to him.

"What if I told you I'll let you leave if you man up and stop that fucking bitch ass crying and screaming? I give birth and wasn't screaming as much as you, and that shit is real pain. I swear men will never understand the pain of cramps or contractions. So, stop crying and tell me who's left." Iris said while pointing the Mac 10 at him.

Gunjan held in his pain and inhaled hard, sucking in air as if that'd help him fight the excruciating pain, he was in. "My little brother's left. Please don't kill him. I'll do anything, please." Gunjan pled.

Iris smiled. "Okay, bet. I'll let both of you live; but you now belong to me and will do as I say. Am I clear?" Iris asked.

"Yes! Yes! You're clear." Gunjan replied.

"Habib! Habib!" Iris shouted.

"What?!" he replied with an attitude while hunting for Amit.

"Don't kill the boy, bring him with us!" Iris shouted.

Habib sucked his teeth while standing in Amit's room staring at his empty bed and was about to shoot it. "First, she wants me to kill everyone she comes across, and now she wants me to take them with us. This bitch doesn't know what she wants." Habib said while bending down and looking up under the bed, grabbing Amit by the leg nonchalantly, as if he knew he was hiding there the whole time. Amit squirmed and twisted as he tried to break free while screaming. Habib punched him in the face twice, causing Amit to lose consciousness as he walked down the stairs holding him.

"Damn you're getting mean." Iris said noticing his act.

"Okay, let's go. Come on little boy; and don't be crying in my truck." Iris said to Gunjan.

Gunjan got up off the floor and followed her. He looked back at his father's body one last time and stared at his mother's body at the door. "I swear one day I'll kill them both." he mumbled under his breath while thinking about how he'd kill Iris and Habib. Iris pulled the pin to a skinny, long grenade and tossed it behind her. It turned out not to be a grenade but some kind of flare that spit fire as it spun around in a circle. The spark hit the wooden floor and the house slowly went up in flames as the sound of police sirens screeched through the night air.

"Time to go home boys." Iris said as she started up the Cadillac and smiled while looking at her new family sitting in it before they pulled off.

Chapter Eight

Harmony B groan in pain as she kicked the bamboo stick that was posted in the ground repeatedly "I'm the weapon! I'm the weapon! Ugh!" she shouted as the pain in her shin drove her crazy. She stopped for a second to rub her legs as Rose entered the room.

"Why are you training so hard and trying to break your damn legs? Just practice with some weapons or something." Rose stated.

"Because what Layla said was right. We won't always have weapons at our disposal, and we must train ourselves to be the weapon. I done kick this fucking bamboo stick over four hundred times today and it still ain't break; but when I finally master breaking it, my legs will be stronger." Harmony replied.

"Yeah yeah. You still do too much; but I can't wait to start doing missions. I need to get my money up. I want to be able to live like a queen." Rose reply.

"Is the money the only reason you agree to train with Layla, become a Teflon Diva and leave the cartel?" Harmony asked.

Rose put on some gloves and begin to hit the punching bag. "No. I got tired of being the punching bag for my ex Benjamin. Tired of feeling weak, being treated as if I don't matter, and that I'm not strong enough to survive in this world. Learning these new techniques and skills from her make me feel like a new person. I'm more confident in myself. The money is just a Bonus." Rose said then laughed. "What about you? What's your reason?"

Harmony put her down then lifted it and began to kick the bamboo stick. "I have two brothers that live in Florida. It's bad out there. I came to New York to earn more money with Blue Banger and thought I was going to move them up here, but it's just as bad or worse with the killing. I want to earn enough money to buy a new place for them somewhere safe; and learning these skills to keep them safe while making an income." Harmony said then kicked really hard, snapping the bamboo stick half.

"Oh shit! You did it!" Rose shouted with excitement.

Harmony was breathing heavy and couldn't believe she did it. The sound of clapping caused both girls to turn to see Layla and the new girl Red Banger sent called Red Velvet.

"Now add two bamboo sticks, and don't stop until you break that one." Layla ordered.

"Wait, wait. I just was able to be able to break one, shouldn't I continue to master that?" Harmony asked out of breath.

"Remember what I told you, the more you train your body, the stronger it will become. Soon your legs will be strong enough to break a grown ass man in half. Go through the pain and struggle now." Layla said.

"I don't know what the big deal is. She only breaking a stick with her legs." Red Velvet said while stuffing a Snicker candy bar into her mouth.

"Well, we all not 350 pounds and can just run into a stick and it will break." Rose said, causing her and Harmony to burst out laughing.

"Oh, you bitches think you're funny? I'll take your big mouth on and show you what I do to skinny as hoes." Red Velvet said, stuffing the rest of the Snicker into her mouth and placed the candy wrapper into her pocket. Rose looked at Layla for the okay.

"Go head. It can't hurt too bad to fight one another. It's how you learn to fight different opponents with different styles." Layla said and smiled.

Red Velvet was 350 pounds of pure fat, and her face was blacker than the rest of her body. She kind of looked like the fat girl from the movie Precious, you know, that same one that plays on the show Empire. She had short, fat stubby arms. and wasn't that tall at all; and her stomach led the way when she walked. She would be a beautiful person inside but had a nasty attitude.

"To be honest, I don't know why you allow her to be a part of the team. If a situation come up when we have to run, Red Velvet here will take two steps and be out of breath; and we'll be stuck trying to save her fat ass." Rose said and grinned before swing kicking. Red Velvet dodged it. "Oh, you got some reflexes on you huh." Rose said sarcastically with a spinning around house kick, aiming for Red Velvet's face, then a swipe kick.

To her surprise, the big woman backstepped, dodging them all.

"Oh, fuck this shit." Rose said as she stepped back then ran and leaped up in the air to kick Red Velvet in the face. Red Velvet grabbed her leg, locking onto it then began to swing her around in a circle.

"Ohhh! Ahhh! Ahhh! Let go! Let go!" Rose yelled as she got dizzy, the room spun around, and she got nauseous. "Stop, I just ate. I'm gonna throw up!" Rose shouted.

"Let go? This is what you wanted." Red Velvet said and let go. Rose went flying at high speed and hit the wall in the larger room.

"Ugh! You bitch! That's why your fat ass is named after a cupcake. Why not just call yourself velvet fat ass?" Rose said while lying on the floor trying to get her head to stop spinning.

She heard what sounded like stomping, but by the time she realized that it was Red Velvet running it was too late. Red Velvet had leaped in the air, spread her arms. and legs and landed right on top of Rose; knocking the air out of her and almost cracking her bones.

"Get off me! Get off me! I can't breathe!" Rose tried to scream but couldn't inhale. Like an anaconda, every time she exhaled more pressure from Red Velvet's body came down, making it hard for her to take in air. "Help." Rose said weakly.

"You know what, I'll take your idea. Everyone can start calling myself Velvet. Yeah, I like that." Velvet said as if she wasn't a few seconds from squishing Rose to death.

"Go help her." Layla said to Harmony B.

Harmony smiled, started off walking then picked up speed and with all her might kick Red Velvet in the leg. It sounded like thunder clapping in the sky on a rainy day.

"Ahhhh! You little bitch, I got something for your ass!" Red Velvet said, popping up off of Rose onto her feet and start swinging on Harmony but missing.

Harmony send five quick punches into Red Velvet's chest, but it had little effect on her. "What the fuck?!"

Harmony shouted, realizing her blows did nothing to the obese woman, and she'd somehow grabbed her by the shirt. Pulling her in, she punched her three times in the face dazing her, then squeezed her tightly in a bear hug.

"I'll break every bone in your body."

"For you to be a fat bitch you're strong as hell." Harmony groaned in pain.

"How can we beat Miss Kung Fu Panda? Everywhere we hit her seems. to do little to nothing to her." Rose groaned as she got up off the floor.

"Easy, stop aiming for normal spots and start aiming for vulnerable parts. If this were a man her size, you'd have to find his weak spots." Layla said.

"But she don't got no balls." Harmony said, feeling as if her back was about to snap in half.

"Then really thought about what." Layla said, then Harmony head butted Red Velvet in the nose, causing her to release her grip.

"You fucking bitch!" she shouted in pain, holding her nose.

Harmony looked at Rose and nod her head. Rose took off running then leaped up and kicked Velvet in the back of the head, sending her flying forward into an upper cut punch from Harmony.

"You small bitches think y'all can jump me as if I'm some punk?!" Red Velvet yelled with her eyes watering up from the blow she received to her nose not too long ago.

Rose kicked her in the back of the leg, causing her knee to give out, dropping her to a knee. Harmony pulled back her leg, and with all of her might kicked Red in the side of her face, knocking her to the ground with incredible force.

"Whoa! Whoa! Stop! I didn't say kill each other. We're still a team!" Layla shouted.

"You said fight." Harmony said breathing hard.

"Yeah, but between Rose's punch and your damn legs, y'all will kill someone. Y'all getting stronger. Red Velvet is new and only been training a few weeks. Well, her new name is Velvet." Layla said smiling. "Velvet are you okay?" Layla asked.

"Hell no! My head is killing me. You let those bitches jump me. That shit ain't fare." Velvet said rubbing her jaw and the side of her face.

"You actually were handling them well on your own. There's no telling how good you can get. You have few week spots because of your juiciness." Layla said.

"Just say fat, that's what it is. In fact, I want some chicken and a container of ice cream." Velvet replied.

"Chicken and ice cream? Do that even go together Velvet?" Rose asked.

"You being funny again? You want to fight some more?" Velvet asked, easing off the floor.

"Naw, it was a serious question; and after fighting you, I've found a new respect for you. I see your more than just tech-support. You get down, and I'm sorry for any disrespect. I do have a big mouth, I can't help it; and you want a thing of ice cream? Don't you mean a pint of ice cream?" Rose asked.

"No, I meant a thing of ice cream. I don't care, whatever. Everyone else calls it a pint or a bucket. I call it a thing of ice cream okay; and I Accept your apology." Velvet stated.

"I'm sorry too Velvet, just for laughing at big mouth Rose. She has that effect; but she was right, I have a new-found respect for you after fighting you." Harmony B said.

"Thank you." Velvet replied.

"Well I'm going for my walk." Layla said.

"Yeah yeah. If you're not back in a half hour we know to look for you or run." Harmony stated, wiped her face with a towel and went back to kicking a new bamboo stick. Rose followed her lead and punch the wooded practice dummy. The skin on her knuckles had hardened and her punch was getting stronger and stronger.

"Fuck that training shit, I'm going cook some chicken and eat a thing of ice cream. I'll save y'all some chicken for when you come up." Velvet stated.

Layla smiled knowing this was her knew family as she rode the private elevator to the first floor of her brownstone. She grabbed her hooded black peacoat with brown fur and her black Timberland boots, using a key card to unlock her door to get out.

It was six clock and it was still getting dark early. People was rushing, coming and going to work or just handling their business, but it was the same faces every day at the same time. Layla had memorized everyone, and only few new faces popped up once in a while.

She walked three blocks over, turned, and just like that you went from luxury brownstones to normal buildings, and then the hood. She walked into the Chinese Restaurant and smiled, seeing they had her order ready. Like clockwork, she paid for it and headed back the way she came just as the snow began to fall. She checked her back, crossed the busy street and walk to into Central Park. Even though it was cold as hell and getting dark fast, that did little to stop people from being outside. Couples on horse carriage rides could even be seen going up and down the main road in the park. Layla walked a different trail until she spotted who she was looking for, the young girl in a dark blue dry bubble jacket and matching scully sitting on a bench. As she walked toward the girl something caught her eye. An older woman walking her small Yorke, but that wasn't what was strange. What was weird was the 6'3 man following behind her with an all-black hoodie and gloves on. He looked around to see if anyone was watching, but the look in his eyes said he really didn't give a fuck, power walking behind the old lady. Her small dog turned around to warn her and start barking. He stepped toward them, pulled his leg back and kicked the tiny Yorkie as if he was a football player trying for a field goal. The Yorker flew up high and traveled a few feet in the air before crashing into the top of some trees and getting stuck.

"Ms. Pepper Pot! No!!" the old woman shouted, not believing what happen to her only real friend in the world. "My baby! Oh, my baby!" she screamed.

The man pulled out a gun and pointed at the woman. "Shut the fuck up and give me your money!" he shouted while snatching the pearls off her neck, then snacking her pride by digging around in her purse, taking the cash he found and a credit card.

"You have my things, please leave me alone and let me go help Ms. Pepper Pot. She could really be hurt you monster." the old woman seethed, more concerned with her dog's life than her own.

The tall creepy man licked his dry peeling lips and said, "I'm not done with you yet. In fact, you're coming with me. I'm gonna take you to a nice quite spot, and if you scream, I'll kill your little dog. Come on." the tall creepy man said yanking at her arms.

The old woman's heart raced, and she felt as if she could have a heart attack at any time, but her fear of the man harming her dog was more than the fear of her losing her life. Everything happened so fast, in the matter of seconds, but Layla already know what was taking place. She prepared to run to get to the man, that was just a few feet away, but the girl on the bench had bet her to it. She ran at top speed, and before the tall creepy man could register what was happening, the tiny 5'2 girl was now standing in front of him. He looked down at her strangely trying to make out the situation and wondered why she was bold enough to run up knowing he had a gun in his hand.

"Oh, I get it, you want to come and have fun with me and the old crow huh." he said then pointed the gun at the young girl, a mistake he'd so regret.

The young girl grabbed his wrist and twisted it, causing him to scream out in pain and drop the gun. "Ughh! Ahhh you little bitch! Let go! Let go!" he shouted.

"Okay." she said then kicked him in his balls with all her might.

"Oweeee!" he groaned, doubling over in excruciating pain as tears came to his eyes. She spin-kicked him in the face while he was bend over for good measure.

"Leave now and get your dog. I'll handle this." the young woman said while picking up the old lady belongings and taking the credit cards and money out the tall creepy man's pocket while he rolled on the ground still holding his scrotum. She passed the belong to the old lady.

"Why thank you child." the older woman said and walked off before looking back. "You be careful. I'm going call the police while I get Ms. Pepper Pot. She's stuck in that tree and been out here in this cold for far too long." she added before continuing on.

"You little bitch! I'll kill you!" the tall creepy man yelled as he recovered.

The young woman kicked the hand gun far in to the bushes. "How you going kill me, huh?" the young woman asked sarcastically.

"Oh, you think you fancy ha, because you know that Jackie Chan tv shit; but let me tell you something, that shit only works on tv, not in real life. In real life bad guys got weapons hoe." the tall creepy man said and pulled out a large kitchen knife from inside his jacket pocket. "I'm going carve you up real nice, and while you bleeding out, I'm going fuck you." the tall creepy man said while licking his dry lips.

Layla stood back watching the whole time. *'Should I interfere, or should I just watch and see what happen; but if she gets killed it's my fault, because I didn't help her.'* Layla thought to herself, but still not moving, waiting to see the outcome.

The tall creepy man swung the knife down as if he was trying to stab the young girl in the head. She stepped back just in time, then he swung it sideways at her face.

"I'm going cut up your pretty little face bitch, then find that old bitch." the tall creepy man said then spit on the ground and began to swing rapidly, trying to stab her while he screamed. "Stay still little bitch!"

The young woman kept dodging his blows, knowing one hit from him, her life would be over. She watched every attack he attempted and noticed he was starting to breathe hard, probably from smoking to many cigarettes during his life. Each swing was coming slower and slower, and she only had to use half her energy to get out the way. Her eyes opened up wide as she saw her opportunity and grabbed his hand that held the knife. With his own hand, she guided it upwards and forced him to stab himself. The blade tore through his black hoodie and into the fat of his stomach.

"Ugh! No, you bitch! No!" he groaned as he tried to pull his hand free of her grip but couldn't, so he let go out the knife that was still inside him.

The young woman held on tightly to his right hand, but with her left she grabbed the handle of the kitchen knife that was still inside him and pulled down with all her might.

"Ahhhhhh! Ahhhhhh!" the tall creepy man screamed out loud at the top of his lungs in agonizing pain as his stomach tore open.

What seemed like hot steam came from his now open wound and his intestines fell out like spilled spaghetti on to the ground smoking hot.

"You bitch." he groaned as he stumbled around trying to hold on to his stomach, but the wound was too big. The smell of his inside left the smell of feces lingering in the air. He then fell face first with his mouth open, landing in his own intestines. He tried to speak but ended up just taking in a mouth full of himself as he died with his eyes open. The young woman dropped the knife, then turn around to head back to her bench.

"Bitch get the knife!" Layla shouted.

"Huh?!" the young woman said, finally noticing her for the first time.

"Get the knife hoe and come on." Layla said, fanning her toward her.

The young woman turned around, grabbed the kitchen knife and ran toward Layla with it.

"Put it in the Chinese food bag." Layla ordered, and the young woman did as she was told. "Now let's go before the police come; and how come you never told me you knew how to fight like that Suyung? I've been bringing you food for a month and you never told me." Layla said as they walked at a fast pace, blending in with the rest of people walking the streets.

"You never asked." Suyung replied as she followed Layla and they stopped in front of a beautiful five-story apartment building. "Wait, I'm trouble. I don't think it's good for me to come to your place." Suyung said with fear in her eyes.

"Listen, you just stabbed a man and gutted him open like a fresh fish. You have blood all over your jacket, and the police might be liking for someone that fits your description. I know that old lady won't tell, but who knows who else seen you kill him. You have to lay low; and whatever's going on with you and your life, I'm pretty sure you don't want no run ins with the law. Am I right or am I right?" Layla asked.

Suyung exhaled. "Okay, you're right. I'll stay maybe for the night." she responded.

"Good. I've been trying to get you here for a month to help you. Who knew all it took was you cutting a psychopath to do so?" Layla said as she lifted a secret panel on the front door, took off her gloves, placed her thumb on the scanner and the door opened. Suyung eyes raise and she looked on in amazement. "So, you live in some high-tech building on some future shit huh? How much you pay in rent for your apartment?" she asked.

"I don't." Layla replied as they entered the building. The entryway was made of white pearl marble that led to a black elevator.

"You don't?" Suyung asked confused.

"I don't pay rent, I own the whole building." Layla replied and Suyung's mouth opened wide.

"You never told me that." Suyung said as they rode the elevator to the fifth floor and got off. The fifth floor was set up like a penthouse apartment and very luxurious with the finest money could buy.

"There's two bedrooms. up here. You can have my guest room. If you stay longer, you'll have to go on one of the other floors with the girls. It's three bedrooms. on each floor. There's a children's area on the first floor and a bigger kitchen." Layla said.

"You told me about the girls, but never that you were living like this." Suyung said.

"Did it matter? Would have you still came when I ask you every day we met?" Layla replied. No, I wouldn't have. I'm more trouble than you can handle, and I don't want to get any one hurt." Suyung replied.

First the first time Layla could see how beautiful Suyung really was. She had beautiful brown skin and was mixed with black and some Asian descent, which you clearly could see by her eyes and face. She had tattoos on the side of her face that traveled down to her neck, which was completely tatted up. Even though she had the Asian eyes and face, she had black girl lips; full and juicy. *'If this bitch cleans up, she would be one of the baddest bitches I know. I don't know who's sexier, her or Harmony B.'* Layla thought to herself then snapped out of her train of thought.

"It's time you talk to me Suyung. Every day for the last month I've been bringing you food and sitting with you. I tell you little things about myself, but you tell me nothing. You refuse my help but take the food. You'd rather sleep on the train or bus then go back to your bench; but by the way you fight and speak, I can tell you're educated. Most people would be fooled by your tattoos, but I know better. I see through the fake you, I see the real you. You're desperately trying to hide from the world. Why are you hiding from the world? Why are you living on the streets? You can trust me. I used to be like you, moving from foster homes to foster home, until Tess found me." Layla said.

"I'm not ready to talk. I'm only here for a night. I appreciate your hospitality and friendship but respect my wishes please and just let it be." she stated. "May I take a shower? I've been washing up in the women's shelter every other day, and their bathrooms. are nasty as hell. You never know how dirty other women can really be."

"You don't have to ask here Suyung. There's a master bathroom in the guest bedroom; and while you were shutting me out and not answering my questions, I ordered you some clothes. They'll be here tomorrow. We have to burn the things you have now and get rid of the knife. No evidence, no time." Layla said as she got up and walked away, disappointed Suyung didn't open up to her.

Suyung got out the shower and saw an off- white silk two-piece pajama set waiting for her on the queen-sized bed. After drying and find bodying lotion, she put it on and then found a new brush on the dresser. She brushed her long her black hair that came down to her back, thinking of the dye she used to color it green or purple.

"And my father's thought I was ratchet as hell." she mumbled to herself but got bored fast in the fancy big room.

Leaving the room to look for Layla, she looked around what seemed like a large condo but didn't find her, so she made her way to the elevator and look at the buttons; but something was off. She lifted the panel and saw a scanner. Blowing on the scanner, she saw a thumb print. She used the silk button-up shirt she had on and pressed gently against it.

"Basement floor." a voice said through the speakers of the elevator.

"This place is so weird. All this time she's talking about me not sharing my life story, it seems. Layla been hiding more than a few secrets of her own." Suyung said as the elevator stopped, and the door opened. "Wow! What the fuck is this, the bat cave?" she said out loud.

The basement was large with tall vaulted ceilings, bright white lights and six black motorcycles lined a wall. There was a cage filled with an arsenal of weapons; guns, swords, knives, and some weapons Suyung couldn't identify. Then there were two training rooms. with glass doors; one with blue mats on the floor, mirrored walls and two treadmills. The second one had blackstrap floors and three human shaped practice dummies that you punch. Inside the room Layla could be seen practicing kicking one of the dummies and doing punching combos to his face. Suyung entered the room.

"I see you found your way down here. There's more to you than meet the eyes mama Suyung. I've seen you fight. How about if I beat you right now, you tell me who you really are and your story." Layla said while never looking at her and still punching the dummy.

"Ha!" Suyung bust out laughing.

"Why are you laughing?" Layla asked.

"Because you can never beat me. I'm undefeated." Suyung replied.

"So, is it a yes?" Layla asked.

"Sure, I'll say yes, knowing you're not going to win. Where the gloves?" Suyung replied.

"No gloves, it's a fight!" Layla shouted then ran and did a jump kick that missed. Suyung moved fast, but Layla bent down, and swipe kicked her. Suyung fell onto the mat and bounced back up.

"You're fast. I like that." Suyung said and took her stance before attacking.

She managed to use her index finger and pointer along with her thumb to grab Layla's stomach and scratch it, ripping three lines into her.

"You know Eagle style Kung fu." Layla said, rubbing her stomach and seeing the blood on her hand.

"That not all I know. Come on." Suyung said.

"Ahhh!" Layla screamed then attacked with a round house kick, then folded her hands up like claws and swung, catching a piece of Suyung's thigh. The strength of her fingers and nails ripped through the cream silk pajama pants and tore in to Suyung's flesh. She leaped back with anger on her face.

"You know Kung fu as well." Suyung stated.

"My mother taught me all styles." Layla said.

"But have you mastered one?" Suyung asked, ripping the left arm sleeve of the pajama shirt and tied it around her tight. "See, I know all style as well, but my father made me master one style; and I never lost a tournament, since the time I was three years old." Suyung said before attacking.

All Layla could see was feet coming at her head back to back. She use her firearms. to block it four times but had to backstep as she receive a kick straight to her stomach that knocked the air out of her.

"What the fuck?" Layla said, but received two kicks to the face, knocking her to the ground.

She looked up to see Suyung jump up in the air and her foot coming down. Harmony B, Rose, and Velvet had seen the practice match on the security camera and made their way to the basement and were now watching the fight outside the glass door from the training room.

"Shit, I didn't think no one could beat Layla. Should we help?" Rose asked.

"Shit, she didn't help me when y'all jump my ass." Red Velvet stated.

"Shut up, that was different; but I think we should just watch and see the outcome. If she keeps getting her ass whipped, we may need the new girl to teach us." Harmony stated.

Layla rolled and the kick missed her head. "Shit, you know Taekwondo, and know it well." Layla said as she got off the floor.

"Yes. I'm half Korean, we invented Taekwondo. I've been in tournaments since I was three as a professional fighter, and never lost. Like I said, you never stood a chance of winning." Suyung said.

Layla held her guard up, knowing she couldn't take much more of her blows. Taekwondo was known for its kicking style and powerful punches. 'I've got to watch her feet.' Layla said to herself while Suyung continued her attack.

"You're good Suyung, but I was taught by the best." Layla said and used her elbow to hit Suyung in the thigh.

"Ahh! Ahh! Fuck!" Suyung yelled and limped backward.

"This ain't no tournament, this is a street fight bitch. Bring your best moves!" Layla shouted then kick Suyung in the chest and sent another elbow into her shoulder, causing Suyung to scream in pain. She looked around and saw a long wooden staff hanging on the wall next to more wooden practice weapons. She turned around and ran, jumping on the wall to grab the long bamboo staff.

"You said treat it like a street fight, right? Well in a street fight you pick up any weapon or object you can and bust someone's ass with it." Suyung said and began her attack.

"Ahhhh!" Layla screamed as she used her forearms. to block the swing from the left, then block from the right, but the staff came down on the top of her head. The staff was fast, yet flexible, like dangling a Twizzler.

"You bitch! Oh shit!" Layla screamed as Suyung hit her in the calf muscle with the staff then began to attack her feet.

It kind of looked as if Suyung was trying to sweep her feet with a broom, but that was not the case. She was swing from side to side trying to hit Layla's feet hard enough to break it or hurt it bad. Layla backpedaled fast, then jump on the wall and grab a wooden sword. Noe when Suyung attacked, she was able to block the blows without injuring herself.

"Oh shit, it's on!" Red Velvet said while eating a thing of chocolate ice cream with a fork.

"This shit do look like one of those old Kung Fu movies." Harmony said as Layla attacked Suyung, but she was to good and fast with the staff, managing to hit Layla twice in the chest.

"This bitch is really good. We might have to jump her to beat her. I don't think none of us can beat her one on one." Rose said, not believing her eyes.

"Speak for yourself. A little more training and I'll kick that bitch in half with one blow." Harmony said.

"All that's a waste of energy. That bitch fast, I'll have to stay on her ass. That'll clam her down while I beat her ass." Velvet said while stuffing more ice cream in to her mouth.

Suyung spun the staff around was able to knock the wooden stick out of Layla hand then hit her in the neck with it. Layla leaped back and ran to the wall to grab the closet things to her, the spikes on her Teflon diva body suit. Two gothic style gloves that had plastic spike on them that travel along her for arms. and down to her elbows.

"I think Layla's gonnna lose. She done fucked up and picked a weapon with no reach. That other girl can beat her and keep herself safe with the distance between her and the staff. Our boss lady stupid." Velvet said while licking the inside of the pint of ice cream.

"You're wrong. The fight's over, I've seen her use that kind of weapon before. Layla's strength is in her forearms. The new girl messed up by letting her put those gloves on. I'm out. I'm going upstairs to watch tv." Rose said and turned around to leave.

"Wait, you not going to stay and finish the fight?" Harmony asked in shock.

"Naw, I've seen it before. I'm going to watch reality TV, stretch my legs, and do some sit-ups. I'll see y'all later." Rose said as she walked to the elevator.

'Layla's smoked, I have the advantage.' Suyung thought to herself and swung her staff at Layla's head, but she blocked it easily with the spiked gloves. Using her forearms., Layla blocked every blow Suyung attempted, then used the staff to spin close to her.

"How… How'd you do that?" Suyung asked as she now stood face to face with Layla, who then punched her in the chest then face knocking her off balance and yanked the staff out of her hand.

Before Suyung could react, her world went black from a blow to the face. She laid out on the black mat leaking blood, fast asleep. Layla wiped the blood from her mouth, walked over to the first aid kit and grabbed a pill. She walked over to where Suyung was laying, bent down and cracked the pill open under Suyung's nose. The strong-smelling salt woke Suyung right up.

"Ugh God! What is that? It smells horrible." Suyung said getting up off the floor.

"It's smelling salt. Are you okay?" Layla asked.

"Yeah, besides feeling like I got punched with a brick. How about you?" Suyung asked.

"Shit, I haven't had a fight that good in a long time. I think you blacked my eye and bust my damn shoulder blade; and you didn't have to hit me on top of my head with the staff. That shit still stings." Layla replied.

"You said it was a street fight." Suyung said as her bottom lip swelled. "Where the hell you learn Wushu from? I see you have mastered a style." Suyung stated.

Layla held her head down. "The woman I called my mother. She had us learn Kung Fu, but secretly taught me different styles, style she only knows. I wasn't finish training, she was teaching me Tai Chi and Buddhist Palm, but I only had a few lessons before she died." Layla replied.

"How did she die? She seemed like a great woman." Suyung asked.

"I killed her." Layla said and walked off.

She took the elevator to the building's roof. The snow had long stopped falling and stuck to the ground. The air was cool and there was an occasional crisp breeze. Layla walked to the six-person hot tub she had added to the roof.

'Tess would have been so mad at me if she knew I was so out in the open and really paying attention to my environment, but she's not here now. I'm the new Tess, the new boss. This is my team. I can write and have my own love story with my own Bless. No more watching and wishing. My team is almost big enough where I can take over the whole city. So, what we're not like Vanessa, Ebony, Iris and Tess. They grew up together and preached that loyalty shit but look what happened; still one of them crossed them all. I didn't have to grow up with the women I have now, but we will grow tighter and be stronger then the Teflon Divas. Matter of fact, we need a new name.' Layla said to herself as she heard the roof door open and reach for her small 380 handgun that was outside of the Jacuzzi but put it down with when she saw it was Suyung.

Suyung took off her robe and had on a yellow two pieces swim suit. Layla noticed that her body was covered in tattoos. One was a dragon Tattoo eating a man on her back.

"You can't be Japanese Yakuza. You're not Japanese, but your tattoo's definitely Asian gang related." Layla said now picking the gun back up and looked at Suyung suspiciously.

'Did someone send her to kill me? I have killed two Yakuza crime families with Tess in Japan.' Layla thought to herself.

Suyung sat down in the jacuzzi, letting the bubbles relax her body. "I'm ready to tell you my story now Layla. You've been kind to me when no one else has. I'm Suyung Lee, I'm the daughter of Kim Lee, head of the Korean Yakuza Shutan. The second world's largest organized crime syndicate family, with over 100,000 members." Suyung said.

"Are you here to try to kill me? Meeting you was no accident, was it?" Layla asked.

"Huh? I have no idea who you are. You found me, showed kindness and brought food to me every day." Suyung replied.

"If you're Shutan, you're pretty much a damn crime lord princess. Why are you living on the streets and in shelters?" Layla ask with a confused facial expression, trying to decide whether to believe her or to try to kill her.

"I was the outside child. The one my family was ashamed of. My father slept with my mother, a beautiful African-American lawyer that worked with him and had me. When my step mother found out, she had my mother killed when I was two. She wanted me dead, but my father stopped her and took me in. He raised me to be strong and fight, while my older half-sister was spoiled and entitled to the lifestyle that came with being a Yakuza princess. She barely trained and killed for fun. Me, I worked and trained hard to earn my father's respect and love. If there was a problem, I handled it myself. If someone didn't want to pay, they monthly allowance to my family, I made sure they paid. I became the goon and the boss. My father finally saw that his beloved wife and oldest daughter weren't shit. They were trying to control things behind his back and stealing millions of dollars. When we found out, he changed his will, left all the companies in my name, and was going to make me head of our Yakuza family when he died. He told a few of our trusted soldiers. On the night he went to confront my step-sister and his wife, my father's Lieutenant Eun-kyung killed him and had 100 of my father's loyal soldiers killed. I was able to escape because my father had a few secret warriors that did survive who took me and hide me but had to disappear. They will come out and fight with me if I'm ready to claim what's mine, but I'm not ready yet." Suyung said.

"Why don't you just go back and kill your step mother, sister and this Eun-kyung?" Layla asked and Suyung began to cry.

"I want to avenge my father's murder, but it's my fault he's dead. When he wanted to first kill them, I stopped him from doing it. I loved my sister at the time, she's my blood. I wanted him to talk to them first to see why they betrayed him. Him talking and not acting caused his death. Killing my mother and sister is almost impossible, they run the Yakuza now, and are well guarded 24/7; but they truly can't rule until I'm dead. They've been trying to get the companies out my name, but my father made it so only I can sign them over or there's proof of my death before it goes to another family member." Suyung said.

"You can kill them. I can teach you. There are ways to kill people from afar. I can teach you." Layla said.

"Really; you can teach me? What you know about killing; and it's not just that. I know I can get half of the Yakuza to follow me, but the other half won't. They judge me and call me a Mutt, because I'm half bread. I look blacker then Korean, just look at me. My father had three members killed for calling me a nigga." Suyung said.

"First of all, your black is beautiful; and you need to embrace both sides of you, not just one. You grow up Korean, I'm gonna nurture the black girl magic in you. When you do go back, you will make them follow you. If they don't, they will die; and what do I know about killing? I'm the last Teflon Diva." Layla said.

"Wait, what?!" Suyung said. Every criminal organization knew about the Teflon Divas. They were the ones you hired to kill the unkillable, to touch the untouchable. No crime family or boss was safe if someone hired the Teflon Divas to kill them. "I thought all the Teflon Divas was killed. Shit, I thought y'all was a myth. A ghost story until my father hired y'all to kill a Japanese Yakuza Boss. My father received a package with the Japanese boss' head and his accountant's in a box." Suyung said. "This explains a lot. The high-tech building that looks normal outside, your money and your fighting skills; it all makes sense now. I have so many questions." Suyung said.

"No, I beat your ass, so I ask the questions; and I have two more for you." Layla said.

"Sure, what is it?" Suyung replied.

"If all your father's companies are in your name, why were you sleeping in shelters and on the streets instead of using some of the money?" Layla asked.

"My father main base of operation is in San Francisco. That's where I ran from, hiding in small towns in California. I used my bank cards a few times or try to withdraw money from the teller. I figured if I got enough cash out from the bank teller, I can stay low and only spend cash money, no cards. My step mother and sister track every time I use the card and send Yakuza men to bring me back or kill me. They really want me alive so I can sign the main business over. It's the one business that if I die goes to no one. I got caught by them twice going to a bank teller, and the last time I had to kill three of them. I was only able to get away with enough money to take a train from California to New York. Living like a bum kept me off their radar." Suyung replied.

"Okay. My next question is, will you join me and be a Teflon Five? I promise when the time is right, we'll kill your family." Layla said.

"Hell yeah!" Suyung replied without any thinking about it.

Chapter Nine

Everything That Glitters Isn't Gold

"It's been over seven months since I been back, and I still haven't gotten the courage to approach him. I should just do it and get over with it. This is what I want right?" Layla said to herself as she sat in a black 2016 Mustang stick shift muscle car, with dark tinted windows.

"Girl, if you don't go over there and get that dick, I will. Short niggas and skinny niggas seem to love them a thick bitch." Red Velvet said. Layla almost pulled the small black transmitter out her left ear.

"What you mean thick? Bitch you fat, no disrespect. All kind of men love them obese type of fat women. Y'all keep them warm in the winter, and summer time there gone." Rose said and bust out laughing, causing the other women to laugh.

"Watch your mouth Rose before I bust your ass again. The next time I get my hands on you I'll put you in a bear hug and squeeze you so hard until your eyes pop out your socket. Don't test me." Velvet replied.

"Whatever." Rose replied.

"Y'all working my nerves, having a four-way conversation and girl talk in my ear. Y'all supposed to be my backup, just in case anything pops off while I decide if I'm going talk to my ex or not." Layla replied.

"Girl please. You been sitting in that car for twenty-five minutes watching your ex in front of that building. You better go out there and show that man what he been missing in his life. Some pussy so good it can't be replaced, no matter how hard a man tries. Shit, I know mine is." Harmony B said.

"That's it, I'm taking this shit out my ear." Layla said, causing the other women to laugh.

She dug in her ear to remove the transmission, placed it in the cup holder, then her passenger car door opened.

"Didn't I say stay down the block." Layla said without looking left. She finally turned her head left to see which one of the women defied her orders and already knew it was Rose's ass.

Layla's eyes opened wide, her stomach began to turn and bubble with knots. Fear consumed her body and her hands began to shake.

"You can't be real. You can't be real. I… I killed you." Layla stuttered and couldn't believe her eyes.

"No little one, you didn't. Did you close your eyes when you took that shot; because you never missed before at that distance." Iris said, sitting there looking pretty with a huge smile on her face.

Layla studied her to make sure she hadn't lost her mind, but it was Iris, she just looked a little different. Her hair was now a dark Burgundy and she was dressed in a dark blue body suit. Layla thought back to the day she shot her and Tess and remembered closing her eyes when pulling the trigger. *'Wait, does that mean Tess is still alive?'* Layla thought to herself.

"See, I can tell by the look on your face your starting to put together that you missed your target. That you didn't hit us in the heart but in the chest; and I can tell by that dumb look you're wondering if Tess made it. I was hoping the same since Bless is missing as well. There was no sign of his body anywhere, but that was a pretty bad fall off the cliff into shark infested waters. A Haitian fisherman pulled me out just in time. For a while I thought she could be alive, but she's yet to have popped up; so, she must be dead, and I blame you. You killed the love of my life bitch, so I'm going chop you into little chunks of meat and feed you to some kids I have trapped. They'll be so hungry they won't even care that they're eating human, or a bitch like you Iris said.

"This shit can't be real, what the fuck! Your dead!" Layla shouted then punched Iris in the jaw but wasn't so lucky with the next blow.

Iris blocked three punches, pulled out a knife and tried to stab her five times, but Layla used her firearms. to block the blow. The sound of metal crashing into metal echoed through the car.

"You still have your good Teflon suit I see." Iris said through clenched teeth, knowing the knife she was using wouldn't do the job. She'd have to use her kombu knife but couldn't reach it.

"How the fuck you find me?!" Layla shouted as they continued to through blows at each other.

"Easy, I just kept an eye out on Famous. I knew you soft ass would come looking for him. You've been hard to find lately, and I forgot Tess had taught your little prissy ass how to fight secretly. I always thought I would have to kill you up close, but you gotten good at hand to hand combat; but I'm still a sneaky bitch." Iris said while pulling out a small grenade from her hostler on her belt while still trying to stab Layla. She tossed the grenade on Layla's lap. "Bye now." she said and hopped out the Mustang with speed, as if she stole something.

Layla looked down, grabbed the grenade, and tossed it out the car window just as it exploded. The impact of the explosion pushed her car out its parking space, put a dent in it and broke her driver's side window, sending glass flying towards her.

"Fuck! Fuck!" she screamed then grabbed the ear piece, putting the small transmitter in her ear.

"Who the fuck is that? I'll handle her." Rose said. She and Harmony were a block away on purple motorcycles with their helmet on watching Layla's back. They heard the whole conversation through Layla's transmitter and saw the explosion. Rose hit the throttle and the motorcycle sped off. She popped a wheelie, hit the brakes hard in front of iris and hopped of the back. Removing her hamlet, she pulled out a Glock 40, aimed and fired four shots.

"Who the fuck is this?!" Iris said as she dodged three of the shots. One hit her in the leg, putting a small dent in her bullet proof body suit. "Who are you bitch?!" Iris asked, grabbing her wrist and twisting it, causing Rose to drop her gun, then front kick Rose in the stomach. Rose backpedaled.

"No, don't fight her. You're not ready. Y'all not ready." Layla said in her transmitter while coughing and speaking. The explosion had her head spinning and she'd inhaled too much smoke. She could barely see or speak, and she felt as if she'll cough up her lung at any second.

"Fuck this bitch, she not that good." Rose said as she fought back, spin-kicking Iris in her face then threw a combo of punches. Two of them hit Iris in the chest.

"Wait, that style is familiar." Iris said out loud as rage filled her body.

Harmony had ridden up the block, took off her helmet and held it tight in her hand before swinging it hard at Iris' back.

"Ahhh! You bitch!" Iris raged.

Both Harmony and Rose attacked Iris at the same time. She became enraged, putting more power into each punch. She sent a right cross to Rose's jaw, punching her so hard she stumbled sideways, lost her balance, and stood there dizzy.

"You taught these bitches our style?! How fucking dare, you!" Iris yelled as she upper cut Harmony B, hitting her in the chin, then grab her arm and flipped her over her back to the ground hard. She then began to stomp and kick Harmony all over her body.

"You taught these bitch our style?! They'll never be us! Never! You fucking hoes! I'll kill you all! Layla, you fucking dumb bitch. I'll chop your head off, watch. You scary ass hoe. You got them thinking you're tough. I'll show you a goon! I'll show you a real-life beast!" Iris yelled then pulled out a 380-hand gun from her ankle holster, aimed at Harmony's head and moved to pull the trigger; but two bullets crashed into her from her side, hitting her rib cage and denting her armored body suit.

Suyung continued to fire wildly with the 9mm Taurus as she pulled out on her motorcycle and jumped off without turning it off, spin kicking Iris in the face. They then began to fight, going blow for blow. Iris tried to shoot her every chance she got, but with them being so close together fighting, Suyung was able to knock her hand out the way each time. Iris was able to knock the gun out of Suyung's hand, but that little to stop her attack. Suyung sent kick after kick, and never slow down.

"You're much better fighter then the other bitches. I'm going have to kill you first and fast. I'm getting to old to be hanging with you sluts." Iris said before she scream, and the grey Cadillac Escalade sped up the block with Habib driving and Gunjan hanging out the passenger side window holding an Ak47. He squeezed the trigger. sending a hail of bullets in their direction.

"Everyone run! Where no ready for this kind of battle. Code yellow!" Layla said before Harmony, Rose, Suyung and herself pulled out a skinny long tube from their pockets.

Pulling the pins, they tossed them into the street. They began to spin in a circle on the ground, releasing a thick yellow smoke what filled the block, making it impossible to see. Harmony, Rose and Suyung took off running and hopped on their motorcycles before speeding off. Layla restarted her Mustang, stepped on the gas, and drove out through the thick yellow smoke to see that Iris was holding on the hood tightly. Layla stepped on the gas and swerved the car from side to side to try to shake her off.

"You think you can lose me that easy little bitch? I invented the smoke gas escape. You better come up with some new tricks to beat me hoe." Iris said and pulled her Glock 26 9mm pistol with the extended clip from her side holster. With one hand she held tight to the hood as she aimed at the windshield. Bullets slammed into the windshield and bounced off.

"It's bullet proof bitch! Now get off my car." Layla said, stepping hard on the gas to pick up more speed.

"I bet the whole car isn't bulletproof. You're not that smart yet." Iris said and started to climb up on the hood of the car onto the roof. Aim down, she started shooting holes through the roof.

"What the fuck! Suyung, I need you drive next to me." Layla shouted into her transmitter.

"Oh, it's Suyung." replied Iris, seeing her pull up to the side on her motorcycle and start firing wildly at her as they drove across the Brooklyn bridge.

"Turn onto the highway!" Layla shouted.

"Ahhh!" Suyung let out a loud scream that could be heard through her helmet as a bullet ripped through the flesh and muscle of her right shoulder, causing her to lose grip and the bike to swerve. She was losing control, but she fought the pain and quickly gained control of the bike.

"Suyung, I'm coming!" Layla said, opening her car door. It hit another car on the highway, causing it to fly off into the road.

Layla prepared to jump out her car and onto Suyung's bike. as she leaned her head out. Iris grabbed a handful of her hair.

"Where you think you're going bitch? We'll die together before I let you get away. I'm gonna fucking kill you, I swear!" Iris shouted through the wind as she held on to the hood of the moving car and Layla's hair at the same time.

The grey Escalade rammed into cars, knocking them out the way as it caught up to Layla's mustang. Habib rolled down the window, aimed his Ak-47 and squeezed the trigger, sending a hail of bullets in to the direction of the Mustang. The bullets bounced off the car and ricocheted everywhere.

"Stop shooting you idiot. Certain parts of the car are bulletproof and one of those bullets will hit me!" Iris shouted.

Harmony pulled up alongside of the passenger side of the Escalade and punched Gunjan in the face twice, knocking his gun from his hand. She tried to pull him through the window, but he was to strong.

"Stop! Stop! What are you doing?!" Gunjan yelled as he pulled a knife and started swinging.

He missed the first two times, then jammed the knife into Harmony's hand. She pulled her hand out the window and focused on driving the motorcycle. She then pulled the knife out and throw it. The knife cut through the air heading for Gunjan's face, but he put his arms. up just in time as the knife jammed into his left forearm.

"Fuck, I missed!" Harmony spat as he pulled the knife out, then pulled out another handgun from up under the seat and aimed at her. Harmony sped off before he could shoot.

"Fuck this." Layla said and hit Iris' hand hard, causing her to loosen her grip and let go of her hair. Layla leaped up in the air and jumped onto the back of Suyung's bike.

"Nooo! Noooo you bitches!" Iris shouted as the Mustang headed toward a traffic jam.

She stood up on the hood, turned around and jumped off the Mustang as it crashed hard into the back of another car, flipped over then continue to roll over into three other cars, crushing and killing the people inside. Iris had managed to grab the driver side mirror of the Escalade and climbed through the back window.

"Fuck! We're stuck. We're not getting through that traffic or that accident in this." Habib said.

"You're right. Back up and get off the next exit before the police come. Next time we'll be ready for that bitch and those fake ass Divas." Iris said while watching Layla and her team zoom through the traffic on their motorcycles with ease.

"Who the fuck was that?!" Rose shouted as they rode their bikes into their building and down the elevator to the basement.

"Yeah. you didn't tell us nothing about some psycho crazy chick that could fight as good as us." Harmony said.

"As good as y'all, that bitch was better. I watched the whole thing on the highway security cameras. That bitch bust y'all ass; even Miss Kung Fu Ming Lee over there." Velvet said, sitting at a desk with an iMac desk top and stuffing her face with ice cream.

"My name ain't Ming Lee you fat whale bitch, it's Suyung. Respect me as I will repeat you." Suyung said while holding her shoulder.

"Who you calling a fat whale bitch? I'll beat your skinny want to be black ass!" Red Velvet said jumping out the chair out of breath with vanilla ice cream all around her mouth, dripping down her chin.

"Uhmmm. I'd like to see you try. Like I said, respect me and I'll respect you bitch." Suyung replied.

"What/! I'm gonna squish your little ass!" Velvet yelled and charged towards Suyung.

In one smooth move Suyung spin-kicked Velvet in the neck and then the chest, causing her to stop breathing. Velvet stopped dead in her tracks, gasping for air and holding her neck and chest as if she was having a heart attack and choking at the same time.

"Help! Help!" Velvet said weakly while dropping to her knees, gasping for air. Layla tapped Velvet in the back twice and she caught her breath.

"Oh, hell no! I'm going fuck up little Ming Lee." Velvet said as she eased off the floor.

"That's what got you down on your knees the first time. The woman asked you to respect her, and I advise you to do it. We all should." Layla stated.

"But that bitch…" Red velvet began but was cut off.

"But nothing. We're grown ass women, no time for buts. Just respect each other, that's it. Now we got bigger problems. to deal with." Layla said as she grabbed the first aid kit and sat next to Suyung. "This going to hurt. I have to pull the bullet out, it's jam in your shoulder. Then I'll stitch you up. Harmony, you'll be next." Layla said.

"Why don't you just take both them to the hospital?" Velvet asked.

"For you to be our technical support member, you really don't know a lot. It was a big shout-out on the Brooklyn bridge and FDR Drive. Anyone going to a hospital for a gunshot wound will automatically be flagged by the police. In this business you have to tend to your own wounds, so you better start learning; but if you do get hurt too bad, you'll have to go to the hospital in a different city or state from where you did dirt at." Layla said as she used tweezers to dig around Suyung's shoulder until she felt the bullet and pulled it before pouring alcohol on the wound.

"Speaking of getting hurt, who was that psycho bitch? I shot her a few times and so did Harmony. The billets bounce off her easy, as if she had on the same suit as you. I thought they don't make those just for anybody." Rose said with a confused look on her face.

"Yeah. She said we stole her style. She fought just like us, as if we trained with her every day, and knew our moves before we did them." Harmony stated.

Layla took a deep breath. "That was Iris. She was like a big sister to me, and part of the original Teflon Divas. She knew most of your moves because she's one of us. It's the same fighting style all the Divas must learn, but we all must pick one style to master that goes with our personality and strengths, which y'all be working on. Going against an untrained person is easy but fighting someone skilled and trained like you will be kind of like the fight y'all had today, a real battle. Iris is the reason the original Divas are dead, and she won't stop until she kills me as well; and now ya'll. The good news is where stronger together. She had trouble fighting you three at the same time." Layla replied.

"Can you beat her?" Harmony ask as she took Suyung's place on the couch after she sewed her up.

Layla squeezed and touched over Harmony's hand to make sure no bones were broken, then opened the wound. "The good thing is nothing's broken and you didn't damage any nerves." Layla said.

"Can you beat her?" Harmony asked again.

"No, she can't. That why her ass didn't answer yet. I say we cut our losses and let that psycho bitch have her way with her. This has nothing to do with us." Velvet said while holding a new pint of ice cream and digging her spoon in it, stuffing it into her mouth. Layla's face turned red.

"I'm starting to see why the others really don't like you, but I be trying to give you the benefit of the doubt because I judge people on their actions and not what others say. Red Banger vouched for you and said I'll need a computer geek as part of my team, but I'm slowly doubting it; but for your information, I beat her once. She underestimated me, not knowing my mother had train me in a different style of fighting. Can I beat her again? I won't say yes, or no. Iris is a female warrior, she adapts to any situation like a true Teflon Diva. Now she knows I can really fight, I'm sure she's training harder, which mean I've got to train harder as well. Now as for you leaving, you're all welcome to leave at any time. I won't beg for any friendship. If we riding together, we riding til death." Layla replied with anger in her voice.

"You know I'm staying. You have my back, I got yours." Suyung said.

"Yeah, I'm riding til the wheels fall off." Harmony replied while trying not to scream as Layla stitched up her hand.

"Bitch, where I'm going? You're all I got." Rose said while laughing.

Red Velvet twisted up her face expression and fought her urge to spit ice cream on Rose. "Listen, I'm down, but I'm not like these fake bitches. I been waiting for us to do some jobs and get our money up. We're not children, and not going be living off your dime. I need a come up, and I'm good at what I do. I can make any legit cards and driver licenses. I already made three each for all of you. I can hack any computer or server and access all kinds of shit. I feel it's time for me to get paid." Red velvet stated.

"I see you'll never really be part of this sisterhood Red Velvet, but you do have a point on the money issues. It's time we do a job or two and make some money." Layla replied.

"I thought Teflon Divas was assassins, not robbers." Suyung said.

"We are, but we're going rob this week." Layla replied.

"What about that psycho bitch?" Harmony asked.

"I'm going make sure y'all be ready for her next time. Rose, come with me." Layla said.

"What about us?" Harmony and Suyung said simultaneously.

"I know y'all would come with me no matter what, but I need the both of you to rest. I'll be okay, I have an order to pick up. Layla replied before she and Rose rode the elevator upstairs to change clothes, then left the building.

"Where we going; and do you think it's safe for us to be walking around on the streets like this? You got the Cartel after you and that psycho bitch; and to be honest, she scares me more than the cartel. She looked like she enjoyed all the drama at the shootout. It was as if she was at home and we were the guests visiting in her house." Rose said as she had flashbacks of Iris' smile and crazy looking eyes, looking like a kid in a candy store when she was fighting.

"We won't be on the street." Layla said as they turned Down 110th street and walked a block before the car alarm went off to a Black Audi Q7. Layla walked to the driver's side and hopped in.

"Shit girl, who's truck we stealing? It's nice as hell." Rose said as she hopped in the passenger side and touched the peanut butter leather seats.

"We're not stealing, the truck is mines." Layla replied.

Huh? When, how? I been passing this truck every time I went to the store or Dominican restaurant for food. It's always parked in a different spot, and some white guy be moving it from one side of the street to the other." Rose said.

"Yeah, he works for me. Always have more than one way to get away. Always have homes and vehicles no one know about. My mother taught me that." Layla said.

"It seems. your mother was a smart woman." Rose replied.

"She was." Layla said as she pulled off in traffic.

Less than twenty minutes they were in Chinatown and Layla was parking the truck. "Why are we here? If you wanted good Chinese food we could've went back to Brooklyn; or if you want to be cheap and buy bootleg bags, we could've hit 14th Street up. I have the hook up over there. All the bags and sneakers look legit for a great price." Rose said.

Layla looked at Rose and shook her head. "No, we're here to pick up some supplies. I ordered some things and now they're ready." Layla said as she exited the truck with Rose following behind her. They walked down the busy street and entered the White Tiger Chinese restaurant.

"I thought you said we weren't here for food; but if we're not, can I order take out anyway?" Rose asked while smelling the delicious food being prepared.

"Sure, you wait here." Layla said as she walked toward the kitchen where two Chinese men in black suits guarded the door.

Layla looked around and noticed some of the customers eating was really hired henchmen waiting to attack. "Ms. Wung Shu is expecting me." Layla said in Chinese.

The guard listened to the orders they received in their ear pieces then waved Layla in. Rose look at Layla as if she wanted to follow, but Layla shook her head no. 'Where this bitch got us? Half the customers in here have guns. Hmm, that why she bought me here, to be back up I guess." Rose said then sat down at a table and cordially looked around, waiting for anything to pop off.

Layla walked through the kitchen and was led into the deep freezer where the back of it opened up to reveal a secret entryway. Layla walked down the stairs to a large room to see an old lady sitting behind a desk drinking tea.

"Nice to see you again. Layla said in Chinese and bowed her head to show respect.

"It's good to see you again as well little one. You have grown so much from the first time Tess had brought you here with her." Ms. Wung Shu said as she stood up to walk over to Layla and hug her. Layla embraced the older woman as if she was her very own grandmother. "You're on a dangerous path little one." Ms. Wung Shu said after releasing her from her hug.

"I know. That's why I'm here to get some things to help me. I wire the funds your account." Layla replied.

"I know, I checked. I have suits for all of your girls and yourself. The new suits are improved with magnets. It can help you jump higher, throw your blade or weapons and they return to you. With your new suit I added more spikes. Now you're a human porcupine. The spikes come out on your back, legs and forearms. when you flex your muscle or press a button. I design them to shoot at target and return." Ms. Wung Shu said.

"What's this with the suit make us jump higher mess?" Layla asked curiously.

"Like I said, it's more magnet technology in each suit. The force of the positive magnets creates a strong push force. With the push of a button that will make whoever's wearing the suit run faster, and jump higher, but you're going need more than that to win the battles ahead. When I thought all the Teflon Divas was dead, I sold the suit technology to a few clients. The Russian Syndicate got six suits, the Asian Mafia got five. So does the Japanese Yakuza, and the Koreans got three; but that's not the worse part. I sold three to the Santiago Cartel, who I'm sure will be coming for you." Ms. Wung Shu said.

Layla's eyes open up wide with horror and her heart raced. Now all the enemies of the Teflon Divas were now equipped with the same gear that set them apart.

"If it's any consolation, they don't have the full version of magnet technology suits like you do. I only made six of those and you're taking four. That leaves me two. I've got 10 of the normal Teflon suits left." Ms. Wung Shu stated, and Layla just stood there in shock not believing her ears. "I have a bad feeling." she added.

"You think?" Layla replied.

"Yes. Not because of your enemies, but because I feel the power you have will change you. I mean is changing you. I can feel your chi, and it's not the same. Don't let the power get to you. In the suit case with your gear I added an ancient Chinese recipe that can be used as a weapon or as a way to escape your mind. If you mix it right, the potion can cause mind lost for maybe four months." Ms. Wung Shu stated.

"Why would I want to lose my mind and forget who I am? How will that help me?" Layla said sarcastically.

"You can run away, stay low, and use the potion to erase your mind; and you can add the memories you want. You can use it to always control your enemies. They will forget who they are and believe what you say." Ms. Wung Shu.

"So, you pretty much give me a mind control potion mixed with amnesia." Layla said with her right eyebrow raised. "Uhmm, I don't think I'm going need that." Layla said while grabbing the two large metal suit case off the table.

"The path you're going down you're going need every tool you have at your disposal. I wish you the best; and choose the path that will make Tess proud of you little one. Choose life, not just power or love. Love yourself first more than anything else." Ms. Wung Shu said as Layla left.

"Yeah yeah, love my self-first. Yes, all the Fortune cookie mess. I get it." Layla said as she exited the secret room.

"No, you don't get it." Ms. Wung Shu said, knowing Layla wasn't the same person she was before.

Chapter Ten

New Weapons to Kill a Baby Diva

"I should follow that bitch and end this now." Iris said as she watched Layla and Rose exited the White Tiger Chinese restaurant, both holding long metal suit cases. She already knew what was in them.

"Do I kill her now before she gives those young bitches suits and they become more of a problem? What do you think Habib?" Iris asked. Habib sat in the passenger seat with his head down thinking of his daughter.

"Huh, what you say?" Habib replied as her voice snapped him back into reality.

"Should I attack or wait?" Iris asked again.

"Don't do it, it's too much of a fight. If she calls backup, it's no telling how big this could get. It's all about timing. I say we catch them one by one off guard." Habib stated.

"As must as it hurt me to say it this, your right. I need to kill these bitches one by one, like I did my last team." Iris said as she watched Layla pull off. "I should follow her, but there will be another time. We're here to shop." Iris said.

"I just want to go home. I want to see my brother." Gunjan said in the back seat of the Tahoe crying.

"You're a man now, stop all that damn crying. Get it together and realize the better you do the better your brother Amit will be treated. I even hired a full-time stay at home nanny for them. See." Iris said and pressed a button. The iPad came to life after reading her thumb print. "Sires call big head brats." Iris said.

A live video feed popped up and a short, dark brown Mexican woman was banging on a door crying and screaming, "Let me out! Let us go! Please!" the woman screamed repeatedly. Habib's daughter and Gunjan's brother could be seen in the living room crying holding each other.

"Lupe, what I tell you about all that screaming? You're scaring the kids bitch, and I don't want that. You came to the interview looking for a full-time nanny job, and now you have one. I'm not understanding what the problem is." Iris' voice boomed through the surround speakers in the house.

"You lie! You lie! You said nothing about being trapped here. Let me go!" Lupe shouted while looking into one of the cameras on the wall.

"Bitch shut up and get your ass to work. Clean and cook for those kids and maybe I'll set you free one day." Iris said.

"Fuck you." Lupe said in Spanish.

"Okay, you asked for it. As a matter of fact, you all asked for it with all that crying." Iris said, pulling a small black device with five red buttons on it, pressing the top button.

"Ahhh! Ahhh!" Lupe start screaming as electrical currents traveled all through her body.

She started shaking uncontrollably as if she was in a black Church and caught the Holy Ghost. She hit the floor and her body flopped like a fish out of water.

"What are you doing to her?" Habib asked with his eyes wide open, glued to the iPad.

"Oh, I placed a small device in her that pretty much sends electric currents through her body, almost like taser. The funny thing is, I put them in the kids too. Watch." Iris said and pressed the second red button on the control she had. Esha and Amit were holding themselves crying on the couch crying as electric shocks went through their little bodies.

"Ha ha! They look like little puppets break dancing." Iris said before she burst out laughing so hard her stomach hurt.

"What the fuck?! You monster! Stop! I'll kill you!" Gunjan yelled and grab the shotgun he had seating on the seat next to him. Iris quickly pressed the third button causing Gunjan to buck and foam from his mouth while twisting up and looking like something out of a horror movie.

"I put one in all you motherfuckers. Don't you ever raise your little fucking hands to harm me again or I swear I'll fucking cut out your brother eyes and feed it them you. Do you hear me asshole?! I can't believe this fool tried to bite the hand that feeds him." Iris said while looking at Habib who was looking back at Gunjan, then at the iPad at his child.

"Are you feeling froggy too motherfucker? If so jump; or do you know better?" Iris said, with her finger about to press the fifth red button.

Tears welled up in Habib eyes as he contemplated whether he should try to kill her or not. "No, but please stop hurting my child. Stop hurting my family, please." Habib begged.

Iris smile showing off a set of white teeth. "For you baby, sure. Besides, we've got bigger fish to fry." Iris said then pressed the other four buttons, turning off power to the shocking device.

"Esha!" Habib cried out watching his daughter moving slow on the floor.

"Lupe, you get your ass back to work. Wash and feed those damn kids, keep that house clean and stop banging on that damn door. The house is sound proof with an extra layer of metal on it, so stop stressing yourself the fuck out already. Am I clear?!" Iris shouted.

"Yes! Yes!" Lupe said in Spanish and got up to start cleaning.

Iris hit the button on the iPad shutting it off. "Okay boys wipe your puppy dog tears. What's left of your family is safe. Now it's time to work."

Gunjan sat up straight and used the back of his hand to wipe his mouth and grabbed the mp5 Machine guns.

"The guns are in a secret compartment on the floor. We're gonna need them. Whatever y'all do, do not hesitate to kill, and body shoots will leave you dead. Aim for the head only or hands, but mostly the motherfucking head; and remember, if I did your family will starve to death, but I seriously doubt that. I think since I added nanny Lupe, push comes to shove she'll eat the damn kids; turn they're asses into a taco or fajita real fast. The shit people do to survive is crazy, trust me. If you don't believe me just look at you two." Iris said and hopped out the truck with an mp5 with a suppressor attached in her hand.

There were two guys in front of the White Tiger Chinese restaurant in plain clothes trying to blend in. Iris raised the Mp5 to her hips. The two men turned their heads, saw her coming with a gun in her hand and went to reach for their guns inside they're jacket blazers but were too slow. Iris squeezed the trigger and sent a hail of bullets into their chests, killing them instantly.

"Come boys, it's time to have fun."

Habib and Gunjan was full of anger and rage from seeing their family tortured. They just wanted to hurt anyone. Both men ran into the restaurant and opened fire, sending a spray of bullets into unsuspecting victims. eating in the hibachi restaurant, enjoying their family time. They didn't know what was happening until the bullets hit them due to the suppressor on the guns. A Caucasian family was at a table enjoying their meal when two bullets split open the blonde husband's face and top of his head. He fell forward face first and his brain oozed out onto the flat grill and start cooking. His dark-haired wife screamed, but a bullet entered the back of her skull and came out her mouth, crashing into their fourteen-year-old son's left eye, killing them both instantly. The chef at the table toss a knife at Iris, which she knocked it down with the side of her gun before it could hit her. Gunjan aimed at the cook and fired. The bullets tore through his white chef's shirt, but he stood there unharmed and smiling.

"You bitch ass niggas!" He shouted in a deep Chinese accent then bent down and pick up an uzi.

"I told you, aim for the head!" Iris screamed while jumping for cover as the chef aimed and squeezed the trigger, sending a hail of bullets in her direction.

Habib's heart race at the thought of Iris dying. *'If she dies my child dies!'* he screamed to himself. He aimed and blew four holes into the chef's face, then roll on the floor and pop up shooting three more henchmen that was disguised as customers. He spun around and opened fire, killing another Chinese henchman and five customers. More men could be heard coming from the kitchen. He pulled the trigger, but all he heard was a clicking sound. Tossing the mp5 to the floor, he pulled out his twin Glock 17's with extended clips to hold more billets that iris modified for him to shoot like a machine gun. He aim, squeezed the trigger, sending bullets tearing through the faces of the men as they exited the kitchen; their faces being torn to shreds before having a chance to react.

"Shit, maybe I need to piss him off more often. Look at this bastard kill right now, turning in to the Indian Rambo or one of those Bollywood action heroes. Shit, all that's missing is the signing and him breaking out dancing and it would be perfect." Iris said before she burst out laughing as she ducked behind a table; grabbing a giant grilled shrimp off the table and bit into it while watching Habib as if he was a star in an action movie.

Habib put one of the guns in his side hosteler and grab one of the oil bottles at the hibachi table they use to make the fire roar for entertainment while they cooked. He used the grill fire to set the top of the plastic bottle on fire and ran into the kitchen sliding on the floor through the door, squeezing the plastic bottle hard. The oil squirted out like a blow torch, setting five henchmen on fire. They screamed and panicked as they ran in circles. Two dropped to the floor and rolled around. Habib sent bullet through the cheek bone of one of the men and the other one right in the nose. A bullet entered the neck of the third one, causing blood to gush out like a busted sink pipe. Blood flew everywhere uncontrollably. One of the men that was on fire had gone out. He sprang up, knocking the gun out of Habib's hand.

"Oh shit!" Habib shouted as the man leaped up in the air then began sending kicks his way.

'What the fuck?! How am I blocking this fast ass fucker's kicks? He's like a midget ninja! Oh crap!' Habib thought to himself as grabbed the henchmen's right leg as he kicked, bringing his elbow down onto his knee cap. A loud crack could be heard echoing

throughout the kitchen as his leg broke. The henchmen screamed and leaped back when Habib released him. He swung, trying to punch Habib, but he caught his fist mid-swing then broke his arm. Stepping closer, he grabbed the back of the man's neck and then his chin before twisting in one swift move, snapping his neck like a twig. His body went limp and make a loud thumbing sound as it hit the hard floor. Habib looked down at the dead man in amazement. Shooting a person was one thing but being able to kill in hand to hand combat was something else.

'How am I able to do this? All that training with that crazy bitch taught me something. I move faster than them and my body reacts to each attack as if she was attacking me; but fighting her is way harder than this.' Habib thought to himself while starting at his hands, then look over to see Iris eating from a small plate of grilled shrimp while leaning on the kitchen door watching everything.

"You're doing good. I love this movie. Well, that's what it feels like; but you forgot one." Layla said while smiling and took another bite of a large shrimp, moaning softly from the taste as the last Chinese henchmen had rolled out the blazer, he was in that was on fire. He grabbed a razor-sharp steak knife and was coming down hard with it, aiming for Habib's back. Habib turn sideways and kicked behind him, striking the henchmen in the chest.

"You son of a bitch! You killed Won! I'm going to turn you into sweet-and-sour chicken!" he yelled in a deep Chinese accent and charged at Habib swinging the knife.

"Shit! Shit! Help!" Habib yelled as he stepped backwards quickly, moving out the way of the knife and running around a steel prep table.

"No, you got this. Just stop running." Iris said while looking around for something to drink. "All those damn shrimps made me thirsty." she said to herself out loud.

"You're worried about something to drink? Shoot this guy, he's trying to kill me!" Habib shouted while running around the table.

"You haven't realized it yet huh?" Iris asked as she found a cold can of Sprite on a counter close to her.

"Realize what? That I'm about to fucking die while you drink a Sprite." Habib said as he jumped over the table, barely escaping being stabbed in the neck.

"You haven't realized that you don't need to run. Those months of training with me have paid off. You should be able to read most people's fighting skill levels. Well not all of them. That's how that bitch Layla surprised us the first time, but that's off topic. You should see or feel their skills level and know how to beat them; and if you still unsure, I just do something sneaky and still will." Iris stated.

"Skill level? What the fuck are you talking about? This ain't Mortal Kombat r Dragon Ball Z. If this man stabs me, I'm dead. There's no coming back or hitting the restart button!" Habib said, running around the whole kitchen.

"Good. Now that you know that, use it. If that man kills you, it's over for you and your daughter Esha. If you die, I'll just press my button and electrocute her to death. I don't have no need for her without you, and all this running around starting to bored me. You're a grown ass man playing tag in a restaurant kitchen. Kill this man now or I'll kill Esha in two minutes.

"What?!" Habib yelled and stop running. Looking Iris in the eyes, he knew she wasn't bluffing.

That one second of him not paying attention, the henchmen jammed the knife into Habib's chest. Habib let out and short scream.

"One-minute left." Iris said nonchalantly and rolled her eyes.

"The henchman pulled the knife out Habib's chest. "You killed my friend Won you bastard! Now me will kill you!" the henchmen said in broken English and went to stab Habib once more.

Habib blocked the attack easily. Soon both men were standing still just swinging at each other, looking as if they were smack boxers. They were moving so fast trying to hit each other but just blocking each attack, you would've thought your eye were playing tricks on you.

'I'm doing this.' Habib thought to himself. "Oh shit, Esha!" he said out loud, realizing he had no time to pep talk himself. He looked at the steel table with his one good eye, smirked and grabbed a meat tenderizer. It looked more like a fat wide chrome hammer with little spikes on it.

He faked a punch then swung it, hitting the man in the head with it. The hencman stop fighting all together as he looked dazed. Habib let go of the meat tenderizer to see it was stuck in the henchman's head. Habib yanked it free with a disgusted look on his face, as if someone had passed gas. As soon as he yanked it free blood poured out of the man's head like a sprinkler system. The squirts became larger with each beat of his heart. Habib and Iris' face's both remained twisted up as if they smelled something nasty as they watch the henchman stumble around the kitchen with a dent in the side of his head and thick red blood squirting everywhere.

"Okay, one second left." Iris said, tilting her head to the side still watching.

"Ahhh!" Habib shouted and smashed the hencman in the face with the meat tenderizer.

The henchman fell to the floor. Habib jumped on top of him screaming while swinging over and over, denting in the henchman's face, breaking the bones in his skull and jaw. He continued to pound until the henchman's face was unrecognizable. It looked like beat up hamburger meat with boneless chicken breast mixed up in it.

"Okay, okay. He's dead.' Iris said as she fought to urge to vomit; but it was Habib couldn't hear her. He keep repeating, 'No one's going hurt my daughter! No one's going hurt my daughter!" while beating the henchman's head in even more. Gunjan finally entered the kitchen. "Make yourself useful and guard him. If anyone comes up the stairs but me, shoot them in the head." Iris said.

"What stairs?" Gunjan asked. All he saw was a kitchen with no more rooms.

Iris went to the deep freezer, found the hidden control panel and used the computer inside her watch to break the code. The refrigerator door moved to the side to reveal a secret stair case. Iris reloaded her mp5 and cautiously walked down the stairs. As she got closer, she could the light of the huge room. Reaching the last steps, five ninja stars came spinning toward her. She dodged the two that were aimed for her face, and the third one hit her mp5, causing her to drop it. The forth one hit the wall on the stair case, and the fifth cut through her body suit armor, jamming into her stomach.

"Ahh! You short bitch! Fuck! How'd it pierced my armor?" Iris asked herself while trying to pull the star from her stomach.

"First of all, dummy, I invented your suit, as you know; so, all my weapons can cut through them. All the suits made for the Teflon Divas. From the look of how deep that ninja star went in you, you've got the Kevlar body suit and not the rare Teflon metal suit. This is going to be easier than I thought." Ms. Wung Shu said and laughed before sending three more ninja stares towards Iris.

Iris hit the ground and rolled. While rolling, she grabbed the mp5 and yanked the ninja star that was deep in her gut out. She groaned in pain, hopped up on one knee, outstretched her right arm and squeezed the trigger. A hail of bullets sprayed out the gun. Ms. Wung Shu jumped around the room like a rabbit on crack.

"How the fuck is she moving that fast?" Iris asked herself while trying keep her eyes on the old woman dress in an all-blue silk two-piece pajama set.

Ms. Wung Shu run up the side of the wall and jumped off it as it was normal. "Got you." Iris said as she seized her opportunity, and a rain of bullets crashed into Ms. Wung Shu's chest and stomach, ripping and tearing open the blue silk shirt but bounced off her body.

"You think your bullets could stop me? I invented the suits, you think I wouldn't have my own on?" Ms. Wung Shu said and smiled.

"No, I was actually planning on it with your Mrs. Miyagi ass." Iris said and squeezed the trigger again, aiming for her face.

She crossed her arms. in a x shape and covered her face, blocking the bullets with her forearms. Iris then threw the ninja star that she pulled out her stomach and hit Ms. Wung Shu in the thigh.

"Ahhh! You little bitch!" Ms. Wung Shu screamed before pulling the star from her thigh and blood began to squirt out.

"You'll be dead in ten minutes from bleeding to death. I hate the femoral artery. I calculated my attack you old bitch." Iris said as she stood up while holding her stomach, applying pressure to her Wound.

"I always told Tess you were a sneaky snake; but you're not as smart as you think you are." Ms. Wung Shu said then hit her thigh with her index and pointer fingers then squeezed. The bleeding from her wound completely stopped.

"What? How?! How the fuck did you stop the bleeding? That's impossible!" Iris yelled, looking on in shock as she began to panic.

"You've got a lot to learn. I see Tess never told you about the Heaven Touch. Too bad you'll understand the true power of a real diva." Ms. Wung Shu said then pulled out one of those all school hand fans you see people use in church.

Ms. Wung Shu flipped open the fan, fanned her face then threw it. Iris' eyes opened wide as it sped towards her. She moved to the side but was slow and the fan cut of a piece of her hair.

"You old bitch! I'll kill you, I swear!" Iris shouted and heard something cutting through the air behind her. She ducked just in time before the fan could chop off her neck, and it returned to Ms. Wung Shu, who caught it with ease.

"What in the new boomerang bullshit is that?!" Iris shouted and knew she was too hurt to kept ducking something so fast for a long period of time without getting hitting.

She raised the mp5, squeezed the trigger and sent bullets flying in Ms. Wung Shu's direction and threw one of her kombu knives at her. Ms. Wung Shu ran the best she could. Even though she'd stopped the bleeding from her leg, it was still injured and cause her to move a little slower. She threw the fan and it slammed into the mp5 cutting it in half. Ms. Wung Shu ran up on iris and touched her six times on her shoulder with her fingers, then front kicked her in the chest, sending her flying backwards. Stretching out her arm, she called the fan blade back to her. Iris hit the floor and rolled quickly back up to her feet. She tried to use her right hand to pull out her next knife, but her arm wouldn't move, and she couldn't feel it at all. It hung there as if it was out of sockets or dead.

"What the fuck you do to me? What have you done to my arm? Why I can't move it?" Iris shouted.

"The heaven touch is a pressure point technique. There are over 10,000 pressure points in the human body, and I just used four to turn off the blood flow to your arm. If I don't turn it back on in 15 minutes, your arm will die and have to be cut off. You never stood a chance against me snake." Ms. Wung Shu said.

Iris' mind raced once she heard pressure points. *'Tess showed me two moves with pressure points, but I brushed it off. What is it again?'* Iris thought to herself then smiled while raising her hand up. She grabbed her knife with her left hand and threw it at Ms. Wung Shu's head. She counterattacked by throwing her fan, knocking both the knife and fan out the air. While that was happening, Iris took off ruining, grabbed her next knife off the floor and placed the blade in her mouth to hold it. Using the index, pointer and pinky fingers with her left hand, she pressed real fast on her right shoulder, returning the blood flow to her arm. She grabbed her knife and before Ms. Wung Shu knew what was happening, Iris took the knife out her mouth and jam both blades into the top of her skull. She let out a weak scream before she collapsed to the ground. Iris looked on in amazement to see that the woman's chest was still going up and down.

"You under estimate me, and under estimated the bond I shared with Tess. No matter how many people tried to get her to turn against me, she never would. Oh, and she showed me a little of that pressure point bullshit when she first started learning it from you, but I only paid attention to three movies; the main one was how to unlock the moves. See Tess loved me, and no one loved you. You'll die alone." Iris said then pulled her blades out of her head, putting one in the hostler and chopped her hand off with the other.

Taking the hand over to the desk, she placed it on the desk scanner and secret a room open up, revealing weapons, suits in the walls and metal suit cases.

"Gunjan come down here!" Iris shouted.

Gunjan rushed down the stairs and stopped as he walked past Ms. Wung Shu. "Why must you kill old people?" Gunjan asked, feeling bad for the old woman, who reminded him of his own grandmother.

"Shut up and grab the a few of these suits. Put them in the suit case and grab the black suit case. That's special for me; and that dead old lady on the floor. She would've kicked your ass and turned you into Chinese food in a heartbeat. Do you want to be someone's Hibachi meal?! Well do you?!" Iris shouted.

"No, no. I don't want to be food." Gunjan replied.

"Well in this world you have eat or be eaten, so we about to eat." Iris said as she grabbed a few things; but couldn't care much because of the wound in her stomach.

Gunjan carried five suit cases by himself that were filled with weapons and Kevlar and Teflon amour style suits. Iris reached the top of the stairs and her eyes opened up wide at the sight of Habib still on top of the henchman's body, banging what was left of his face to a pulp.

"Stop! Stop! It's time to go. We need to feed Esha, okay!" Iris shouted.

Habib stopped swinging, dropped the meat tenderizer and stood up. "Yes, feed Esha." he said, grabbing some of the metal suit cases from Gunjan and made their way out to their truck.

Iris inhaled the cold air. "It was a good night shopping. We need to do this more often." she said and hopped into the back seat as Habib pulled off.

"Ugh! Ahh!" Ms. Wung Shu moaned as she laid on the cold floor and could feel her life fading away. She coughed a few times and moaned in pain, then felt a pair of soft hands gently touch her face. She tried to open her eyes but couldn't. Where Iris' knife had stabbed her in the head had damaged most of her brain. She was unable to control her body but wondered how she could still control her thoughts. She then felt soft lips on her forehand and tears fall down onto her face.

"I knew you would come. I've been waiting for you my dear, but as you can see your too late. Ugh." Ms. Wung Shu said while coughing up blood but never opening her eyes. I need you to finish me off and say the code. It will revise your suit, and a flash drive of how to recreate all my technology as well as the secret handbook of the heaven touch. Here, you don't have much time before the police come." Ms. Wung Shu told the woman.

She could feel the woman's tears on her face, falling down on her like rain. The woman lifted Ms. Wung Shu's head up and kiss her forehead once more. Ms. Wung Shu smiled, then a loud smacking sound echoed throughout the room as the woman snapped her neck. She stood up and wipe the tears off her face as she walked to the desk.

"The last Teflon Diva." she said, and the desk turned bright purple before moving to the side to reveal a secret compartment in the floor. A purple metal suit case popped up to reveal a razor-sharp chain, whips, and an all-black armored cat suit. The woman closed the case, grabbed it and quickly made her way out of the restaurant as police sirens could be heard approaching.

Chapter Eleven

Small but Feisty

As Sabrina peeled the meat off the chicken bone, food was the last thing on her mind at the time. Flashbacks of her sister dying played in her mind, along with thoughts of killing Catalina. Bronx Sound View Project walls were made of concrete. Sabrina spat on the chicken bone and rubbed it back and forth. It made a grinding sound as she continued to rub the chicken bone until it became a sharp point, like an ice pick. She touched the top of it with her pointer finger. "Ouch!" she exclaimed as it pricked her finger and it start to bleed. She sat up off the small twin-size bed, grabbed the white sheet off the bed and tore a small thin piece from it. She wrapped the thin piece around the end of the chicken bone tightly, making a handle for it so it won't slip when she uses it.

"Hey, you done eating?"

Sabrina quickly put the chicken bone up under her shirt into her waist band. "Yes." she said as a Flacco came into the room and grabbed her plate off the bed.

"Damn. You were that hungry you ate the bone too?" Flacco said. Sabrina didn't say anything. "You have a nasty attitude little bitch. If it was up to me, I would have been killed you. I don't know why Catalina just won't give me the order to kill you." Flacco said.

"She must think more of me than you. Why else are you here babysitting me? It seems. like you going lower and lower on the position line. You better hope I die, because when I grow up it's my birth right to control the Santiago Cartel. It's my last name punk; and when I do, I swear I'm going to kill your kids, your family, your dog; everything you love!" Sabrina screamed.

Flacco held his Chihuahua Tutu in his arms. "I'm getting really tired of your little ass. I bet if I kill you like we did your baby sister Catalina won't mind." Flacco said and Tutu start barking wildly as she jumped out his arms., onto the bed and start snapping at her.

"Get your small ass dog before I kick it! Get your dog!" Sabrina screamed.

"You kick my dog I'll kill you!" Flacco shouted. "Tutu come her girl. Come here." Flacco called out to his dog. Tutu ran up on Sabrina and bite her on the ankle.

"Ahhh! Sabrina hollered and kicked Tutu in the face, sending the dog flying off the bed on to the floor, causing Tutu to make a whimpering sound.

Flacco moved at the speed of light and back smacked Sabrina so hard she hit the wall. "You hurt my tutu I'll kill you, you little bitch; and Catalina won't know I did it." he said as he grabbed the dirty pillow that was on the floor and pulled down her flat on to her back.

Sabrina's head was spinning from her head banging against the wall. Before she could realize what was taking place, Flacco had placed the pillow on her face and was pressing down with all his might. She tried to scream but couldn't as she gasped for air. She kicked, wiggled and squirmed, but Flacco pushed down harder. She tried to bite the pillow and suck in oxygen through it, pulling on it as if it was an inhaler. I'm going die.

'This how I'm going die? God no! First my father, then my sister, now me.' Sabrina thought to herself as she felt her body go weak, slowing her bucking and kicking. Her mind raced and then she started reaching for Flacco's belt, loosening it without him knowing, and pulled it out the loop. She then pulled out the jail made knife she made out of a chicken bone from inside her waist band and swung wildly.

"Ahhh! Ahh! Fuck! What is that?!" Flacco screamed as Sabrina jammed the chicken bone into the side of his stomach three times, then once in his rib cage. When she pulled it out, a gush of blood poured out, causing Flacco to loosen the pressure on the pillow. Sabrina wiggled up from under the pillow, put the belt through the buckle then threw it around Flacco's neck, turning it into a noose.

"You skinny bastard!" Sabrina shouted and pulled the belt hard before dragging it to the door and tied it around the knob. Running around him, she stabbed him in the back of his right thigh six times until blood was squirting everywhere.

"Stop! Please stop!" Flacco cried out in pain as Sabrina started to work on his left leg, stabbing it ten times. "Just stop! Please stop! God help me!" Flacco cried out and tried to stand up but couldn't. All the muscles in his legs was torn to shreds.

He laid in a pool of blood, slipping every time he tried to stand and holding his side as blood continues to poor out. Tutu barked loudly in the corner. Sabrina went over to her and tried to grab her but was bite on the hand. Moving fast, she grabbed Tutu by the neck, picked her up and stabbed her repeatedly with the chicken bone.

"Noooo! Not my Tutu! Not my Tutu!" Flacco scream on the floor with his arms. stretched toward her. Sabrina tossed Tutu's dead body in front of Flacco. "You're just like her. You're everything like your damn cousin Catalina!" Flacco cried uncontrollably while holding Tutu's dead body. Sabrina walked behind him then stabbed him in the neck.

"Ughh!" Flacco gasped for air and tried to scream but couldn't as blood rush out his body and he fell forward dead with the belt around his neck still holding his head up.

Sabrina pushed his heavy body to the side and opened the door to peek her head out. Loud Spanish music played in the apartment they kept her in. She crept out to see a man with his back facing her on a couch smoking weed, and a woman on her knees with her head in his lap, which was going up and down. Sabrina tiptoed over and could see a gun on the cushion next to him. She leaned over the couch to reach for it and could feel eyes on her. She turned her head to see the man's eyes were wide open now and staring dead at her without moving. He looked down at what she was reaching for and sat up to reach for the gun.

"Ahh!" Sabrina yelled and sent the sharp chicken bone through his hand.

"Ugh! he groaned in pain, pulled back his hand to see the jail made knife stuck in, and yanked it out to go for his gun but was too late. Sabrina was now griping the 38. Revolver and had it pointed at his head.

"Put that down little girl! Just put it down! You're not going use it…" he said.

His words were cut short by the loud boom coming from the gun before a bullet pierced his head above his right eyebrow before another went into his nose, killing him instantly. The woman that was between his legs screamed at the top of her lungs. Sabrina aimed and squeezed the trigger, blowing off the top of her head. She fell back and her body bucked shortly then stopped. Sabrina's heart raced as she scanned the room and saw a man running out a bedroom with a gun in his hand and no shirt on as he fixed his pants.

"What's going on out here?" he asked over the loud Spanish music but felt something hit him in the stomach.

He looked down to see that he was bleeding. He grabbed his wound and looked up to see Sabrina holding the chrome revolver standing across the room. She squeezed the trigger once more, sending a bullet into his chest. The man dropped to his knees, fell sideways and died with his eyes open.

"I'll kill you all! I swear; for my father and sister." Sabrina cried.

She went back over to the couch, grabbed her chicken bone knife and tucked it back into her waistband. She walked to the front of the apartment with the gun leading the way and slowly open the door to peek her head out. She looked up and down the hallway before running out the apartment and down the long hallways to the door at the end that lead to the stair case. She tried to push it open, but it wouldn't budge.

"No! No!" Sabrina cried out, then realized it was an elevator she had run pass.

She ran to it in the middle of the hallway and pressed the button multiple times. "Come in come on." she mumbled as she anxiously waited. A ding sound echo through the hallways and a smile spread across her face as the elevator made it to her floor and the door slowly opened.

"No!" Sabrina shouted as the door fully open to reveal Catalina standing there looking at her phone.

Sabrina raised her gun and squeezed the trigger. Catalina looked up just in time to block her face with her arms. The bullet went through her pink blouse shirt and hit the Teflon body armor she had under it. She lowered her arms. to see a teary-eyed Sabrina holding the gun squeezing the trigger to the .38 repeatedly, but it was empty.

"Why you little bitch! How you get out? I was just coming to check on you!" Catalina shouted.

Sabrina's face balled up in anger, she pulled her jail made chicken bone knife out her waist band and ran at full speed. She poked Catalina in the stomach, but the chicken bone broke in half. Sabrina look at the cracked bone strangely trying to figure out why it broke so easily on her but did the job on two grown men. She looked up at her where she had stabbed and could see another suit underneath the blouse, before Catalina side kicked her in the face so hard, she fell sideways and lost consciousness.

"Now let me see how the fuck you escaped when Flacco and his men are supposed to be watching you. You can't find good help these days." Catalina said while dragging Sabrina on the floor by her leg until she reached the door and kicked it in. "Flacco how she get away?!" Catalina shouted while entering the room.

She dropped Sabrina's legs and looked at the two dead bodies by the couch, then another dead man holding a gun by the bedroom door. "What the fuck?

She did all of this; and with a damn chicken bone huh." Catalina said out loud before walking to the bedroom where Sabrina was being kept. Catalina tried to open the door, but it felt like it was dead weight behind it. She pushed it even harder until whatever was behind it moved. She squeezed into the room and noticed blood was all over the floor. She looked behind the door to see Flacco string up by the neck with his belt tied to the door; his Chihuahua Tutu stuff sideways in to his mouth.

"That girl need seriously therapy. She's only eleven, this is just too much killing, even for me; but if she's this ruthless now, imagine when she gets older. I don't know if I should be proud and keep her and proud or just kill the little bitch before she figures out how to kill me. Naw, I'll keep her around. It will be fun seeing who she'll become." Catalina said to herself with a smile. She looked at Flacco one last time then exited the room. "Uhmm, I never liked Flacco any way. Looks like I'm gonna have to keep you closer you little demon." Catalina said then panicked when she didn't see Sabrina where she left her.

She scanned the living room and noticed the dead guy by the bedroom door. The gun that was in his hand was gone.

"Fuck! Fuck! Not now Sabrina, I got shit to do and you already fucked up my outfit for the day. Now I have to change it." Catalina said frustratedly.

She checked the second bedroom of the house and still no Sabrina. Catalina stepped out into the hallway to see the elevator button had been pressed, but no sign of Sabrina. Her heels could be heard clicking on the hard floor, echoing down the hall as she checked the locks on each apartment making, sure they weren't broken into. The whole project building was a drug front, and she'd made the tenants move out years ago. When she reached the end of the hall, she could hear a squeaking sound, as if was running their bare feet on the floor. Catalina followed the sound and looked up to see that Sabrina had somehow shimmied up on the wall with her bare feet and was in the corner in a split, using the pressure of her feet to hold her up there. Every so often she would slip an inch and you'd heard the weird squeaky sound that sent chills through your body like someone scratching a chalkboard with long nails. Sabrina smiled as she aimed the gun at Catalina, holding the big handgun with both hands tightly and squeezed the trigger repeatedly. Bullets slammed into Catalina's chest and came toward her face. She blocked them, but the impact of each bullet sent her back.

"Die! Die! Why won't you just die?!" Sabrina cried while crying, trying to aim at different spots on Catalina, not understanding while she didn't fall over for good.

The billet would hit Catalina and hurt her, but there was no blood. *'She's got something on that's protecting her. I saw it. I've got to aim for her head.'* Sabrina said to herself and focus her shots at Catalina's face.

"Okay, now you're pissing me the fuck off little cousins! Getting shot hurts, even with amour!" Catalina shouted while holding one arm up to block her face.

She reached behind her back to pull lose one of the blade rings and threw it. The blade cut through the air with incredible speed and sliced the 9mm in half. Sabrina's eyes open up wide as she looked at what was left the gun in her hand, only the handle. The blade returned to Catalina and she threw it again. This time she flexed her wrist and held out her hand as if to say stop, looking like a school crossing guard. The ring stopped in front of Sabrina's face and hovered, spinning in place, waiting for its next orders.

"Are you going to come down and behave, or am I going have to use my friend there to cut off your legs then your hands?" Catalina asked sarcastically.

"Umm, yeah. I'll come down." Sabrina replied, not wanting to deal with whatever was spinning in her face now. She slid down the wall.

"Come, let's go." Catalina ordered then close her fist. The ring return to her and she placed it on her back.

"What is the armor you have on; and that frisbee thing. It's cool, what is it? Kind of reminds me of a movie I saw with my dad called Torn." Sabrina said, her curiosity peaked.

"I'm not telling your ass. All you're doing is trying to figure out how to kill me. I'm not gonna help with that." Catalina replied as they entered the elevator and rode it down with Sabrina staring at her, studying the suit under her clothes as best she could.

Chapter Twelve

Young Divas on The Rise

Harmony B took a deep breath then took off running towards the wall the, running up on it, flipping backwards four times, then hopped up.

"What the fuck? It's like the suit pushes me. I can feel a force, like someone holding my back and saying go bitch, at top speed. This shit amazing! Where has this been my whole life?!" Harmony perked with a smile on her face, showing off her set of perfect white teeth. Her dark skin seemed to glow and look smooth to the touch.

"That's just one of the benefits of the new body suits. There's magnet technology in them that make you jump higher and push you. It also helps you run faster." Layla said.

"Good, because we all know miss thick thighs Harmony could only jump but so high." Rose said and laughed, causing everyone else to join in.

"Yeah yeah. I'll bust your ass in a fight though." Harmony replied.

"We can see." Rose replied with a smirk on her face. They both looked at Layla for the go head. Layla nodded her head, giving them the go sign as she and Suyung stepped back. All four ladies were dress in their new Teflon Diva body suits; everyone but Red Velvet, who sat outside of the training room mad, staring at them through the glass wall.

"They all get some special suits and all I get is this new damn high-tech laptop. So, what it can hack any system. What if I wanted to be out there fighting too? What if I didn't want to be behind the mic directing them away from danger. I can bust most of those bitch's ass if they don't jump me." Red Velvet said to herself and scraped her spoon at the bottom of the pint of the chocolate ice cream container. Damnit, I'm gonna need another thing of ice cream." she mumbled while sucking on the spoon.

"Remember ladies, each suit was built to your abilities." Layla said.

"What you mean by that?" Rose asked.

"I mean the suits were made to enhance the strengths of the individual. Each was specially made for you, and to help you with weakness you had in your style. Just don't kill each other." Layla said.

"How, ain't we indestructible and can't be hurt?" Rose asked.

"No, you're not fool. Any Teflon metal can cut through your suits. There's bullets and weapons out there in there in the streets now made of Teflon that can harm us; and even your own personal weapon. Each suit has its own weapon." Layla said.

"Weapons? We have weapons where?" Rose asked and started feeling around her suit, finally feeling two handles on each side of her belt. She grabbed them and a sword unfolded from each one of them. "Oh, this is so fucking cool!"

Harmony looked around her body suit, feeling for anything out of place, and felt nothing. The only thing that felt weird was her forearms. felt tight, as if the shirt on the suit was squeezing them. She fixed her forearm muscle and two sword-like blades came out of the suit, still attached to the forearms. on the suit.

"Fuck, this is so cool! I'm like Wolverine or something."

"No, you're more like Blanca." Layla said.

"Who the hell is Blanca?" Harmony asked.

"From Street Fighter. God, y'all never played Street Fighter. I'm starting to feel old, or I hung with Tess too long as a child." Layla said as all three of the girls looked at her, not knowing what the hell she was talking about. "Just fight." Layla said while holding her head. Harmony took off, leaping in the air and spin kicking Rose in the face and chest.

"No fair, you had more practice than me I your suit; but I got something for your ass." Rose said and began to attack. She swung both her swords and Harmony blocked with her arm blades, attacking her. "I see you finally got something to help you reach with them short arms." Rose said.

"Huh!" Harmony said mad and got caught off guard as Rose swop kicked her, knock her off her feet then jump in the air and came down with her knee to her chest before rolling off her.

"I'm goanna fuck you up." Harmony said as she roll off the floor flexing her muscles in her left forearm, causing the blade to shoot out like a bullet, cutting through the air at incredible speed.

"What the fuck!" Rose said as she just managed to block it. "How the hell you do that? You didn't say her suit could do that." Rose said looking at Layla.

Layla shrug her shoulders. "I didn't know. Like I said, all your suits are made different." she replied.

"Well that's not fair." Rose said and threw her sword at Harmony. Harmony block it with the right arm blade, the only one she had left. "I'm hating. I'm gonna whip that ass." Rose said then stopped when she saw the first the blade, she threw was now flying through the air coming at her handle first. She caught handle with ease. "Oh yeah, this is so fucking cool. This must be the magnet thing Layla was talking about."

"How did you do that? How'd you make it come back to you?" Harmony asked with a confused look on her face.

"It had something to do with me flexing my wrist and hand." Rose replied.

"Hmm." Harmony said then flex her left wrist and forearms. The arm blade that shot out returned back into the socket of the forearm of her suit. "This shit here is some real ninja assassin shit!" Harmony shouted.

"Hello! No, this some future shit here." Rose replied before throwing her sword at Harmony, who block it and ran toward her swinging both arms., looking like a human pair of scissors.

Rose backstepped and blocked most of the moves, but each blow was faster and stronger. She hesitated on kicking, thinking her leg might get chopped off, so she threw her swords and called them back to her hand repeatedly, which Harmony blocked with ease. Rose's heart race knowing she was about to lose the fight. She looked down at her chest while blocking Harmony's blows and noticed what look like a button on her breast. She pressed it and long round barrels popped up like a bracelet around her wrist.

"The fuck is this?" she asked. "Time out! Time out!"

"There's no time out Harmony!" shouted and continued her attack.

Rose balled both her hands into a fist aiming for Harmony's chest. A loud bang went off as shotgun pellets few out the barrel bracelet and hit Harmony in the chest, lifting her off her feet, down onto her back, damn near knocking her out.

"That's fucking cheating! No one said we were using guns! This bitch got shotgun barrel bracelets." Harmony groaned in pain.

"Holy shit! I got guns for hands!" Rose perked and smiled.

"Yeah, I told Ms. Wung Shu you couldn't shoot for shit." Layla cracked and laughed. Red Velvet squinted her eyes then stomped off to the elevator and got on.

"What's her problem?" Rose asked.

"She's upset the creators of the suit didn't make her one. They made her a Kevlar suit, but velvet didn't want it; but she got a one of a kind laptop that can hack any system." Layla replied.

"Shit, then I don't know what she's mad for. I'll trade the dummy my suit for her laptop and show her what to do with it. I'd start by hacking a bank or two and wiring millions to my account." Rose said and bust out laughing.

"Umm, you on your own girl. I like this shit. No, I love it." Harmony said, looking over herself as if she just got dress to go out for a party and was looking like a meal to eat.

Layla looked at Suyung and said, "Go ahead." Suyung smiled and walked in between Rose and Harmony.

"I been dying to see what your slim, pretty ass got. You look too cute to be trying to fight." Rose said.

"Don't let the looks fool you. She's pretty but got to be crazy. Why else would someone tatt there face and neck when they're as fine as her? That means something mentally ain't right. I took Psychology classes about shit like this." Harmony B stated.

"Umm, y'all talking like I'm not here. Less talking, more fighting." Suyung said, backflipping toward Harmony and tried to swipe kick her.

Harmony jumped up, causing Suyung to miss her legs, but Suyung was faster. While Harmony was still in the air, Suyung managed to leap off the floor and kick her in the chest then her face.

"This bitch fast!" Harmony shouted while blocking her face as Suyung set a hail of different kicks at her.

"She made be fast, but she can't beat my swords." Rose said and charged Suyung's back.

Suyung moved to the side and dodged Rose's blades. Harmony flexed her wrist and her arm blades popped back out. Suyung back flipped three times and stopped to pull out a small chrome bar that was the size of the palm of her hand.

"How you going bet us with that?" Rose asked with her right eyebrow raised.

Suyung smiled, pressed a button making the small chrome bar expand a sharp to protrude from the top, turning it into a long spear. Suyung wasted no time attacking. She moved the spear around gracefully but with power at the same time. Rose tried to block every swing with her swords and dodge the spear head, trying not to get poked. Suyung spun her spear around, causing Rose to lose grip of her swords, then knocked them out her head and across the room. Rose flipped sideways, stretched out her hands and the blades came back.

"Huh! Nice try, but they always come back. What do yours do?" Rose asked on one knee while smiling. Suyung smirked.

"I'll show you." she said. Out of nowhere, Rose saw the spear tip on Suyung's staff shoot out at her like a bullet.

"What the fuck!" Rose hollered and blocked it, slapping it to the left. Her eyes opened wide when the spear returned back to the staff in Suyung's hands.

"That's not it. Watch." Suyung said and began to attack Harmony who was on the other side of the room; but the crazy part was Suyung hadn't moved an inch. Her spear expanded at will, getting longer and longer; and she was using it to send attack after attack at Harmony. She would shrink the spear then expand it again. There was no telling how far it could reach or when it would be a normal size staff or get super long; giving Suyung the advantage that no one could get close to her.

Harmony flexed her wrist and shot her arm blade at Suyung before running at full speed toward her. With all her might, she side kicked her in the rib with her shin. The blow sent Suyung flying sideways.

"Ughh! What the fuck was that!" Suyung said in pain, holding her ribs.

"That was Harmony's special gift. More metal was added to the lower part of her legs, making it a little heavier; but she won't notice it giving more power to her side kick." Layla replied.

"Damn, really?" Harmony said looking down at her legs.

"Yeah; but remember you are the weapon and the suit is just to enhance what you already can do. You broke that bamboo stick with your legs, without a suit. Keep that in mind Layla said.

"These weapons and suits are the shit. I can't wait to really use them." Rose said, then something caught her eye.

Her facial expression twisted up and she stood in a fighting stance. So did Harmony and Suyung once they saw what Rose was looking at. Layla's heart raced seeing the seriousness in their faces. She turned around to see a woman in a purple Clock Hoodie with a purple ninja mask over her mouth and nose, leaving her eyes out; but you couldn't see her eyes because of the hoodie. She gripped a Glock 40 in her right hand.

"Iris!" Layla shouted, and everyone in the rooms. heart dropped. The last encounter with Iris she was more than they could handle, but maybe now it would be a fair fight. Layla wasted no time. She flexed her muscles and her suit filled with different size spikes like a porcupine about to attack. Iris pulled out a sword that was made of fat razor blades stuck together as Layla flexed her muscle and sent sixteen spikes in her direction. Iris used the razor blade sword to block each spike as if it was nothing. The spikes hit the ground then returned back to Layla's body suit. She flexed again, shooting more this time. Thirty razor sharp spikes flew at Iris. She flipped backwards then sideways, all while swinging the razor blade sword blocking all the spikes. Before Layla could call back the spikes to her suit, Iris flipped four times toward her and had put the gun and razor blade sword away. She was now standing face to face with her. Layla threw a punch then a jab, trying to hit her with everything she had.

'Wait, this isn't right. Iris is good, but not this good. She's blocking my attack too fucking easy, and her fighting style isn't as aggressive. It's calmer, yet powerful; something I was supposed to learn. Could it be?' Layla thought to herself while fighting even harder but got hit in the rib and chest with the palm of Iris' hand. She backpedaled then fell to her knees gasping for air. Before she could get up, Iris squeezed her thigh then poke it with her index finger three time and then her pointer finger. Layla tried to get up and recovery to

counterattack but couldn't move and was still trying to breathe.

"Buddhist palm and the Heavenly Touch. It can't be! I killed you." Layla said, barely able to speak and breath. Her throat was dry.

"Get this bitch!" Rose said. and her and Harmony attacked at the same time, pulling out their weapons.

Harmony used her arm blades like scissors, trying to take Iris' head straight off, while Rose try to chop her legs off; but Iris jumped and spun in the air, dodging both their blows.

"Enough is enough." she groaned and pulled out two razor blade swords, pressing a button on the handle. The blades expanded to 40 inches and became loose, turning into whips. Harmony and Rose stopped their attack and looked at the whips in awe.

"What the fuck is that?!" Rose asked.

"It's whips." Suyung said, gripping her spear as she got into her fighting stance.

"No! You won't win! No!" Layla mumbled, still having issues breathing. She held her chest and try to move, but her legs wouldn't listen to her mind.

"You said that last time, but we ready for this bitch." Harmony said, flexed her muscles and shot both arm blades at Iris.

The blades cut through the air at incredible speed. Iris twirled the razor blade whip and knocked them both down with ease then flexed her wrist and the end of her left whip locked around Harmony's ankle. She yanked tight and fast, pulling her toward her.

"Help!" she screamed and try to call back her arm blades, but Iris leaped up in the air, kicked her in her chest then hit her in the ribs with the palm of her hand before poking her in the stomach seven times with her index finger and pinky. She grabbed and twisted it, then let go.

"Ahhh! Ahhh! Fuck! Ahhh!" Harmony screamed at the top of her lungs while on her knees holding her stomach.

"What? What's wrong?" Rose looked on with a confused look on her face but ready to fight.

"Somehow this bitch gave me what feel like cramps in my stomach, but they're ten times worse. Ahhhh! Ahh fuck! Fuck make it stop please! Make it fucking stop! Ahh!" Harmony shouted while rocking back and forth on her knees with both her arms. wrap around her stomach.

"Ahhhh!" Rose screamed and threw both her swords at Iris.

Iris pressed a button, her whip retracted and turned back in to the razor blade sword. She quickly blocked both swords with her own. Rose called her swords back while running towards Iris. They went head to head swinging and blocking, trying to hit each other, but blocking every move. Suyung pointed and shot the spear head out her staff. Iris saw it from the corner of her eye and moved, but not before the spear slid pass her face and hit the inside of her hoodie, knocking the purple cloak off her. Suyung and Rose both stopped fighting for a second and look at Iris strangely. Now that the cloak was off, they could see that Iris was a different complexion, and a totally different woman. She was shaped like Iris and similar in weigh, but she was clearly black. They was still unable to see her face clear because of the purple ninja mask that covering the lower half of it.

"Ahh ughh! Ahhh!" Harmony's agonizing screams. of pain echoed throughout the room. Rose look at her friend and her anger consumed her.

"Who are you?!" Suyung shouted.

"Who cares, she hurt my friend! Let's fuck this bitch up!" Rose shouted, placing her swords in their hostler and pressed the button on her chest to bring her shotgun bracelet out of her suit.

She raised both arms. and aimed, but before she could fire, the woman's sword turned back in to a razor blade chain whip and she snap her wrist. The whip wrapped around both her arms. and she yanked hard while running towards Suyung as Rose fired. She could control her aim as her arms. were led to face Suyung.

"Ahhh!" Suyung hollered as the shotgun pellets slammed into her stomach and chest, send her flying backwards into the wall.

"No!" Rose screamed, seeing she'd hurt her friend, but felt her body being yanked and controlled by the whip around her arms.

The woman pulled her close and did the same move that she'd done to Harmony on Rose's stomach. She unwrapped her whip from around Rose's arms. as she dropped to the floor and screamed in excruciating pain.

"Ahhhh! Ahhhh! You bitch! You filthy whore! Ahhh!" Rose screamed as her stomach cramped up worse than she'd ever felt before.

Suyung shook off the pain she was in and jump kicked, aiming for the wannabe's face, but the woman blocked it. Her eyes open wide as Suyung continued her attack, moving faster and faster, sending kick after kick. The woman blocked it but knew she actually had to put in work.

"You're not like the others. You trained much longer and your Wushu technique is superb, ss if you were born with it." the woman said, then Suyung kicked her in the face, grabbed her arm and flipped her, slamming her hard to the ground hard.

She came down with the heel of her foot, aiming for the woman's nose hoping to break it. The woman rolled and dodged it just in time.

"Yes, I'm better than you and will fuck you up for hurting my friends. Undo what you did to them!" Suyung shouted and got back in her fighting stance.

"They have to learn to undo what I did to them themselves; and as far as you being better than me, hmmm, maybe one day or maybe never." The woman said and stood in an ancient Buddhist Palm stance.

"Ahhh!" Suyung screamed as she attacked, feeling confident that she would win after her last move.

Suyung raised her left eyebrow while sending punch combinations at the woman then kicks, but this time it was different. The woman moved like the wind, and moved with each attack, dodging every blow like it was nothing. Then Suyung felt the woman's palm hit her on the side of her head then her chest.

"Ughh!" Suyung's head spun and felt like a church bell was now ringing inside her head. Suyung grabbed her head and applied pressure on her temples, hoping that would ease the pain.

"Better than me, not yet young diva; but you're a great fighter." the woman said, fascinated as she walked up to Suyung calmly, poking her in the stomach with her index finger six times and once with her pointer finger before she grabbed what she could of her flat stomach and turned.

Suyung eyes open up wide and she started to cry while screaming. The pain in her head couldn't compare to what she was now feeling. She dropped to her knees and wrap her arms. around her stomach while screaming.

"Help us! Help us!" Rose shouted looking at the woman.

The woman turned her back, walked toward Layla and look at her.

"Remember you're the weapon, not the suit. If you want the pain to stop, do what I've done backwards." the woman said and removed the mask that covered her lower face and stood there waiting.

Screams. from all four women echoed throughout the basement. Layla's face twist up as she gained the strength to grab her own stomach, pinch it twice and poke the same spot the woman had done. A second later the pain went away.

"Ugh, why? Why did you do that?" Layla asked while getting up.

The woman looked at her as if to say don't question me but answered her question any way. "So, you can learn." the woman replied. Layla rolled her eyes and ran towards Harmony, Rose and Suyung. "Stop, don't help them or we'll fight again." the woman said, pulled out her razor blade sword and pressed the button on the handle to turn it into the chain whip.

Layla stopped in her tracks. Her face twisted up with anger and despair. "We can't leave them like this!" Layla shouted.

"Watch your tone; and you know I know best baby. If they want the pain to stop, they have to do it themselves." the woman stated firmly.

It took everything in Layla's body not to listen. "Concentrate! Please concentrate and work past the pain." Layla said with tears in her eyes, watching her team in pain.

Harmony tightened up her stomach and did the steps the lady did to her backward. "Ugh." she groaned in relief as she hit the matted floor, rolled onto her back and breathed heavily.

Suyung was the next one to follow the steps and undo the pressure points the woman hit to undo the damage. "

"Help me please! It hurts so much! I can't take it!" Rose shouted.

"Help her." Harmony said mad while looking at the woman.

"No. She must do it herself." the woman said.

After ten minutes of Rose screaming, Layla, Suyung and Harmony couldn't take anymore. Layla nodded her head giving the go sign. She and Suyung attacked the woman, sending flying kicks to her face while Suyung side kicked her in the ribs.

"Ooou!" the Woman screamed and grabbed her rib.

Suyung sent a round kick in hopes of hurting her more before she recuperated but wasn't so lucky. The woman caught Suyung's leg in mid-air and twisted her ankle. While holding her leg she quickly kicked her seven times with force.

"You like to kick people in the fucking ribs I see. How does it feel?! Huh?! How does it fucking feel?!" the woman shouted with each kick, finally letting Suyung go as Layla through a right jab, aiming for the woman's face. She bobbed her head to the left making the kick miss.

"Really?!" she perked while looking at Layla.

Before Layla could react, the woman had poked her in the neck with four fingers, causing her to choke, then punched her in the rib. She turned Layla around while removing her belt and began to spank her with it on her ass.

"Fucking hard headed; and you helped raise more hard-headed ass bitches! A hard head makes a soft ass. Didn't I always tell you that?!" the woman screamed while whipping Layla's ass.

Layla was moving her ass side to side trying to get away. She turned sideways and round house kicked the woman.

"Stop! I'm grown now, you can't be doing that no more!" Layla shouted while crying tears of shame and embarrassment.

Her pride hurt more than the pain her body felt. She looked over at her girls to see Suyung on the floor holding her ribs but watching the whole thing. Harmony had snuck over to Rose while everyone was fighting and did the pressure point moves in reverse on Rose's stomach, undoing what the woman did to her. Both her and Rose look at the woman as if she lost her mind.

"This shit don't seem right. She's not you but has our fighting style, but better; and she's whipping your ass with a belt. What the fuck is going on here? If she wanted us dead, we would be dead. Who is this woman?" Rose asked while getting up from the floor.

Layla held her head down. "She's my mother...or the woman that raised me. Her name is Tess."

Chapter Thirteen

Back From The Dead

"Wait, what the fuck?! You told all of us your mother was dead. That you were the last Teflon Diva and we were the new ones. What's going on?" Rose asked.

"Yeahl and why the hell did she try to kill us with cramps from hell?" Harmony asked.

"She was trying to teach us something." Layla replied with her head still down.

"Iris gotten pages from the book of Heavenly Touch, pressure points, and Kung ku; and trust, causing pain with it is child's play compared to what this style can really do. It's best y'all learn to reverse most of the moves rather than wait until later." Tess stated.

"You had no right to do that. You could've warned us! Rose shouted.

"When someone's trying to kill you, you think they're going warn you? I don't think so. Your friends think they helped you Rose, but all they did was cripple you. For future battles, you'll be the only one that can't come out of the move. It's like being in a headlock and you don't know the way out, so you'll get choke to death." Tess replied.

"Stop! Just stop! We need to fucking talk Tess, in private." Layla said.

The ceiling seemed to help Tess's chocolate skin shine, something her and Harmony shared, but Harmony was two shade darker; a perfect chocolate bar. Tess raised her left eyebrow and stared at Layla as if she had lost her mind.

"I know I been gone for a while, but it's wasn't okay then and it sure isn't okay now to curse at me Layla. Remember who I am and remember who you are." Tess said looking at her, wondering why she was getting so much animosity and attitude.

'Maybe she's hurt. Layla's always been a little sensitive when it comes to me and love, but she never *spoke to me like that. I raised her to always speak to me as her mother and friend, never like I'm someone in these streets.'* Tess thought to herself as she walked to the elevator and Layla followed. Harmony, Suyung and Rose just stared at Layla as if they were waiting for her to give an order to attack Tess, even though they all knew they weren't ready. The elevator door shut behind them.

"Say what y'all want, I kinda like Layla's crazy ass foster mother." Harmony said.

"Why? That bitch played herself by doing all that." Rose replied.

"Because she had a point. In order to beat her or beat someone more skilled, we have to learn what they know and be faster. Shit, Suyung was faster than her, I saw it; but the lack of knowledge is what got her beat. It's what got us all beat to be honest." Harmony B stated.

"Yeah yeah. I still want to whip her ass and kill Iris. I don't care what you say." Rose replied.

"I never said I didn't as well. I said we got to get better." Harmony said while smiling, showing off a set of perfect white teeth.

Layla sat on her all white couch with her legs shaking, bouncing up and down as if she had bad nerves. "How?! How could this be? I thought I killed you." Layla said with tears streaming down her cheeks.

"That day you took the shot, you did it with your eyes closed. The bullet was nowhere near my head or Iris', but the impact of the billets sent us both over the cliff. I lost consciousness, woke up on a beach, and was taking to the same hospital where we lost Ayana and Iris. It took me months to heal, but still didn't get out the bed. The loss of Ayana and Iris broke me. I was depressed and didn't want to go on, until he came and found me. Somehow Bless was still alive and talked me out of the state of depression I was in. We've been in Harlem for a while and I've been watching you from a distance. I would have left you alone, but events have changed with the death of Ms. Wung Shu." Tess stated.

"So, you been alive the whole fucking time?! Did you ever think of telling me? It's been 11 months and you just going let me think I killed you?! Now you trying to walk back into my life like nothing happened?! Really Tess! Put yourself in my shoes." Layla replied while crying. She couldn't believe her ears.

Tess sat down in the couch next to her. "I'm truly sorry baby. My mind wasn't right and hasn't been right since I lost Ayana.

"So, losing one child is an excuse to neglect the other one? You didn't give birth to me, but you're just as much as my mother as you were to Ayana. Are you saying you love me less because I'm not your blood?" Layla asked.

"No, that's not it. You're my child even if we're not blood. I raised you as mine, but the loss of any child is enough to destroy any parent. No parent should have to outlive their children." Tess replied.

"I don't believe you. You never once questioned what shooting you did to me, and never once asked me. You been sitting back just watching the whole fucking time!" Layla shouted.

"I'm not going tell you again Layla, watch your mouth. Don't you curse at me." Tess said, trying not to lose her patience. "I came back because I think Iris killed Ms. Wung Shu. I spotted her only once since I've been in New York, but she's hard to track. All me and Bless can think about is killing that bitch. She killed children, our children, and she have to pay. I went to Ms. Wung Shu to get new suits for myself and Bless but was too late to save her; but now you done built me a new team. New Teflon Divas. Young savages. That's even better. I can train them a little more and we can use them to finally get rid of Iris." Tess said while holding back tears and daydreaming, looking as if she was staring in to space but was staring at nothing. Memories of her daughter's face danced around her head.

"What you mean built you a team? These women follow me, they're my team. You had your turn and look what the fuck happened. Your own best friend crossed use, killed so many members of your team then killed your child; and she's still walking around. You think I'm going let you bring that negative energy to my team, fuck no!" Layla cursed, and in a blink of an eye Tess backslapped her in the mouth.

"Ouch!" Layla groaned then flexed turning on the spikes in her body suit.

"Come on now, do you really want to do that? It's not a good idea for anyone to pull a weapon on me, family or not. I'll treat them like a stranger in the streets and beat their ass." Tess said calmly.

"Well that's what the fuck I am, a stranger to you. That's what I've been these last 11 months, so don't stop treating me like that now; but I swear on God, you put your hands on me one more time you're going have to kill me because I won't stop trying to kill you Tess." Layla said and jumped up off the couch ready to fight. "I want you to go! Get out my place, get out my life. I've been living in your shadow for years, but not anymore. I'm free. I'm free to do as I want, I'm free to find love. I'm free to live my own life, not yours. My own damn love story. This is my team Tess, not yours. I need you to go! Go back to acting like I don't exist, acting like I'm not your daughter; acting like your dead, because I can deal with that. I can understand, but you being alive the whole time and the only excuse you have is you lost a daughter? Well you just lost another one!" Layla shouted.

"Wait! Why do you feel this way? You know what, I think it's best I leave before we both say things we don't mean." Tess replied while walking to the elevator.

"I meant everything I said. I wouldn't want you to piss on me if I was on fire. You're dead to me Tess! Deadddddddd!" Layla shouted.

Tess enter the elevator with tears in her eyes. "I love you." she said as the elevator door shut.

Chapter Fourteen

Trust no Bitch

"I'm telling you, the plan's going to work." Rose said into the two-way transmitter that was in her ear. She sat in a black Cayenne Porsche truck with Layla in the passenger seat. "Just don't be nervous, that's all." Rose stated.

"Nervous? Bitch please. It's nothing to get a man to think of nothing but me. Like Layla always says, a weak man thinks with his dick; and any man looking at my thick ass will do just that. Okaaaaay!" Harmony B said into her transmitter for everyone on her team to hear.

"I don't care what y'all bitches talking about, y'all better not fuck up this pay day for me. My bank account is running low and you hoes out play fighting and letting old bitches whip your ass." Red Velvet said into her two way. She sat back in her blue chair in front of her desk with the master hack laptop in front of her and a pint of birthday cake ice cream. She was taking big scoops and stuffing it in her mouth.

"First of all, they not old bitches, they're in their middle thirties; and I don't see you trying to fight one of them. You just sitting behind your desk eating snack as always." Rose replied.

"Whatever bitch. Just make sure to get my money." Red Velvet replied and rolled her eyes while breathing heavily then digging up her nose, eating the booger then scooping some ice cream into her mouth. "Yummy. They need to make that a new favor. Add more salt to ice cream that taste like boogies. Maybe I'll invest my share of money in to that." Red Velvet said, speaking out loud.

"Uh, what?" Harmony, Suyung, Rose and Layla said into their transmitters simultaneously.

"Umm, naw. Nothing. Y'all didn't hear nothing. Get back focused on getting that bag and not thinking about taking my ideas." Red Velvet replied. "Shit, thirsty bitches will steal the rug from up under your feet. I know they'll take my ideas and try to run with it. Not today Satan." Red Velvet mumbled under her breath.

"Yo, she's bugging." Rose replied.

"Yeah. It's time." Harmony said, pressing a button and the hood of the beat-up Honda she and Suyung was in started to smoke.

They pulled over in front of a building that had a group of young Spanish thugs shooting dice. Harmony stepped out in an all-black dress with splits on the sides that showed of her thick, voluptuous chocolate thighs. She walked to the hood of the now smoking car, popped it open then bent over. Suyung stepped out the passenger side in a yellow dress.

"Please don't mess this up y'all, we don't have on our body suits." Harmony said in a low voice.

"And that should be less dangerous or more dangerous?" Layla replied in her earpiece.

"More." Suyung said through her teeth, smiling as she went under the hood as they both bent over extra hard, showing off their shapes.

"That right. A woman is the weapon. We're stronger, smarter and more dangerous; and without your suit you have more to lose." Layla replied and had flashbacks of Tess saying the same words to her. She shook her head to get the images of Tess's face and voice out her mind. "It's my time." she mumbled to herself.

"Aye, yo mami, you need help?" one of the thugs playing dice shouted. He stopped what he was doing and walked away from the other six guys standing there. "I asked if you need help." he said, now standing behind them.

"I don't know. The car just started smoking. I don't know what's wrong with it." Harmony said and came from up under the hood.

"Damn, you a bad chocolate bitch." the man said.

"Excuse me." Harmony said while looking at him funny.

"I mean no disrespect. I'm just saying you're a pretty for a dark skin woman, that's all. Anyway, my name's Rico." the young thug said.

He was slim built and light skin with two long fish tail pony tails in his har and four teardrop tattoos under his right eye. He had on black jeans with a matching pair of red and black Jordans, and a yellow leather bomber jacket.

"Why do guys say that you look beautiful or pretty for a dark skin girl as if dark skin women ain't just naturally beautiful? What, their color makes them ugly?" Harmony asked with her face balled up.

"I didn't mean nothing by it. I just normally don't fuck with dark skin women. I didn't find them attractive, until now. y preference in women is usually more like your friend; that brown skin and exotic features. Where you from Miami? You from a tropical Island or Japan or something?" Rico asked while looking at Suyung.

"No fool. I'm from America, born and raised here; and I'm not fucking Japanese. I'm black and Korean." Suyung said while rolling her eyes.

"Umm, y'all bitches are really sucking at flirting." Rose said into the transmitter.

"Shit, easy for you to say. You're not dealing with idiots. Besides, hood niggas with money like to show it off and can't understand why a bitch don't want them, then they throw more money." Harmony B whispered.

"Huh? What you say?" Rico ask looking at her.

"I didn't say nothing, but it's getting cold out here. Can we wait inside somewhere or hold your jacket?" Suyung asked.

"For you baby, you can have both; if you not afraid of a thug." Rico replied and took off his jacket, placing it on Suyung. Both Harmony and Suyung noticed the shoulder hosteler he had on holding a 45 handgun. "Come follow me and I'll call you a cab."

"Okay." both girls said as they walked onto the sidewalk and passed the group of men shooting dice.

"Damn mami!" "Damn you a bad bitch." "I see you Rico." the men took turns shouting as they entered the building's lobby.

"I only got sixty dollars, let me get four bags please." a skinny dirty looking Mexican fiend said, looking like he was barely able to stand and was about to hit the floor at any second.

"No fool. $60 get you three as always. Stop fucking playing with me before I kick your poor fiend ass!" a tall brown skin Spanish guy with a black bandanna tied around his head shouted. He stopped shouting to look at Suyung and Harmony walked by. "I see you got some fine hoes with you." he said with a cheese smile on his face.

"Shut the fuck up Pablo!" Rico said then winked his eye and give him a smirk, letting him know not to say too much.

Rico lead them down the hallway to apartment 1C, pulled out a set of keys and let them in. Harmony try her hardest not to twist up her face in disgust. The apartment had a weird smell and was dark. They were led to a living room that held an old, brown sofa set. The sound of a big dog barking could be heard coming from one of the rooms. in the back. Harmony looked down at the couch and thought to herself, 'I think I see can see the cum stains on it.'

"Please have a seat while y'all wait for the tow truck and I'll fix you a drink." Rico said and walked off to the kitchen and returned with two glasses of Sprite. "Here, drink up."

Harmony looked at Suyung and shook her head. The first thing you learn as a woman is never drink something you haven't seen poured, and never drink what you leave surrounding by people you don't know.

"Well, it's okay love. I see you don't trust me." Rico said while touching Suyung's hand then let his hands rest on her shoulder before he shook Harmony's hand.

'Something's not right. Why did I feel dizzy when he touched me, and my stomach's saying run? Don't let this fool touch me anymore.' Harmony thought herself. She looked down at the palm of his hands. He held a small cream rectangle paper in them.

"What's that?" she mumbled while stumbling backwards.

Layla pulled out her phone and pressed a button that linked eye camera contacts that both Suyung and Harmony had on.

"Don't let him touch you, he has Tads on his hands." Rose said as her heart raced.

"What's Tads? Layla asked.

"It's hallucinogenic acid. People put it on their tongue and let it dissolve. It gets you high as hell and have you seeing things bitch." Rose stated.

"Get them out of there now." Layla said.

"No, we go it." Harmony said in a weak voice as she fell back onto the dirty sofa next to Suyung, who's head was hanging, and she look like a drop fiend.

"Yeah, now the real fun about to start." Rico said as he removed the Tads from the palm of his hand and tossed them on the floor. "These shits never fail. They're better than that date rape pill. The drugs soak through your pores and give you one hell of a ride."

Rico said while unbuckling his pants and three more men entered the room. One of them was Pablo, who pulled a forty-dollar bag of coke out his pocket, sprinkled some on the back of his hand, and sniff it off.

"Damn, your dick can never get hard without the coca." Rico said then laughed.

"You're just mad because the L coca gets me up. I fuck longer then you, and I'm about to fuck the shit out the pretty dark skin bitch then finish off with the Chinese one." Pablo stated with a grin on his face as pulled down his pants.

"We need to go in now and help them." Rose said.

"No, the hell we don't. Y'all better not fuck up my money!" Red Velvet shouted into her transmitter.

"Red has a point. If we go in now the Santiago Cartel will send more men than we can handle at one time. Harmony, Suyung... get the cocaine from that Pablo guy. It will speed up y'all heart rate and reverse the drug that in your system." Layla stated.

"I knew I should've gone." Rose said with anger.

"It wouldn't have worked. Every cartel member knows your face and mine." Layla stated.

"I told y'all you should've sent me. Then Spanish niggas love a fat bitch. They all be wanting a BBW. They say I look like that girl that be on Empire, so they want my goodies even more. I be fighting them skinny Spanish niggas off of this Milky Way." Red Velvet said.

Rose rolled her eyes. "Shhh, I need to make sure Harmony and Suyung are okay and you talking about your damn Milky Way. Now's not the time." Rose replied.

"Fuck what you thought. It's always good time to talk about my Milky Way." Red Velvet replied.

More of the hallucinogen acid was in Suyung's system, making her unable to move. She could hear the men laughing and talking, and her friends in her ears speak. Then she could hear the sound of fighting. Harmony pushed herself off the sofa and hit Rico in the balls.

"Ahhh ughh! You bitch!" he shouted while bent over.

She slapped the bag of coke out of Pablo's hand and it landed on Suyung's lap, then she poked Pablo in the eyes with her pointer and index finger.

"Ahhhh!" he hollered and rub his eyes.

There was two more men in the room, but Harmony couldn't focus or stand up straight. The bald-headed man swung with all his might, punching her in the stomach.

"Ahhh, fuck!" she yelled at the top of her lungs as she was knocked down to the ground and hit her head. She could feel a pair of hands pining her legs down and another set holding her arms. down.

"Oh yeah, we going fuck her stupid then slit her thought and put her in the trash can. No one will ever know," Rico said while still rubbing his balls as he leaned down to get on top of Harmony.

"No! No! You small ass dick asshole, get off of me! No!" Harmony shouted and squirmed but was too weak to put up a good fight.

"Suyung sniff! Sniff it now! Do it do it now or we're coming in Rose and Layla both shouted commands simultaneously as their hearts race.

"Voice. So many voices." Suyung mumbled, looking down at the coke for the first time that was sitting on her lap.

"Do it! Do it now!" she heard the voice in her ear yell.

Suyung grabbed the plastic bag of cocaine, dumped some in the palm of her hand the size of a golf ball and dropped her face into it. She sniffed slowly at first, trying to drown out the voices she was hearing. A smile spread across her face and her eyes popped open wide like a child that had too much sugar. The pace of her heart beat speed up. She sniff again and bust out laughing Her laughter caused Rico, Pablo, and the two other men to stop their attack on Harmony and look at her.

"Son look, she's tweaking. She's bugging the fuck out! I think I'm going fuck her first." Pablo said.

Suyung pop up out the chair laughing, sounding like a cute Japanese girl gone crazy. She stood in front of Pablo, smiled, grabbed his dick and twisted it.

"Ah! Ah! Ahhhhh!" Pablo screamed and try to pull free then swung, trying to punch her in the face,

Suyung caught his hand mid-swing, twisted it then flipped him to the floor onto his back.

"Ahh! What the fuck!" Pablo shouted as Suyung stomped the heel of her shoe into his balls, popping his scrotum and squirming one of his balls before stomping on his neck.

The heel pierced his neck, putting a thick hole where his Adam's Apple used to be. She squashed it completely, pulled it out, and blood poured from the open wound. Pablo bucked on the floor and shook uncontrollably his blood poured from his body. He tried to use his hands to cover his neck, but it did nothing to stop the thick red blood from gushing everywhere. The two bald Latino men that were holding Harmony down released her arms. and feet.

"You bitch! You mother fuckin' pussy ass bitch!" one yelled and swung at Suyung.

Suyung smiled, ducked it with ease and punched him in the neck. She grabbed his arm, held it tight to balance herself and make sure he couldn't run as she unleash a series of sidekicks to his face, chest, and legs. He screamed and groaned while trying to pull away and block his face, but the kicks to his stomach hurt just as much if not even more. He bent over and began to rock.

"Ha ha!" Suyung laughed and grab the bag of cocaine off the couch just as the guy violently vomited on it.

Suyung looked over her shoulders and toss the bag of coke to Harmony as she took off her heel and plunge the point of it into his right temple while he was bent over throwing up what he had to eaten not too long ago. He stood still, as if he was frozen in time, with the heel of Suyung's shoe in his brain. It was as if he couldn't process a thought. She pulled the heel out of his head, causing him to fall over on to the couch and into his own vomit. He was still breathing, but not moving. Suyung laughed as she bent over and began to beat him repeatedly with the heel all over his face.

Harmony had managed to gather enough strength to grab the bag of cocaine off her chest, place it to her nose and inhale deeply. Her eyes opened up wide and smile spread across her face.

"What the fuck!" Rico said, looking at Suyung beat his man while he was on top of Harmony. He heard a giggle and looked down at Harmony to see her smiling. "Yo, these bitches are geeked the fuck up! We got to kill that bitch now!" Rico shouted to the guy that was holding Harmony's legs.

Harmony looked at Rico with lust in her eyes. He grinned.

"I knew you wanted it." he said pulling his dick out his boxers and tried to stare into Harmony's eyes. It's too much crazy shit going on here." he said, noticing his dick wouldn't get hard.

Harmony opened her mouth wide and locked down on his nose. "Ahhh! Ahhh! Get off her off me!" he screamed at the top of his lungs and began to punch her in the face, but she felt none of his blows.

He reached for the gun in his shoulder hostler, but Harmony grab his hand and bit down hard like a pit bull dog locking onto a thick piece of rope and refused to let go.

"Ahhh! Ahhh!" Rico yelled as his eyes watered up and tears began to pour out of them.

Harmony grabbed the gun out his shoulder holster and kneed him in the dick while pulling back hard with her teeth, tearing off a larger piece of his nose.

"Ugh! Ahhh!" Rico hollered in excruciating pain and rolled over with one hand holding where his nose used to be as blood rushed out the open hole. With his other hand holding his testicles, he rolled around on the floor like a hurt puppy.

Harmony got up as the last bald thug walked up behind Suyung with a knife. "Hey, you." she said then whistled.

The guy turned around to see the gorgeous chocolate complexion woman with blood all around her mouth and jaw smiling. She spit something at him that hit him in the face. Curiously he looked down at the object after it bounced off his face and hit floor to see it was Rico's nose.

"Huh!" he said in shock then looked back up to see Harmony gripping Rico's 45mm hand gun aiming at his head.

"Bye bye." Harmony said and squeezed the trigger, sending a bullet slamming in to the bald man's head. His whole face split in two like a cracked egg as he fell sideways, sending brain and bone matter spilling out onto the floor.

The whole time Layla and Rose were watching everything from the laptop and the camera contacts that Suyung and Harmony had in their eyes.

"What the fuck was that, a damn horror movie?" Rose asked, but they seen and heard the gun shots, just like the other six thugs outside shooting dice. They pulled their guns and prepared to run into the building.

"It looks like it's show time. Let hurry and wrap this up, it's going to get hot now." Layla said as they pulled up across the street.

Both holding black and brown AK-47's, Rose stood on the passenger side of the Porsche truck by the hood using it as cover and Layla used the driver's side door as they look at each other and squeezed the trigger of their guns simultaneously; sending a hail of bullets that tore through the bodies of four of the thugs standing in front of the building. Two of them managed to dodge to the ground at the sound of the gun shots.

"We being hit! We being hit!" one of them shouted into his iPhone repeatedly before ten more men ran out the building firing back, and three black Lexus' pulled up in front of the building with more Santiago Cartel soldiers.

"Damn it! Hurry guys, you don't have much time left." Layla said into her earpiece while still firing.

She sent six bullets through one of the cartel henchmen's face. The bullets traveled out of the back of his skull and slammed into the neck of the man standing behind him, killing them both instantly. Stepping back behind the truck next to Rose while reloading, Rose shouted as she ducked low behind the truck to reload her AK. She loaded a new 100 round magazine and slid one to Layla's feet.

"Their girls, nothing but women. We having a gun fight with helpless women. You three go left. You two go right and sneak up on the side of them; and try not to kill these bitches. We should shoot them in the leg and fuck them to death." a cubby, bald head cartel solider wearing a black button up shirt and sunglasses with tattoos on his face and head said.

Layla held her breath, aimed and squeezed the trigger, sending one bullet flying out the gun and into the tattooed man's mouth. Before he could hit the floor, she squeezed the trigger twice, sending a bullet into his right eye and one in his left; making a fake smiley face as he hit the floor dead.

"Umm, bitch how you did that?" Rose asked in astonishment.

"I'm a fucking snipper before I'm a warrior." Layla replied while flexing her forearm, making the spikes pop up and shot out her suit at full speed towards Rose.

"Layla no! What you doing?!" Rose screamed and panicked before she closed her eyes then opened them again. The spikes turn inches before hitting her in the face, zoomed past her and slammed into the chest of a cartel solider that was creeping up behind Rose for the perfect kill shot. The spikes pulled out his body and went back in to Layla's suit before she shot them again.

"Use your swords while shooting, it's too many of them. They're like roaches, just keep coming. If you flex your arm and forearm muscle a certain way you can control which way the swords go; like a remote control for a drone or toy car. That's how I made my spikes go past your head." Layla said while shooting three cartel soldiers and her spikes tore through the passenger side of a car and went through the driver's side, fulling up the cartel solider that was hiding there with twenty spikes. When Layla called her spikes back, it looked as if the man had been stabbed in the face and body a thousand time with an ice pick or screwdriver.

Rose grab one of the handles on her said holster and a sword folded out. She tossed it and the magnet in her suit pushed it with incredible force as it slammed into one of the Cartel soldier's stomach, lifting him up off his feet and pinning him to the brick building wall.

"Ahhh! Ahh fuck! Get me down! Get this thing out of me!" he screamed while trying to pull the sword out of him but, it was of no use.

One of the Cartel soldiers ran over to him, grabbed the handle of the sword and pulled. "It's jam in there." he said in a deep Spanish accent.

"Rafael, help me! Please help!" the cartel solider shouted in Spanish.

"Stop moving Jesus, you're making it worse. Quit panicking so much!" Rafael shouted over the sound of the constant gunfire.

"It hurts! I can feel it ripping my insides!" Jesus shouted while crying and squirming all around.

"You're over reacting. If you stay still, we can get this thing out of you." Rafael replied; but Jesus wasn't over reacting.

His body weigh couldn't be held up by the sword alone, so the more he moved, his body lower down onto the sword. The sword started from his stomach, but the razor-sharp blade made of Teflon had sliced upward and was now in the center of his chest.

"Stop moving! You're making it worse!" Rafael screamed.

"Ahhhhhhhh!" Jesus let out a loud piercing scream that could be heard over the gunfire, which caused the Cartel soldiers, Layla and Rose to look left over at him and Rafael. Jesus had slid all the way down and his body sliced in two, like a gutted fish.

"Ahhh! Ahhh!" Rafael screamed in horror as he looked at his friend standing there with blood rushing from his body. His top half along with his face split in two and his arms. were still moving.

Layla flexed her arm and spikes flew out her suit. Seven slammed into Rafael's back, knocking him forward into what was left of Jesus, which was still moving around like a zombie, knocking both of them on to the ground. Rafael began to cough up blood.

"Fuck." he groaned as he took his last breath.

Rose called back her sword and toss it again as three more black trucks pulled up and more Cartel soldiers hopped out with machine guns.

"Shit! Shit! Y'all need to hurry the fuck up!" Rose shouted into her earpiece.

"Ha ha." Harmony and Suyung burst out laughing.

"Bitch are y'all tweaking?" Rose asked.

"I don't know what that is, but I'm high as hell. I feel like I drank seven caramel cappuccinos and two dark coffees. I'm hype as hell. This can't be good for my heart. I'm never doing this shit again. Harmony B replied with her eyes wide open.

"Yo, y'all better move. Police are on their way. I jammed most of the cellphone towers so no one can call them, but someone how a call got through. Y'all running out of time hoes, and I'll be pissed if I don't get my cut of money. You bitches better get y'all act right." Red Velvet said through the transmitter.

"Shut up bitch! Let you try to move around this high." Harmony said then aimed down to finish off Rico and noticed he was gone, but a trail of his blood smear on the floor lead out the front door of the apartment.

"Hurry get the money! It's on the fourth floor, apartment 4b. The police are coming!" Rose shouted while still firing.

"Not before we kill that rapist Rico." Harmony stated and looked at Suyung.

Suyung went over to the kitchen and pulled the gas line out the stove, letting gas seep through the air, then pulled a lighter out one of the dead Cartel soldiers pocket and set the couch on fire.

"That will get rid of all evidence, but it will explode in a few. Suyung said.

"Good." Harmony replied as they left the apartment.

Gunshots outside of the apartment could be heard, making it sound like a battle field; but the sound of keys jingling, and Rico crying could also be heard on the stairwell.

"Hurry!" Suyung shouted ask they ran up two flight of stairs to see Rico had opened up two of the apartments while nervously shaking while holding where his nose used to be and a set of keys in the other head as he opened a door.

"Don't move." Harmony said and raise the gun to the back of his head.

Rico dug in his pocket and spun around, pulling out a clear jar full of a blue liquid that look like a perfume Bottle and sprayed it on Harmony and Suyung's clothes. Harmony front kicked him in the chest, knocking him backwards, causing him to drop the bottle which broke. Suyung snatched the keys out of his hand.

"What the hell did you spray us with?" Harmony asked.

"Ha ha! You die now bitches." Rico said.

Suyung kicked him in the mouth. "My friend asked a question. What did you spray us with?" Suyung ask as she prepared to kick him again.

"Stop! Okay, okay. I'll tell you." Rico said while blood dripped through his left hand as he covered what was left of his nose. "Y'all stupid chicks not street smart or never heard of Black Ice?" Rico asked.

"I heard of Black Ice." Harmony B replied.

"Who's Black Ice? I'm not from around here. I'm from San Francisco." Suyung replied.

"Oh, trust bitch, even on the West Coast Black Ice is well known. There's no place in the world he hasn't touched, but he's a notorious serial killer that chops up the toughest thugs and bosses. He kidnaps women, rapes them and breed them with his children. Oh yeah, he has hyenas on steroids ss pets and attack dogs." Harmony stated while keeping the gun pointed at Rico.

"Oh yeah, I heard of him. We call him something else in Korean: but what's that got to do with the stuff he threw on us?" Suyung asked with her face twisted up, still feeling hyped from the cocaine she sniffed.

"Stupid bitches. He been creating a new drug called Blue Mist. It's mixed with bath salts, crack, crystal meth, and some other stuff he won't say; but it sells faster than heroin and cocaine. They can sniff it, or they can smoke it. The liquid they shoot it up or drink it and the smell of it drives them crazy. I seen them rip a person in half trying to suck the liquid off them." Rico stated.

"Huh? What the fuck that have to do with us?" Suyung asked.

"Stupid bitches." Rico said then laughed.

"What's that?" Harmony aske.

"What's what? I just hear the shooting outside. You're freaking me out." Suyung replied.

"Shhhh, listen." Harmony said. The sound of weird moans and grunts could be heard coming from two of the three apartments doors Rico had opened.

Harmony's eyes open wide as a tall skinny dirty looking man came out. His eyes were blank, as if he wasn't there, but he was. The smell of feces lingered in the air, and one look at him you could tell he was a dope or crackhead. Two more men came out the room behind him with the same blank stares, then a woman wearing a trash bag as a dress came out of the apartment on the left with four more people dress in trash bags behind her. The smell of urine was strong in the air.

"Ha ha!" Rico laughed.

"Ugh!" the lady wearing the trash bag dress charged Suyung. Harmony raised the gun and fired, hitting the woman dead in the center of her chest. Her frail, drug abused body flew back onto the ground. Harmony aimed at another one of the crackheads that had no shirt on but dirty blue jeans, shooting him in the stomach. He bent over and hit the ground.

"This was your plan, to have frail crackheads attack us?" Suyung asked.

"You haven't been listening fools. Blue Mist has bath salt in it." Rico stated.

"Oh shit, run!" Harmony said as she grabbed Suyung by the arm, aimed at Rico and squeezed the trigger. His head exploded like a watermelon being dropped off the rooftop. "Come on!" Harmony shouted.

"Why are we running? They're just crackheads." Suyung said and pulled her arm free.

"I'm from Florida. Guys out there use bath salts. It turns them into some type of living zombie. They try to eat people, and only head shots can kill them. They're energy Level is higher than we are on this damn coke right now." Harmony stated.

"Bitch, that sounds like some made up horror story shit." Suyung said then laughed.

She stopped laughing when the woman wearing the black trash back got up. She had a huge smoking hole in her chest. She screamed and attacked Suyung. Before Suyung could react, the woman bit in to her forearm.

"Ahhh! No No! This bitch gonna give me AIDs!" Suyung screamed as she panicked and start punching the woman in the face repeatedly, but the woman reuse to losing her grip. She was locked on.

Harmony aimed and squeezed the trigger, sending a bullet into the center of the woman head. Brain matter and blood flew into Suyung's face and open mouth as the woman fell backwards.

"Come on!" Harmony shouted as more blue mist crackheads start to chase them. She ran up a flight of stairs, turned around and squeezed the trigger, but the gun made a clicking sound. "Oh shit! Hurry up!" Harmony shouted then kicked two of the crack head in the chest, sending them flying backwards and slowing the other ten that were trying to get to them as they sniffed the air. Six more came out the apartments.

"Oh shit, this isn't good. Fuckin hurry!" Harmony shouted.

Suyung found the right key that she'd taken from Rico and opened the door to apartment 4b. She and Harmony both ran in and locked the door behind them as the blue-eyed crackheads bang on the other side like will animals.

"That not going to hold them. They're going to bust through that door." Harmony said as she backpedaled.

They heard a growling sound behind them and turned around to see two Great Dane; one blue, the other grey.

That had to have been at least five feet tall each and looked to weigh over one hundred pounds.

"That explains why this place smells like shit and piss I guess." Suyung said and shrugged her shoulder. The sound of the door behind them could be heard being forced open.

"They'll be in her any second. How we gonna get past the two Hujos? We can't stand here forever. We have to find the money and go." Harmony B said while standing completely still and looking one of the dogs in the eyes. "You remember that move they did on the Wonder Woman movie? You run toward me and I'll toss you to the table behind you. You grab the kitchen knives on it, throw one to me and we kill these big mutts." Harmony stated.

Suyung looked at the brown table behind the two large dogs. Two jars full of what too looked like Blue Mist rested on it and a pound of weed, as well as two kitchens knives, scissors and a small pile of money.

"Ummm, why won't you just let me throw you?" Suyung said, unsure of the plan as the dogs continue to growl and step closer, as if they wanted the women to react or run.

"Because stupid, I weigh 160 pounds solid. All my weight's in my butt and I'm thick. You over there slim built, barely weighing 120 pounds, with your little booty." Harmony B replied.

"How about we vote on it, or play rock paper scissors?" Suyung said just as the door to the apartment finally give in and the blue eye crackheads fell on top of each other to get in.

They looked behind them down the narrow hallway and could see the crackheads getting up on the floor and rushing in while knocking each other down.

"Never mind, I'll go." Suyung said and didn't hesitate.

She jumped and kicked the right hallway wall right next to her to give her a boost higher into the air. Harmony locked her fingers together as Suyung landed in the palm of her hands, and with all her strength she pushed up; pushing Suyung higher in the air as she did a back flip and landed on the dirty table. The two Great Danes seemed confused as they watched the whole thing.

"I have an idea. Scale the wall!" Suyung shouted as she gripped one of the jars of the liquid Blue Mist.

The narrow hallway walls were close together. Harmony jumped, did a half split and used her feet and hands to scale the wall, climbing up on it each by inch. Suyung tossed the glass jar at the dog on the left. The jar slammed into the dog's head and cracked open. Blue Mist covered his body and the floor. The dog on the right bark then growled, showing his huge teeth as he ran towards Suyung. Suyung quickly grabbed the kitchen knife and threw it. The knife cut through the air and hit the dog in the chest but did little to slow the large beast of a dog down.

"Oh shit! Oh shit!" Suyung panicked and tossed the next knife, this time hitting the dog in its left foot, causing him to stop and cry in pain.

She took the opportunity and tossed the next jar of Blue Mist at him. If the smell of the Blue Mist was driving the crackheads crazy and dying for a taste, the fresh smell of it now in the small apartment sent them in a frenzy. Three of them attacked the dog on the right, biting him and trying to suck the blue mist off his skin. The dog tried to fight back and sunk his teeth into one of the crackheads faces and shook it from side to side. His attacked was slowed down as six more crackheads wearing trash bags started to bite him all over, ripping away at his fur and flesh. He howled in pain as a pair of teeth ripped into his neck. He fell to the ground and bled out slowly while feeling each bite the now eight crackheads took out of him; ripping away at his skin and meat as if he was a bucket of Popeye's chicken. The dog looked at the one crackhead he killed and seemed to smile a sad smile as he died. The other dog on the left that had the knife in his chest had seen what had happened and got the fuck on; running down the narrow hallway trying to make it past the blue eye crackheads that were rushing in but got trapped and surrounded. Ten sets of teeth bit into him and sucked the Blue Mist off his skin as he fell to the ground howling as Suyung and Harmony watched in horror.

"Bitch let's go!" Suyung shouted.

Harmony snapped out of the daze she was in and hopped over the blue eye crackheads that was feasting on the dog closet to the kitchen and ran down another hallway to a bedroom with Suyung shutting the door behind them.

"What the fuck was that?!" Suyung asked.

"I don't know girl, but we're not next on the menu; and they broke down that steel front door. This wooden cheap door not going do shit to hold them back, and they will come for us. We still smell like that stuff, whatever it's called. Blue Mist or some shit." Harmony stated.

Suyung turned around and smiled. "I don't think it will be a problem bitch. Look." Suyung replied.

"You call me one more bitch, I'll feed you to those crackheads myself…" Harmony stopped short as she turned around to see a long table with four money counting machines, money stacked up on the table and ten black duffle bags.

"Guess we found the money." Suyung said.

"These fools really think there untouchable. Not nearly enough security for this type of money if you ask me." Harmony stated.

"Did you forget about the damn hyped up crackheads that eat people? Yeah, I say that's the best security money can buy." Suyung returned.

"Yeah, you're right." Harmony said as she walked over to a closet and opened it to see a few guns on top of a dirty blanket; a sawed-off double barrel shot gun with six bullet shells, two black Smith and Wesson 45's, and a tec-9 sub machine gun. "Why do fucking gangsters have the most ghetto guns and never no bullets?" Harmony said.

"Let me see." Suyung said as she walked to the closet. "Well, I'll take the tec-9. I didn't know people still used these guns. They jam so much." Suyung added and pulled out the clip. "There's only twelve bullets in and it holds fifty." Suyung said while shaking her head.

"Well there's only eight bullets in each of those Smith and Wesson's." Harmony said as she heard what sounded like growling and banging at the door. "Fuck it, beggars can't be choosy." she said and grabbed one of the 45's, opened one of the duffle bags of money and placed it on her neck and zipped the bag halfway. She then took the six shotgun shells, placed four of them in her bra and two in the bag. "Okay, I'm grabbing three duffle bags." Harmony said.

"Just take two, they're too heavy and going slow you down. We got police on the way and fucking blue eye crazy crackheads. Ain't no telling how many Cartel soldiers we have to get pass." Suyung said as the door behind her bust open and shredded to pieces as three crackheads barged their way in.

"Duck bitch!" Harmony shouted as she raised the sawed-off shotgun and squeezed the trigger.

The shotgun roared to life and the recoil from the forces of the gun pushed her back some as pellets flew from the gun at full speed, slamming into the chest and head of two of the crackheads; ripping larger holes the size of golf balls inside them, taking half their face off. Suyung aimed at the third one, squeezed the trigger and the bullet ripped off the top of his skull, killing him instantly.

"Go! Go!" Harmony shouted as more of the blue eye crackheads were trying to get pass the three dead bodies that blocked the door. Harmony ran to the room window and realized she couldn't open it.

"The chair! Use the chair! Here!" Suyung said while passing her a metal folding chair that was next to the table and the black duffle bags of money that were under the table.

Harmony swung with all her might and bust out the window with the chair. "Let's go!" she shouted as Suyung grabbed two duffle bags as more blue eye crackheads entered the room.

They both carefully climbed through the broken window onto a rusty fire escape.

"Come, come on!" Harmony shouted while running down each flight.

"Shut up! I'm right behind you." Suyung said.

Both were still feeling the effects from the cocaine they sniffed, and the world was moving in slow motion to them. The sound of grunts and groans caused then to look up to see two blue eyed crackheads climbing through the window, and a third one peeking its head out.

"Why are they still coming after us? Like come the fuck on! Pssst!" Suyung said while sucking her teeth.

"It's the liquid drug that fool Rico threw on us. It's on these dresses. We have to get rid of them and wash our skin as soon as we can. If not, they're going keep coming as if we're the dealers. I can't, front that Black Ice is one smart motherfucker; but he couldn't make the crackheads smarter instead of killers?" Harmony said as she reached the second flight of stairs.

Suyung looked up and fired, hitting one of them in the chest twice. She squeezed the trigger again and a bullet ripped open the neck of the third one, causing him to tumble down a flight of stairs.

"Head shots only. You're wasting bullets, but that neck shit did work." Harmony stated as they climbed down the metal ladder to the side of the building.

"Oh shit, police are here. We gotta go. Whatever you do don't go through the front." Layla said as she and Rose threw four smoke grenades and they went off, release thick purple smoke in the air; making it impossible for the Cartel soldiers and the six police cars that pulled up to see As Layla and Rose hopped into the truck and speed off.

"Fuck! Fuck!" Harmony spat while trying to think fast.

More gun shots could be heard coming from over their heads. Suyung looked up to see two Cartel soldiers climbing out through the broken window pass the blue eye crackheads, heading down the fire escape shooting.

"Fuck! Do we ever get a break?!" Suyung shouted and fired back.

The bullet missed the Cartel solider and hit one of the blue eyes in the jaw, breaking it off completely. "Eww!" both Harmony and Suyung said while running and looking back. They cut through the side alleyway of the buildings and Harmony saw what she was looking for, the side of another building. They cut through and ran into another alleyway.

"I love the fucking Bronx, I swear. All the buildings and alleyways connect for two or three blocks." Harmony stated.

"Fuck you mean? My heart is racing and I'm out of bullets. I think we lost those guys." Suyung said while bending over and breathing heavily.

"We didn't lose them. It's only a matter of time with those crackheads acting like blood hounds. Put down your bags and help me with this." Harmony said while grabbing two old pipes that belonged to a fence and walked over to a manhole.

"You can't be serious." Suyung said and rolled her eyes.

"It's this, die, or get caught by the police. Ummm, I choose this." Harmony stated.

"Just the thought of shit on my feet is nasty." Suyung replied.

"Umm, bitch wasn't you living in the street as a bum when Layla found you?" Harmony asked while she and Suyung used the pipes to pry open the manhole.

"Yes, but I was a clean bum. Don't you ever forget that." Suyung replied and caused both of them to laugh.

The laughter was cut short as a hand grabbed Suyung in the shoulder. She spun around and swung the pipe, hitting a blue-eyed crackhead in the face, causing him to stumble sideways. She bent low and hit him in his calf muscles, causing him to drop to his knees.

"Batter up!" She shouted and swung, hitting him in the head so hard it crushed the side of his face and skull. He hit the ground but eased back up as four more blue eyed crackheads came running towards them.

"Over there!" two of the Cartel soldiers said as they pushed past the crackheads shooting.

"Fuck!" Suyung shouted before picking up the skinny crackhead man who's face, she banged in and use him as a shield.

"Here!" Harmony shouted as she took the tec-9 out of Suyung's duffle bag and tossed it to her. She aimed and squeezed the trigger, causing rapid gun fire to sound off, kinda like a sprinkler coming on only for a second and then stopping.

"What the fuck!" Suyung shouted and look at the gun as if was broken, then remembered it was only twelve bullets in it.

She looked up to see that the head of one of the blue-eyed crackheads was split open and one if the Cartel soldier's legs and pelvis area was now pouring out blood.

"Ahhh! Ahhh!" he hollered and screamed while rolling around the ground.

"Let's go." Harmony said while throwing all five duffle bags down the manhole.

Harmony pulled the shotgun shells from her bra, popped open the double barrel and loaded the bullets in just as three blue eyed crackheads and a cartel solider approached. She squeezed the trigger and the shotgun roared, blowing the arm off one crackhead and a leg off of another, before jumping down into the sewer.

"Eww, what the fuck!! Harmony yelled while her face twisted as the smell of feces overpowered her nose.

"Bitch let's go!" Suyung said, grabbing two of the duffle bags full of money.

Harmony threw a bag on her right shoulder than one on her left and grabbed the third one.

"I'm telling you, leave it. It's slowing you down." Suyung said while running and looking back at Harmony struggle, barely able to hold the shotgun and the bags at the same time.

Gun shoots echoed and bullets flew pass their heads. "I'm out of bullets!" Suyung shouted.

"I've got two more shotgun shells in my bra and the 45 with four bullets. We gotta make it work.

They ran and turned a corner and came to a stop. Harmony placed one of the duffle bags down in the dirty sewer water, opened it and took out the .45, passing it to Suyung. She took the two shotgun shells out her bra and reloaded the shotgun before she noticed a shotgun bullet in the duffle bag. she grabbed it just as the Cartel solider turned the corner. Harmony raised the shotgun and squeezed the trigger. Her eyes opened wide as a basketball sized hole opened up where the Cartel soldier's chest used to be.

He looked down at his now smoking chest and yelled, "Motherfucker!" in Spanish before putting his left hand through the large hole, as if to see if it was really there. His face twisted up in rage, causing Harmony look at him weird.

"How the fuck is he still alive?" she asked out loud as he stumbled and backpedaled before he raised his gun and aimed at her face. Suyung aimed and squeezed the trigger, sending a bullet in to his mouth, which blew out the back of his head.

"Well that did the job." Harmony said as his body slumped into the shitty sewer wall.

Before she and Suyung could share a laugh, a crackhead turned the corner and tried to bite her.

"Fuck!" she screamed, pulling her arm back just in time as six more turned the corner. She hesitated to reach for the duffle bag.

"Just leave it!" Suyung shouted.

"Damnit!" Harmony said and left the bag. "This isn't my day. I smell like shit and I'm being chased by crackheads." She added as she squeezed the trigger and blew the legs off a crackhead before tossing the sawed-off shotgun, hitting another in the face.

"I'm out!" she shouted.

"I got three left." Suyung replied as they turned another corner and it looked to be a dead end, but it wasn't. The sewer dropped two feet down into a pool of dirty water and floating shit. "Oh, hell no!" Suyung said.

"For once I'm with you girl." Harmony said, but seven blue eyed crackheads started to run down the tunnel towards them as if someone stole their crack pipe.

Suyung aimed and a bullet entered the eye of one on the left, killing him instantly. She squeezed the trigger twice and one bullet slammed into the chest of the one in the center looking like he was leaning the pack, doing nothing to slow him down. The next bullet slammed into the nose of the blue-eyed crackhead on the left. His legs buckled and his body dropped dead as if someone had pressed a button to turn him off. Suyung squeezed the trigger once more to only hear a clicking sound.

"I'm out! Fuck!" she yelled as she tossed her gun toward the running crackheads.

"Fuck it!" Harmony shouted, turned around and jumped, landing in two feet of shitty water. "Eww! she shouted while spitting water out her mouth.

Suyung's face twisted in disgust and she jumped as well. "Ewww! I can't believe I'm swimming in shit. My pussy's in shitty water!" Suyung cried as they struggled to walk in the water, slowing them down. Suyung looked back to see if the crackheads followed suit.

"Looks like they're not following us." she said.

Harmony looked back to see four blue eyed crackheads looking down on them and sniff the air before they turned and walked away. "This shitty water must smell too bad and even they're smart enough not to jump in it, or the dirty water washed off the Blue Mist we had on us." Harmony stated as they climbed into a tunnel, walk down it and came out the manhole in a city park.

"Layla, come get us. We're at St. Mary's Park." Harmony said into her two- way transmitter.

"On the way. I thought I lost y'all. We couldn't hear nothing once y'all went in those tunnels." Layla replied.

"Please just hurry." Suyung said, and before she knew it a black x6 BMW pulled up. Rose rolled down the passenger side window.

"Eww! You bitches look like y'all went through hell." Rose said while a huge smile on her face as Harmony and Suyung walked to the trunk of the truck and pleased the four duffle bags in it then hopped in the back seat.

"What the fuck! Y'all stink! Oh my God, roll down the windows!" Rose shouted.

We can't. We can only crack them. we don't need people seeing our face. We just robbed the Santiago Cartel in broad daylight, shot at police officers, and left a whole crime scene with police killing the Cartel soldiers in a shootout we started. Do I need to remind y'all of that?" Layla stated.

"No, no. We're good." they all said simultaneously.

"But can you hurry up and get home, I've never felt so disgusting a day in my life." Suyung replied.

"Y'all do know we going have to hose you down before you enter the building right." Layla said.

"Any clean water would be my friend right now. I don't care." Harmony B replied as they rode in silence and Rose held her nose tightly.

Chapter Fifteen

Moneys Not The Root to Evil! Greed is!

"Ahhhh! You let them get away with my money?!" Catalina shouted while slamming both her hands on her desk.

"It's not like that boss." Miguel said. He stood there matching from head to toe in a light green button up shirt, with red and green colored hair to match.

"So, what is it like?" Catalina asked while raising her eyebrow and trying to control her anger.

"Rico and Pablo tried to help some sexy girls whose car broke down and took them inside the building. The next thing I know a Grey Porsche truck pulled up and two chicks with machine guns start shooting at us and killing every one. Luckily, I was in the bathroom when everything went down. Back up came, but these chicks were like female Rambos or something. They took everyone out until the police came. That's when I broke out, ran through the back of the alleyway and saw Mateo and Diego shooting at the girls Rico brought in to the apartment building not too long ago. The girls had a few duffle bags, and the blue eye crackheads was chasing them as well. I shot at them but saw a bullet rip Mateo's lower half a part. I'm telling you, I don't think he had his dick no more. I could hear 5.0 coming in the alleys, so I took off and ran into the building on the left into my homegirl Felicia's House." Miguel said while sweating. He used the back of his hand to wipe it away.

"So, you mean to tell me, instead of y'all dropping off the monthly income to the next stash house y'all all keep it there; and because y'all let those bitches in the building because Rico was thinking with his dick I'm out of eight million dollars? No one knows how much the police took, so who's to blame? Who's going pay me back my money?!" Catalina asked.

"Umm, I don't have that type of money, but I can find those bitches, kill them and get the money." Miguel replied.

"How I know you just didn't take my money or a duffle bag yourself and took it to that girl Felicia's house, huh?!" Catalina shouted.

"No boss. I didn't do that." Miguel said with his hands raised.

Catalina reached behind her back, grabbed the ring blade off her chair and threw it. It spun through the air like a frisbee with incredible speed and sliced off Miguel's Left hand from the wrist while he held hand his up. His eyes opened wide as he looked down at his hand and began to scream at the top of his lungs. Catalina hopped over her desk and side kicked him in the face before spin kicking him in the chest, knocking him to the ground.

"Stop fucking screaming like a little girl! If I wanted you dead, you'd be dead." Catalina said.

"Wait. What you going to do with me?" Miguel asked nervously.

"You're going get back my money and kill those bitches that took it." Catalina said as she stared at Benjamin and Tito, who were standing on the far side of the room. "You two fix him up and have him ready to fight; and go check his story out…and check that girl's house he went to. If she has my money, kill her. I'm tired of playing with these young hoes. Put a five-million-dollar contract out. Let it be known that we'll wire the money or pay cash for anyone that can lead us to them. It's time to kill these new young Teflon Divas. They're feeling themselves a little too much, and anybody can get touched!" Cartel shouted and Benjamin smiled.

"Yes, I've been dying to see my ex Rose. It's about time we had a face to face. I'm on it boss." Benjamin replied quickly as the thought of his hands wrapped around Rose's neck choking the life out of her brought him joy.

Sweat dropped down Layla's forehead into her mouth as she breathed heavily. She was amazed at how good Rose and Harmony had gotten so fast. She looked at Suyung to let her know she was ready to attack. Layla took off running and slid low across the mat for two seconds, causing Harmony to look down. While she wasn't paying attention, Suyung leaped into the air and stretched out her legs to kick Harmony in the chest but was kicked while still in the air by Rose.

"I got your fast kicking ass now. You didn't see that coming, did you." Rose said, proud of herself while talking shit but should of being paying more attention to the fight. Suyung bounced off the ground and did a spinning round house kick.

"Fuck! You broke my nose!" Rose yelled as she used her hand to block the first kick but the second one landed on the right side of her face.

Now she and Suyung were going blow for blow, punching and blocking each other's moves until Suyung kneed Rose in the stomach, causing her to bend over in pain. She was about to receive a knee to the face, but Harmony kicked and block Suyung, only to have

Layla's arms. wrap around her from the back; lifting her off her feet and slamming her onto the floor.

"Ahhh! Bitch this ain't wrestling." Harmony B said and rolled out the way as Layla tried to kick her.

"No, it's a fight, and there no rules in a fight. It's live or die. Win by any means necessary." Layla said as she continued to try to kick her while on the floor or hit her with the back of her heel, but Harmony keep rolling.

"You know what, your right." Harmony replied and tried to sweep kick Layla, but she back flipped out the way as Harmony popped up and with her index and pointer finger hit Layla in the stomach six times then grabbed it squeezed, and twist. Instantly Layla started to scream and dropped to the floor.

"You little dirty bitch, you know how much this hurts. Why would you do it; and how'd you remember how to? Ugh!" Layla groaned in excruciating pain, as it felt like she was on her cycle, but ten times worse.

"You said there was no rules; and I'll never forget that move. That shit was the most painful experience in my life. Worse than the first time I tried anal sex; but I bet every time that move happen to you it don't get no better, unlike sex. I'll never let that shit happen to me again and not know how to undo it. I don't know why they called this style the Heaven Touch. You sure it's not called a day in hell; or a year's worth of periods in one day?" Harmony B said and laughed at her corny joke; but from the corner of her eyes she could see Rose and Suyung going at it and Rose losing. Suyung's kicks were just too fast for her eyes to keep up.

Harmony ran toward them. Rose turned said ways to embrace Harmony and took a kick to her cheek bone. Rose opened the plan of her hands and Harmony jumped on it with one foot and leaped up in the air as Rose punched her up and came down with incredible force, first punching Suyung in the eye.

"Fuck! That's real fucked up Harmony. How you going use the same move we did together on the Santiago Cartel men?" Suyung shouted then felt Harmony hands on her stomach.

"No no! No, you better not!" Suyung yelled, but it was too late. "Ahhhh!" she yelled out at the top of her lungs in pain and dropped to her knees holding her stomach.

"Nice move sis. That shit hurt." Rose said, smiling because her and Suyung won the sparring match as she leaned her arm on Suyung's shoulder then looked down when she felt fingers on her stomach. "Oh, hell no bitch!" she yelled and tried to back step, but it was too late. She took a few steps back and began to cry. "You fucking bitch! Why? Why?!"

"Because it can only be one winner; and Layla mother was right that day she came in. Tess, or whatever her name is. If you can't reverse the move you deserve to lose; and judging by how long y'all taking to do so, I was the only one paying attention."

"No, you weren't; and don't mention that woman's name in this house again. You don't understand the hurt she put me through. It's always about her." Layla said standing up slowly after she reversed the heaven touch move on her stomach. A second later Suyung stood up.

"You're really going have to tell us the deal with her and that crazy bitch Iris. You can't leave us in the dark. You know all our secrets and more. We will fight with you if you say so, but it's clearly a lot of history there. We should know why and what we fighting for." Suyung said while rubbing her stomach.

"That why I love Rose, she doesn't ask why, she just bites when I tell her to attack." Layla replied.

"That's because Rose just likes to fight. She don't care who, it could be one of us. She likes a good fight, but deep down we all know it's because of the issues she had with her ex mentally and physically abusing her.

She never wants to feel weak again, so she jumps in head first." Harmony B replied.

"Umm, stop talking about me in a third person as if I'm not here. Ughh this shit hurt! I can't undo it, help me Harmony!" Rose cried out in pain while rolling around on the floor.

"No, you have to figure it out. You can still feel my fingers on your stomach throbbing. I know you do because I did. Clear your mind and push the pain out. You're a woman, that's what we do best; then repeat what I did backwards." Harmony stated.

"We should help her." Suyung said.

"No, she'll help herself. Harmony is right on this one; but I still don't want to speak about those bitches." Layla replied.

Rose took a deep breath and fought the pain she was in then repeated every spot she felt Harmony fingers hit then twisted. "Oh God! Thank God!" Rose said while whipping her tears away and getting up. "Naw, but they have a point, you have to tell us more." Rose stated.

"There's nothing to say." Layla replied while walking through the glass door of the training room and sat on a couch next to the weapons room.

Harmony followed her out, pulled out a pre-rolled joint and lit it up. She inhaled deeply then exhaled the smooth cannabis smoke before she passed it to Layla.

"Naw, I don't smoke." Layla replied.

"This isn't smoke, it's aromatherapy." Harmony said.

Layla took the blunt, pulled on it three times then passed it back as Suyung and Rose came and sat on the couch across from her. Harmony took two pills and passed it back to Layla. The weed had begun to relax Layla's mind and body.

"Iris was like an aunt to me, but she crossed the originals Teflon Divas and killed them all one by one without us knowing it was her. She was like the snake that snuck open on you and swallowed you whole before you realized it was happening; but I understand why she did it in away. In her sick mind she loved Tess. the woman that raise me like a mother. The woman who taught to me taught and how to shoot. Shit, I almost forgot I'm really a snipper first. She taught me that to keep me away from harm. So, I guess I could watch her back and still play a major roll. No one knew I knew how to fight as well as I did; but Tess... my mother's not what she seems. Maybe that's why Iris went crazy. Tess has a way of her making you love and trust her; but when it comes down to it, she will throw you away for her man Bless or her biological child. She told me to shoot her to kill Iris. I closed my eyes and made the shot, but I missed they're hearts. Deep down I did it on purpose I guess." Layla said and hit the blunt again.

"So, why you hate her so much?" Rose asked as Layla stood up and passed the blunt to her.

"Shit, where do I start? For years all I wanted was my own life, my own love story. What she had. I was tired of watching her love story… her life, I wanted my own; but I couldn't because we were on the run from the FBI. That's when the Teflon Divas became the most dangerous assassins in the world. If the world was going to treat us like criminals, then so be it. We'll be the best; but back to why I hate her. Damou, the love of my life is in Brooklyn, and I couldn't contact him or go back, but somehow Tess always ended back up with Bless. Let me tell you, this nigga been shot, stabbed, forgot who he was…shit straight out of a damn soap opera; but always find his way back to Tess." Layla said then paused a minute.

Suyung lit up another blunt and rested her head in the plan of her hands while leaning forward as if she was watching a good movie.

"It sounds like to me you needed a Bless. That's what was wrong with your love story. You said he did everything and found his way back to Tess, but Damou didn't do the same." Harmony stated.

"Shut up! That's not the fucking point." Layla said as her face turned bright red. "Damou had no way of finding me or the money, Bless did." Layla replied.

"Umm, sounds like an excuse if you ask me." Harmony replied.

"Excuse me!" Layla said with her face twisted up.

"Like I said, it sounds like an excuse if you ask me. I'm a real friend, so I won't hold my tongue. You might can beat my ass, but I'm going keep it real sis. If a man wants you, there's nothing he won't do to get you or keep you. It's their job to be the hunters and go after what they want. We're the prize. I'm just stating facts." Harmony said while raising her head. Rose and Suyung both give her the look as to say shut up. They wanted to hear more of the story before Harmony ruined it. It was already hard enough to get her to open up and talk. Luckily the weed helped.

"Like I said, it wasn't that easy. Tess never let me leave, never let me live my own life; even when we were traveling the world. They fucked who they wanted when they wanted. Me, I was treated as a kid. I'm twenty-five years old, but that wasn't the worst part. The worst part was her having me think I killed her. I been here in New York for eleven months and she didn't once try to reach out and tell me she was alive. As far as I'm concerned, she's dead to me. She was more hurt at the loss of her real child, more than she cared about me, the daughter she adopted. Because I'm not blood doesn't mean I deserve to be treated like a second-class citizen. I say fuck them all. They're dead in my eyes; and if they get in my way, I'll lay them down. It's my time go live my best life." Layla said.

"No matter what, I have your back." Rose said.

"I do too." Suyung replied. "That Damou nigga still ain't shit, but I still have your back girl; through thick and thin.

"Aww, look at y'all bitches." Red Velvet said while getting off the elevator and entering the huge basement with a pint of cookies and cream ice cream, sucking on a plastic spoon. "You bitches are soft as hell. I been watching y'all the whole time on the security cameras."

"We soft like that jiggly ass stomach of yours huh? You always talking shit and eating ice cream while doing it." Rose stated.

"Whatever. It's better than do what y'all doing, down here giving each other period cramps from hell as if it's a game and then taking about y'all feelings. Oh, my step mother wants me dead, my boyfriend used to beat me.

The woman that raised me loves her actual child and man more than me. That's weak as fuck. We should be getting some more money." Red said while walking closer, stuffing more ice cream in her mouth.

"Where hot. We just robbed the cartel for eight hundred thousand a piece. We need to lay low before hitting her or anyone else." Layla stated.

"Shit, we would have had a million dollars a piece of Ms. Harmony over there didn't lose a duffle bag; and speaking of my money, where is it?" Red Velvet asked with an attitude.

"Let me see you try to survive with the Cartel chasing and shooting at you along with crazy zombies ass crackheads while crying three duffle bags full of money. I doubt you'll be able to run a block like that." Harmony B replied.

"Is that a fat joke bitch?" Red asked and threw her pint of ice cream on the floor. "Because if it was, I'll knock you fuck out!" Red said balling up her fist and stepping closer.

Harmony crossed her legs and sat on the couch. She inhaled deeply and close her eyes before opening then. "I'm really starting to lose my patience when it comes to you hoe. It wasn't a fat joke, it me stating facts. If I couldn't run and escape with all three duffle bags, I know you wouldn't. I'm really starting to question you as a person. We all joke with each other but you're the only one that takes it serious." Harmony B stated.

"That's because I'm not the playing around type. I'm the steal your man and bust you in the face type of bitch; and you keep playing with me that what I'm going do! Knock your motherfucking teeth out." Red Velvet said through clenched teeth.

Harmony smirked. "You not gonna keep threatening me. That's your second time doing it, it won't be a third. You were only hard to beat the first time Red, and that was because I was still learning, but I came along way from that. We all have. You act real funny style, I swear. At times I don't know why you on the team or why you even got a cut of that money. What did you actually do? You supposed to be technical support but didn't warn us when the police was coming, and you didn't hack the street light system to crash cars to slow the Cartel or police down. You probably were just listening to everything like you always do, eating fucking ice cream; and I'm tired of you always passing gas and acting like it's not you. Bitch say excuse me. Bitch everyone farts, but you walk past and don't say shit; and a bitch can taste it in the air. If you stop eating all that damn ice cream, you wouldn't be so damn gassy!" Harmony stated as Rose passed her the blunt.

"Fuck this and fuck you! I told you I would knock your teeth out!" Red yelled while charging toward her with her fist up.

Just as she reached the couch Harmony jumped up, stepped on Red's large stomach, pushed off of it and did a back flip as she swung and missed. Harmony land on the cushion, standing on the couch and sent a knee to Red's chain.

"Ughhh! You hoe!" Red screamed as blood flew from her mouth.

Red wiped her mouth and look up to see Harmony standing right in front of her. She felt fingers on her stomach then felt Harmony grab and twist.

"Ughh! Ahhhhh! Ahhh!" Red scream in excruciating pain as she fell onto her butt, holding her stomach. "Oh my God! Make it stop! Make it stop! Please make it stop! Ahhh!" Red screamed as her stomach cramped up in tight knots worse than she ever felt in her whole life.

"I warned you about threatening me with your Precious looking ass!" Harmony shouted as she bent over and kicked her in the back of the leg.

"That's enough Harmony." Layla said as she got off the couch and bend over Red to undo the heaven touch on her stomach. "We're a team and he have to start acting like it; and Red we're too hot right now to do another robbery. We gotta stay low, then hit them again." Layla stated before she walked off headed toward the elevator.

Red groaned as she stood up, scrambled to the weapons room and grabbed a Glock 17. She pulled back the chamber, placed a bullet inside and step out the weapons room aiming at the back of Harmony's head as she, Suyung, and Rose walked to the elevator to get in it with Layla. Layla was zoned out, thinking of what Harmony had said. If a man really wants you, he'll come to you no matter what. "He should've looked for me or found some way to reach me." Layla mumbled to herself then looked up to see the girls coming. Her heart raced when she saw Red pointing the gun.

"Harmony! Side flip now!!!" Layla shouted.

Harmony wanted to hesitate and question her, but the urgency in Layla's voice told her not to. Harmony side flipped just as Red squeezed the trigger. The bullet flew out the gun and missed Harmony's head by an inch. Red's face twisted up in anger as squeezed the trigger repeatedly, sending billets flying out the gun.

"Shit! Shit!" Harmony said while flipping left to right without using her hands to flip and dodge the bullets.

"Bitch stay still! I'm gonna kill your ass!" Red shouted.

"Red, stop!" Layla shouted, but Red continued to fire as if Layla didn't say a word.

Rage and the look of death were in Red's eyes as three bullets slammed into Harmony's back while she was in the air flipping, knocking her off balance. Rose and Suyung looked at Layla as if to say why the fuck we not helping or moving. Layla shook her head and they both knew why.

"This shit still crazy." Rose said while stepping back next to Layla.

"I can't believe she took it this far." Suyung said while shaking her head.

Red continued to fire at Harmony stiff body on the floor and stepped closer. "I'm going empty this whole clip in your ass." Red said through gritted teeth as she stepped closer.

Something in her body was screaming no, that something was wrong, but she ignored the feeling and stepped even closer; which is when she noticed that there was no blood anywhere.

"Wait. I'm sure I hit this bitch seven times." Red mumbled to herself, then eyes open up wide as she realized what was going on.

Harmony had on a dark purple satin pajama shirt with the matching pants. The bullets had torn through four spots in the button up shirt and a few in the thigh area, but underneath the pretty purple satin pajamas you could see a skin-tight back body suit. It was hard to notice at first because it was only two shades darker than Harmony's smooth chocolate skin. Red looked up and could see Layla in her red satin pajamas, Rose in her royal blue and Suyung in her cream. None of them look worried or scared that she'd just shot Harmony, but for the first time she could see they all had there Teflon body suits under their pajamas. Her mind raced. *'They must have had it when they were training.'*

"Fuck no!" Red yelled and aimed at Harmony's head while she was still lying flat on her back not moving.

Harmony rose up like the Undertaker in a wrestling match before Red could squeeze the trigger. She raised her arm and flex the forearm muscle on her left arm and the blade slid out of the forearm of her suit and flew at incredible speed and force, slamming into Red Velvet's huge stomach.

"Ughhhhh!" Red screamed and try to grab it when it hit her stomach but slice the palm of her left hand deeply as the blade tore and ripped through her intestines before it went right through her and came out her back, slamming her into the brick wall behind her.

"You fucking bitch." Red mumbled and look down. Hot steam could be seen coming from a wide-open wound as blood began to squirt out and hit the floor.

Reds facial expression twisted up with the look of pain and shock. She grabbed her stomach as her eyes water up and tears traveled down her cheeks. "You fuckin bitches! I hate you all! I hate you!" Red screamed and raised the gun again, aiming it at Harmony who was sitting on the floor straight with her arm raised.

"Fuck you bitch! Fuck all of you!" Red velvet shouted while crying.

"Red, don't do it." Layla said as Red used the little bit of energy she had to try to raise the hand she had the gun in.

"Red, no! Stop!" Rose shouted, because all of them knew what would happen next. Harmony don't! Layla please."

"Fuck that. I'm supposed to sit back and let this fat bitch kill me? It's not happening Layla. I don't care." Harmony replied as she stared Red in the eyes.

"Fuck you; you black ass tar baby hoe!" Red shouted.

As if her scream gave her more energy, Red finally lifted the gun and aimed. Before she could squeeze the trigger, Harmony flexed her muscles on her left arm she had stretched out. Red could hear a sound coming from behind her as the forearm blade that was stuck in the wall shook free and flew backwards as if someone pressed rewind on the tv, taking off at top speed. Red twisted her head around to see what the noise was and tried to move but wasn't fast enough. The sword slammed into her back and traveled through her backwards out of her stomach, leaking blood and guts from it, then entered back into the slot on her forearm. Red spun around dramatically in a full circle in what seemed like slow motion and lasted for damn near an hour before she hit the floor hard.

"Harmony!" Layla shouted and ran out the elevator with Suyung and Rose fast behind her. Rose helped Harmony off the floor as Layla bent down next to Red. "Get towel now, and duct tape!" Layla shouted.

Rose and Harmony didn't move an inch. Suyung took off to the weapons room to grab a few white towels and grey duct tape, then rushed back to hand it to Layla.

"Ughh! I don't want to die." Red cried out as she lay twisted on the floor looking like a sea lion out of water and unable to move.

"You won't. Just hold on." Layla said to her. "Suyung there's morphine and a medical kit in the weapons room as well. Grab it." Layla said while tapping towels to the two large slices in Red's back and applying pressing to the wound in her stomach area.

She was doing her best to slow the bleeding, but blood was rushing out fast as if she took three gallons of milk out the fridge, dropped them at the same time and they burst open everywhere. There were puddles of thick blood everywhere, that Layla was now kneeling deep in.

"Give me the morphine!" Layla shouted and Suyung tossed it to her.

Layla caught the small military style needle, peeled open the military style sterile pack and jammed the needle in Red's arm, pushing the morphine into her system.

"Help me. You hold the towel; keep pressure on the wound. I have to seal her wound and stop the bleeding so she can get to a hospital. If not, she won't make it." Layla replied.

"You should just let the bitch bleed out. She never liked any of us, and I'm sure she wouldn't piss on us if we were in fire. She's not part of this sisterhood, it's all about the money for here while we actually care about and love each other Layla." Rose stated.

"Either help or shut the fuck up. She's still one of us, we just can't let her die." Layla said while sewing up the first wound then threaded the needle before she started sewing up the next wound.

"Ugh! Ugh!" Red gasped for air as if she couldn't catch her breath as she kicked her feet.

"Relax. Just relax and hold on. Breath." Layla said then felt Red's body go limp.

Layla eyes open up wide and a tear escaped them. She leaned over and touched Red's chin, moving it to see if she got a reaction then touched her wrist for a pulse. There was none. Layla stood up with her pajamas soaked in blood.

"Why you so mad? She attacked me. She tried to kill me." Harmony said, not understanding why Layla was looking so devastated.

"Yeah, but you know you had the skills to stop her and disarm her whiteout killing her; and both you just stood there and let her bleed out like a stuffed pig." Layla said while walking away with Suyung following behind her.

"Umm, what we supposed to do with her, we can't leave here there?" Harmony asked.

"You killed her, you dumb the body. It's no longer my concern" Layla said as the elevator door shut.

"Now how in the hell are we supposed to move her big ass?" Harmony asked.

"Umm, what you mean we homie? You killed her. My back ain't strong enough for this job." Rose said with her left eyebrow raised, looking down at Red's body.

"Stop playing and help me. You know I wasn't wrong. Layla would've done the same thing if someone tried to kill her. That's what she trained us for. Red never once act like she was a part of this team." Harmony said.

"You said this already. You don't have to sell me on the reason why you killed her. It sounds like you trying to convince yourself more than anything. The bitch pulled a gun on you, you killed her, end of the story. So how we going to move her?" Rose asked.

"I got an idea." Harmony said before she went in to the weapons room and came back out pulling two Dolly's. "We'll scoop her up in these dolly carts, take her to the small white van Layla owns and drop the body off then come back and bleach down the floor to clean up all this blood." Harmony said.

"It sounds like a plan to me." Rose replied. "Ugh, help shove her over." Rose said as she scooped the dolly half way up under Red's body.

Harmony went to the other side of Red and pushed her hard, rolling her body to scoop onto both dollies'.

"Damn this bitch is heavy." Harmony stated.

"Shit, I honestly think we should've chopped this bitch into tiny pieces before doing this." Rose replied while grabbing black trash bags and duct tape.

"Naw, that would be too messy, it's already too much to clean. My body's already sore. That fat hoe shot me seven times. The suit protects our body from the bullets penetrating, but the impact of that shit hurts like hell. It feels like it breaking your bones. I can barely move." Harmony replied.

"Just shut up and move faster, I'm ready for bed. I might even try eating a pint of ice cream before I go to bed in memory of Red here." Rose said, causing both her and Harmony to bust out laughing.

They used the dolly carts to drag Red's body to the elevator, down to the building lobby and out the door. Rose had grabbed the white cargo vans keys when they were in the basement. She walked down the block, crossed the street. Rose hopped in, started it up, then drove it down the block. Even though it was one o'clock in the morning, a few people could be seen moving about. As Rose pulled up to the body, she looked at

Harmony standing there smiling nervously behind the dolly cart and what looked like a broke down sofa couch wrap in a black plastic bag. They just keep it moving.

"Fuck, this butch is heavy." Rose grunted as she and Harmony push together, and after the sixth time finally got Red in the back of the van.

"Let's go." Rose said as they hopped in the van and took off. Should we just dump her in Central Park? It's right across the street. Rose asked.

"That was a stupid thing to say. You sure you use to be Cartel my friend? That's way too close to where we live. We need to burn here or something." Harmony replied.

"Burn her? That takes forever. I been to Haiti and cooked a whole pig. That shit takes hours. I don't think we can burn a body for hours in New York City, and the next option is to bury her. I don't feel like digging no hole. I'm muthafuckin tired; and besides, you killed her." Rose said then sucked her teeth. "We can just drop her body on the street somewhere." Rose then said.

"Naw, that's not good. I have an idea, drive to the Hudson river." Harmony said with a smile on her face.

"I see where you going with this." Rose replied.

Ten minutes later they park under a bridge and looked around, making sure no one seen them then use the dolly carts to drag Red's body to the pier and roll her into the river.

"Damn that was a workout. Let's burn the van and go home." Harmony said. "We can we burn it next to a chicken spot in Harlem, I'm fucking starving and got to feed these thick thighs."

"Sounds like a plan to me." Rose said as they hopped in the van and pulled off.

A thick fog filled the New York air. "I swear I hate this job." Frank, a tall Caucasian man said while adjusting his hat.

"What's there to hate Doug? We get Harbor patrol; cursing the river at night drinking great coffee." Frank replied while brushing his mustache down with his hand.

"Yeah, drinking coffee all night's not bad, but what make it's so great being on a boat drinking at night?" Doug asked.

"Because the air in the water is even better." Frank stated while moving the larger head light on the middle-sized boat from side to side looking for anything suspicious in the water.

"Looks like we got another one though. Damn I love this job. Let's fish it out and call it in." Frank stated.

"See, you got issues. How can you enjoy this? This will be tenth body we found this week." Doug replied with disgust on his face.

"Shit, that's the best part. We never know what shape the dead person is going be in. If the fish ate their eyes, or if they got their arms. and legs chop off; or oh, you remember that guy we found a month ago with rocks in his stomach. It was as if whoever killed him shoved rocks down his throat hoping the guy would sink and stay at the bottom. Dumb assholes." Frank said as he used the fishing crane and net to pull the body out of water and place it on the deck.

"Damn, this a big one. I wonder how they killed the poor big guy." Doug stated.

"Well let's find out. I bet the fish ate his eyes already. If I win, you're buying breakfast when we get off." Frank said while pulling out a folding pocket knife and sliced open the plastic.

"Well it looks like you lost the bet. He is a she and it looks like she's still got her eye balls." Doug said looking over Frank's shoulders.

"It's still a chance I can win. It's not over to the fat lady sings, let me lift her eye lids to make sure her eyeballs aren't gone." Frank said then placed his index finger and thumb on the woman's eyelid, peeling the right one open. The other eye opened and the woman moved.

"Help me! Help me!" she said in a weak voice while stretching her arm out.

"What the fuck!" Frank shouted while hopping backward away from the woman then jumping onto his feet. "Call it in! We need an ambulance now, not the forensic science truck!" Frank shouted, unable to believe the woman was still alive.

"The cold water must've helped her somehow and kept her alive instead of killing her." Doug said out loud.

"Yeah, but will she make is the question." Frank replied. "Stay with us miss. Do you know who did this to you?" Frank ask while holding the woman's hand as Doug drove the boat to the pier where you could see the bright lights of the ambulance and the two EMT's standing beside it with the stretcher waiting to help.

"Yes, I remember; and I swear they'll pay the woman back." She said weakly while crying, unable to move.

"What's your name?" one of the EMT's asked as Doug, Frank and the two workers loaded the woman off the boat and into the back of the ambulance.

"It's Red. Red Velvet." the woman said before losing consciousness.

Chapter Sixteen

Playing a Dangerous Game

"I still can't believe Harmony killed Red. Are we destined to repeat the same mistake as Tess and her team, killing each other off? No, that can't be so, because everyone on Tess's team really loved each other. Others a little too much." Layla said to herself while smoking an exotic weed called wedding cake in a pre-rolled blunt. She was in the basement of her building in a room set up like a laboratory. She could hear Rose, Harmony and Suyung practicing shooting in the small shooting range courses they had down there. Layla was dressed in a black crock top and tight Fashion Nova jeans with black Gucci sandals on her feet, showing off her pretty French pedicure. She looked down at the book Ms. Wung Shu had given her and the ingredients for an accent Chinese drug. Ms. Wung Shu told her the drug will make anyone do what you say and forget certain things about themselves, but it only last seven days at a time before you'll have to drug them once more. Otherwise the persons memories start to come back, and they start to fight the control you over them.

'This stuff is very deadly in the wrong hands. It's pretty much mind control; and from what I'm reading you can put memories into the mind of the victim that were never there, and they will believe it with all their heart. My question is why did she give this to me? Was it because she knew in her heart Iris was alive and was coming to see her and she didn't want her to find this formula? Shit, all the damn problems. this can cause if she discovers this formula. Hmm, I wonder." Layla said out loud to herself while smoking the blunt.

She left the lab, went into the weapons room and grab two small devices, one that looked like a black electric taser, and went back into the Laboratory. It took her an hour to make the formula, and another to take apart the device and putting it back together. She loaded the device with what looked like sewing needles she'd dipped into the formula and placed the device in her pocket before she left the lab.

"Where you going boss lady?' Rose asked.

"To run an errand. I'll be back in a few." Layla replied.

If you're not back before it gets dark, I'll track your phone and come looking for you." Rose said then put back on her headphones and went back to shooting targets dressed as masked robbers.

"You think she still mad at us?" Harmony asked, taking off her headphones.

"Huh?!" Rose shouted.

"Stop shooting and you can hear!" Harmony shouted back.

"Okay, what?" Rose replied.

"You think she's still mad at us?" Harmony asked.

"Yes, she's still mad. That's why she's been so standoffish, you killed a member of our team. I'm not saying you're wrong, because I don't know what I would've done in that situation, maybe kill her too. We could've broken her arm and kicked her off the team and out the house. She didn't belong with us. She really wasn't one of us, but Layla would never see it that way. She believed she could help everyone, even the ones that don't want the help." Suyung said and went back to shooting the target shape as a business man in a suit holding a sword and uzi, thinking of her half-sister and step mother.

The sun was shining bright as Layla walked through Central Park. It was just turning twelve o'clock, but the park was still full of people on a Monday. She walked to the Central Park garden. The beautiful flowers were blooming everywhere. The smell of sweet honey was in the air along with bees flying. The garden was mostly filled with couples and elderly people sitting on benches, looking at flowers or sitting on the cherry blossom. trees as their beautiful pedals hit the ground.

Layla spotted an older woman with beautiful grey hair and a nice brown complexion, pulled out the k12 and squeezed the button. "I hope this don't kill the poor lady." Layla said to herself as the small needle flew out with speed and pierced the woman's shoulder.

"Ouch! What fuck was that?! A bee stung me!" the woman said in Spanish.

"Let me help you." Layla said and sat next to the woman before swiftly pulling the small needle from the woman's shoulder, placing it in her back pocket. "Are you okay?" Layla asked and stare at the woman, who looked stuck in a daze and mannequin-like.

"Would you do what I tell you?" Layla asked curiously.

"Yes, I would." the woman said in a stiff voice.

"Hmmm. What's your name, how old are you and where you from; and talk normal." Layla said.

"I'm Delilah. I'm fifth two years old and I'm from Puerto Rico. I have a nice piece of land with a good house." Delilah said in a deep Spanish accent.

"Give me your phone and unlock it." Layla demanded. Delilah dug in her purse and passed Layla her phone.

"When I stand up and walk away, you will go back to being your normal self and will forget this conversation ever happened, until seven days from now on Sunday. You'll call me and say it's time for your medicine, and I'll tell you where to meet me so you can get stung by a bee again okay." Layla said.

"Yes." Delilah replied.

Layla passed her back her phone, stood up from the bench and walked away. She looked back to see Delilah staring at the beautiful cherry blossoms. falling just like she found her a few seconds ago.

"Hmm. That was a corny test of what this formula can do, but I might be able to use her later. I'll never know; but how would Iris test it out. Ahhh, I know." Layla said with a smile as she walked out of the garden area and saw a middle age Caucasian couple walking holding hands while the woman ate ice cream.

The man was tall with dark brown hair and slim build, but one of those skinny guys that had muscles like they lived in the gym and want to be bigger but only get definition. The woman was short. 5'2 with blonde hair, and they looked very in love, stopping to kiss every few feet and take selfies.

"Awww, how cute. No one loves me like that. Let's see if I can fuck this up." Layla said and pointed the k12 device at the blonde hair woman as she walked behind the couple and pressed the button, hitting the woman in the back with the needle.

"Ouch!" she screamed and step forward real fast as if someone shoved her.

Layla carefully walked until she was right beside her, snatched the needle out her back, leaned over and whispered in the woman's ear, 'Rip his dick off, he's a cheater.' Layla then power walked ahead of the couple with her head held down, found a bench on the right of the walking path and sat down to watch what would happen next. The blonde-haired woman stood frozen like a statue for about five seconds.

"Baby what's wrong? Are you okay? baby do need to go to the emergency room?" the man asked while looking at his girlfriend look stuck, then he shook her a little.

"You fucking cheater! You fucking cheater!" the woman shouted and started clawing at his face.

"Brittany stop! What are you talking about, I never cheated? You can check my phone!" the tall slim guy shouted back while trying to hold her hands. She was like a wild animal; uncontrollable and stronger than normal.

"You're lying David! You fucking cheated on me!" she screamed even louder while still attacking.

David use all his strength to try to hold her, but she broke free and dug her nails deep into his face and scratched down hard, tearing the first layer of his skin and digging deep into the white meat.

"Ahhh! Ahh! You crazy bitch!" David yelled at the top of his lung as the burning sensation on his face was too much to bare and he swung, punching her in her right temple. The hit sent Brittany flying sideways to the ground. "Oh shit! I'm sorry baby. I'm so sorry, it was a reflex." David said while bending over to check to see if she was okay and pick her up. When he did, Brittany leaped into his arms., wrapped her legs around his waist and her arms. around his head before squeezing tightly.

"Bri! Brittany what's got into you?! What's wrong?! Get off me! I haven't cheated. I love you!" David yelled while trying to shake her off. Brittany opened her mouth wide and sunk her teeth in to David's neck.

"Ahhhhh! Ahh you fucking bitch!" David yelled out in excruciating pain. People walking by stopped and pulled out their phones to record and take pictures. "Help me! Help! Someone please help me!" David yelled and ran up to two people holding their phone with Brittany still attached to him like a leech.

He punched her in the rib repeatedly and could hear what sounded like one cracking. Layla saw a snap back baseball hat on the bench across from her, so she casually walked over to it, put the cap on and pulled it low before walking a little closer to the crowd of people starting to form. David panicked and spun in circles, punching and trying to shake his girlfriend off. Brittany yanked with all her might and pulled back a chunk of flesh from his neck. Blood began to rush out of it fast like a leaky water hose.

"Ughh!" David groaned in pain and his eyes opened wide as he held the side on his neck when felt Brittany teeth sink into his left side of his neck.

David's heart raced as blood poured out the open wound on the left side of his neck and knew she was about to rip another hole into his neck with her teeth. He panicked as he looked around and realized no one was going help or call the police. They were just hanging around, continuing to recording until the worse happened. David looked at the concrete walkway and jump up in the air spreading his arms. and feet before he did a belly flop onto the hard concrete with Brittany hanging on the front of him like a swaddled. David heard something on Brittany pop, but that didn't loosen her grip on his neck. David stood back up, ran to the closest bench and stood on the very top of it before leaping off it.

"Ouchhhhh!" the crowd of people said simultaneously.

This time the back of Brittany's head could be heard smashing in, causing her to loosen her grip around him and release her teeth. David stumbled, stood up and looked down at Brittany's body twitching.

"What the fuck is going on?" Davit said to himself and fell backwards onto the ground. His head felt woozy from the loss of blood and he could barely move. He did his best to keep his hand on his neck, but it did little to help as blood continue to rush out as he laid flat on his back.

"Help me! Help me!" he mumbled weakly.

Brittany got off the ground slowly. As she got up, the crowd of people could see the back of her head was dented in, and her blonde hair was missing spots, as if had been pulled out. Dark red blood the color of Burgundy was leaking down her back. She limped towards David, bent down to her knees, and started unbuckling his gray shorts.

"Stop! Stop!" Davit said weakly and tried to fight her off with his right arm but couldn't. She pulled down his shorts to his ankles, then pulled down his boxer briefs. "What you doing?! Fucking help, me! Call the cops! Call 911!" Davit shouted while crying.

A dark skin heavy set woman out for her afternoon walk had stopped to see what everyone was recording and squeezed her way through the crowd. Her mouth dropped wide open when she saw all the blood and David on the ground. She pulled out her phone and called 911.

"Hello police. There's a woman attacking a man out her close to 110th street in Central Park." the woman said and then continue to watch as the 911 operator talked in her ear.

Brittany grabbed his dick and gripped it like a bitch trying to snatch other another woman's hair. "What you doing?! Stop!" Davit shouted as her nails dig into his pink flesh. He thought things couldn't get any worse. As his head started spinning, Brittany bent over and bent his dick to the side before she started biting into the base of it, chomping on it repeatedly like a beaver chewing until they chop down a tree.

"Ahhhhh! Ahhhh!" David began to holler at the top of his lungs as her teeth rip away layers of flesh and muscle.

Brittany stopped biting and held her head up to see that David's penis was pumping blood and hanging on by a piece of skin. She grabbed his dick in her hand and twist it around in a circle until the skin popped and ripped it off. After she snatched it off, she stood up and turned around to face the crowd. Her eyes met with Layla's right away.

"See, I snatched it off, like you said. "I snatched the cheater's dick off." Brittany said while walking toward the crowds like her legs was broken.

Layla tried to backpedal into the crowd but knew that wasn't going to stop her from coming. If her boyfriend breaking her ribs and almost cracking every bone in her body, including smashing her skull in didn't stop her from doing what she was told, nothing would.

"Forget what I said! Forget it all!" Layla shouted while blending into the crowd.

The sound of Layla's voice over everyone else's caught Brittany ear and she stood frozen as if she was in a trance, then snapped out of it.

"David! David what's going on?" she mumbled while looking at all the people around her with their phones out recording her.

She turned around to see David laying in a pool of blood, a big hole in neck, and an even bigger hole in his groin area.

"David! What happened?! What happened?!" Brittany yelled then looked at her hand to see that she had his penis in it.

She tried to open her hand to drop it, but she couldn't. She then made a step toward David's body, but her nervous system that was dormant while she was in a trance had now started to function. The pain she hadn't felt before came at her all at once, like someone pulling your tooth with pliers and breaking your arms. and feet.

"Ahhhh! she screamed and began to cry as the pain from her leg being broken as well as four ribs, and the back of her skull smashed in.

"Police! Freeze! Put your hands up!" two police officers shouted and pulled their guns on Brittany.

The crowd scattered while some stood back and kept recording. Layla couldn't believe her eyes. 'This shit a fucking biological weapon.' Layla thought to herself then turn around to walk away, whispering attack them while leaving. Somehow through all the screaming and the police shouting at her, Layla's voice became the only voice she heard. Brittany stood frozen for a second and the pain went away, then she looked at the cops. The two police officers looked at her strangely as she stood there covered in blood, blood around her mouth, and a tight grip on a dick. They gave each other a knowing stare.

"This one going to have to go to Bellevue psych ward. I think she's losing it." one said.

"I think she's already lost it. Watch out!" the other police officer yelled as Brittany screamed and came running towards them swinging the dick.

The police officers opened up fire. Bullets tore through Brittany's chest and stomach ripping her apart, and five went into her face as well as three more bullets into her shoulder and arms. She hit the ground like a ton of bricks and was dead in seconds.

Chapter Seventeen

Leave no Evidence or Friend Behind

'Maybe I should just burn the book Ms. Wung Shu gave me. Without it and the locust flower, no one will know how to recreate it. It's too powerful for one person to control. Why the fuck would she give this to me? I have three locust pedals left. That's enough to make a teaspoon worth, but I can do a lot of damage with this and make my wishes come true. Fuck it, I'm keeping it.' Layla thought to herself as the hot, sudsy water filled her soaker tub. She opened her robe and step in the tub.

'Damn I needed this. I have too much shit on my mind. Is this what it's like to be Tess; to have so much on your shoulders? I have to keep my team safe, and I'm still not fucking happy yet. I wasted close to two fucking years staying low and training my team and have yet to touch Damou. That was the whole point of me coming back, that and to bury Tess and Iris' daughters. Now I got a fucking Cartel trying to kill me, Iris' psycho ass out there trying to kill me, and Tess wanting to take over my damn team. If it's not one thing it's another. I just want to be loved and free.' Layla thought to herself as she submerged herself under the hot water but popped up and wiped the bubbles off her face. She grabbed the tv remote from the side of the tub, turned on the tv that was mounted on the wall in front of her, and flipped through the channels. Each channel was a live video feed from a security camera on each of the four floors of the building not including the basement.

"There's Rose in the kitchen, always eating." Layla said as she watched Rose on the first floor in the kitchen cooking.

Layla flipped the channel again and was now watching Harmony on the couch on her apartment floor watching tv with a shiny metal toy between her open legs, moaning.

"Is that a Rabbit or the Bullet? You know what, I don't even want to know." Layla said to herself and quickly changed the channel before Harmony climaxed.

She could now see Suyung in her bathroom dying her neon green. "To each its own girl. To each its own." Layla said, talking to the tv knowing Suyung couldn't hear her.

Layla reached her hand out the tub to grab the lighter and blunt full off wedding cake. She sparked it up and inhaled deeply. "Fuck. Harmony and Rose got me smoking more and more if this shit. I'm starting to like it way too much." Layla said to herself then exhaled.

She smoked half the joint before putting it out and submerging herself in the hot sudsy water.

Catalina sat in the back of a Lincoln Navigator with Benjamin next to her and Tito in the driver's seat. Catalina stared at Layla's building as twenty black trucks pull up, cutting off traffic that was coming up and down the street. Men dressed in dark blue shirts with Uzi's and shotguns along with handguns hopped out and ran towards the building.

"They'll never see us coming, until it's too late." Catalina said as she hopped out the truck dressed in her all black Teflon body suit with two Glock 17's in her hands followed by Benjamin and Tito. 50 armed men entered the building's lobby.

"They're alarm won't go off?" Benjamin asked.

"Naw, our inside person give us the blue print of the building and hacked their security system." Catalina replied then began to give orders. "A group of you take the stairs and three of you come with us." she said and entered the elevator with Benjamin and Tito along with three other Cartel soldiers. Benjamin exited onto the first floor, and the three Cartel soldiers got of the second floor. Tito got off on the third floor.

Rose hummed while cooking. She checked the oven twice, looking at the chicken wings she was baking and went to the cabinet to get the box of Idaho potatoes before going back to the stove and poured them into the hot boiling water. Rose sang along to 'Reggae to' a song by sin Pijama while dancing and shaking her hips.

"You always could shake your ass good to some Reggaeton." Rose heard a voice say over the music that caused her heart to race. Her body began to sweat as fear consume her. Her hands shook nervously as stood in the kitchen. She slowly turned around to see Benjamin standing there in an all-black suit with a matching tie, holding a sword in his left hand.

"You look like you seen a ghost baby." Benjamin said then smiled. "Uh yeah, because you do. You betrayed me mami, and for what? To be dancing naked in a fancy apartment. So, this why you betrayed me and let a stranger kill me? I was the one to take care of your ass." Benjamin said with his face twisted in anger as he stared at Rose.

"It was to get away from you. I was tired of getting mentally and physically abused. That's not love; or me being scared to speak because I might say the wrong thing to upset you and you beat me. Yes, I wanted you dead, and still do." Rose said while gaining her courage back slowly.

"So that'd what you learned over here, how to talk back? I'm going enjoy this." Benjamin said while dropping his sword and unbuckling his leather belt. "I'm going beat you like old times, while my boss and team kill your friends. I don't know why she's so worry about y'all, but today will be the last day any one will ever hear of the Teflon Divas." Benjamin said then move closer to her as he raised the belt high over his head and prepared to come down with it with all his might.

"You're dead. I'm not the same bitch or woman you knew before!" Rose shouted and grab the pot of boiling mashed potatoes that was popping. She swung it, tossing the hot mashed potatoes all on his face and chest.

"Ahhhhhh! Ahhhhhhhhh! Benjamin shouted at the top of his lungs as the steaming hot mashed potatoes burn through his skin.

Before he could process a thought, Rose attacked, hitting him in the head and face with the pot. "You think you'll beat me again?! Fuck you! You'll never just whip my ass again and I just lay there crying! Not again! Never again!" Rose said with each swing.

Benjamin used his forearms. and he blows to soften the blows from the pot. "Enough!!" Benjamin said in a deep voice before grabbing her wrist, twisted it then flip her over his shoulders, causing her to land hard on to her back.

"Bitch what thought? I was just going let you hit me!" Benjamin shouted but then felt his feet lift up under him as Rode swipe kick him. He fell on his ass with a stupid, surprised look on his face.

"It looks like you learned a little more than talking back…" Benjamin began, but his sentence was cut off by a side kick to his face.

'What the fuck?! Is this bitch fighting me back?! Is she really beating my ass? Hell no, this can't be.' Benjamin thought to himself as he rolled and hopped off the ground to see Rose standing in a fighting stance with her hands up.

"Okay, let's do this." Benjamin said as took off his jacket and toss it at her, causing her not to see for a second as he front-kicked her in the chest, sending her flying backwards; but she quickly recovered, jumped up in the air and punched him in the face then the neck. Benjamin grabbed his neck as he coughed and choked while trying to gasp in air.

"You bitch!" he wheezed and started to realize he had to really fight her.

His brown skin started to turn red as he got angry and began to send combo attacks, sending three punches toward her face. Rose dodged them all with ease but let out a slight scream as he right hooked her, punching her in the ribs, then once in the mouth and nose. Rose stepped back, spit out blood from her mouth and wiped the blood from her nose.

"I used to think you hit hard, but after fighting my girls I've come to realize you hit like a bitch ass nigga." Rose said then spit in his face. Blood and saliva splashed in to his eyes.

"You nasty bit…" Before he could finish crushing her out, Rose attacked; running and jump on the kitchen counter before leaping off it in one move and sent a flying knee into his jaw. Benjamin stumble backwards, but before he could recover Rose was on him like white on rice, sending blow after blow to his face and stomach. Benjamin did his best to block all of them but couldn't.

'Where the hell did, she learn how to fight like this? She fights better than a damn man; and how the hell did she get so fast? I can barely see her hands or when she going to attack next so I can counter attack. This can't be.' Benjamin thought to himself then started gasping for air again as she punched him in the neck.

"Ughh! Aight, stop punching me in my neck!" Benjamin screamed weakly, removing his hand from his neck and Rose punched him is his Adam's Apple once more.

This time he choked on his own saliva and his turned bright reddish brown as he tried to back away.

"Oh, don't run now daddy. You remember all the times you beat my ass and treated me like shit and talked about how you hate the Haitian side of me that wasn't a real Dominican; and you hate that my skin complexion was a little darker? You'll beat the black out of me, right?!" Rose asked, picking up the leather belt off the floor that he had dropped when they start fighting. She wrapped it around her hand, leaving the buckle end hanging out.

"I thought you'd understood being mixed. You're half Japanese and half Dominican, but you hide it and you're ashamed of who you are. I just realized your weak. Weak minded and a weak ass person all together. I can't believe I used to be scared of you!" Rose shouted.

Benjamin smiled. "You should be. Like you said, I hide who the fuck I am." he stated while spin kicking Rose in the rib.

She attacked him but something was different. He block her blow and hit her repeatedly.

"What style is that?" Rose asked out loud as she rolled off the floor.

"You reminded me of who I was. I'm a fucking Samurai master!" Benjamin shouted.

"Fuck you!" Rose screamed and grabbed a kitchen knife off the counter. She aimed for his heart and came down with all her might.

"Die fucker! You have no heart!" Rose said as the knife connected with his chest and snapped in half. "What the fuck?!" Rose said and step back and look at the broken knife in her hand. She then stare at the white button up shirt he had on and notice the dark suit underneath.

"Wait, what?" Rose asked as her mind raced and she knew he had body armor on.

"That's the motherfucking second time you tried to call me. You won't get a third." Benjamin said and pulled out a baby 9mm from the small of his back and aimed.

"Oh hell no." Rose said and swing the belt, hitting him in the head with the buckle.

"Awww!" Benjamin shouted. Rose beat him repeatedly, causing him to drop the gun as the buckle hit his hand, the top of his head, and his arm. "Ohh you bitch! he groaned in pain and scrambled to the floor to pick up the gun while taking hits to the back but couldn't feel them because of his armor under his clothes. He began to fire wildly sending billets everywhere.

"Oh shit!" Rose said while jumping left and right looking like she was playing dodge ball, and quickly took off toward her room as Benjamin aimed for her back. She shut the door, pushed her dresser up against it and grabbed her Teflon Diva bulletproof body suit out the closet along with her ear transmitter. "We're under attack! I repeat, we're under attack!"

On the second floor Harmony was practicing doing splits in some skin-tight shorts that rode up her ass and showed off her butt checks. She then practiced some kicks in the living room while watching a tv show, 'Are you the one?'

"Nope, that fool isn't the one for you. He slept with three girls in the house on the same day. Don't you kiss him girl! Don't do it! Eww, she did it!" Harmony said, talking to the tv as she heard the elevator ding, letting her know someone was coming.

"Rose girl, you missed so much! This fool Brian slept with Kelly, Stephanie, and Keisha; and now kissing Samantha, all in 72 hours. See, that's why I could never be on one of these hook-ups shows. I catch feelings too fast and liable to beat the nigga's ass along with the woman's ass. Out here servant community dick. I'm good; but why you so quiet? Did you finish cooking or bring me a snack? I got to feed these thick asses thick of mines." Harmony said and turn around to see three brown skin Spanish men staring at her. One had an uzi, the other a 45 handgun, and one a shotgun, aimed straight at her. Harmony raised her hand and tried to think fast.

"What are we waiting for? Let's shoot this bitch and find the rest." the short one on the right side.

"Naw, that will be a waste homie, look at her fucking thighs. Them shits chocolate, thick and smooth. I never seen no shit like that in real life, only on Instagram; and 80% of the women's body on there be fake plastic Barbie want to be bitches. Her body you can tell it's really. I have to taste it and try it before we kill her." the tall man in the middle said, and Harmony could tell he was the leader out of them.

"Naw, I'm with Chico. Our orders are to kill these bitches fast and find the money they took. I don't think it's a good idea to play with Herb." the guy on the right said in Spanish.

Harmony smirked because she took Spanish classes and spoke it fluently. She started to slowly touch her small breast and her flat stomach, then rub on her thick voluptuous thighs. Harmony knew she had the body and face that drive men crazy. She was short with barely no breast, which she hated, but it fit her perfectly. She was thick but had no stomach. All her weigh went straight to her thighs and ass. You would think she had her body done, but you could tell it was all natural. She did her best not to show it off, but there was no hiding it. Being seductive came easy to her, and for some reason brown skin men and white men went crazy for her; but she was only attracted to strong, intelligent dark skin men with nice teeth.

She stared at the Cartel solider that was in the middle and stuck her finger into her mouth, sucking it slowly. She pulled her two fingers out her mouth covered in saliva and let it drip down onto her, face then stuck her finger back into her mouth, twirling her tongue around them. All three men could feel their dicks slowly raising and soon trying to bust through there jeans. Harmony stepped closer.

"Fuck this." the guy on the right said then hit Harmony in the head with the back of the shotgun.

Harmony saw stars and everything went black before she lost consciousness and her body collapse on to the floor. It felt as if she was a sleep for hours, but it was only seconds. The sound of the three men's voices woke her, but she kept her eyes closed.

"What the fuck you do that for!" the guy in the middle yelled.

"Man listen, I don't trust her. We still can fuck her while she's knocked out, then kill her." the guy with the shotgun replied.

"I don't want to fuck her while she's knocked out, that's not gonna big get my dick up. It's like fucking a corpse. I want her moving and touching me. She was with it." the guy in the middle said angrily.

"It's all the same to me. I bet the pussy still get wet. I'm with Pepe. We should keep her knocked out and tie her up. You haven't heard the stories of what two of them did inside one of the stash houses. I think she was the one in the building. She's the only dark skin one I seen so far." Chico replied.

"She's moaning. Just watch as soon as I get my dick in her. Just tie her feet and arms. up when I get started." Pepe stated as he bent down on one knee with the shotgun in his left hand, using it as a cane to balance his weight while pulling down her shorts. He stopped when he saw Harmony's eyes pop open and she punched him in the throat.

"Ughhhhhhh!" he gagged and gasped for air while choking.

"Dude, you okay?" Chico asked, hearing Pepe choke.

Harmony grabbed his tongue while it hung out his mouth and pulled, then bent up as if to go kiss him but locked her teeth onto his tongue and bite down, hard ripping it away.

"Ughh! Ughhh!" Pepe made a weird sound, trying scream as blood poured out his mouth from where his tongue used to be.

Harmony grabbed the shotgun as he crawled away backwards, pumped it and aimed at Chico, squeezing the trigger. The shotgun roared and send pellets crashing into his chest, lifting him up off his feet.

"Oh shit! You bitch!" the guy in the doorway yelled and started to fire.

Harmony rolled on the floor over and over, just being missed by his bullets buy an inch, until she was behind the couch. He stopped firing and inch slowly toward the couch.

"You thick little bitch! We could've had some real fun before I killed you. It's a shame, you're going to be such a loss." he said before he eased closer and then peeked over the couch like he was playing tag. "I got you!" he shouted, aimed and squeezed the trigger, sending bullets flying then stop when he realized she wasn't there.

Pepe could be heard making mumbling sounds. "Mmmm! Mmm!" he said loud repeatedly while pointing and holding his mouth at the same time.

"What! What is it! Fuck! I can't concentrate with you making all that damn nose!" the guy said and looked at Pepe for the first time. He squinted his eyes when he realized he was pointing and turned his head to look down to see what he was pointing at.

Harmony had crawled around the couch while he was talking and was now on the floor on the side of him on her back with the shotgun and fired. Boom! The sound of the shotgun echoed throughout the floor as she blew off both his legs, tearing them to shreds. He fell to the ground backwards, hollering at the top of his lungs. Harmony stood up and walked over to him.

"Hmm, what a waste. You were a cute papi. I might've let you hit if you didn't try to kill me or under different circumstances. Now we'll never know." Harmony said while holding the shotgun with one hand, aiming down at his head and squeezed the trigger. His head exploded, sending blood, bone, and brain matter flying everywhere.

"Ewww!" Harmony said then saw Pepe holding his mouth and his eyes wide open as if he seen a ghost or his own death.

He stumbled as he tried to stand up but slipped in his own blood on the grey marble floors. He looked at Chico's body slumped over, like a rag doll and tiny holes in his chest. He looked at the uzi still in his hand. *'I got to get to it before that bitch kills me. I knew we should've just shot her when we got the drop on her.'* Pepe thought to himself and eased off the floor. Harmony ran on her tiptoes, jumped and kicked him in the back. He flew forward and hit his head, losing consciousness. He could feel his pants being pulled along with his boxers.

"No! No!" he moaned weakly with his eyes still closed.

"What was that you said about me? Oh yeah, I remember. Raping and fucking an unconscious woman is the same as raping one while up. She still moans once that dick inside her. Yeah, that's what you said."

Pepe could hear Harmony's voice as he fought to open his eyes and get up but couldn't. He then heard Harmony spit and coldness hit but checks as they were being spread apart before he felt something cold and wet by his ass.

"Ahhhhhhh! Ahhhh!" he screamed in pain as Harmony jammed the barrel of the shotgun up his ass.

"I guess you were right." Harmony said with a smile on her face as his eyes opened up wide and he tried to squirm away, but it was too late.

She pushed the barrel of the shotgun even deeper, then pull the trigger. Pellets rip through his insides and cause his chest and neck along with is jaw, to explode. He lost control of his bowels and shitted all on the shotgun, getting a little on Harmony's hand.

"Ewww! That was so fucking disgusting. I'm never going to do that again." Harmony said out loud with her face twisted up as she wiped her shitty hand on his clothes then went over to Chico and wiped her hand again on his shirt.

She grabbed his uzi, went to the kitchen sink, poured dish detergent in her right hand and scrub her hands in the sink over and over. The sound of the elevator dinging let her know someone else had come to her floor. She grabbed the uzi and ran toward the elevator in the living room to see five Cartel soldiers about to step out of it. She aimed and squeezed the trigger before the Cartel solders could raise their guns. The uzi spit bullets out rapidly, sending bullets speeding towards the bodies of all five men. Bullets riddled the bodies of the soldiers as two managed to get off a shot, but it was only their nerves reacting from being torn to shreds before the uzi began to make clicking sounds. Harmony looked at it and said, "Damn that was fast." She walked over to the elevator, tossed the uzi on the ground and saw another shotgun, this one was short barrel pump. She picked it up and ran to her room to grab her Teflon Diva body suit before she ran back to the elevator, stepping over the dead bodies as she entered it before she quickly work her voluptuous body into the suit.

"Ughh! Ugh!" the sound of grunts of pain made her look down at the elevator floor to see one of the soldier's was still alive with holes smoking out his back and trying to claw over the other dead bodies to get out the elevator.

"I would ask you to press the button so we can go to the third floor, but I've got a feeling you wouldn't do it." she said sarcastically before stretching her left arm down toward him, flexed her muscle and her blade shot out, piercing his skull; sticking his face to the right side of the elevator wall, killing him.

She flexed her wrist back and the blade returned back into the slot of her arm in her suit and disappeared as she pressed the button for the third floor.

Suyung was drying her hair in the bathroom mirror thinking, 'This came out very nice.', when a sick feeling bubbled in her stomach and she knew something was wrong. She spin-kicked and hit something hard in the chest that caused her to bounce back.

"What fuck." She looked to see a tall brown skin man, about 6'4 tall, wide and fat; but not the regular fat, his fat was tight. He looked like a sumo wrestler or a Hawaiian; a stocky, massive man with his jet-black hair pulled back in a ponytail. His large frame of a body blocked the whole doorway.

"Hmmm, I'm going have fun with you." Tito said in Spanish.

"Huh? Oh, hell no with your big ass. You should feel bad for even trying to fight me, I'm the size of one of your fucking legs." Suyung said then grabbed a rat tail comb and flipped it around to stab him in the neck. He blocked it and the point went through his hand.

"You fucking put a splinter in my hand." Tito said while looking at the piece of comb jammed in his hand and pulled it out.

Suyung looked around and tried to think fast. She pulled off her sock, grabbed two bars of Pink Dove soap before stuffing them in and tying it in a knot. She rushed to the toilet bowl and grabbed the thick Porcelain cover on the back of the tank. She put the sick holding the soap in her packet and grabbed her bottle of Nair.

"So, you gonna hit me with that huh? I'd like to see you try little bitch!" Tito shouted.

"Okay." she replied then aimed and squeezed the bottle of Nair, sending the pink thick chemical flying into Tito's face.

"Bitch, you sprayed lotion on me?! I'm going enjoy fucking you and killing you!" Tito said while wiping the lotion off his face and some got in his eyes. He made a strange face as he felt his face start to burn.

"What is this shit?!" he asked as his face continued to burn. "Ughh! Ahh! What the fuck?!" he cursed in Spanish while wiping his face repeatedly before he ran to the bathroom sink, turned the water on and scoop some in his hand to splash on his face.

"You don't have no sisters huh." Suyung said as she stood on top of the bathtub, leaped off it and cane down with all her weigh and smashed him in the head with the porcelain tank lid. It shattered to pieces and he fell into the sink face first; breaking the sink and pipes, sending waters squirting out of control everywhere, where she left him lying.

"The bigger they are, the harder they fall. Just big for nothing ole type of nigga. Reminds me of an ex-boyfriend. I swear." Suyung said and rolled her eyes as she stepped over him and out the bathroom. "Now to find out what the fuck in going on around here." she said to herself.

"I'm big and quick, and fast." Suyung heard a voice coming from the left side of her ear that gave her chills. Before she could react, she felt a huge hand grab her by the back of the neck and left her up while choking her.

"If you weren't trying to kill me, I would find this very fucking sexy." she said with spit flying out her mouth while gasping for air as Tito lifted her with both his hand and toss her in to the living room wall.

"Damnit. You a strong big one huh? Well I'm going beat your big ass, out here hitting girls. What the fuck is wrong with you?" Suyung said as she eased off the floor and looked up to see Tito charging towards her. "What the fuck dude!" Suyung said as she jumped, and front flipped over him using his shoulders. "Dude you're like a rhinoceros." Suyung said then felt his hands wrap around her ankles before he spun her in a circle three times and released her.

"Ohhhhh fuck!" Suyung screamed as she crashed into the kitchen counter. "I'm getting really tired of you throwing me around like a damn rag doll. I'm a got damn person, not a toy." Suyung said as she stumbled to get up and her head spun.

She smiled when she saw the kitchen knife set on the counter. She grabbed four knives and threw all four at once. Two crashed into the center of his chest and bounced off. The other two went toward his face. He put up his forearms. and they slammed into it and broke into pieces.

"Fuck. You got armor? This day can't get any worse. I didn't finish dying my hair, you messed up my damn bathroom, my damn relaxation time, and now you have armor. Enough is enough!" Suyung shouted and ran towards him.

Tito stood there in shock. His whole life he'd only seen people run from him but never towards him. 'This bitch done lost her mind.' Tito thought to himself.

"What can this little woman do to me?" he said out loud and smiled as Suyung got closer, pulled the sock with the two bars of soap out of her sweat pants pocket and swung it hard, hitting him in the left cheek with it.

"Ouch!! You bitch!" he yelled as he spit out a tooth.

Suyung ran behind him and hit him in the back of the head with the soap-filled sock. He stumbled forward as she right to the right side of him and swung hard, hitting in the temple with it. "Ahhhh!" he groaned in a deep voice. "You little bitch! Stay still!" Tito shouted, using his forearms. to cover his head and try to keep his eyes on Suyung who was running around him in circles and hoping like a rabbit.

He tried to anticipate her next move but couldn't. Then he punched and out of luck connected with her jaw. Her legs buckled from up under her and she collapsed to the ground.

"What the fuck was that?" she mumbled weakly as Tito bent down, took the sock out her hand and threw it across the room before holding her down by her neck. He bent down, licked her face and spit out another tooth.

"You put up a good fight to be only 120 pounds. I like you." he said in her ear before licking from her cheek to her forehead.

"Ewww! Why you licking me like a damn puppy?!" Suyung shouted as he choked her tighter and pick her up by her neck before slamming her back down on to the floor, knocking the oxygen out her chest.

Suyung gasped for air as he licked her face once more. Ding! The sound of the elevator stopping on the third floor could be heard. Tito turned his head to see a sexy, short chocolate woman with short hair standing there.

"Hello and goodbye." Harmony said as she raised the shotgun and squeezed the trigger. Bright red and orange flames came out the muzzle of the gun as Tito used his arm to protect his face. Pellets blast into him, knocking him sideways.

"Suyung! Suyung! Are you okay?! Harmony shouted.

"Ugh! Ahhh!" Suyung cough before answering her. "Yeah. You just saved me from being licked again." Suyung replied.

"Licked?" Harmony asked with her right eyebrow raised.

"Yeah. This fool kept licking me like a damn lost puppy dog all in my face. I don't even like dogs. Shit, my father's side of the family eats them." Suyung said while rolling her eyes and getting up. She then turned her head at the sound of Tito groaning on the floor and starting to get up.

"Oh shit. I forgot to remind you he has body armor on under his clothes something like ours." Suyung said while running past Harmony.

"Where you going?" Harmony ask and wonder if she should start running as well.

"Keep him busy. I'm going to get dressed and put on my suit. Be careful, he's fast for a big guy; and don't let him lick you, his breath stinks. I can still smell it. Okay, bye now." Suyung said and ran into her room.

Tito stood up and looked at Harmony with blood dripping out the corner of his mouth as he licked his lips. "Mmm, chocolate." he said and bent low like a football player before he charged at full speed while making and x with his arms. to cover his face.

"Oh shit! Oh shit, oh fuck!" Harmony shouted repeatedly from seeing the large Sumo wrestler looking man running towards her. She panicked and backpedal as she cocked back the shotgun, putting a new bullet in the chamber and firing; but it did nothing to stop him from coming at full speed.

"Suyung! He's fast! You didn't say he was fast and big!" Harmony said as she took off running around the living room with Tito chasing her.

"Umm, yes I did. Just run circles around him. I don't think he has that many brain cells. He's a little slow on the thinking side. Outsmart him, I'm almost done!" Suyung shouted from her bedroom while getting dressed.

"What the fuck! Harmony shouted as she ran and jumped over the living room couch, still gripping the shotgun tightly in one hand.

Tito ran one way and she ran the opposite, looking as if they were playing a game of tag. Tito continued to chase her around the couch and became frustrated.

"Enough!" he shouted then stomped. He stomped so hard it shook the floor and building.

'It's one of our suits." Harmony thought, realizing that the suit he had on was powered by magnets, and it increased the strength of his legs by the magnet pushing the opposite direction. Tito kicked the couch and it slid towards Harmony.

"Fuck!" she screamed, and front flipped over it as it slammed into the wall behind her and broke in half. The tv that was mounted on the wall fell off onto it. Harmony turned her head and look back at it, only to turn her head back around to see Tito rush her. His shoulder hit her breast, knocked her to the floor and stepped on her while still running.

"Little bitch!" Tito said in a deep Spanish accent as he turned back around and prepared to charge her once more.

'Oh God. I can't have that heavy fucker step all over me again, he'll break my ribs." Harmony thought to herself while coughing, but her body was too hurt to move. Tito smile like a wild bull that'd seen red and was ready to attack.

"I'm fucked!" Harmony moaned as Tito took off and ran toward her to stomp her out then stopped as something hit him in the side of the head hard.

"Ughh!" He rubbed his face and turned around to Suyung dressed in her Teflon body suit holding a chrome spear staff "I'm getting really tired of y'all hitting me." Tito said before Suyung front flipped and hit him on top of his head then try to stab him in the face with the spear. He blocked it with his forearm.

"It took you long enough. Damn, now I know how a man feels when I get ready for a date. Did you put on your makeup as well?" Harmony said sarcastically and rolled off the floor as Suyung continue to attack Tito.

"This big motherfucker just won't go down!" Suyung shouted while swinging the spear at Tito, trying to beat him as if he'd stolen something.

"I got an idea! You remember what we did at that stash house? How we got rid of the evidence?!" Harmony shouted.

"Yeah!" Suyung said while hitting Tito on the hands as he tried to protect his head.

Harmony ran into the kitchen, went to the stove and pulled it back before kicking the tube to the gas line, letting gas leak lose in the third floor.

"Come get me fat boy." Suyung said to Tito.

Tito's rage took over and he charged Suyung, chasing her into the kitchen. She stopped short and spun while bending low and stretch out her staff, causing Tito to trip over it. He tumbled forward and ran into the fridge.

"Now!" Suyung shouted while running to Harmony.

Harmony aim and fired. Pellets hit the stove, but nothing happened.

"What the fuck! Do it again!" Suyung said as she started to panicked and Tito punched the refrigerator.

Harmony aim at him and squeezed the trigger. The pellets from the shotgun pushed him back an inch but did nothing else to him.

"This fool the fat Terminator." Harmony said then aimed for the stove once more then fired.

Boom! A loud explosion went off, sending Harmony and Suyung flying backwards. Fire engulfed the kitchen and living room and began to spread fast.

"We've got to get out of here. Head to the basement!" Suyung said while getting off the floor.

"Yeah. Layla said if anything happened the basement was the escape route." Harmony replied.

"What about Rose?" Suyung asked.

"We'll stop and get her on our way down." Harmony replied as they both stepped over the dead bodies and entered the elevators, pressing.

As the elevator door closed slowly, they could see movement in the kitchen. Tito was moving rubble off him. He started at them with death in his eyes. Half his face was badly burnt, and his hair has burnt completely off. He stood there surrounded by fire just staring at them until the elevator door shut.

"That man scared me. I thought I had some crazy ex's." Harmony stated.

"Bitch, you didn't even experience the worse part. He didn't even lick your damn face like a lost puppy. He freaked me out. We got to find a way to kill that motherfucker, or I'm going to have nightmares of his tongue for life. Eww!" Suyung said and shook as if she was shaking off a bug off her shoulders.

The loud expression shook the building. Layla pulled her head up from up under the water. She looked at the tv screen mounted on the wall and could see Cartel soldiers enter the building like roaches, armed with machine guns.

"How the fuck did they get pass my security? The alarm didn't even go off." Layla said to herself while stepping out the bathtub. She grabbed a towel and the Glock 26 from up under the sink cabinet. She stepped of the bathroom to see a dirty blonde-haired woman standing in her bedroom door with three armed men behind her standing in the living room section. Layla raised her gun and wasted no time. The first bullet zoomed pass the blonde head woman's face and entered the right eye of one of the of the Cartel solders and exited out the back of his head, tearing through the neck of the Cartel solider stupid enough to stand behind his friend. She then aimed at the woman and put three bullets in the center of her chest. The last Cartel solider took off running and Layla squeezed the trigger. The bullet burst open the back of the Cartel soldiers head. He fell forward and died before his body hit the ground.

"What the fuck is going on around here?" Layla asked as she enter her bedroom and grabbed her Teflon diva suit.

She wiggled her way into it fast, pressed a button and a secret compartment opened revealing guns and grenades. She grabbed the black mp5 machine gun, a smoke grenade, and a flash grenade.

I'll teach motherfuckers not to break into my damn house. I feel so violated." Layla said to herself and could hear something cutting through the air with incredible speed that sounded like a long whistle. Her body told her to duck, so she did as something just miss her head and hit the wall in front of her where she kept her weapons.

Layla looked up to see a spinning ring the size of a frisbee stuck in her wall. While staying low, she turned around to see the blonde hair woman standing there with a smile in her face.

"We haven't been properly introduced dear. I'm Catalina, head of the Santiago Cartel. Your team killed my cousin, and that was a good thing. It made me boss, but I couldn't have any loose end just walking around. You were the last Teflon diva, so we thought; but then you had to make things even worse, starting your own little diva club and robbing me. Why did you rob me? I'm so curious. You're from the original diva team. I heard y'all were beyond rich from all those assassinations you did." Catalina said with her hands on her thighs.

"It was practice bitch for my team; and we going rob you some more after I kill you." Layla said then tumble rolled forward, hopped up with the mp5 and sent a hail of bullets all over her body.

"Huh! What the fuck?!" Layla said as the bullets bounce off Catalina. Layla rolled right as the spinning blade ring that was in the wall try to slice her in the back. It barely missed her, went straight to Catalina and she caught it with a smile on her face, while staring at the shocked expression Layla wore.

"Teflon Diva technology; but how?" Layla said with a confused look.

"The old bitch sold it to me. Really, I heard she sold it to a lot of crime underbosses. The secret Is out. The Teflon Divas won't be the only ones with the Teflon metal or technology. So, nothing will make y'all so special anymore." Catalina stated.

Layla stared at her with hate in her eyes. "See, I'm going tell you where you fucked up at bitch." Layla began as flexed her muscles and the spikes in her suit pop out from her arms. and chest. "The first mistake you made was coming into my house!" Layla shouted then flexed her muscle, sending a spike from her chest shooting towards Catalina.

"Oh shit!" Catalina shouted while backpedaling and using her ring blade to block what looked like twenty middle sized black spikes.

She knocked most of them down and turned sideways to dodge the others. Layla jump up and kicked Catalina in the chest before sending punched to her jaw and stomach.

"Ugh!" Catalina groaned in pain as she swung the hand with the ring blade in it, hoping to cut her.

Layla caught her arm mid-swing, twisted it and pressed down, trying to break it. She applied pressure to Catalina's elbow.

"Ahhhhh!" Catalina shouted, feeling as if her arm would break in half by the joint.

"Second, you fucked up if you think it's the suit or technology that makes a Teflon Diva. We are women that have survived the harshest things life has thrown at us. It's not the weapons that make us, we are the weapons bitch!" Layla said as she raised her hand high and came down with all her might onto Catalina's elbow. A loud snapping sound could be heard followed by high-pitched scream.

"You broke it! You broke my arm you bitch!" Catalina said while pulling away from Layla, holding her arm.

She let her broken arm go, took the ring blade out of it and throw it, then grabbed the second ring blade that was on a holster on her back and throw it as well.

"Shit!" Layla perk as she bent backward as if she was trying to do a back flip, then side flipped as the two spinning ring blades came at her from different angles.

Layla flexed and sent spikes at the ring blade, but her spike was knocked down by the ring blade as it was nothing.

"Kill her!" Catalina shouted as seven of her soldiers entered the fourth-floor penthouse style apartment from the staircase. "Kill that bitch!" Catalina shouted once more while holding her arm as she watched Layla hop around like a ninja.

"Fuck! Fuck! I can't keep this shit up." Layla said to herself out of breath.

She flexed while doing a back flip and five spikes entered the chest of one of the Cartel soldiers. His body shook and he fell forward dead. The other six soldiers opened up fire with uzis, sending a hail of bullets in Layla's direction. Four hit her in the side by her rib but bounced buff; but the pain from the bullets had slowed her down for a second to long, as one of the ring blades sliced the side of her right check.

"Ahhh! You fucking bitch! Not my face!" Layla screamed as she became even more enraged and charged toward Catalina, only to be stopped by a hail of bullets to her legs and chest.

"Aim for her head! Shoot that bitch in the head!" Catalina shouted.

Layla pulled out the flash grenade from her belt hostler, pulled the pin and tossed it. It exploded instantly and the bright flash was like staring straight at the sun on a summer day. The flash blinded everyone in the room but Layla, who had closed her eyes. She stood low as the sling blade rings continued to cut through the air. Layla ran back into her room, shut the door and swiftly entered the walk-in closet. She grabbed a Draco mini sub-machine gun, pressed a button and the wall of her shoe rack moved, revealing a secret pathway with had a long polo that lead straight down. She entered the room and the door closed behind her. She grabbed her black transmitter and put it in her ear.

"Everyone, if you can hear me, make it to the basement now. You have five minutes before the building explodes. Hurry!" Layla said before grabbing the polo and holding on tight as she quickly slid down three stories, gripping the pole tighter as she came closer to the ground.

"Who designed this shit? It's more dangerous than the motherfuckers trying to kill me. This is real smart." Layla said, trying to slow herself down and with her legs wrapped around the pole. She squeezed them tighter and was able to stop.

"We're on our way, we have to stop and get Rose first." Harmony said into her earpiece.

"How the fuck did that bitch get pass my security? This would've never happened to Tess like this. She would've seen them coming and been ready along with the whole team ready. What the fuck am I doing? I can't lose my team or position, I just got both." Layla said to herself.

"Ahhh!" Catalina screamed while still holding her broken arm. "Break the door fucking down!" she yelled with a mix of tears and rage in her eyes.

'I can't believe I let that little bitch broke my arm. I'm gonna fucking kill her and everyone she loves.' Catalina thought to herself as her men broke down Layla's room door and entered cautiously with their guns leading the way.

"The bathroom clear!" one of the Cartel soldiers shouted.

"She's not here." another said.

"Stupid, it's a secret door in her closet. Open and use it. Find that bitch and kill her!" Catalina shouted. "I can't believe I have such stupid assholes working for me. No wonder I'm getting robbed by a group of women, we've got more sense." Catalina said while shaking her head.

"We got it open!" she heard one of them men say.

"Well go get here stupid!" Catalina shouted back while rolling her eyes.

Layla could hear talking from the secret entry way to the basement she'd just left. She went back to hear a man suddenly scream like a little girl or a kid on a roller coaster as he slid down the pole. Layla could hear more than one man sliding down. She raised the Draco machine gun, squeezed the trigger, and bullets flew out the gun wildly. Two went through one of the guys legs, causing him to let go of the pole.

"Ahhhh!" he screamed as he flew three stories down and hit the hard basement floor, breaking his spine and left leg. It was folded backwards in a weird angle. "Ughh! Ughh!" he groaned in excruciating pain.

Layla looked at him with both her eyebrows raised. "You scream like a little girl." she said before she sent a bullet into his nose, cracking his face in half.

She then looked up and continue firing, send a hail of bullets into one of the soldiers that had almost made his way down the pole and into the basement. Bullets riddled his body, sending chunks of his flesh flying everywhere as he hit the floor, went into convulsions and died.

"I'm not going down there! Hell no!" The remaining four Cartel soldiers said from the fourth floor in Layla's closet as they looked down the secret pathway.

Catalina throw her spinning ring blade weakly, but the magnets in her suit pushed it with great force. The ring blade cut through the air like a shiny frisbee, slicing off one of her soldier's head and continued to travel and enter the mouth of a second one, cutting the top part of his head. His body stood there moving from side to side and his head moved up and down as if he was trying to talk but couldn't, because he no longer had the rest of his mouth. His body fell backward into the secret tunnel and down it, landing inches from Layla feet.

"You two get down there; and call more men before you do. I want this bitch dead." Catalina said through gritted teeth.

"Si. Yes boss." both men said simultaneously in Spanish before one called for more backup.

Ten more men entered the fourth floor from the stair case. "Something's not right." Catalina mumbled to herself as she felt a strange feeling in her stomach and could smell something like gas leaking through the building. "Maybe I'm going crazy; but fuck it, I always listen to my stomach." Catalina mumbled to herself and headed for the staircase.

"Boss where you going?" one of the soldiers asked.

"Don't ask me damn questions! Who's the boss, you or me?" Catalina said while gripping her ring blade tight, waiting for him to give the wrong answer.

"You're the boss. I'm sorry." the solider said and lower his head.

"Good. Get in there and kill that bitch! That is your job, make it happen!" Catalina barked and continued making her way to the stairs and down them fast.

"Girls, hurry. I don't know how much longer I can hold these guys off. They're like roaches, or a thirsty dude standing on the corner every day and you keep telling him no you're not feeling him every time you go to the store; but he's still talking, and you can't get rid of him. Ugh!" Layla said.

"Shit, I know the type. In Florida they be at the damn gas station trying to talk to you and sell their mixed tape to you at the same time." Harmony replied.

"We're on our way." Suyung said. "I can't believe y'all talking about men being thirsty at a time like this." Suyung added while looking at Harmony.

"What, they don't do that in San Francisco?" Harmony asked.

"No. My father would kill any man if they talked to me. I could only marry or talk to a man he picked for me, but he got killed before he could do so." Suyung replied as the elevator stopped at the first floor.

"Damn. It sounds like if we live through this you need to get you some dick. Try a hood nigga or a corporate thug. Those them ex drug dealers turn business men. Mmm girl! They'll fuck the shit out of you; and know how to treat you." Harmony said with a smile on her face as if she was reminiscing. The sound of banging brought her back to reality. "Come on." she said to Suyung as they walked through the living and passed the kitchen to see a bald-headed man in a black suit with a long Katana sword in one hand and a handgun in the other, pounding on Rise bedroom door.

"Come out bitch, don't run! Come the fuck out! Show me more of what your learned Rose. Don't be afraid now!" Benjamin shouted.

"This should be easy." Harmony said and took off running, but Suyung stopped for a second to study the sword in his hand and the way he gripped it.

"No, slow down. Let's make a plan first. He's a Samurai." Suyung shouted, but Harmony was already at full speed with a smile on her face.

Harmony leaped in the air to kick him in the back, but Benjamin spun, grabbed her leg and tossed her into Rose's door.

"What the fuck just happened?" Harmony asked while trying to get up, but Benjamin swung down, aiming for the center of her head.

Suyung threw her spear and it stuck in the door, just missing Harmony's head by an inch, but blocked Benjamin's blow as he came down. His sword hit the staff and bounced back.

"We have to fight him together. He's holding back who he really is to catch us off guard." Suyung said running toward them.

Harmony rolled backwards, hopped up off the floor and yanked Suyung's chrome spear out the wall. She began to jab at Benjamin in the stomach and chest, but he used his sword to block it effortlessly.

"Rose! Rose! Are you okay?!" Harmony shouted.

"Yeah!" Rose shouted back from behind the bedroom door.

"She won't be once I get my hands on her." Benjamin said.

"We'll kill you before that happens." Harmony said and throw the spear behind Benjamin into Suyung's hands. She tried to stab him in the back of the neck, but he moved his neck to the side, turned around and began to fight her, Sending blow after blow with his sword.

Harmony flexed her muscles and her Wolverine-like forearm blades sprang out and she swung at Benjamin.

"You go high, I go low!" Suyung shouted while attacking Benjamin's legs, then tried to stab his feet while harmony tried to slice off his head.

He moved fast, blocking both women's weapons. He aimed the gun he had in his right hand at Harmony. She swung and slice it in half in the blink of an eye just as Rose popped out her bedroom in her Teflon Diva body suit, holding her double swords. She ran up on Harmony's back, front flipped off her shoulders and came down hard with both swords. Benjamin blocked it, but Suyung poked him in the chest with her spear, and Harmony's blades struck his calf muscle but there was no blood.

"Why is he not bleeding? I know I hit him." Suyung said as Benjamin backed away.

"Me too." Harmony said as all three women stood side by side in their fighting stance.

"He has Teflon body armor on under his suit; but remember what Layla said, our weapons are made of Teflon. If we keep cutting and poking at it, we'll be able to destroy his armor and kill his punk ass!" Rose stated.

"But doesn't that mean his sword will be able to cut through our armor as well with a good hit." Suyung said.

"Shut up!" Harmony and Rose said simultaneously.

"Think of the cup half full." Harmony said.

"So, you hoes want to jump me huh." Benjamin said then pressed a button, causing his sword to split in half and turn in to two swords. He pressed another button and both swords began to glow a bright red. "Come on! Thought you weak bitches was going jump me! Let's do this!"

Harmony looked at Suyung then turned her head to Rose. "You can't tell me your ex don't have a small dick. He's just too fucking cocky and arrogant." Harmony stated.

"He does; and a weak ass stroke too girl. Let's fuck him up." Rose replied, causing all three women to burst out laughing.

"My chest hurts." Suyung said, as she laughed a hard and a tear came from her eye.

"Stop laughing at me!" Benjamin shouted and ran toward them as he threw one of his swords at Suyung, who was bent over laughing the hardest.

"Suyung watch out!" Harmony shouted and pulled Suyung by the shoulder closer to her, causing the sword to miss her by an inch and slam into the wall.

I'll kill you fucking Teflon bitches!" Benjamin shouted as his sword returned back to him and he swung at Rose and Harmony at the same time. They blocked his blow as Suyung used her spear to try to poke him in the neck. He blocked her blow and swung back.

"This fool is fast. Is he this fast in bed?" Harmony said while trying to sweep kick him, then aimed for his balls and slice up but her kick was blocked while Rose swung her double swords with anger.

"He's gotten much faster, and I didn't know he could fight this good. We going have to move as one to take him down." Rose said.

"Well fighting him is better than fighting the other one with armor. He kicks your face and tries to turn you over with his foot as if he was a pickup truck." Suyung stated while continuing to swing her spear.

"There's another one with armor?" Rose asked with a confused look on her face. As soon as she did the elevator dinging at a stop could be heard.

Harmony and Suyung along with Rose jumped back from Benjamin and looked past him to see who was steeping off the elevator. Rose looked first.

"Oh, I see. Yes, meet Tito." Rose said as she looked at Tito's half burnt face. Then the side door to the stairway burst open and eight Cartel soldiers armed with AK-47's stood next to Tito, spreading out.

"Umm, I think it's time we go and use that secret door in your room." Harmony mumbled.

"Uh, yeah. Yeah, I think your right." Rose stated.

Suyung reached behind her back and grabbed with look like a handful of small silver metal balls then tossed them in the direction of Tito and the soldiers. The balls exploded and a thick pink smoke filled the room, blinding everyone in it but the Teflon Divas. They took off running into Rose's bedroom and entered her walk-in closet. She pressed her thump to a black scanner that was on the wall, and the secret door open revealing the long pole that lead straight to the basement.

"Who's first?" Rose asked. Harmony looked at them both.

"Are you bitches serious?! We got Tweetle D and Tweetle Dumb out there with Teflon armor and weapons, fucking cartel soldiers with assault rifles and y'all gonna hesitate on going down the dark hole to get away? Y'all stay here if you want." Harmony said and jumped on to the polo to slide down.

"Okay, rock paper scissor to see who's next." Rose said to Suyung. Suyung rolled her eyes.

"Just fucking jump already!" Suyung shouted.

Rose shrugged her shoulders, jumped onto the pool and slid down it. Just then the room door burst open and Tito came running at Suyung at full speed with six cartel soldiers right behind him.

"Oh shit!" Suyung shouted and threw her spear.

It cut through the air and entered through the mouth of the one of the soldiers, lifting him off his feet and pinning him to the bedroom door like a poster.

"Hell no!" Suyung yelled seeing Tito running towards her and the thought of him licking her face played in her mind. She jumped into the tunnel. "Fuck the pole." she said and knew she would land on her feet, but something stopped her. "Ahhhh!" she screamed out in pain as her head yank back and she could feel a huge hand gripping her by her hair.

"Help! Help!" she screamed and wiggled.

Rose and Harmony looked up. "Suyung! Suyung!" they both shouted not knowing what to do as Tito pulled her back up into the closet by her head and held her face to face while staring at her smiling, Suyung poked him in the throat with four of her fingers, causing him to choke and cough at the same time. Tito pulled his head back and headbutted Suyung in her forehead so hard it sounded like two cars crashing into each other. Before Suyung could scream out in pain she lost consciousness, passing out. Tito threw her onto his shoulder and walked away.

"No! We got to go back and get her!" Harmony shouted while looking up.

"There's no time." Layla said looking at her watch, grabbed three mp5 submachine guns and some clips to go with them before passing one to Harmony and the other to rose.

"They got Suyung. The big dusty looking motherfucker got her! We have to go back and get here now!" Harmony shouted.

"Yes, we have to save her." Rose agreed.

"We will get her back, I promise, but not in this building. Now isn't the time. This place going to explode in less in two minutes. Grab some grenades and let's get going. Now!" Layla shouted and hopped on one of the black KLR 650 dirt bikes. Rose ran into the weapons room, grabbed a one-shot mini grenade launcher and the bullets that go with it that were on a belt. She placed the belt around her waist just as four cartel soldiers jump downed the tunnel.

"Shit!" Layla said, aiming and squeezing the trigger, sending a hail of bullets into the face of one of the cartel soldiers, shredding his face into pieces.

The second cartel soldier panicked, putting his arms. up to his face as if that would protect him. The bullets ripped through his forearms. and into his cheekbones before coming out the back of his head.

"Let's go! Get on the bikes!" Layla shouted while still shooting, trying to kill the other two cartel soldiers that were ducking and firing back.

"I don't know how to ride!" Rose shouted over the gun fire.

"I made yours automatic, just get the fuck on!" Layla shouted just as a loud explosion went off on the fourth floor, then the third, killing the cartel soldiers that was on those floors, starting a fire.

"Oh shit!" Harmony said and hopped on one of the klr 650s. Rose did the same as the second level exploded.

"We on dirt bikes in the basement, the roof about to come down on our heads and the only way out is the elevator! Where the hell are, we going to go?!" Rose shouted.

"You always have to have a good exit and escape plan." Layla said as Tess words echoed through her mind. She pressed a button on her bike and the rear wall of the basement slowly lifted up, revealing a pathway.

"Now that's some top secret, James Bond secret agent shit." Rose said as the first floor exploded; but not before two more cartel soldiers jumped down into the basement.

"Let's go!" Layla said as she twisted the throttle and the bike took off with Harmony and Rose following behind. The four Cartel soldiers in the basement looked at each other. The building was shaking and ready to fall apart at any second. The smell of smoke was in the air. The basement ceiling was engulfed in a blazing fire that seem like it was following them and dancing at the same time. They looked to see two dirt bikes and one street motorcycle was left. The tall cartel soldier shot the guy that was standing next to him in the knee cap. He fell to the floor screaming and his gun was kicked from his hand.

"No! No! Don't leave me! Help me! Help me!" he screamed in Spanish as the other three cartel soldiers started the dirt bikes and the motorcycle and took off. They looked back at him on the floor with one hand holding his knee and his other hand stretched out asking for help as the ceiling collapsed, falling on top of him killing him instantly before burring the path as the ground shook.

"Where the hell you got us? We have to go back for Suyung. She can't be dead." Rose said.

"We're in the sewer tunnels; and Suyung is alive." Layla stated.

"How?! How the fuck do you know? We just left her." Harmony said and stopped her bike. Layla stopped next to her, then Rose stopped.

"Harmony has a point. How you know she's still alive? We just left her." Rose cried.

"There was nothing we could do at the time. I promise we'll get her back. We're sisters for life; and if both you bitches shut up and listen, you can hear her breathe and that dickhead Benjamin talking." Layla replied.

Harmony looked at her strange but then listened carefully to the two-way transmitter device that was in her ear and smiled. She could here Suyung breathing and Benjamin talking.

"Why are you smiling?" Rose asked.

"Just shut up and listen. Layla was right. It's low but you can hear Suyung breathing, and your abusive ex." Harmony replied.

"You grabbed the wrong one. I needed you to grab Rose. Benjamin said in an angry tone.

"No, he did good. They will come for her, trust me; but first, take the transmitter out her ear and throw it out the window." Rose could hear Catalina say and then what sounded like the car running over the transmitter.

"She's alive! I heard everything. We can get her back, but what's that sound I'm hearing?" Rose asked.

"What sound?" Harmony asked.

Layla listened carefully and could hear the sounds of engines speeding in their direction. "Go! Go! We're being followed. Ride ahead of me. I'll try to slow them down!" Layla shouted.

Rose and Harmony hit the throttle on their dirt bikes. The front tire of both bikes lifted up doing a wheelie, riding in the back wheel as they took off. Layla gripped the handle of the mp5 with her left hand as she peeled off, following behind them.

"Why we running? We can take them out and go find Suyung." Rose said through her transmitter.

"True, but we don't know how many there are. We already got caught off guard and underestimated them. There's no telling how many got Teflon metal or suits. We're not invincible, so we gotta out think them; think ahead of them and control the situation." Layla said out loud, mostly talking to herself as bullets zoomed past her head.

She looked back to see two cartel soldiers on dirt bikes firing at her with an uzi. "You fucking bastard!" Layla shouted in Spanish and aim. She squinted her eyes and fired a single shot. The bullet flew out the gun with incredible speed.

"Ah, you missed bitch!" one of the cartel soldiers shouted then try to hit the bike to slow it down because her dirt bike was going too fast, splashing them with the dirty, stank sewer water.

"What's wrong with this thing?!" he shouted as Layla fired again, this time hitting his handle bars.

"Harmony, smoke grenade! Now!" Layla shouted.

Harmony didn't hesitate and threw to smoke grenades behind her that exploded midair, releasing a thick purple smoke, making it impossible to see. Layla rode straight through it and made a hard-left turn.

"Now!" Layla shouted and all three Teflon divas turned left just in time, missing the brick wall that was in front of them by a few inches. "I never miss." Layla mumbled to herself.

The first shoot she took she hit the brake line of the cartel soldier that was on her tail. The second shoot she disabled his handle bars, so he'd be unable to turn. He rode at top speed, unable to slow down or stop, and now couldn't see because of the thick purple smoke.

"You bitches tricks won't work on meeeee..." were the last words he said as he slam in to the brick wall at full speed, breaking every bone in his body. He laid there twisted up with his body mix with some of the dirt bike parts. He made a weird gagging sound as the dirt bike caught fire. He could smell gas on him from the gas tank leaking out on him. His eyes opened wide as the fire traveled quickly to his body up to the gas tank before exploding. He was dead before he could scream out for help. The bright fire made the other two cartel soldiers that was behind him slow down as they rode through the thick purple smoke. They stopped and looked at their friend, roasting like a piece of chicken on a BBQ grill on a hot July day.

"Damn!" one of them said and made the sign of the cross with his fingers, touching his own head then chest and left shoulder than right before pulling off.

"I think it's only two left!" Layla shouted.

"I got the next one." Harmony replied and slowed down her dirt bike.

She carefully stood up on it then flipped around, sitting on it backwards while still twisting the throttle to keep up speed. She could see the next cartel soldiers clearly as he aimed his uzi. Harmony raised both her arms., flexed her muscle her left forearm blade shot out, hitting the front tire of the dirt bike the cartel soldier was riding causing it to stop short and flip forward.

"Ahh! Oh shit! Ahh!" the soldier screamed in middle air, feeling as if time was slowing down as he flew in the air knowing he will lead on his face; but that wasn't the case and he soon wished he'd just crashed.

Harmony flexed her forearm muscle and the right sword blade shot out and went straight through the cartel soldier's neck, severing his head from his body. His head jerked and landed in Harmony's arms. She flexed once more, and her forearm blades returned to their slots. She held the head tight and flipped back around on the bike then hit the throttle.

"How the hell did you do that?" Rose asked.

"What, shoot his head off? The target practice we been doing all week." Harmony replied.

"No, not that shit. How you ride the bike backwards? That was some crazy shit." Rose said.

"Girl, I keep telling you I'm from Florida where we ride four wheelers and dirt bikes all day. My brothers taught me." Harmony replied.

"So, everyone knows how to ride good but me." Rose said twisting up her face.

"I'm from Brooklyn and all they do is ride dirt bikes. It's like breathing to us." Layla replied and shrugged her shoulders.

The sound of gun shots could be heard hitting melt pipes in front of them. "What the hell?! It's still one left!" Layla shouted while looking back at the tall cartel soldier riding the black motorcycle.

"We gotta to lose him. We're about to come to the end of the sewer tunnel and then we'll be up in the train station terminal for the number 3 line. We'll be in the Bronx!" Layla shouted.

"The Bronx! The Bronx, really? I thought you were smart. You took us to the one place Catalina has on lock down?! I hope that means where going straight for Suyung." Rose replied.

"Now's not the time to discuss this Rose; and this escape plan for this house was designed before my time and the drama we're having now with Cartel. Just take out the last guy!" Layla shouted.

Rose sucked her teeth, bent low and looked back while holding the mp5 and squeezed the trigger, her bike swerving while doing so.

"I can't concentrate, keep my balance and ride this thing at the same time!" she screamed.

"You better learn!" Harmony replied as they made a right turn into a tunnel. The stinky smell in the air wasn't as bad, a bright light could be seen down the next tunnel, and they were now riding on bumpy train tracks.

"Okay, his bike not gonna keep up on these rough tracks. Let's go. Layla said and twisted the throttle, speeding up the dirt bike.

She soon saw a flight of stairs and rode up them onto the train platform. "Move! Move!" Layla shouted while beeping the horn on the dirt bike, getting the people out the way that were waiting for the train. Layla rode up another flight of stairs, popped a wheelie and went through the thick black metal grate meant for people in wheel chairs or women with strollers to enter the train station. Harmony and Rose were right behind her as people scream, panicked and moved out the way. They rode up one more flight and was outside.

"You really brought us to the damn south Bronx." Rose said while shaking her head and looking at the street sign that read 149th Street and third avenue. Two masked Cartel soldiers ran up. One grabbed Harmony from behind and tried to pull her off the dirt bike while the other punch her in the face.

"Get off her!" Layla shouted and flexed, causing five spikes to came out her suit and enter the back of the cartel soldier that punched Harmony.

"Ahhh! Ahhh!" he screamed and stumbled around, trying to reach the spikes that was in his back, but couldn't reach them.

Layla flex her muscle and the spikes yanked out of his back and came toward her. She sent them back out, and this time they went straight through his back; ripping through his flesh and organs before coming out his chest and stomach. He wobbled, fell to his knees, then to his face. Rose grabbed the handle of her sword that was on her side hostler. The blade folded out and she stabbed the soldier in the back of his head. His eyes open wide as he released the bear hug, he had on Harmony. He fell sideways as Rose pulled her sword out the back of his skull.

"Let's go!" Layla shouted and they peel off.

"How did they find us so fast?" Harmony asked.

"I don't know. It's like they knew about our secret exit. I don't know how that can be, because I just learn about it since we been living there." Layla said, really talking to herself as they zoomed through traffic. She looked behind her to see two black BMW X6 trucks and a dark green Hummer behind them. "Shit! They're on our ass!" Layla said.

"Yeah; and look, our little friend that was following us from the sewer tunnel is with them as well." Rose stated as all three of them looked back to see the soldier on the motorcycle.

"Shit. We not going be able to out run him. He's going to be too fast on that street bike." Harmony stated.

"He'll be faster but won't be able to do what we can do sis. Remember what you on. We gotta out smart them. Split up now!" Layla shouted as she turned down one block.

Harmony kept going straight and Rose turned left, going up another block. One of the black BMWs X6's followed Layla. A cartel soldier wearing with a yellow bandanna covering the bottom half of his face hung out the passenger side window with an AK-47 and opened up fire. Radom people walking up and down the sidewalk began to scream and run. A few off them even pulled out their cellphones and stood up straight to record.

"I'm get like ten thousand likes on Instagram, watch." a thirty-year-old man said before a bullet went through his iPhone and exited out the back of it before hitting him in the chest, tearing his heart to shreds. He was dead before he hit the ground.

A woman ducking for cover pulled out her phone and cover the dead man with her body while crying. "I can't believe this is happening! It's the middle of the day and their shooting, killing incent people." she said as a stray bullet bounced off the brick wall building and blew a hole in the side of her head the size of a golf ball. Her body went limp as blood poured out her skull.

"We've got to be careful shooting. These maniacs are killing innocent people." Layla said into her transmitter.

"Harmony, Plan b now!" Layla said.

"Umm, what's Plan B? Y'all got plans while I'm trying to out run a huge fucking Hummer that's running over cars like it's the damn Hulk; and guess what guys, it has the nerve to be green." Rose replied.

"Just keep going, we got your back." Harmony stated.

"Y'all do remember I really don't know how to ride this damn thing right? Every time I twist the throttle to go faster the damn bike lifts up and does a damn wheelie." Rose replied.

"You can use that; but give us a second." Layla replied. "Harmony you in place?" Layla asked as Harmony cut through an alley way and the second black BMW X6 stopped because it couldn't follow.

"I'm about to be." Harmony zoomed and cut through the alley way with ease on the dirt bike and came out on the other side on the next block. She smiled because she was now behind the BMW truck that was on Layla's tail.

"Okay, I'm ready." Harmony replied and twisted the throttle on the bike to lift up, doing a wheelie. She held it up and ran the bike into the back of the truck. While standing she ran and jumped on the roof of the BMW X6.

"Huh? What the fuck was that?" the driver asked, and the other three men looked behind them to see the dirt bike now bouncing and dragging on the street with the back wheel still spinning.

"I think one of those bitches tried to run her bike into us." one of the soldiers in the back seat said, causing everyone to bust out laughing.

"Dumb girls. Don't they know a bike isn't stronger than a fuckin' truck? Stupid." the drive said in Spanish.

"Something's not right." one of the soldiers in the back seat said as he looked back and could see the other BMW with members of the Cartel family in it. They were hanging out the window with their guns pointed toward them.

"Why Manny and them pointing their guns at us like they tripping' ready to fire on us homes?" the other soldier in the backseat said, causing all four men to look back and see that Manny and the guys in the other trucks were pointing.

"They're pointing at something. What is it?" the guy in the passenger seat said, then his phone ring. He pulled his iPhone out his pocket and looked at the name on the screen.

"Stupid you're not supposed to bring your phone when we do a hit, only a cheap burner. Police can track where you phone been. You don't watch Law & Order?" the driver said while keeping his eyes on Layla and the road, trying to get close enough to hit her back tire.

"No. I don't watch tv, it makes you soft; but it's Manny calling, should I answer?" the guy in the passenger seat asked.

"Both of y'all stupid. Did anyone else bring their cellphone to work, while we killing people?" the driver asked and the other two men in the backseat raised their hands.

"Stupid!" he shouted. "Answer the phone." he told the guy in the passenger seat.

"Hey Manny, what's up? Huh? I don't understand what you mean. She who?" the soldier in the passenger seat said with a confused look on his face.

"What?! What did Manny say?" the driver asked.

"He sounds like he going crazy but kept saying she's on the roof. She's on the roof. I looked out the window at the buildings we passing and ain't see no one on the building roofs aiming at us or nothing." the passenger stated.

The driver's mind started to work. "The dirt bike that crashed into the back of us, did y'all happen to see the chicks body?" he asked.

"No. She must've rolled over to the side." one of the soldiers in the back seat answered.

The driver slowed down as his mind race. "No, she didn't! She's on our ..." he began shouting, but his words were cut short as Harmony broke the grass sunroof and jumped in, landing in the backseat between the two cartel soldiers.

"I thought you'd never slow down so I could pull this shit off." Harmony said and elbowed both of them in the nose then crossed her arms. like an x and her forearm blades sprang out like claws, entering both men's neck at a weird angle and travel up to their brains before the tip of the blade pinned them to the truck doors. Their bodies twitched and their feet kicked then stopped.

The soldier in the passenger turned around to get a good aim as Harmony pulled out her bloody blade from one of the dead soldier's head and sliced off his hand.

"Ahhh! Ahhh!" he hollered before using his left hand to open the door and hopped out the moving truck. He hit the ground hard and rolled before he stood up and began running for dear life while holding his wrist.

"Your friend was the smart one? Are you going be smart as well?" Harmony asked and smiled, showing of her perfect set of white teeth.

"Fuck you bitch!" he shouted, turned around and fired three shots into her chest.

"Ahh!" Harmony screamed as the impact from the bullets knocked the wind out her chest and she felt as if someone hit her with a baseball bat. "Ughh! Ughhhh!" she gasped for air as the cartel soldier raised his gun.

"You're a pretty chocolate bitch. Damn shame I got to kill you. I almost forgot, I got to shoot you diva hoes in the head." he said then smiled. Before he could, his left eyeball popped out his eye and onto Harmony's lap.

"Ewww! Oh, my fucking gosh!" Harmony said, flicking it off her lap as a spike entered the back of his skull and pushed his eyeball out the socket. "You're just fucking nasty Layla." Harmony said in her transmitter.

"Bitch get the moving. We don't have time for that; and remember no one's driving." Layla said as she turned back around and continue driving the dirt bike.

"Oh shit!" Harmony said, flicking off the second eye ball off her lap and climbing into the front passenger seat.

"Ughhh!"

"Oh shit!" Harmony spat, surprised the guy in front seat was still alive.

Harmony grabbed him by the legs and with all her strength pushed him into the back seat then quickly clawer to the driver seat and grabbed the steering wheel just in time as the truck side swiped a few cars parked on the side of the road.

"Help me. Help me." the soldier groaned in pain, feeling around the back seat.

"Man, this some freaky shit. I think I'm gonna through up. He's still alive, moving around like a damn zombie." Harmony said.

"Hold that shit in and let's continue with the next step, just like we did in the tunnel. On the count of three." Layla said before she grabbed a handful of the small sliver balls from her hostler and throw them behind her. Thick purple smoke covered the street.

"One…two…three." Harmony said and pull two grenades from her hostler, pulled the pin and throw them in the backseat.

She pulled the emergency brake and turned the truck sideways in the street covered by the thick smoke. She climbed up through the sun roof, jumped and landed on the back of Layla's dirt bike, grabbing her waist.

"They getting away!" Manny said.

"Wait, I don't think you should be driving this fast. We can't see in this smoke. Why fucking purple smoke? I swear you can tell they're fucking girls. Who throws purple smoke everywhere? If they were smart, they'd be throwing bullets." Manny said.

"Manny, slow down." the passenger said.

"Fuck that! We going get them hoes." Manny said then hit the black X6 at full speed causing the airbags to pop out.

"Ughh!" "Ahh!" All four men in the truck groaned in pain.

"I think you broke my nose." one of them said from the back.

"My fucking arm's broken! I told you to slow down, we couldn't see the pass the damn smoke stupid; and I smell gas." the passenger seat.

"Oh shit! Ain't that PJ? It looks like he got no eyes and mumbling something." Manny said, squinting his eyes to see. "He got something in his hand. Oh shit!" Manny yelled when he realized it was a grenade. The grenade exploded, blowing up the first truck then the second one, killing every inside.

"Damn men are stupid." Harmony said.

"Nothing upstairs at all." Layla replied.

"Umm, if y'all done laughing and giggling can y'all fucking come help me before I get run the hell over by this Hummer?" Rose said while cutting through the cars in front of her as the Hummer behind her ran over each car or push them to the side with ease.

"Oh shit, I almost forgot about you. We're on our way Rose, what block your on now?" Layla said then speed up as Harmony held on to her tight. "If I was gay this would turn me on." Layla joked.

"You joking but shit, you'd be surprised how many straight women want to try this chocolate; but sadly, I only love dick. Anyway, what's the plan to get Suyung back? I'm worried about her." Harmony said.

"Me too; and no plan yet, but we will get her back. We just have to be ready; and like I said, we have to out think them because they have armor now. We have to use our brains, not our strength or straight shooting. We'll lose." Layla replied.

"Umm, y'all still not here and this truck gaining on me; but since where talking as if nothing going on and as if I don't have cartel men trying to kill me and wondering where the fuck is the police when you need them. I was thinking how they got past our security and knew the exit to the escape route. Could it be your old member, that crazy chick Iris? Could she be working with the Cartel?" Rose asked as she popped a wheelie and jumped onto the side walk, riding up it as the hummer knocked parked cars in her diction, missing her by a few inches.

Layla popped up behind the Hummer. "We're here sis. Let me think." Layla said riding faster.

"Think? Shot that shit." Harmony said and snatched the Mp5 from the strap around Layla's neck and aim at the back of the Hummer, sending a spray of bullets toward them.

The bullets crashed into the rear window of the Hummer, bounced off and came back straight towards

Layla and Harmony. Layla swerved the bike and the bullets barely missed their heads.

"It's bulletproof." Harmony said with a surprised look on her face.

"Duh. I was trying to tell you that. That's why I said let me think." Layla said.

"Well think fast!" Rose shouted as the hummer bumped her back tire. The dirt bike wiggled and swerved as she fought to keep control. "Help!" Rose said.

"You going to have to jump!" Harmony shouted as the driver stepped on the gas, accessing the trucks at full speed and slammed into the dirt bike, crashing the bike in to a building wall and smashing it.

"Rose! No! No!!!!" Layla shouted as tears pour down her checks. "I can't., I can't lose two of them in one day. This can't be." Layla said to herself as she stood there stood, not moving the dirt bike.

Three green Honda Accords pull out behind them along with the cartel soldiers that had shot them on the motorcycle. Two men each hopped out the Hondas.

"The boss said she'll give a bonus if we bring one back alive." one of the cartel soldiers said.

"Fuck that. I've seen and heard too many stories about these bitches and what happens to men for underestimating them and hesitates on trying to kill them. Not me. I'm not about to be a story someone tells saying some ninja hoes killed me." a short stocky man said named Alex.

"Fuck that, I want the bonus. The boss said $300,000 for one of these bitches alive. That big gay rapist Tito got one." a middle-sized man named Julio said. "Oh, and please don't tell Tito I called him big and gay."

"Oh, so you're scared of Tito but not these crazy bitches? You're dumber than I thought." Julio replied.

"Whatever. Let's go. Vamonos." Julio said in Spanish, charging towards Layla and Harmony.

Harmony quickly jumped off the back of the bike. "Layla, snap out of it!" she shouted as Julio upper cut her in the jaw, making her bite her tongue.

"Ooooou, you bastard!" Harmony was barely able to say while swallowing her own blood. She spin kicked him, but he dodged it.

'What the fuck? My body must be tired, all this fighting and running. I should've easily landed that kick, but I'm moving slow. I'm not going be able to keep this up much longer. I'm gonna need to rest.' Harmony thought to herself as reality set in that she had over her exhausted herself.

She punched one of the Cartel soldiers in the eye then flex and her forearm blade popped out. She stabbed him in the stomach, but to her surprise the guy grabbed the blade with both hands, holding onto it as she tried to yank it free to free up her arm to fight. He looked Harmony in the eyes like a deranged mad man.

"You die with me bitch." he said in Spanish as blood leak out the side of his mouth and a guy ran up on Harmony from the left side, punching her in the temple. Her world went dark as she seen stars.

"Layla snap out of it! I need help! Help me!" Harmony cried out, but Layla stood there stuck, sitting on the dirt bike staring at the Hummer as two men hopped out of it.

"I just let them die. This isn't how it's supposed to be. It's supposed to be my love story, my crew, me living my best life, not this. Not this." Layla said repeatedly as she stood there broken.

The two Cartel soldiers that hopped out the green Hummer both smiled and raise their guns, knowing Layla was going to be an easy kill. They squeezed the triggers to their uzis simultaneously, just as Tess jumped down from the five-story building's roof to the fire escape and in front of Layla. Just before the bullets could kill them both she swung her chain blade whip, blocking all the bullets flying their way. The bullets bounced off her chain whip as if she was swatting files, She snapped her wrist, flicked the chain whip and it wrapped around one if the cartel soldier's neck. She pulled with all her might, causing the razor blades on her whip to cut through the meat and fat of his neck like a hot knife through butter, then snapped the bone of his neck. Tess flexed her wrist once more, twisted and turned, pulling his head off his body; but it was still wrapped in the, like a string with a hand ball tide to the end of it. She swung it at Julio as he tried to punch Harmony in the face. The dead man's skull hit him on the head so hard you could hear a cracking sound echo through the street. Tess swung again and hit him in the nose with the head.

"Ahhh! Ahh!" Julio scream like a little girl who'd just seen a hard movie as he backpedal, not knowing whether to hold his head that was throbbing or his nose that was dripping blood.

"Use your weapons! Use your swords! You can't be tired. Tired means death. Get mad and use it. You're a woman, not a weak ass cry baby man!" Tess shouted to Harmony.

See Tess fight and hearing her words of encouragement, Harmony felt a new level of anger

"She's right. I'm fighting for my left and my friends life." Harmony said as she looked up at the man that was still alive, holding her blade and arm inside his stomach smirking at her.

"You know what?" she said.

"What you black bitch?!" he shouted.

"You forgot I had a left arm, and so did I for a second." Harmony said, smiling as she swung, and her left forearm blade popped out like claws before she chopped half the guy's face off.

"Ohhhh!" "Oh shit!" "That's just nasty!" a few of the cartel soldiers said. One took off running down the block, "Fuck this! Fuck that, I don't want to be in a gang no more!" he shouted while running down the hill.

Harmony front kicked the dead guy body, pulling her right arm and sword out his stomach before taking her fighting stance as two guys ran toward her. She spin-kicked one and bent down to spin, chopping the left leg off the other.

"Ahhh!" he screamed and fell to the ground as he pulled out a 9mm handgun and aim for the side of Harmony's head.

Tess snapped her wrist and the chain blade whip wrapped around his arm. She yanked and it ripped completely off. She flicked it with the whip over to the other cartel solider by the Hummer, who caught it and stared at it before jumping up and down then dropping it.

"Fucking bitches!" he shouted as Tess pressed a button on the handle of her whip, retracting it and turned it into a sword made of razor blades.

Tess ran up on the guy slicing up and down like a true samurai, making thick blood rush out his body. He spun around in what seemed like slow motion. Tess raised her eyebrows and just looked at him like he was stupid as he fell to the ground and died.

"Fucking men. They can be so damn dramatic, I swear." Tess said out loud.

Julio made it back to the car and stood next to Alex. "Here." Alex said, passing him an Ak-47 with an extra clip as he looked at the other two soldiers standing beside him.

"What the fuck is this going do? Them hoes are bulletproof and move too much and too fast for a head shot." Julio spat while wiping his nose with his shirt.

"If you had listened to me the first time, we wouldn't have lost four men, and you wouldn't be hurt. You don't fight these type of people head on. That's like trying to fight a professional boxer hand to hand, knowing he's going kick your ass. Boxing is what he does. Well these ninja bitches, killing people with their hands is what they do, so we out smart them stupid." Alex said as he raised his Ak-47 that had a scope on it, aimed, then fired.

The bullet the size of the gunman's index finger flew out the gun, cut through the air and slammed into the left side of Layla's back, ripping through her bullet proof suit and came out her stomach before entering the hummer in front of them. Layla fell sideways off the dirt bike as blood poor out of her.

"Layla!" Tess screamed and ran over to her. Harmony did the same with tears streaming down her face.

"How? But how? Nothing can get past our armor body suits." Harmony said as Tess held Layla's head off the ground.

"They have Teflon bullets." Tess said in a distant tone.

"Oh shit! Why you didn't tell me from the start we could just shoot these bitches?" Julio said with a smile on his face, licking the blood off his lips from his nose.

"I was trying to tell your stupid ass that. Now can we kill them before they figure out how to kill us first. Alex said.

"Hell yeah! I'm with you." Julia replied.

"Shoot your blades repeatedly, it will give us cover!" Tess shouted.

Harmony raised her arms. and flexed, releasing both her forearm sword blades like bullets. The four Cartel soldiers ducked as the blades slammed into the car them came back towards Harmony and went back out again. Julio ducked behind a Honda and fired wildly, raising the gun over his head as he sat on the ground sending bullets everywhere.

"Julio don't waste the bullets, we only have so many of them. The boss said she paid more for those bullets then buying a neighborhood." Alex said, ducked behind a car close to Julio.

"Fuck that, I'm gonna kill these hoes!" Julia shouted.

"Get up Layla get up, I can't carry you. You have to snap out of it." Tess said.

Layla look up at her as she bled out. "It was supposed to be about me mommy. It was supposed to be about me, my happy ending. I was supposed to be you; and have what you have." Layla cried, still stuck in a trance. "I was supposed to be the last Teflon Diva." Layla mumbled as her eyes rolled into the back of her head.

"Shit! No, stay with me! Stay with me!" Tess said then stood up and dragged Layla by both arms. to the

Hummer. She opened the back door and roll her into the back seat.

"Ughh! Ouch!" the sound of moans could be heard over the gun fire. Tess looked at Layla and knew it wasn't coming from her. She bent down and couldn't believe her eyes. Rose was up under the Hummer twisted up. Rose open her eyes to see the chocolate complexion woman with thick long hair reaching out to her.

"I know you." Rose said weakly, barely able to open her eyes.

Tess pulled her from up under the truck and rolled her onto the floor of the back seat of the truck, then she grabbed two smoke grenades off of Rose's hostler belt.

"Glade to see she taught y'all something and keep the same Teflon routine." Tess said as she pulled the pins off the smoke grenades and rolled then towards the Hondas. They exploded and thick purple smoke covered the air, providing cover for Harmony.

"Come get in the truck!" Tess shouted. "That's new. When y'all start using colored smoke? These new divas. Now I know I'm getting old." Tess said as Harmony hopped in the passenger side of the truck and Tess backed the Hummer off the building wall and the dirt bike before stepping on the gas and peeling off.

"Follow them! Get those hoes!" Alex shouted and hopped in the Honda.

"Fuck! Something's wrong with this truck." Tess said as the left wheel wobble a little.

"Well we need to do something. We got a fuckin' angry papi on our ass, and you know damn well we not out running there Hondas. You know they be putting all kinda shit in those little engines." Harmony stated as bullets ripped through the back of the truck.

"Fuck! We're all dead." Harmony said.

"No, we're not. Not today." Tess said as she turned and rode on the side walk as the Hondas try to pull up on her side by side. She drove through a green light and entered a city park.

"We got those bitches now." Julio said, hanging out the passenger window with the Ak-47, sending a hail bullets into truck window. We got these bitches! They'll never be able to out run us!" Julia yelled with excitement and felt himself get hard with the thought of shooting the Teflon Divas.

The three Honda drivees never noticed the smooth matte black Mercedes Benz truck that was speeding on the grass through the park behind them. The driver stuck his left arm out the window. In his hand he gripped a chrome 50 caliber desert eagle handgun. He squeezed the trigger once, and the hand cannon roared. A bullet hit the gas thank of the Honda in front of him, causing it to explode before flipping forward in the air and crashing down upside down; smashing the roof and the Cartel soldiers inside, killing them instantly. The driver of the Benz zoomed past the smoking car while keeping his eyes locked on his targets, the two remaining Hondas.

"Oh shit, we have company." Alex said looking through his review mirror and could see the fire coming from the third Honda, and the black jeep bouncing and riding on the grass with ease.

Alex tried to see who was in the truck, but the front window shield was tinted, making it impossible. "We gonna have to stop chasing those bitches and focus on that jeep behind us Julio." Alex stated.

"No! Fucking hell, no! We're too close to killing them hoes. Just drive faster, there as good as dead; and the bonus for killing them will be all ours. Just look at the Hummer bro. The front wheel is about to break off at any second." Julia replied.

"You keep talking about this bonus, but if where dead we can't spend money stupid. The jeep behind us has a fucking cannon as a handgun!" Alex replied.

"So, what. We have Ak-47s and they shoot faster than any handgun." Julia spat and fired more shots in the Hummer's direction.

"Fuck this, I'm not dying because of you." Alex said and cut the steering wheel left, cutting through some trees.

"Are you crazy?! We gonna lose them!" Julio yelled and grabbed the steering wheel. Both men fought over the wheel, punching each other.

"You want it so bad, fine." Alex said as he opened his car door and jumped out. His body hit the ground hard, but he tuck and rolled. He quickly stood, dusted his clothes off and power walked to the other side of the city park while looking back to see if anyone followed him.

"Pussy! God damn pussy!" Julio yelled while holding the steering wheel to keep the car from crashing. He hopped in the driver's seat and turned the car around.

The driver in the Benz looked at the second Honda swerve and go left. He shrugged his shoulders and aim at the one in front of him. Squeezing the trigger, the 50-caliber bullet cut through the air, crashed in the back-window shield and the back of the skull of the driver. Jis head exploded into tiny little pieces like a cracked egg dropped on the kitchen floor. Bone and brain tissue matter splashed on the front windshield as the car rolled to a slow stop, and people in the park record what look like a headless man driving.

"Damn! Who's that helping us? Harmony asked while looking back, then looked in the back seat and onto the floor to see Layla and Rose both not moving.

Tears began to flow down her cheeks. She tried to wipe them away with the back of her hands, but they kept falling.

"Ahh!" Harmony let out a slight scream as the Hummer was bumped sideways, the left wheel completely fell off, and Tess continued to try to drive it.

"I got you now." Julio said while driving and sticking his Ak-47 out the window. He drove right beside them and squeezed the trigger, sending a spray of bullets through the passenger side window.

"Get down!" Tess screamed, grabbing Harmony by the head and pulling down to the truck floor before getting down herself as bullets flew past their heads.

Julio never looked in the review mirror at the Mercedes barreling toward him at full speed and crash hard in to the back of the Honda.

"Ahhhh!" Julio shouted as his body buckled and his shoulder blade broke as he went through the front window shield. "Ughh! Help me! Help me!" he continued to cry out as he lay on top of the hood unable to move, feeling as if every bone above his waist was now broken; and most of them was.

He laid on his stomach trying to move but couldn't. His face held tiny little pieces of glass and some were in his mouth, that he was sure he'd swallowed. He coughed up blood and pieces of glass as he could hear a car door open then slam shut hard.

"Help! Help! Please help! Someone call the police! Call the Police! Help me!" Juli yelled and was able to wiggle his way out a little; but the more he moved, the more in pain he was. "I got to get away. I can't die like this." he said to himself, and somehow moved enough that his body weight and blood caused him to slide down head first off the hood of the car into the grass.

"Help! Help!" Julio screamed with the little energy he had left as he lay in the grass.

He stopped screaming as his body trembled in fear and pain as black Timberlands boot stopped inches away from his nose. Using his eyes only, he traced from the boots to a black pair of jeans, to a man that stood there wearing a black tight hoodie on that showed his muscular frame. On his face was a black matte mask. All you could see was his eyes and death in them.

"Ahh no! No! Please don't kill me!" Julio screamed while crying as he stared at the barrel of a chrome Desert Eagle.

His pleas fell on death ears as the man squeezed the trigger and the sound of the large caliber gun echoed throughout the park and blocks away. People in their apartments jumped from the sound of it as the bullet exploded Julio's head, leaving nothing but blood and bone fragments everywhere.

The man in the mask placed the gun in his hostler and swiftly ran to the Hummer.

"You okay?" he asked as he opened the passenger door.

"Yes; but grab Layla and the other girl." Tess said getting up off the floor.

"I'll help carry Rose." Harmony said.

Tess laughed slightly as the man in the black mask and hoodie grabbed Rose and Layla, tossing them on his shoulders as if they weigh nothing and took them to the back of seats of the Benz.

"Well damn." Harmony said and got turned on.

"Let's go." Tess said as she hopped in the passenger seat of the Benz and the man in the mask got in the driver side with Harmony in the back. "Drive fast. Get them to the hospital in Brooklyn." Tess cried, looking back at Layla.

"I'm on it." the man with the mask said and peeled off, cutting through the park as police sirens could be heard coming in their direction.

"Now they want to show up." Harmony stated.

The masked man took off his hoodie and mask as he drove down the block and two police cars passed him by. Something caught his eye.

"Baby how far that chain blade whip thing you got reach?" he asked.

"It expand to about 20 feet if I press a button and retract it. It can reach pretty far, why?" Tess replied.

"You see that guy in the sky-blue hoodie walking behind that girl with the grey wig? He jumped out the Honda that was trying to kill you. Look how nervous he is; looking back and forth then putting his head down. I don't think he recognizes the truck." the man said.

"Are you sure it was him?" Tess asked.

"I'm positive." the man replied.

Tess roll down the passenger window and grabbed her whip. She pulled the whip close to her chest then flick her wrist, snapping blade whip out the passenger window. It whistled through the air before making a snap sound and returned back to Tess dripping blood.

She wiped the blood on the truck's carpet floor. Alex stood there with his eyes wide open. Everything happened too fast. He turned to see a beautiful dark skin woman with her hair in a ponytail smiling at him, and a huge dark skin man driving the truck.

"Ughhh" Alex made a funny sound while trying to suck in air but couldn't. He touched his neck but felt nothing but a big hole and a wet spot. He looked down at his hand soaked in his own blood as it pumped out his neck. He looked on the sidewalk next to him and could see the large chunk of what once his neck was, noticing the tattoo that was on his Adam's Apple that read Elizabeth, his first girlfriend's name. *'Did that bitch just rip my throat out?'* was Alex's last thought as he fell forward, and his body start to shake like a fish out of water.

"Say hi to your friend." Tess said and rolled up the window. "Bless drive faster. Get us to the hospital now." Tess said with concern in her voice. "I can't lose another child."

"Yes baby." the man said as he stepped on the gas.

Chapter Nineteen

I Want What's on Your Plate and I Intend to Get it

"Damn." Layla moaned as she opened her eyes. Her head throbbed as if someone was beating on it with a hammer. She looked around and didn't recognize the room she was in. There were big bright windows shining light in, but you couldn't see in or out, and they had a cloudy tint on them. The ceiling in the room was tall, making Layla feel as if she was a toy in a doll house. She looked down at what she had on, and it was a set of her favorite pajamas; a purple silk button up shirt with the matching pants. Layla tried to sit up and a sharp pain traveled through her body.

"Ouch! What the fuck!" Layla said.

She scooted up, leaned against the headboard and unbuttoned the bottom half of her shirt to see her stomach was fully wrapped. She lifted her pants to see she had something connected to her vagina to collect her urine in a clear plastic bag. She pulled the tube out of her and took the plastic bag half full of urine and placed it on the night stand next to her bed, then pulled the iv that was in her arm out. She looked up at the iv bag.

"What were they pumping into me?" Layla asked herself as she read it was a form of saline, pure clean water with salt.

Layla eased to the edge of the bed and slowly placed pressure on her feet as she stood up but collapsed to the floor.

"Why my legs so damn weak and my stomach killing me?" Layla said in pain and used the bed to stand back up straight until she fully got her balance.

Looking around the room for a weapon, she spotted the handle of a black 40 caliber handgun that was under her pillow.

"Tess!" Layla said as her mind flashed back.

From the time she was fourteen, Tess would leave a knife and a gun under her pillow, kiss her forehead and say, "If you stay ready, you never have to get ready. Be prepared for the fight before it happens, and you'll always be okay baby." Layla's mind snap back to reality as she grabbed the gun, felt around and smiled when she found the small folding knife. She placed the knife in one pocket and the small powerful 40 caliber hand gun in her right pocket before slowly inching out the room. Once out, she realized she was on a catwalk style Terrance She turned her head left and could see three rooms. She turned right and could see three more. She walked to the edge, grabbed the rail of the balcony and looked down. It was an open area with a kitchen on the far side, living room areas on the right, and floor mats in a practice area where Tess and Harmony was fighting each other while Bless was in the kitchen cooking what smelled like curry chicken.

"What the fuck." Layla mumble as found the stairs and walked down them.

"Again!" Tess shouted as Harmony charged at her.

She did a front flip and a round house spin kick. Tess blocked then swiped low, trying to take her off her feet. Harmony jumped just in time, raising her leg high until her knee was touching her chest and held her leg then let go with incredible force. Tess rolled over and the blow just missed her.

"Good move, but wrong timing. Wait next time until your opponent is hurt and moving slower, then that move will be perfect." Tess said as she hopped off the floor and send blow after blow of short punches.

Harmony backpedaled and blocked them, trying to keep her eyes on each strike. *'How is this bitch so fast? She's older than me, she can't be this fast. I got to be quicker than her.'* Harmony thought as she blocked the blows and then did a spin back hand punch Tess blocked with ease then hit her in the ribs twelve times with short powerful punches.

"Ugh! Harmony screamed as she twisted up and pretty much ran to the other side of the fighting mat. "Fuck, that shit hurt. How do you do that? It's not even a full punch." Harmony said while still rubbing her ribs.

"You've got short arms. Your strength is in your legs." Tess replied.

"Why does everyone keep saying that? My arms. are normal size." Harmony replied with an attitude.

"The short punch will be good for you, and it takes time to master. It's called the one-inch punch, and it's stronger than most punches; but you need to master your foot work. Your thick ass thighs can break a man's legs." Tess said and smile. "But use the chain blade whip I gave you. Being short or having short arms. won't matter if you can grab you opponent with the whip." Tess stated.

"What if I cut you or hurt you?" Harmony replied.

"You won't. Now go!" Tess shouted.

Harmony grabbed the chain blade whip off the hostler on her waist and snap it. It made a clinging sound like a guy wearing three Cuban chains at once that were touching each other. Harmony snapped her wrists, sending the blade towards Tess. Tess dodged it and moved to the side.

"Move faster and make the whip an extension of your arm and hand. Act as if you're dancing with it." Tess said.

Harmony snapped her wrist three times and Tess back flipped out of its way with ease.

"Okay, see you think I'm playing." Tess said then ran full speed toward Harmony.

Harmony backpedal and swung the whip side to side but missed, and before she knew it Tess was standing in front of her punching her in the face four times then jump up in the air and kicked her in the chest. Harmony stumble sideways but kept herself from falling. The taste of copper was on her tongue, letting her know the inside of her mouth was bleeding. Rage filled her face as she spun in a circle with the whip and it wrapped around Tess's right leg. She twisted and pulled then flicked her wrist. Tess went up in the air and was thrown across the room. Before she could get off the floor Harmony swung down on the floor as if she was going to give a child a beating with a belt. Tess rolled and rolled as the chain blade missed her by inches.

"I see I made you mad. Good, use it." Tess said as she pulled her chain blade whip off her hostler and swung, making Harmony jump back. Tess swung it again and Harmony rolled on the floor, hopped up then did three front flips with no hands and swung the chain whip the same time as Tess. The chain blades hit each other than twisted up and locked into each other. Both Tess and Harmony pulled, looking as if they were in a battle of tug war. "Ugh!" Both grunted while pulling. Tess let go and ran full speed toward Harmony, jumping up in the air and wrapped her legs around her neck while sitting on her shoulder. She leaned back twisting and turning before flipping Harmony to the ground onto her back, knocking the air out her lungs. Tess went to stomp her out and Harmony spin-kicked on the floor, trying to sweep Tess's feet. Tess jumped back, giving Harmony enough time to get up, then Harmony screamed,

"Ahhhh!" and side kicked Tess's thigh with all her might.

"Ahh shit!" Tess yelled in pain then punched Harmony in the neck and drop kicked her with both legs in the chest.

Harmony laid on the floor trying to breath as Tess rub her thigh. "Shit, you're pretty fast to be so thick." Tess stated.

"You're just as thick. Well, not as thick as all of this. Harmony said playfully and touched her own ass while still laying on the floor. Both women were covered in sweat and burst out laughing.

"What the fuck is this?" Layla asked, causing Bless, Tess and Harmony to look at her.

"You're up." Harmony said with a joyful smile on her face and got off the floor running toward Layla and hugged her.

Layla embrace her then pulled away. "What's going on here? Layla asked, looking Harmony in the eyes, talking with her facial expressions without saying a word. 'You know I hate her, so you hate her.' is what her face said.

"It's not liked that Layla. Shit went crazy when we escaped the safe house." Harmony said, trying to explain.

"No need. My beef isn't with you, it's with them." Layla said while looking at Tess and Bless. Bless smiled.

"Hey Layla. "I'm cooking Curry chicken with white rice tonight and that red wine you like to go with it." Bless stated.

"What the fuck! You just gonna stand over there like nothing happened." Layla said as her face turned bright red.

"Oh yeah." Bless said, walking out the kitchen area and over to Layla and hugged her tight.

Layla pushed him off. "I wasn't talking about that. How the fuck y'all acting as if nothing happened? You got shot in the fucking head for the second time. Nigga, how are you still alive?" Layla asked with a confuse look on her face. She looked at Bless' head and could see a slight dent as well as a dark scare the size of a pea.

"The first time I got shot, Ms. Wung Shu came to the hospital. I was close to her grandson, so when the doctors were fixing my skull, she paid them to use her metal. So, my forehead and right side of my head have Teflon melt attached to my skull under my skull. No one knew, not even me; because Ms. Wung Shu left after the surgery and I woke up without my memories. I didn't find out until the day I got shot in the head by Iris again.

I thought I was dead, but the bullet knocked me out. I woke up with the bullet hanging halfway out my forehead and pulled it out. Then I went to the hospital thinking you all were dead and got x-rays. That's when they told me I had metal plates in my head, but metal they never seen before and put two and two together. I went back to Haiti to recover and found Tess there as well." Bless replied and shrugged his shoulder. "Come taste this curry." he said grabbing Layla by the hand. Layla pulled away.

"Fuck! What the fuck! This some bullshit. Some real life bullshit. Things just come easy to y'all huh? You and Tess just magically find y'all way back together no matter what, even though fucking death. Then you bustards that call yourself my family let me believe y'all was dead; and now we just gonna sit and eat like nothing happened. This is bullshit. No, I don't forgive y'all. This is my life, I'm done with y'all. Tess and Bless only care about Tess and Bless!" Layla shouted. "That's not true, I love you. I stayed away to let you live your life." Tess replied.

"That's more fucking bullshit you spitting, because you could've told me you were alive sooner and still let me discover life on my own; but no, you let me think you were dead and now you're lying to me because before you did you were in a bad place because if Ayana's death; the only daughter you care about." Layla said while a stream of tears flowed down her cheeks.

"Layla it's not like that. You need to sit down." Tess said.

Layla's head began to spin, and she stumbled. "No. No, I want to get out of here and away from you. Where's Suyung? Where's Rose?" Layla asked while holding her head.

"Rose is in the back of the warehouse practicing shooting with a ruffle and silencer. Her right hand broke, so she has to learn to shot to be helpful. No hand to hand combat." Tess said.

"A warehouse?" Layla asked while holding her head.

"Yes, this building is a warehouse. I had it design and remodeled in Flatland Brooklyn. No one will find us; and Suyung was taken by the Cartel." Tess replied.

"What? She was taken and you let me sleep away? I'm not trying to be like you and forget any one on my team; and this is my team, so stop trying to train them. I told you already, you had your divas and fucked that up. This is my squad, my crew... not yours; and you not going fuck them up like you did me Tess. When you start teaching someone else how to use the chain blade whip? You didn't even finish teaching me how to master it!" Layla shouted.

"I'm really trying to be patient with your ass. You keep raising your voice at me and I'm about to pop you on your lips like when you were thirteen." Tess said while trying to control her breathing before she lost her cool.

"I'd like to see you try. I'll fuck you up." Layla replied.

"See, you need an ass whipping bitch. Guess the Cartel whipping your ass wasn't enough." Tess said and moved toward her.

Bless quickly step his massive muscular body between them. "Now clam down ladies and listen to each other talk; and Layla please stop. You know how she get when she's mad." Bless said, talking to Layla in a fake whisper trying to warm her.

"Naw, fuck this. I'm out. Where's my suit? I don't have to listen to y'all no more. I'm my own boss and person. Harmony go get Rose, we out." Layla said. Harmony hesitated for a second but then walked off. "And grab my suit and stuff." she added.

"Where you going Layla? You have no place to go. Just stay here." Tess said.

"That's where you're wrong. You taught me well. I bought a few safe houses in different LLC companies' names. I don't need to stay here, and I won't. It's already been a day wasted, and the Cartel has Suyung." Layla said then saw something in Tess's eyes, as if she was holding back something from her. "What is it? What?" Layla asked.

"It's been seven days you've been sleep. I moved you and Rose out of Brookdale hospital on the first day and brought you here after your surgery. There were complications with your surgery." Tess stated.

"What the fuck your mean it's been seven days? You let me sleep and y'all in here playing while Suyung's somewhere getting hurt." Layla said and start to cry all over again at the thought of Suyung.

"It's not like that. We've got the location and map of her where bouts; but it's a trap, and we need to be ready." Tess replied.

"There's no we. Give me the map; and what complication with my surgery?!" Layla shouted.

"Girl, I keep telling about raising your voice. I love you; but do it again and I swear…" Tess said. Layla rolled her eyes. "I don't know what's going on with you, but you haven't acted this bad since you were a teenager when I whip your ass for rolling your eyes. You act like you don't know who I am Layla." Tess replied.

"I know exactly who you are mother. The woman that had me think I killed her, and the woman that raise me to be her child but never loved me enough to keep it real with me. What complications happened during surgery? You still not telling me." Layla said. Tess held her head down.

"The Ak-47 bullet was a Teflon bullet as you know. It entered your back at a weird angle and came out close to your pelvic area. Some of the pieces of the bullet were still inside you. They got all of it but had to remove your fallopian tube. You won't ever be able to carry a child full term." Tess said.

"Noooo! Nooo Lord, no! Why?" Layla asked as she drop to her knees and started to cry hysterically.

Tess began to cry as well. She knew Layla's dream was to someday stop all the drama and beef they were in, have children and be a family with Damou, but now that we'll never happen. Tess got on her knees and took Layla into her arms. as she cried.

"How could this happen to me? It's not fair." Layla said, breaking Tess's embrace and standing up. She used the back of her hands to whip the tears away, but they kept coming. "No matter what happens you always come out on top Tess, and everyone around you ends up hurt or dead. Somehow your love story always prevails. You and Bless always find your way back to one another, but everyone in your life is just stuck watching and wishing for their own fairytale. I don't believe you! You did this to me bitch!" Layla shouted.

"Baby I know you're upset, but please watch your mouth; and I didn't do this to you. It happened, and now you can let it break you or use it to make you stronger; and my life is far from a fairytale, you should know that. You're not a person on the outside looking in, you've lived through this pain with me." Tess replied.

"Fuck you! Fuck you Tess!" Layla shouted and Tess Kung fu chopped her in the neck. "Ughhh!" Layla backstep and held her throat while trying to breath.

"I told you, watch your mouth. You won't be disrespecting me. I raised your high yellow ass, show some respect. I understand you're hurt baby, but you know how to talk about it without cursing." Tess replied.

"Respect you! Respect you? Why, you don't respect me; and if you put your hands on me again you better kill me mother! Or I'll try to kill you. I swear on Allen on that." Layla replied.

"What!" Tess said and twisted up her face in disgust.

"All you care about is yourself. I wish you never came back. Bless, give me the keys to a car. I know it's always more than one at a stash house." Layla said.

"Oh naw, you grown right? You can find your own way to wherever you going, but you need to leave them girls here before you get them killed." Tess replied.

"How? You got your team killed. I don't think it will be a difference. This is my team Tess. I'm not going keep telling you this. I will grow with them and we'll learn from our mistakes unlike you." Layla said wanting to curse but held back as she headed toward the door.

"You're acting like a spoiled ungrateful child Layla, that's going end up death if you keep taking this path." Tess said, talking to Layla's back.

"Then you'll finally be happy; and only worry about Bless and not noticing you're losing both your daughters." Layla said as she walked out the front door and sniff the fresh night air as she cried.

I'm not understanding what's wrong with her. She's a grown ass woman acting like she's a teenager all over again and I'm telling her she can't go to the movies on a school night or something." Tess said while holding back her tears.

"She's just hurt right now baby. Y'all were talking but it seemed like y'all wasn't listening to each other. She wants her own life without us or you getting the shine. She wants to be the boss for once and can't do that with you; and that's just one issue, the next one is us not telling her we were still alive. We're the only family she has; and the third issue is you do treat her as a child. Now tell me if this curry needs pepper or is it just right." Bless said with a white bowl in his hand and scooped a piece of curry chicken and gravy on the soon, placing it on her lips.

Tess was hesitant to taste. Her arms. were folded, and her face was still frowned up. She tried to stay mad but looking at Bless' set of perfect while teeth smiling at her, his handsome face and smooth chocolate complexion, her mind went to another place as she opened her mouth.

"Mmmmm, it's good; and I like the carrot you added into it, but you don't need to add more pepper." Tess replied.

"I knew you'd like it and I could get your stubborn ass to taste it." Bless said as he walked back into the kitchen.

"I wasn't thinking about the chicken when I opened my mouth for you. I was thinking of something thick and chocolate." Tess said.

"Eww, y'all nasty. Get a room. It's like hearing your parents talking about sex. That's just nasty." Harmony said as she came down stairs with two duffle bags and Rose behind her.

"Shit, I'm not that much older." Tess replied.

"You're in your mid-thirties and won't tell me the right age. Y'all old or getting old and just don't know it; but we're out of here. Thank you for all the help and the lessons." Harmony said.

"Y'all don't have to leave because Layla left. There's still more you must learn. Stay here with me and I'll teach you, then we can save you friend together." Tess replied.

"As tempting as that sounds, our loyalty is with Layla. She took me in and didn't have to. I was her enemy, part of the Santiago Cartel. She could have killed me. I'm with Layla; 'til death do us part. That's my sister. I'm sorry if she's upset with you, and so am I. Thank you for all your help." Rose said as she hugged Tess and kept it moving.

Harmony strung her shoulders and twist up her lip. "It was fun not being the only thick big booty chocolate woman around my team; but it's what Rose said, we're loyal to Layla. My sister not messing with you, so I can't as well; but thank you." Harmony said as she kissed Tess on the cheek and walked off.

Wait ladies. Here, I made three to go plates with curry and white rice; and here. There's a grey 2019 Ford Explorer parked between two cars up the block. Take it." Bless said handing the plastic bag with the plates of food to rose and the truck keys to Harmony.

"Y'all making a mistake." Tess said with her arms. folded.

"Yes, but it's our mistakes to make and lessons to learn, just as you've done. I think that's all Layla wants you to understand." Harmony said as she and Rose went out the front door.

They're making a big ass mistake. They should be my divas, with me training them." Tess said.

"Woman come sit and eat." Bless said as he set up the small table for them.

"How the hell can you eat at a time like this." Tess asked.

"Layla said it, things always workout for us in the end. We found each other once again, and I'm going enjoy every moment, every second I have with you beautiful. Now bring your ass over here and eat with me; and let's discuss buying land and homes on an island or two. A nice get away where we can live our lives out and maybe just maybe try for another child." Bless said and sat down with force a smile on his face as he thought of his daughter that Iris killed. He couldn't hold back any more and his face balled up as a waterfall of tears came down. He tried to use his big hands to cover his face to keep Tess from looking at him as he cried uncontrollably.

"Why! Why she had to take our baby? Why?" he asked repeatedly.

Tess stood up from her seat, walked over to him and hugged him as he sat in the chair crying. she pulled him close, pressing his head against her stomach. She let him cry for a few and shed her tears. Then she dropped to her knees, unbuttoned his jeans and grab his dick chocolate dick before she took the head of it into her mouth. The warm, wet feeling from her mouth sent chills through Bless' body as he tried to hold in his moan. He kept his eyes closed, praying all the hurt and pain in his heart and mind would leave him, if only for a second. Tess could feel his dick growing and getting ticker as she took more of him into her mouth. She twisted and turned her head, moaning while letting the extra saliva in her mouth drip down his shaft. She sucked up and lowered her head then took his balls into her mouth, sucking both at a time, then one by one while jerking his dick off. The spit from her mouth made it easy as she went up and down, twisting and rubbing the head of his dick with her palms. She did that combination for a while before she switched it up.

"Fuck! Mmm, yes baby. Suck that shit! Ssssssss!" Bless moaned as he tried to hold it in, but it was no use.

The more he moaned, the more Tess got turned on. The sound of his deep moans made her pussy throb. She pushed his dick to the back of her throat and made a gagging sound then began to bob her head up and down while jerking his dick.

"Fuck, Fuck yes baby, don't stop. Yes bitch!" Bless screamed as she went faster, twisting her head from side to side and moaning, "Mmmmm."

She could feel him about to climax, so she went faster and started sucking the tip of his dick while jerking it harder.

"Fuckkkkk!" Bless screamed as he held the back of her head and exploded, shooting cum in her mouth and all onto her face.

Tess seductively sucked it up and open her mouth to show him. Bless looked down and got even more turned on as she played with his cum in her mouth before swallowing it, then used her fingers to wipe the cum off her chin and face before sticking them into her mouth.

"Fuck!" Bless said, lifting her up and took off her clothes.

"No baby, I'm sweat. I need a shower first." Tess said.

"Fuck that, I don't care." Bless said, pulling down her leggings to her ankles, turning her around and pushing her forward onto the table; knocking everything on the tablet off of it. He touched her most pussy lips to feel the wetness.

"Mmm." he moaned with excitement as his dick throbbed, feeling as if it was stretching.

He placed the head of his dick inside of her wet pussy and began slow, short strokes.

"Ssss! Yes baby, yes." Tess moaned as his dick teased her pussy, making her even wetter.

She gyrated her whips, whining slowly in a circle. Bless followed her movements, and with each circle of her hips, he pushed a little more of his dick inside her.

"Mmm. Yes baby. Yes… like that." Tess moaned as he held her waist matching her stroke.

He grabbed her ponytail and pushed his dick deeper inside. "Shhh! Oh yes daddy. Get it!" Tess moaned while arching her back, tooting her ass a little higher and getting wetter as Bless gave her long, slow deep strokes; pushing his dick in all the way to the base and pulling it out.

The sensation of his dick sent chills through Tess's pussy and traveled through her while body. 'I can't take it no more. Stop teasing me and fuck me! Fuck me daddy! Fuck me." Tess begged.

Bless' face twisted as he pumped faster and harder as he watched Tess's chocolate ass checks bounce. "Fuck!" he groaned, doing his best not to cum until she did, but the wetness of her pussy drove him crazy. The harder he went the more slippery she became.

"Yes baby, fuck me! This is your pussy daddy. Fuck me. Shh… fuck! Yes… fuck Bless, yes!" Tess screamed as Bless pounded away, moving his hips from side to side.

"Fuck yes." he groaned as Tess's pussy juices began to splash all over his dick.

"Right there! Yes… right fucking there." Tess moaned as she shed tears of pleasure. "Fuckkkk!" she screamed as she exploded, Cumming all on to Bless' thick black thick. Her body went limp as she lay on top pf the table.

Bless looked down at the white creamy cum that now covered his rock-hard dick and smiled. He pulled her hair tighter. "Oh. don't rest now. It's my turn." he said as he began to pound hard and deep. He hiked one of his legs onto the table to get even deeper inside her.

"Oh shit! Fuck. Fuck! You're fucking the shit out of me. Oh, shit baby!" Tess screamed while crying, feeling his dick deep inside her hitting her spots and feeling as if she was Cumming again.

"Grrr." Bless groan and pounded with all his might. "Baby I'm gonna cum. I'm cumin'!" he screamed, letting go of Tess's hair and hips before Tess slid off his dick quickly, turned around and took his throbbing penis in to her mouth just as he exploded.

"Ughh God! Fuck!" Bless moaned as Tess licked up every drop and suck the head of his dick. Bless' body shook as he tried to back away from the warm, sweet sensation of his wife's mouth.

"Oh, you're going nowhere." Tess said as she began to jerk and suck his dick while twisting her hand.

"God! Oh God!" Bless moaned as he exploded once more, and Tess licked it up greedily then stood up.

"Never forget who that dick belongs to." Tess said as she walked away.

Bless turned around and looked at her thick ass and wide hips before looking down at his dick. "It's all yours baby. All yours." he replied, getting hard once more.

"Good, then follow me to the shower." Tess replied with a smirk on her face as she led the way upstairs.

Chapter Twenty

Small Dick Not Enough

"You sure you made the best move?" Harmony asked while looking out the passenger side window.

"You're asking that question as if you don't trust my judgement or you'd rather be under Tess. Which one is it?" Layla asked with an attitude.

"Naw, it's not that. What I'm saying is, are you sure you made the best move not needing your mother and bless help to save Suyung? You're still pretty badly hurt, and the Cartel has an endless supply of dumb men that don't mind giving their life for a dollar and a dream. Not to mention the two dudes running around with Teflon armor and Catalina. Seems. like a lot for us to be missing our fourth member." Harmony replied.

"We got this. I'll have a plan. We don't need my mother's help… I mean Tess's help. It's not required or desired." Layla replied as she pulled up into a building in Flatbush and parked the truck. Harmony looked out the window.

"What's this?" she asked.

"It's home for now. I brought a building in Flatbush because it's nothing but West Indian people that live here, so a Spanish cartel will stick out like a sore thumb. We're safe here. Wake up Rose and let's go." Layla said as she hopped out the truck.

"Rose, get up! Get up!" Harmony said, shaking Rose's thigh.

"Huh! What?! We under attack?!" Rose perked, jumping up ready to fight and punched the back of the passenger seat as a reaction. "Ouch!" she screamed them looked at her hand that was wrapped in a cast. "I almost forget I broke this damn thing." Rose said. "Are we ready to get Suyung?" Rose asked with concern.

"Not yet, but we're at our new spot." Harmony replied, hopping out the truck, grabbing both duffle bags, and opened the back door for Rose.

"I can get my own door. I'm not that broken." Rose said with her face twisted up.

"Next time I'll remember." Harmony said while smiling.

They both followed Layla to the building as a woman with purple hair came out of it. She waved to them and keep it moving. Rose looked at Harmony, she shrugged her shoulders and they both looked at Layla.

"What? I had to rent out the first floor to make it look like a normal building." Layla replied.

On the outside the building looked like every other building on the block, tan brick, with a steel security door you had to get buzzed in to enter; but to trained eyes, you could see all the small security cameras and refocused doors. They entered the building.

"We're upstairs, come on." Layla said, leading them to the second floor.

"What, no elevator?" Rose asked.

"No, not this one." Layla replied as she pulled out keys and open the apartment door.

They entered 2B and walked down a long hallway to another steel door where Layla punched in a code on the digital lock. The door opened and they entered.

"What the fuck!" Rose said as they entered.

"Damn." Harmony said.

"What?" Layla asked.

"This is the same floor plan as Tess's warehouse. There's barely anything different. It's weird, that's all I'm saying." Rose replied.

"My floor plan's even better. I used the Empire Hotel to inspire me. I had the ceilings removed from the second and third floor of this building. Bedrooms. are on the tier up those stairs. That way we can walk around the whole catwalk and see the open concept in the middle with the living room and kitchen. What I did differently and before Tess is our training and weapons rooms. are in the fourth floor. We take those stairs there; and it's sound proof so no one can hear us shooting or fighting." Layla said proudly.

"Umm, I watch jail movies, a lot of jail movies and shows; and to be real with you, this shit look like a fancy pen. I told your mom the same thing about her warehouse."

"What we got good in this joint? I'm hungry." Rose said and went to the refrigerator.

"Nothing yet. There's a supermarket around the block and some good Jamaica food around here. You can go food shopping if you want, keep your tracker and gun close." Layla replied.

"What? There's no delivery boy like the last spot?" Rose asked.

"Naw, we in Brooklyn; the hood. It's pretty, but still the hood." Layla said while laughing.

"I'll go with you. You won't be able to carry much with that broken hand and I'm staying. Shit, Layla may hate her mother, but she's got more of that woman in her than she likes to admit." Harmony said to Rose as Layla came down the stair with two guns in her hand.

"Here. These are Glock 26s. Y'all already familiar with them, but these have been modified. There's an extra red beam, so you can't miss; and they're fully automatic." Layla said, passing the guns to them.

"Huh?" Rose replied.

"That means you can't miss when shooting Rose. They shoot like an uzi or a machine gun, but with less recoil. The kick from it won't make you jerk; and here's an extended magazine. It holds 73 hollow point bullets. Put it in your pocket." Layla said.

"Damn, is my aim that bad?" Rose asked.

Harmony and Layla both looked at Rose. "Ummm, yeah." Harmony replied.

"What you want from the store?" Rose asked.

"Nothing. I can't really eat with the thought of Suyung being trapped. We got to get her. There's no telling what they're doing to here. If it were me, I'd want y'all to come get me right away or pray for death. She probably thinks we forget about her." Layla said while trying not to cry.

"Naw, we sisters for life. We gonna get her back, just not on an empty stomach." Rose replied, meaning every word.

"Why when you said that I thought of Red Velvet talking about she needs a thing of ice cream." Harmony said and burst out laughing.

"Harmony, really! Really?!" Layla said.

"I'm sorry, I know it's too soon." Harmony said and left with Rose.

"Do you think we were wrong for leaving Tess's place?" Harmony ask as they walk down the street. It was seven o'clock and the streets were full of people coming and going, and groups of hustlers on each corner. The night air smelled of weed and gas.

"No, not at all. Yes, we were learning some new shit from her. It's like Layla's the kung fu master and Tess is the grand master teaching us even deeper shit; but like I told her and will tell anyone else, my loyalty is with Layla. Always has been and always will be. You couldn't pay me, teach me new moves or bribe me to change up on her. I'm sorry. Why you ask?" Rose replied.

"Nothing. I feel the same way." Harmony replied.

"Umm. you better. I hope your mind didn't get twisted up because you been training with her or because she's dark skin like you. I'm still black you know. Just not as chocolate as you." Rose said playfully.

"No, it's not that at all. I'm done with Layla blood, sweat, and tears. I think we might need Tess and Bless' help to get Suyung back, that's all." Harmony replied.

"I think we got this." Rose replied.

"Wait, what's that?" Harmony asked as she watched two young ladies on the corner surrounded by a group of hustlers wearing black and blue. Harmony could tell they was Crip or GD gang member.

"Bitch! Bitch!" a bald headed one with a long Muslim looking beard said as he smacked one of the women repeatedly

The woman's friend stood there trembling in fear, scared to move, while the other hustlers in the back were just laughing while selling weed and crack to the customers that walked up.

"Bulldog, no. Please no don't hurt me. I'm sorry! Ahhh! I'll do what you want!" the woman being slapped cried.

"Harmony, you got that look in your eyes. Leave it be sis, we've got enough drama of our own to deal with." Rose said but before she could even fully finish her sentence Harmony was power walking toward the group. "Aww shit! Here we go." Rose said as she did a little skip jump to try to catch up with Harmony and began power walking as well.

Bulldog raised his hand to smack the woman once more and Harmony caught his hand mid-swing.

"What the blood clot is going on? Who you and why you touching me? You want some of this beating here too, huh skank?" Bulldog said as he pulled his hand free from Harmony's grip.

"Stop beating her. If you hit her again, we're going to have problems." Harmony said while looking in to the guy's eyes.

She could tell he must be the leader of this crew and could clearly see why they call him bulldog. He looked just like one in the face. His body was tall and slim, but his face was fat with puffy, saggy checks.

"Bitch please. Who are you to tell me what to do with my property?" Bulldog and all his men laughed. He slowly walked around Harmony. "Hmmm, thick gal too; and sexy. Maybe it's fate. We should have you fuck me, and my team then go make money for us." Bulldog said and his men laughed again.

"I know her face. I see her around." one of the men named Popcorn said.

"Where? Where you see her from?" Bulldog asked in a thick Jamaican accent. "Who are you gal? My next bitch is who you are!" Bulldog stated.

"I'm Harmony. Rolling 60's Crip, east side. OG blue banger." Harmony said throwing up gang signs while staring Bulldog in the eyes.

Rose looked at her in shock but played it cool. Bulldog's men took a step back and got nervous. Everyone knew who the Rolling 60 Crips were in Flatbush, the neighborhood was full of them. Even worse, everyone knew who Blue Banger was and his brother Red Banger; notorious gang members that were nothing to play with. They killed people on sight and were good at it.

"Yeah, that's where I seen her from mon. She used to be up on the other side of Flatbush with them. I seen her beat some chick's ass once. She roll with them

Crips, but I heard she haven't been dealing with them for a year or so now." Popcorn said while smoking a fat blunt rolled in a Backwoods'.

"Fool, I'm still Crip to the death of me; and I'll peter roll on you fools. You think I can't have this hood flooded if I do a Crip whistle? I said leave the women alone." Harmony said.

Bulldog smiled then laughed and walked over to Popcorn, who passed the blunt to him. He inhaled deeply then exhaled the thick white smoke in the air. "See, there's an issue with your treat gal." Bulldog replied

"And what's that?" Harmony asked.

"Blue Banger and Red Banger been missing for two months now, and most of the rolling 60 Crip set looking for them in Virginia. The Crips that was hanging around, we killed them and took over their blocks. See gal, it's a G.D world." Bulldog said, and the seven men behind him screamed, "G.D for life!"

Rose and Harmony both knew of the G.D. gang. It started in Chicago and spread down south, then to New York. They were known for wearing black or blue bandanas and shooting people without thinking twice while screaming G.D. Folk out loud wherever they're at.

"See, you have to pull over here gal. "I'm just gonna fuck you gal then pass the both of you to my men to take turns and make you stand on the corner to make me money like these two bitches." Bulldog said pointing to the young woman that was on her knees covering her face with her arms. with her friend standing next to her trembling. "But now… pssstttt!" Bulldog suck his teeth hard as if he had a big piece of meat stuck in them while staring at Harmony.

"Please no, don't hurt them. Leave them out of it. Y'all go, please. Just run, now." the woman on her knees said to Harmony and shook her head when they didn't take off running. "You want to die?" the woman asked while crying and look at them with sorrow.

"Shut the fuck up!" Bulldog said then slammed the woman that was on her knees so hard that it knocked her down, causing her head to hit the sidewalk.

"I warned you." Harmony said as she walked up on Bulldog.

"You warned me of what?!" Bulldog yelled looking down at harmony, then he gagged for air and held his neck.

Before he could realize that Harmony had punched him, he heard a loud scream that sounded more like a lioness roar before he attacked. Harmony pulled her leg back and side kicked with all her might. "I am the weapon." she mumbled to herself as she screamed and kicked, striking Bulldog in his right leg by his kneecap. The sound of Bulldog's leg breaking echoed through the block.

"Ahhh! Ahhh!" he screamed and fell to the ground onto his left leg and looked at his right leg in horror. It was twisted backwards at an awkward angle.

"You black bitch you! You pussyhole! Ahhh! Oh God!" Bulldog shouted while sitting on the sidewalk looking at his leg, rocking back and forth, scared to touch it.

"Kill her! Beat that bitch ass!" Bulldog shouted.

His men hesitated for a second, looking Harmony up and down standing in a fighting stance. "We can beat this short bitch up." Popcorn said as he charged Harmony at full speed.

Harmony look at him as if he was stupid, stepped to the side, bent down and swiped his feet from up under him before jumping up in the air and coming down with all 160 pounds of her body weigh; sending her left knee into Popcorn's neck, breaking it.

"Wah the rass!" all the men said while Popcorn's eyes rolled to the back of his head as he stopped moving and Harmony stood up looking at them.

"You killed mi brother!" Bulldog shouted and pulled out a gun from behind his waist band and aimed.

"Oh shit! You done it now." Rose said as she pulled her gun fast, squeezed the trigger and sent three bullets into Bulldog's chest.

He fell backwards onto his back trying to breath and choking on his blood. "Fuck!" The other Jamaican G.D.'s pulled out their guns and started firing. Rose and Harmony ducked for cover behind a car. The woman that was on the ground crawled behind the car next to Harmony, but her friend stood there like a dear in headlights not moving but screaming as bullets ripped her body to shreds. She fell forward and died.

"G.D. green light! G.D green light!" the Jamaican G.D. gangster started shouting.

"Why are they shouting that?" Rose asked.

"It means we're in trouble. Switch your magazine, to the hundred proofs. They're calling for backup and telling all G.D. members in the area to attack us." Harmony replied while press the button on her Glock, taking out the ten round magazine and putting it in her pocket before putting the extended magazine in.

"Layla's gonna be mad as hell at us. We didn't get three blocks before we got into some drama. We were supposed to get groceries Harmony." Rose said as she hopped up from the car and squeeze the trigger, shooting one of G.D. gangsters in the head.

"Fuck!" Harmony said as ten more men with black bandanas around their faces came out arm with guns from the building behind them.

Harmony aimed, squeezed the trigger and a spray of bullets came out, hitting two of the men in the face and neck, and three in the shoulders and arms.

"We need to run and find better cover. We can't be trapped here! There in front of us and behind us!" Harmony shouted.

Rose dug in her pocket, felt around and grabbed a silver ball about the size of a golf ball.

"What you supposed to do with that?" the woman asked, wondering why Harmony and Rose weren't screaming or panicking, and where the hell they pulled a gun out from.

"This is going help us." Rose said to the woman.

"Really; that shinny ball is going to save us?" the woman asked.

"Yes." Rose said and threw it in the middle of the street. It broke in half and thick purple smoke filled the air. The wind made it travel through the whole block, making it almost impossible to see.

"Who the fuck are y'all?" the woman asked in amazement.

"We're dead if we don't get moving." Rose replied with a smile on her face.

"Yeah, what she said. Stay low." Harmony replied as bullets slammed into parked cars. The G.D gangsters were shooting blindly and coughing because of the smoke.

"We got to get off the streets." Rose said.

"There." the woman said and pointed to a brick apartment building across the street on the right with the door open to the lobby.

They ran toward the building as two G.D. gangsters ran toward the smoke. Rose aimed, squeeze the trigger, and bullets ripped through the chest and legs of one of them killing him instantly. She aimed at the second one and heard a clicking sound.

"I'm empty!" Rose shouted as the G.D aimed at her, but Harmony squeezed the trigger of her gun first and a bullet slammed into his neck, ripping through his flesh and coming out the back of his neck, leaving two big holes that poured out blood. He fell sideways into the street holding the front and back of his neck, kicking and jerking before he stopped moving.

"Bitch, we're not bulletproof right now, you gotta move faster." Harmony said as they entered the building's lobby.

"Yeah, blame me. It's not my fault the stupid gun run out of bullets fast." Rose replied.

"Wait, y'all normally bulletproof and this right here, what's happening now is normal to y'all?" the woman asked with her eyes wide open.

"Umm, yes and yes." Rose answered as two G.D gangsters ran into the lobby.

Rose slammed one in the face with her arm that had the cast on it, breaking his nose, then kicked his gun out his hand. Leaping up into the air, she double kicked him in the chest with all her might, sending him flying backwards into the small window on the front lobby door. The second G.D. gangster was stuck on stupid, looking at his friend's body folded up, hanging half way out the door window and half way in. Rose ran up on him and punched him in the neck. He choked on his Adam' Apple and tried to raise his arm to fire, but Rose spin kicked him in the temple and knock him out. He managed to get off one shot as he hit the ground.

"Fuck!" Harmony said, holding her ears as all three women's ears rang from the gun going off in a closed environment.

"I think you knocked him out." the woman said.

"Let's go." Harmony replied. "Head to the roof!" Harmony shouted as five G.D. gangsters rushed into the building lobby.

Harmony aimed and squeeze the trigger on her Glock 26. A hail of bullets entered the body of one of them before she heard a clicking sound.

"You remember that heavenly touch thing? Can you do it with your right hand?" Harmony asked.

"Yeah, I should."

"Good." Harmony said as she jumped from the second floor into the lobby and side kicked one of the G.D. gangsters in the chest.

"Fuck! Lord, here we go. I swear my girl's gonna be the death of me." Rose said and jumped down, touching the closet guy to her. She poked him with her index finger then pointer finger before grabbing his stomach and twisting.

"Ahh! Ahh!" he dropped to his knees screaming and crying, causing the other three men in the room to look at him.

They looked at Rose, wondering what she did to him. Rose and Harmony smiled. Taking advantage of the opportunity, they quickly did the heaven touch of two of them. Before both men knew what had taken place, they hit the ground screaming and holding their stomachs. The third G.D. gangster dropped his gun and put up his hands.

"Wah the rass clod. Mi don't want none of that." he said in a deep Jamaican accent before he turned around and took off running out the building lobby. Police sirens and ambulances could be heard.

"We gotta go." Rose said, peeking out the window as the purple smoke start to clear, cop cars filled the block and the G.D. gangsters scrambled like roaches into hiding.

"What they hell did you do to them?" the woman asked as she looked at the three men rolling around the floor holding their stomachs and crying uncontrollably.

"We showed them what it feels like to be a woman once a month." Rose said and laughed.

"Psssst! Psst! Over here." all three women heard a voice say and turn their heads to see an elderly woman with a curly grey wig had opened her door and fanned them toward her. "Come in here and hide for a second babies, before it's too late." the old woman said.

Rose and Harmony looked at each other than Rose looked back outside through the lobby door. Police officers had their guns drawn and were arresting the G.D.s that didn't run fast enough as more officers turned the block in to a crime scene, blocking it off and were now heading to the building they were in.

"Why are they coming this way?" the woman they saved asked.

"Umm, could be the fact we have a guy hanging out the lobby door, or the fact that the guys on the floor haven't stopped screaming and crying like little girls; but yeah, we got to go." Rose said.

"What about them? Won't they tell we went into the lady's house" the woman they save asked.

"No, they won't be able to talk; and if we don't reverse the move we did, it will kill them in an hour or so." Harmony said as they entered the elderly woman's apartment.

"I'm Ms. Crane." the elderly woman said as she shut and locked her door. "Go sit in my living room and just wait an hour until this dies down Chile. Watch some Law and Order with me." Ms. Crane said, leading them to her living room.

Harmony smiled once they reached it because Ms. Crane's furniture had plastic on it, and it reminded her of her grandmother's.

"Just take a seat. I don't have to worry about y'all messing anything up, I have that good plastic on my couches." Ms. Crane said as she sat down. "Are y'all thirsty? You should be after all the butt kicking. What was that stuff; that Judo or Kung fu karate mess? Y'all sure whipped some ass. It was like watching a movie!" Ms. Crane said loudly, getting excited.

"Yeah, I am thirsty." Rose replied.

"Well, you're no guest. I'm too old to be walking back and forth, the kitchen is over there on the right. I got some fruit punch Kool-Aid in the refrigerator. Help yourself." Ms. Crane said.

"I sure will." Rose said getting up.

"No need for you to act all shy. All that fighting, who won't need something to drink." Ms. Crane said.

"Rose, bring a cup back for me and ummm... You know, I never got your name, or didn't have time to get it. I'm Harmony and as you know, that's Rose in the kitchen. I'm always shouting her name for some reason. She's like the ratchet sister you never had; and speaks her mind a lot." Harmony said.

"I heard that! You lucky we in Ms. Crane's house, I almost called you bitch girl." Rose said from the kitchen.

Harmony and the other woman both shook their heads because Rose cursed anyway without thinking. "I'm Jessica, but my friends call me Jess. Bulldog just killed the last person I called a friend; Crystal." Jessica said and held her head down, trying to fight back her tears.

"Oh child, things like that happens every other out here; but what was new was seeing y'all stand up to these thugs and men out here. Forty years living in this building and I have yet to see anything like that. No, I'm lying. It was a girl, I forgot her name, that everyone in Brooklyn was scared of it. Starts with a T. Her and her girlfriends had the hoodlum's. shook. Think her name was Tessa or something like that; but girl, I was looking out my bedroom window, saw you kick that man and break his legs… I damn near choked on my peppermint." Ms. Crane stated.

"We appreciate you Ms. Crane; but I got a feeling in my stomach and think it's time to leave. Is there a way out of here in this building without going to the front block?" Harmony ask as Rose entered the living room, passing everyone a cup of Kool-Aid.

"Girl, you were supposed to use the plastic cups. No one has time be washing dishes. I could use that time watching the Have and Have Nots or my soaps." Ms. Crane stated.

"I'm sorry." Rose replied.

"But yes. My second bedroom has a back window. Y'all go through there and can walk through the ally to the next block. The police not gonna be looking too hard. They never do." Ms. Crane said as she eased off the chair and lead them to the back bedroom.

Harmony opened the window, kissed Ms. Crane on the forehead, then climbed out the window before Rose and Jessica did the same. They walked through the alleyway like Ms. Crane said and was on the next block; then walked three blocks over, made two rights and was back at their building.

"Where we going? I have no place to go. I was forced to stay with the G.D., where they raped me and made me sell my body." Jessica said.

"You have no family?" Rose asked.

"No, I'm from Jamaica. The only family I had was my brother, who got us to the USA and was killed in a shootout. Then the G.D. kidnapped me." Jessica replied.

"Um, we can finish this conversation inside? The cops and G.D. gangsters are still around." Harmony said as they entered the building and walked up to the second floor.

Harmony pressed a code into the digital lock, and they entered. Jessica walked in and her eyes opened wide.

"Who the fuck are y'all?" she asked as she realized she wasn't in an apartment but something fancy; something big and remodeled.

"We'll break that down to you once you meet Layla." Rose said as she walked to the kitchen and got on her phone. "Oh shit! They got an Uber eats that comes to this neighborhood. Looks like we won't starve tonight." Rose said smiling then looked at the text that was sent 40 minutes ago from Layla.

'I won't be here when y'all get back, needed fresh air and took off my tracker. I'll be back by the morning. Stay low and out of trouble.'

"She's going to be pissed when she get back home." Rose said, tossing her iPhone to Harmony.

Harmony read the text. "She's still hurt. I don't think it's good for her to be out by herself." Harmony said.

"We all need time apart and fresh air now and then. After all that with Tess she's probably stressed out; and the fact we still haven't got Suyung back yet, that's a lot on her mind. It stresses me out every day." Rose replied.

Harmony shook her head. "I'm gonna take a bath. Jessica, pick a bedroom, we have five. You're about the same size as Rose with more ass, but I'm sure she has something that fits you. We have to stay in for the rest of the night." Harmony replied.

"Who! Who are y'all?" Jessica asked.

"We're your new sisters; the Teflon Divas." Rose said.

Chapter Twenty-One

A Love Story to Die For

Layla sat parked on the block in east New York, Brooklyn. She studied every car that went up and down Jerrold Avenue. She went to go pull on the blunt and noticed it went out. she re-lit it and took a long deep pull before exhaling the smoke out her nostrils.

"This shit really do taste like cookies." Layla said to herself. "Why have I been so scared to do this; so nervous. I don't understand. Do I fear I won't have my happy ending, or I won't have what Bless and Tess have? No, I'll have that. I've dreamed about this for years, this was meant to be. I just need a few more pulls of this blunt to calm my nerves. I got this." Layla said to herself as she took three more pulls, put the blunt out and hopped out the truck, walking to the building she'd been watching.

She looked behind herself continuously, making sure Iris wasn't ready to pop out at any given time. a woman and a man walked behind her. Layla's heart raced. She touched the handle of her Glock 26 with the extended magazine, pulled it out and spun around while squatting low.

"Ahhhh!" the woman screamed and took off running in the optimist direction. The man raised his hands.

"Wow, chill! Don't shoot, I'm just trying to get home from a long day of work. I have no money." he said.

Layla looked at the man and could tell he did construction work. His clothes were dirty, and his jeans held white power on them that looked like cement before you mixed it with water.

"I'm sorry; but don't be walking behind people so close. That's how you get your head blown off. You're too big to be walking that fast." Layla said.

"I'm sorry. I'm just trying to get home." the man replied.

"Just go." Layla replied.

The man walked across the street with his hands still up and didn't lower them until he reached the corner and took off. Layla stood up, turned back around and took a deep breath.

"Okay, I'm panicking. I just have to relax; but what if he doesn't like me? That's crazy, what man wouldn't like me? I got to push all these negative thoughts out my mind." Layla said as she walked to the building, pulled out a knife and picked the lobby door lock. She took the stairs to the fourth floor, walked to apartment 4a, and knocked on the door. She stood there with her heart racing. The door opened and Damou stepped out with a Glock 17 handgun in his hand dressed in a red sweat suit. His brown skin seemed to glow, and his bread was thick, full, and looked to have oil sheen in it. He had a black NY snap back hat on, and his light brown eyes lit up when he saw Layla standing there.

"Oh my God! I heard rumors you were alive and back in New York, but I didn't believe it." Damou said, hugging her tight and lifting her off her feet.

Layla's heart skipped a beat and her pussy got wet from the touch of his skin. "Oh my God I missed you." Layla said.

When he broke there embrace, she pulled down his sweat pants, grabbed his short fat dick, got on her knees and began sucking it fast.

"Wait. Wait baby." Damou said while moaning.

"Fuck waiting. I haven't felt a man's touch in I don't know how long because all I could do was dream of you and your dick." Layla said while sucking him faster and felt his dick expand, getting thicker.

"Oh shit. Ssss…" he groaned as he tilted his head back, enjoying her warm, wet mouth.

Layla came up for fresh air and tongue kissed him deep and sloppily. Damou turned her around and wiggled her out her jeans.

"Damn. You been takin' care of yourself. You got thicker, and still have no stomach. Damn." Damou said while pushing Layla forward on the staircase before bending down and sticking his tongue into her ass.

"Oh God, yes. Yes." Layla moaned as his tongue went in and out her asshole then he French kissed it before letting his tongue slowly travel to her pussy.

He took her pussy lips into his mouth and sucked them while taking her clit into his mouth. "Ahhh fuck! God yes. Yes." Layla moaned as she whined her pussy into his face. "God it's been too long. It's been too long." Layla moaned as her body shook and she orgasmed.

Damou came up, wiped his mouth with the back of his hand then stuck his dick inside of her. Layla was waiting for him to push the rest of it inside her. She had not been with a man in a while but had used dildos and vibrators. She could hear Damou pumping away and quickly remembered he had a short thick dick, so that would be all she feels.

"Yes! Oh yes!" she fake moaned and thought about him eating her ass once more.

"What the fuck is going on out here?" Layla heard a voice shout before she turned around to see a short, chubby light skin woman with a bonnet on that look like it never came off her head, holding a frying pan and a kitchen knife. She swung and hit Damou with the frying pan twice.

"I knew something wasn't right, that your ass been out here too long; and this what you're doing? Fucking hoes in the staircase in front of our apartment?! You'll never change!" the woman shouted while still hitting him with the frying pan on his arms. and shoulder, aiming for his head.

"Baby it's not like that! Stop, ughh! Baby stop! Kesha, fucking stop!" Damou shouted while trying to pull up his pants.

Layla continued to watch with a stupid look on her face and slowly worked her way back into her jeans.

"Bitch, what you looking at, out her sleeping with my man. I'll fuck you up too." Kesha said and swung the flying pan at Layla.

Layla side stepped, grabbed her arm and twisted it. "Ahhh!" Kesha shouted and dropped the frying pan.

"You little fat bitch. What the fuck you think you doing?" Layla said with rage in her eyes.

"I wasn't always fat. You trying having three kids and still look nice. I bet you'll find your nigga cheating too!" Kesha shouted and try to stab Layla in the side with the knife.

"You stupid bitch.' Layla said and grabbed her neck then head butt her, bursting Kesha's nose. She shook the knife from her hand, then began to punch her in the face repeatedly.

"Stop! Get off my wife!" Layla heard Damou say before he punched her twice in the temple.

"Ahh! Ugh!" Layla groan in pain and backpedaled feeling dizzy.

Damou swung at her again, but Layla caught it, twisted his arm and front kicked him in to the hallway wall. She swipe kicked him off his feet, and he hit the hallway floor sideways.

"Mommy! Mommy!" A six-year-old boy came out the apartment that look just like Damou, followed by a five-year-old girl that had Kesha's cubby face. The children stood over Kesha and Damou as if they were trying to be protect them.

"Leave my mommy and daddy alone!" the little boy said while crying, looking at Layla in a fighting stance.

"You're married and have children?" Layla asked with her face twisted in disgust and pain.

"Yes bitch. He has four kids. Three with me, and one with his other baby mother; and we don't need baby mama number three on the team, so go!" Kesha shouted from the floor next to Damou.

Layla stare in to Damou's eyes. "You out here having kids like a male seahorse? That's fucking crazy; but that doesn't hurt as much as you getting married. Why you didn't tell me? Why didn't you wait or come looking for me? Bless would've looked for Tess." Layla said with tears flowing down her checks.

"Bitch are you crazy? You attacked me and put my dick in your mouth. What was I supposed to do, not fuck you; but you're delusional. It's been almost seven years since I've seen you. I thought you was dead. I was supposed to stop my life to wait for you and look for you?" Damou said, looking at her as if he was going to spit on her.

Layla couldn't believe her ears. Damou was her true love, her love story. They ran Brooklyn together. They were meant to be.

"Yes Damou, you were supposed to wait." Layla replied.

"You're fucking stupid; and I'm not Bless. I'm not about to be looking for any bitch. Now leave me and my family the fuck alone, you delusional bitch." Damou said as he got off the floor.

Layla took off running down the stairs.

"See what you did; always fucking some crazy bitches. Had one that almost beat our asses, you stupid motherfucker. Get your ass inside and change your damn clothes. You smell like that hoe." Layla could hear Kesha shout as she made it to the building's lobby and out the door.

"Why? Why Lord? Why can't I have a happy ending? A real love life love. Why you do this to me?" Layla asked while sitting in the truck, smoking her blunt while she cried.

After she finished smoking, she opened the ashtray and smoked another blunt as she wiped her tears away.

"Life's never going to be fair. Anything I want, I'm always gonna have to take it." Layla said and took one more pull of the blunt before she stepped out her truck.

"Stupid ass. I swear, if you get another bitch pregnant while I'm with you I'm going leave you this time. I promise." Kesha said.

"I'm not. I'm promise baby. I was weak." Damou replied, and the sound of knocking on the door caused Kesha to stop yelling at him.

"Who is it this time?" Kesha asked.

"I'll get it." Damou replied while pulling the chamber back on his gun, making a bullet jump in to it as he walked to the door.

"Oh no. You won't be getting no doors by yourself now we know your little dirty dick ass would fuck a bitch on the staircase as if your whole fucking family's not right here. I swear I'll never forgive you for that one." Kesha said as Damou opened the door. "It's you again bitch? Didn't you get the picture? He's married and don't want you." Kesha said, stretching out the would m-a-r-r-i-e-d.

"I said go Layla." Damou said and raise his gun, a mistake he wouldn't have time to regret.

Layla punched him in the neck, then the nose. He stumbled, trying to caught his breath, but the punch to his nose made his eyes watery and hard from him to see. He felt Layla's little hand twist the wrist of the hand that held his gun. Layla pointed the gun toward Kesha's head as she stood next to him and squeezed the trigger before she could scream, blowing a huge hole in the side of her head. She collapsed to the floor and died instantly.

"No!" Damou shouted, hearing his wife's body drop to the floor.

Layla punched him in the neck once more then kicked him in the balls before kicking his feet from up under him while holding his own hand with the gun in it towards his face.

"What are you doing? Layla stop! Stop, I love you!" Damou shouted.

"I love you too." Layla said and squeezed down on his finger and the trigger, sending a bullet into his right eye that came out the top of his head. She let go of his hand and he fell back dead.

"No! Daddy!" Damou's son screamed and came running over to his father body.

Before he could reach it, Layla stepped over Damou and in one swift move snapped the little boy's neck. His body made a small thud as it hit the floor. Layla looked at her work and could hear children crying in the back room. She wiped down the door with her shirt, twisted the bottom lock, shut the door and left.

"A beautiful murder scene." Layla said with a smile on her face. "Little dick motherfucker couldn't wait for me? No one will ever break my heart again." Layla said to herself as she got in the truck and pulled off.

Tess laid in her bed fast asleep. Bless looked at her and smiled, knowing she wouldn't be getting up any time soon after the orgasm he gave her in the shower. He began to do pushups to burn some of the extra energy he had, but that didn't seem to help. After doing three hundred, he washed the dishes and cleaned the kitchen.

"Why can't I sleep? This some bullshit. Maybe a jog will help." Bless said to himself then got dressed in a grey hoodie sweat suit, grabbed a 38 revolver and placed it in the hoodie pocket. Putting on his white Beats headphones, he stepped outside. It was eleven o'clock and not too many cars driving by the warehouse areas, mostly hookers with they're dates, fucking in the cars.

Bless jogged at a slow pace, listening to some old DMX and laughing every time he passed a car with a hooker in it fucking. *'I needed this. The run is really clearing up my head.'* he thought. His stomach started to bubble, letting him know something was wrong. He turned around with his 38 drawn, scanned the area and didn't see anything out of place, so he turn back around.

"Oh shit! Why are you creeping up on me? You can get hurt like that. Are you here to see Tess? Y'all really need to talk it out." Bless said.

"No. I'm here to get my happy ending." Layla replied.

"Your happy ending? Oh, that mean you're going to see Damou." Bless replied while running in place.

"No! Tonight, I realize I been chasing the wrong things. I wanted the Bless and Tess love story; but came to the conclusion I would never have that with Damou; or have it unless I take it." Layla responded.

"What are you talking about? If you live life, the right one will find you. Don't go looking for a man." Bless said. "But who's the right one?" Bless asked, looking at her strange.

"You!" Layla said, raising the locust gun and squeezing the trigger. A small needle stuck Bless in the neck. He stopped jogging in place and pulled it out.

"Layla, what are you doing?" he mumbled, feeling light headed.

"You are mine. I wanted the love story with the wrong man. You'll love me like you love Tess. Come on, let's go." Layla said as she turned around and walked to the truck.

Bless stood in a trance for a second then shook his head. "Yes baby." he replied and followed her to the truck before they pulled off.

Tess yawned then reached over to touch Bless but didn't feel him. She patted his side of the bed but didn't feel no parts of his body. *'Maybe he's working out or cooking again. That man loves to cook as much as I love to eat.'* Tess thought to herself, but her body told her something was wrong. She got out the bed, put on her Teflon body suit, put some guns on her hostlers and grabbed her twin chains whips before checking the surveillance camera on her phones. She saw Bless had gone out for a run an hour ago. He did turn on the find my iPhone app to track him, but he was down the block not moving. Tess's face twisted in confusion.

"Why hasn't he moved yet?" she asked herself before quickly running out the warehouse and down the two blocks while looking at her phone to see where he was.

She slowed down and looked at the parked cars in the street. She walked across the street to where it looked like a car had been parked and looked down to see Bless' iPhone and his workout headphones. She picked it up and her heart raced. Her eyes watered up as the worst thoughts came to mind. She looked up and down the block before she stared to cry uncontrollably.

"I can't lose him. I lost my daughter, now him. This can't be!", Tess said then screamed, "Bless!"

Chapter Twenty-Two

'Oh, my fucking God! Oh God! This is what I have been missing!" Layla moaned at the top of her lungs. She had been with a few men, but mostly around her age, never anyone older; and Damou and her sex toys were the only things that'd been inside her for a long time. Let's face it, Damou was a few inches short of having a real dick; but Bless was different. It was as if he paid attention to every detail, every moan and arch she made; even when she grabbed the sheets.

"Oh God! Oh God!" Layla screamed as he sucked her clit then French kissed it repeatedly before inserting two of his fingers inside her, thrusting them in and out. "Oh God!" Layla moan while whining her hips and she orgasmed for the second time.

Bless crawled backwards off the bed, pulled Layla to the edge of the bed and arched her ass.

"I don't know how much more of this I can take. I feel as if I climaxed ten times and had three organisms. tonight. I never in my life had sex this good." Layla said out loud while trying to catch her breath.

"You'll get this good dick all the time. It's you I love, and I will go out of my way to see you smile." Bless replied as he slightly bent his knee and guided the head of his dick into her soaking wet pussy, grinding his hips in a circular motion.

"Ssss. Ahhhh!" Layla moaned as he went deeper and faster.

"Spread your ass cheeks." she heard Bless say in a deep voice. She reached back behind her and spread her cheeks apart.

"Oh God! Oh God!" Layla screamed as he thrust harder and deeper into her pussy, touching spots she never felt.

She let go of her ass cheeks and tried to push his stomach to keep him from going deeper.

"Ohhh! Ahh yes… Oh God! You're fucking the shit out of me! You're fucking the shit out of me!" Layla screamed in pleasure as she tried to squirm away so she could escape his long thick chocolate dick.

Bless grabbed her by her wrists and held them tight. He looked down and all he could see was her brown pretty ass and his chocolate dick inside her, disappearing with each stroke. He began to thrust his pelvis harder and faster while whining his hips at the same time.

"Oh fuck! Fuck! Fuck!" Layla came as he beat her pussy up. She tried to squirm and get away, but he was locked onto her arms., holding them still along her body.

"God! Oh God you hitting my spot! Oh my God!" Layla screamed as she climaxed, creaming all over his dick.

Bless felt her pussy getting wetter and tighter on his dick. He looked at her ass and then down at his dick to see it covered in her cum.

"Yes. You love this dick! You love me right." he said through gritted teeth as he let go of her arms., reached his hand up under her to grab her neck and slightly choke her, all while never stopping his thrust.

"Fuck! Yes fuck!" Layla scream as each stroke was more intense and better than the last.

"Say, cum in me. Say you want me to cum in you." Bless said.

"Cum in me baby. Fuckin cum in me!" Layla said as if she was crying as he pushed his dick all the way in her and began to grind from the left to right, nutting all inside her wet pussy before pulling out and collapsing to bed out of breath.

Layla laid there twisted at a weird angle, looking as if she was broken. Her pussy was throbbing and would send a sweet chill through her body every few seconds.

"Oh my God. I've never been fucked like that. I still can feel you inside me." Layla said, wiping her tears away. "Damn, is this what everyone always said, that dark skin men fuck you better, like they have a point to prove? I been dealing with short dicks and rabbits my whole fucking life, not knowing it's dick like this out there. Damn I love you." Layla said.

"I love you too baby." Bless said as he closed his eyes.

Layla couldn't help but to stare at him, then looked at her phone that read 9 am. "Fuck!" she mumbled to herself. "Now I understand another reason Tess acts as if she couldn't replace you. It's clear, but she can never know I took you. You're mine now, my love story, my man; and after tonight, I'm never giving you back. Bless open your eyes." Layla said and Bless opened his eyes like a robot or someone in a trance.

"You will follow every order I give you. Layla said.

"Yes, I will follow ever order you give." Bless replied without emotion.

When she gave orders to anyone, she used the locust flower on, they were like zombies. After she gave them the orders, they went back to acting normal, and it was as if you could never tell they were being controlled.

"I want you to say in this stash house until I come back, or text you I need you. Stay out of sight; and you are to forget about Tess. She is the enemy and killed your daughter. The thought of her make you think of ways to kill her; but me you love me, will kill for me and always be by my side. Okay?" Layla said, staring at him and wondering if what she was doing will work.

"Yes. You're right baby." Bless said and began acting normal. "I'm going to go take a shower." Bless replied as he got out the bed.

"Okay. There's a burnout iPhone in the night stand. I'll be back later." Layla said as he kissed her deeply and passionately.

She had a big Kool-Aid smile on her face. "Now this is life. This is what love is supposed to feel like. The love story I should have had. Shit! Dick I should've been got. Damn." Layla said as she put on her coat and still could feel Bless' stiff dick in her as she walked.

Layla left the secret stash house in Yonkers, New York with a smile on her face. *'No one will think to look here for him.'* she said to herself as she got in her truck and pulled off. 45 minutes later she was in Flatbush Brooklyn, driving through side streets. "What the fuck happened here? It looks like a war took place." Layla said to herself as she looked at buildings filled with bullet holes, yellow crime scene, police blocking off blocks, and drawing where dead bodies laid out.

"Wait, this better not be Rose and Harmony behind this shit." Layla said to herself as she pulled up on her block, parked and headed into her building.

"1-2-3-4-5-6-7-8-9 -10. Repeat!" Harmony said out of breath, counting her sets as she did her squats in the training room. The smell of bacon and grits with eggs made it hard for her to focus. Her stomach growled.

"Stop it. After we finish two more sets." Harmony said as she looked down at her stomach and continued to do her squats.

Layla walked into the secret stash house and looked at Rose cooking in her underwear. "Umm, I was gone one night. Can y'all tell me what the hell happened that fast? We just got here; haven't been in this neighborhood a whole 24 hours before y'all start killing people." Layla said then noticed a dark brown skin woman come out one of the bedrooms. upstairs. "Umm, who the fuck is this?!" Layla said pointing up to her on the catwalk.

"How you know it was us?" Rose asked, never turning around to look at her while cooking.

"Because dummies, there was purple trees from smoke in the streets; and again, who is that?" Layla asked again, still pointing at the woman that was nervously walked down the stairs.

"Oh, that's Jessica, but we call her Jess. We saved her last night and killed a bunch of Jamaican G.D. gang members. It was Harmony's idea, but a good call. You want bacon or sausage with your grits and eggs?" Rose asked nonchalantly.

"So now we have to move again. We can't stay here with a whole gang looking for y'all. We already got enough people after us. That's it, we're going to save Suyung today and we leaving town, getting the fuck out of New York. We're packing after breakfast; and I want bacon." Layla said as she walked to the kitchen nook, sat down in a chair and Jess did the same.

"Nice to met you Jess. Do you know how to use a gun?" Layla asked with a smile on her face.

Jess smiled back and said, "Yes."

"Umm you were walking like your choochkie was swore. I know that walk. If I didn't know better, I would say you got some good ass dick bitch. Did you finally go visit Damou?" Harmony asked with a cheese smile on her face and walking into the kitchen.

"Damou's dick is too small to have me walking like this. I found someone better to bless this pussy, but I'll tell y'all about it another time; and I hope you don't judge me." Layla replied.

"Judge who? Judge you? Bitch please. I don't know how you keep your legs closed for this long. I would've done had a one-night stand and had someone beat this pussy up. We were staring to worry about you. Shit, Rose disappears and got dick a few times, even your girl Suyung." Harmony stated.

"Stop dry snitching hoe. Damn; but yes, I'm ready to get Suyung back. My stomach been hurting so much lately just thinking about her and what they're doing to here." Rose said as she fixed everyone a plate.

"I feel the same way. The only bright side is, the new Teflon suits can only be removed by the owner; some kinda new technology D.N.A scan with the magnet. To be honest, we haven't really tapped into what the suits can really do." Layla said as Rose stood next to the small tv in the kitchen.

"It looks like a night full of killing in Brooklyn!' A small Chinese reporter said. *"First it looked like a gang war took place in the Flatbush area of Brooklyn, with twelve gang members and one woman dead. There are no witnesses to what took place; but we have another side story to share with you. A murder suicide took place in East New York, involving a with an ex-drug dealer by the name of Damou Jones. He snapped his son's neck and shot his wife in the head before turning the gun on himself."* The Chinese reporter said as she sat at her desk and showed pictures of the crime Scene behind her. A little reddish-brown toned girl sat on the side walk crying, no other older than five.

"My daddy didn't kill my mommy! It was that crazy lady! My daddy didn't kill my mommy!" the little girl said repeatedly as the camera guy zoomed in on her tears then turned to the cops bringing out the bodies.

"It's such a sad thing to see a little girl heart broken, but neighbors have said the married couple fought all the time, and the husband was a known cheater." the reporter said, shaking her head.

Rose turned the tv off and she and Harmony stared at Layla.

"What? Don't look at me. I was with a one-night stand; and the only crazy lady we know is Iris, but it was a murder suicide." Layla replied while eating.

"The love of your life just killed himself and you okay with it? No tears, nothing? You had all of us watch this man for eighteen hours once, and you're acting like nothing happened." Harmony said as she looked at Layla funny.

"You didn't hear the reporter he had a wife? It's not my issue or concern. Besides, I had some good dick last night, I could care less. I only care about us getting Suyung and getting the fuck out of New York before something goes wrong or someone else try to kill us." Layla replied and got up from the table. "Pack your gear. We're moving to the next safe house and going to get our girl." Layla replied.

"How many fucking homes you have?" Rose asked.

"We have one for each of the months in every state we go. You can never be to prepared. If you stay ready you never have to get ready." Layla said.

"You sound just like Tess." Harmony said and smiled, then realized she messed up and cut her smile short.

"I'm not my mother, I'm better. Now let's go be Teflon Divas." Layla said and stomped off.

Chapter Twenty-Three

"Ahhhh! Ahhh!" Suyung screamed in pain as Benjamin punched her in the face repeatedly. He stopped for a second to admire his work. The right side of her face was bright red, knotted up. Her eye was swelling shut and looked to be the size of a golf ball.

"I may not be able to get you out that damn armor body suit until your dead, but I'll find ways to hurt you. So far, a week without food didn't break you down, we'll go for two weeks. You're lucky the human body needs water or you're dead, because you'll go without that as well. You'll tell me everything I need to know. Where is my Rose? That's all I want. I don't want you or even care about what happens to you. I just want you to tell me where your friends would hide." Benjamin said.

"Ha! You don't have no real friends, do you?" Suyung asked while laughing even though it hurt her face.

"Yes, I do. Well one friend, Tito." Benjamin replied with his face twisted up, trying to figure out Suyung's point was.

"Okay, so the psychotic giant is your only friend. It makes sense. So, you'll understand a true friend would never cross their friend or put them in harm. You might as well just kill me already." Suyung said then spit blood out her mouth into his.

Benjamin angrily wiped his face. "Don't worry about that bitch. You'll die soon enough; and you're talking about true friends, but you been here a week, and smell like piss. Your so-called friends forgot all about you! At the end of the day you only get yourself; and when you forget that you end up in situations like this!" Benjamin shouted and pulled his hand back to punch her again before he heard a loud explosion that shook the whole building, causing Benjamin to fight to keep his balance as if he was riding a skateboard.

"What the hell was that?" Benjamin asked himself out loud as the building finally stopped rumbling. Thick purple smoke began to come through the vents in the room and every vent in the twenty-story building.

"That would be my so call friends I don't have. They're coming to kill y'all." Suyung said as she dangled from the wall with her arms. stretched out.

"Let them come. There's over twenty-five hundred armed men in this building. They'll never make it to you." Benjamin spat, turned around and stomped off.

"We both know that's not true, or you wouldn't look so nervous; and when Rose sees what you've done to my face. Hmmm, you really gonna see who she's become. Ha! You weak ass punk." Suyung said and burst out laughing.

Benjamin stopped in his tracks and scowled at Suyung and kept going, leaving the room and locking the door behind her.

"Make sure no one enters that room; and be ready to fight." Benjamin said to the six men that were sitting in the living room of the master suit, coughing.

What is this stuff?" one of the cartel shoulders asked, trying to fan the purple smoke.

"I don't know; but cover your mouth and stay on point." Benjamin replied while leaving the room.

The Breeze Stone was a luxury hotel on City Island, located on beach front property that the Cartel owned. Catalina looked out at the beach view through the floor to ceiling windows as purple smoke flowed out the duct system into each room.

"They're here. Have the men ready. Don't let those bitches reach this floor." Catalina said to Tito.

"Si boss. I'm on it." Tito said in a deep voice and left the penthouse.

Flashbacks of the last fight she had with Layla played in her mind. *'I'm not ready yet. I've got to think. I have to outsmart the young bitch.'* Catalina thought to herself.

The Cartel solider in the hotel lobby coughed uncontrollably, and was unable to see Layla, Harmony, Jess, and Rose walk through the front door wearing purple gas masks that covered their nose and mouths. Their eyes glowed a neon green from the special contacts they had on to allow them to see through the smoke and at night.

"I told you, y'all should've let me work more on the gas. If I had more time, I could've had everyone in the building knocked out." Rose stated.

"We had no time. Let's get our friend; and besides, the gas you made looks like it will slow them down a little and get them dizzy, as well as unable to really see us. That's all we need." Layla replied.

"Less talking more killing." Harmony said as she aimed the matte black AR-15 riffle and squeezed the trigger.

Bullets cut through the thick purple smoke in the air, slamming into the chest of two cartel soldiers and ripped out they're backs before hitting another cartel soldier in the face, killing all three men instantly. Cartel soldiers in the lobby opened up fire, sending bullets in to the smoke blindly. Rose squeezed the trigger to her automatic shot gun, and it roared, blowing a hole in the stomach of one of the cartel soldiers. He ran fast and slid across the floor as Rose slid and continued to squeeze the trigger, blowing the right leg off of one of the cartel soldiers and sending pellets into the pelvis area of the neck of another one.

"Ahhh! Ahhh!" he yelled, dropped his gun and bent over screaming in excruciating pain as Rose stopped sliding.

The screaming cartel soldiers looked at Rose sitting in the marble floor with an incense smoking. "Hi and bye." were the last words he heard as Rose pulled the trigger and tiny metal pellets crashed into his head, exploding it before he fell sideways. Rose twisted up her face in disgust.

"That's just nasty. I don't care how many times I see it." Rose said. "It's all clear!" she shouted.

"This going be easier than I thought." Harmony said.

"Naw, this don't feel right. It's too easy. I'm gonna take the elevator to the eleventh floor and y'all met me there. Stick to the plan and we'll be out of New York in less than an hour with Suyung by our side." Layla said as she walked to the elevator and pressed the button before she entered.

"Let's go." Rose said. harmony and Jess followed behind her, running up the stairs.

"Tell me again why we just didn't take the elevator with Layla?" Jess asked out of breath. "And how the hell y'all move so fast with these body suits on?"

"Yours is an older model, and it's not Teflon metal, it's Kevlar. The metal that's sewn into that suit a little heavier; but be careful, some bullets can easily go through it. Just remember what I said, point and shoot." Harmony replied as five cartel soldiers in the second flight of stairs started to shoot.

"Ahh!" Jess screamed as six bullets crashed into her chest and stomach, sending her flying backwards and rolling down the stairs.

Three bullets hit Harmony's left forearm as she raised it and use it to cover her face, repelling the bullets. Harmony raised her AR-15 and sent a hail of bullets in their dictation. Bullets enter the faces of two of the Cartel soldiers, killing them. Rose squeezed the trigger and blew off the right arm off of one of the soldiers and the pellets few in the face of the one standing next to him.

"Ahhh! Ahhh!" he screamed in agonizing pain and held his face, touching the tiny pellets on it that didn't go deep enough to kill him.

He removed his hand to see what looked like a bullet cutting through the thick purple smoke in slow motion and slammed into the center of his forehead, coming out the back of his head, killing him instantly.

"Jess get the fuck up! We've got more incoming, and we got to go!" Harmony shouted while shooting. Cartel shoulders was coming like roaches, out of nowhere.

"I'm dead! I'm dead!" Jess said, laying at the bottom of the first flight stairs.

I told you that bitch was nowhere near ready; talking about she's dead, she's dead." Rose said while ducking behind a wall.

"If you don't fucking move, you're going be dead. We gotta go already; and I'm not Harmony, I will leave your pretending to be dead ass right here!" Rose shouted while pooping up from her place of cover and shot two more soldiers at once.

"I'm not dead?" Jess said as she eased off the floor and touched her chest where the bullets hit her. There were marks, but no blood. The bullet had slammed into her body suit then fell off.

She eased off the floor and grabbed her Uzi. Her contacts glowed green to help her see through the thick purple smoke and spot Harmony and Rose.

"Let's go bitch." Rose said as she opened the door that led to the second-floor rooms.

Jess ran up the stairs and onto the floor. She turned around and could see three men running down the third flight of stairs towards them. She squeezed the trigger to her Uzi and a spray of bullets tore through the three men, sending pieces of their flesh and blood flying everywhere on the staircase wall. Stopping for a moment to twist her face in disgust, Jess continued to follow Rose and Harmony onto the second floor.

"I don't think we bought enough bullets." Harmony said as she reloaded her magazine and chamber a new bullet in to the barrel.

"Yeah, I'm almost out too." Rose said, reloading her shotgun.

"Jess how many bullets you have left?" Harmony asked.

"I have maybe thirteen in the clip, and another magazine with twenty-five." Jess replied.

"Good, save your bullets with your Uzi to Semi-auto, one bullet at a time. The way we going we'll be out soon, and you can't fight like us yet." Harmony replied as group of soldiers came running down the long hallway screaming. In front of them and behind them was another set of ten.

Rose squeezed her trigger repeatedly, sending buckshot pellets flying through the air, ripping two soldiers apart and blowing the head off the third one.

"Duck!" Harmony shouted as she spun around and squeezed the trigger. Bullets spit out her gun rapidly just as Jess ducked down, ripping through the men's bodies. Their bodies jerked and shook, causing to appear as if they were dancing. Harmony heard a clicking sound, letting her know she was out of bullets, and the barrel of her gun was smoking.

"Ahh!" "Ughhh!" Some of the men she shot were on the floor moaning. She tossed her gun and walk up to them as they squirmed around on the floor. She flexed the muscle in her forearm, causing her blade to pop out. She stabbed one of the men in the back of the head, the next one in the heart, and other in the face. Jess looked on in horror.

"Eww girl, you're just nasty." Tess said with her face twisted up.

"The more you do it, the more used to it you become." Harmony replied as she pushed her forearm sword blade into a soldier's neck and watched him gasp for air as he drowned in his own blood.

"I'm sorry to say, but y'all bitches a little dark. I think the more you do this, death don't phase y'all; and y'all actually have fun with all this drama." Jess replied.

"Life couldn't be better." Rose said as she continued to squeeze the trigger of her shotgun, blowing pieces and chunks of soldiers in front of her. "Come on, let's go." Rose said as men lay on the ground crying, missing legs and arms.; and two of them with half of their face gone.

"We're just going leave them alive?" Harmony asked with a strange look on her face.

"We don't have time. Suyung's on the fifth floor; and the way shit going, we gonna have to start taking the soldier's guns we kill, because I'm down to five shotgun shells and we only on the second floor. We don't have time to make sure every one of them is dead, to be honest. We need to grab Suyung and Layla and get the fuck out of here. We're out numbered. The purple smoke we released into the hotel vent system helped a lot, making them unable to really see through it, and got them coughing; but if I had more time with making it, it would've made them weaker. That's neither here nor there, let's get the fuck out of here." Rose said as they walk down the hallway and stepped over bodies of soldiers squirming around.

They ran up the flights of stairs, and with each flight expected someone to jump out on them, but no one did, and they reached the fifth floor.

'Umm, does anyone else have a bad bubbly feeling in their stomach like me right now?" Rose asked as she opened the door to the fifth-floor hallway.

"Yeah, like getting here was too easy and we're walking into a trap?" Harmony replied.

"Yeah, I feel it too." Jess said.

"Okay. Just wanted to make sure it wasn't just me. Let's go." Rose stated.

"Wait, so we know we're walking into a trap and we're still going?" Jess asked in a confused tone.

"Yes bitch. We got to go get our girl." Harmony replied.

"Y'all some crazy ass hoes, I swear." Jess stated.

"Well, you gonna be crazy with us." Rose replied as they entered the fifth floor and walked cautiously down the hallway, expecting someone to jump out at any given second. "This is the room. 511." Rose said.

"You kick the door open, and Jess aim your gun as I roll in." Harmony whispered.

"Let's get it." Rose said and front kicked the double doors open to room 511.

Harmony jumped, rolled and tumbled on the floor as four men sitting in the living room playing cards jumped up as the door bust open. Jess stepped in the room behind Harmony and squeezed the trigger to her Uzi. Bullets ripped through the jaw and face of two of the soldiers. Harmony stood on one knee as she raised her arm flexing her muscle and her forearm blade shot out; entering the mouth of one of the soldiers, lifting him off his feet and pinning him to the wall. His head sliced in half, and his lower body from his jaw down, slid down the wall leaving a bloody smear. The too part of his head rested on top of Harmony's sword blade, still pinned to the wall.

"That's just nasty." Jess said.

"Hell yeah." Rose and Harmony said, forgetting about the fourth guy. He raised his gun and sent four bullets into Rose's chest and stomach.

"Ahhh fuck! You pussy!" Rose screamed in pain and cursed in Spanish.

Jess aimed at him, sending the last five of her bullets into his shoulder and his back as he tried to turn around and run.

"My nerves are bad. I don't know how y'all so calm, like this shit normal. I'm starting to think I was safer with Bulldog and the G.D. Gang." Jess said, causing Rose and Harmony to stop in their tracks and look at her as if she was stupid.

"See, I told you. We should've kept it moving on that day you wanted to save her. You can't help or save a hoe. This bitch just said she'd rather be pimp slapped and gang raped then fight for herself or the people that risked their life to save her." Rose said, staring at Jessica as if she wanted to shoot her.

"Maybe Rose was right; but we're knee deep in the shit right now, so there's no going back, only forward. I feel stupid for saving you. You could've gone your own way after we saved you, but you wanted to be part of us. A part of our sisterhood. Well this is it. We're fucking assassins. Listen, we don't have time for this." Harmony said in disgust.

"I didn't mean it like that. I'm just saying this shit's not normal." Jess replied.

"Save it." Harmony replied and began to walk.

"Yeah, save it; because normal is for women to be the victim and not fight back. That's normal! Well we're gonna change the standards and teach any woman that wants to learn how to never be weak again. I'll never let a man hit me again." Rose said with fire in her eyes.

"Duck!" Jess said as she saw a group of men running down the hallway about to enter the room with their guns drawn.

Jess pressed the button on the side of her Uzi and the empty magazine fell out to the ground. She grabbed the fresh one from her hostler on the side of her waist and slid it in the gun, all before she could blink and squeeze the trigger, shooting one solder in the eye. She then rolled on the floor and squeezed the trigger, sending a hail of bullets tearing through meat and flesh, shattering the bones in their legs. The men's screams. echoed over Jess' gun fire as they fell forward and sideways. Jess heard the clicking sound, tossed her gun, hopped up off the floor and quickly ran into the hallway. She kicked one of the solider in the face that was in the floor and took his chrome 49 caliber hand gun, shooting him in the back of the head, before walking down shooting the screaming men on the floor in the chest and head.

"Ahhhh!" Jess screamed as two bullets slammed into her back and push her forward.

She turned around to see one of the men crying. His legs were leaking some much blood, Jess wondered how he was still alive. It looked like he was using all his might just to hold up his gun that he was trying to aim. He squeezed the trigger again and Jess lean to the side, causing the bullet to miss her and slam into the wall behind her. Jess aimed and sent a bullet into the center of his head. His face split open, killing him instantly. Harmony and Rose both looked on with their eyes wide open in shock.

"Hmm, it may be some hope for you yet bitch." Rose stated as Jess shot three more men that were squirming around, grabbing two hand guns off the floor and tossed one to Harmony.

"Don't ever think I don't appreciate you both. I was just saying this shit isn't normal; but like you said, you get used to it fast." Jessica said.

"Damn bitch. Okay" Harmony said as they opened the double doors to the master bedroom.

All three women's hearts felt as if it dropped to their stomach at the sight of Suyung stretched out and hung up on the wall, her face badly swelling. She looked up at them at weakly said, "I knew you'd come." and lowered her head. Harmony ran over to her and picked the lock on her chains. Suyung fell weakly to the floor.

"Can you stand?" Rose asked.

"I think so." Suyung replied as Harmony helped her up.

"Did they break anything?" Rose asked.

"No, just a whole lot of punching; and that ex-boyfriend of yours, he's a real dickhead. I can't wait until we kill him." Suyung said.

"Okay, I have a shot of morphine mixed with adrenaline. Once I shoot you with this, you won't feel nothing. It'll take away the pain for about 30 minutes; but once it wears off the pain you feeling now will double and crash down on you like a ton of bricks. Do you feel you need it?" Harmony asked.

"Hell yeah, or I'll be just dead weight. Y'all do know this is a trap, right?" Suyung said as Rose grabbed a bottle of water out the ice bucket and a piece of bread off the table where the four soldiers were playing cards and kneeled next to Suyung.

"Here, drink; and eat this fast; put something in you." Rose said as she fed her.

"Yes, we know it's a trap. We took care of them." Harmony replied.

Suyung gulped down the bottle of water then bit into the bread, eating it greedily. "No, I'm not just speaking about the cartel soldiers. I overheard your big head ass ex Benjamin talking. He said Catalina hired about twenty martial artists. Ouch!" Suyung said as Harmony stuck her with a small needle and squeezed the small pouch on it. "What the fuck Harmony? You could've warned me." Suyung said, rubbing her hand.

"We can handle anything that comes at us." Rose replied.

"Umm. uh oh." Harmony said.

"Uh oh what?" Suyung asked, looking at Harmony as she stared at the needle and pouch attached to it.

"Umm…" Harmony said with an innocent look on her face.

"Ummm nothing. What did you do Harmony?" Suyung asked.

"I gave you the wrong medicine. I gave you the straight adrenaline, and the mixture." Harmony admitted.

"What does that mean? Am I going to die; and who the fuck does shit like that?" Suyung asked.

"No, I don't think you'll die; but you'll feel how we felt when we sniffed that coke last time; very hyper with a lot of energy. I mean a lot." Harmony said with her eyes wide open.

"So, I'm not gonna die?" Suyung asked again.

"Well if your heart doesn't bust after thirty minutes or so, you'll be just fine bitch." Harmony replied as five short brown skinned Asian men entered the room. Two were holding swords, one had two knives, and the other two had hatchet axes.

"I'll handle this." Jessica said and raised her arm as she took aim.

The short Asian man throw his knife, knocking the gun out of Jess' hand and ran toward her while screaming as he jumped in the air; kicking her with his right foot as he spun in the air and kicked her in the chest with his left foot before landing on the ground in a fighting stance.

"Ahhh!" Jessica barely screamed as the oxygen in her lungs was kick out and she flew backward to the floor.

"These guys are different." Harmony said as she got up from Suyung and took her fighting stance.

"Yeah. I guess the tiny men are some of the material artist she hired." Suyung said.

"Here." Rose said and tossed her a short, thick silver stick. "You dropped your staff at the house that day." Rose stated.

Suyung pressed a button and the staff explained to six feet. With the push of another button, the spear popped out. She twirled the staff around.

"It feels nice having it back in my hand; and speaking of feeling nice, you guys, I feel great. Like really great." Suyung said while jumping up and down like a kid who just ate candy.

"We're the Thai gang Lodi, and we're here to collect on the bounty on your heads." the Thai man with the knife said.

"Uhhhhh, less talk, more fighting." Suyung said and charged him.

The Thai gangster with the knife eyes opened wide along with his men, not expecting such a crazy attack right away. Suyung moved faced as she pressed a button and the spear head on her staff shot out, ripping through the heart of one of the Thai gangsters holding a sword, all while she attacked the Thai gangster with the sword. He blocked her first two moves with his knife. The sound of metals could be heard crashing into each other.

The next two moves she'd made, he couldn't block; as she swung low, hitting his ankle and knee cap. He bent down to rub it and Suyung screamed as she hit him on top of his head with her metal staff with the weight of her body behind it.

"Ughhh!" the gangster groaned in pain and backpedal then touched his head. He could feel the blood in his hands, that was now leaking on his forehead. He then felt a big gap in his skull where the staff had dented his head, cracking his skull open.

"Get her! Get her!" The Thai gangster with the knife said.

The men roared as they ran toward Suyung swinging their blades, trying to slice and dice her. Suyung blocked their blows while moving backwards then forward. More men could be heard coming from the hallways before they entered the room with knives and machetes in their hands.

"Ummmm, I know I feel good and all, but anytime y'all want to jump in would be great. I thought this was a rescue Suyung mission, not watch Suyung fight crazy Thai men." Suyung said as she placed her staff on the ground like a stripper pole and held on tight as she jumped, using it to balance herself while kicking six guys in the face.

"Oh yeah. Shit, it was like watching movie for a second. My bad girl." Harmony said as three men attacked her.

She flexed her forearms. and her sword blades popped out just in time to block two machetes as the came down toward her face. The third man tried to stab her in the stomach with his knife, but the tip of the knife broke when it connected with her suit.

"You little mother fucker." Harmony said and side kicked him with her strong legs like Layla and Tess had taught her. The sound of the guy's knees breaking could be heard in the room as he hit the ground. Harmony block and swung, slicing of the head of one of the Thai gangsters and stabbing the next one on the month.

"Why is it so many off them? We need to get out of this room." Rose said while fighting with her double swords.

Her right hand was wrapped up tight, but still wasn't heal. She took the cast off too early, so her moves were a little slow; but since she'd trained with both hands, her left hand made up for it. She poked one of the gangsters in the eyes as he tried to stab her, and another in the neck.

"Why the hell are they screaming? I can barely hear my own thoughts. It's like they scream while they attacking for no reason!" Rose shouted.

"I know what you mean, but we got to get out this room or we'll be trapped." Suyung said as bodies piled up by her feet.

"Shoot your blades!" Harmony shouted.

Suyung pressed the button and her spear head yanked out the dead gangster on the floor, returning to her staff. All three Teflon Divas aimed, flexed or press a button and their blades few with intense force from the magnet. Harmony's forearm blades went through two Thai gangsters, traveling through and coming out their backs before entering two more. Suyung's chrome spear head entered the mouth of one of the gangsters, came out the back of his head and entered the forehead of another before finally landing into the nose of a third one. Rose's double sword sliced through the air like scissors, cutting three gangsters in half. Their blades returned to them as fast as they left.

"Come on Jess, get off the floor. We gotta go before more come!" Rose shouted.

"Who's Jess?" Suyung asked while stabbing one of the gangsters on the floor in the back of his head with her spear.

"Oh, she's the new girl." Rose replied.

"Hey new girl, nice to meet you. I'm Suyung; and feeling very hyper today." Suyung said and bust out laughing.

"Bitch, this ain't no meet and greet. Let's go." Harmony said while shaking her head as they ran out into the hallway towards the stairs to see the first Thai man Suyung attacked holding his head, waiting for them with ten more Thai gangsters behind him.

"Damnit, we don't have time for this." Rose stated.

"Let's get to work," Suyung said began to run, then ran into the wall, slicing three necks while doing it until she was now behind the group stabbing one in the back.

"I'm coming for you big head." Suyung shouted at the Thai gang leader. The look of panic spread across his face as he pushed two of the Thai gangsters in front of him towards Suyung.

"Well, let's go help." Harmony said and took off running toward the gang with Rose and Jess behind her.

The elevator rode to the eleventh floor and stopped. Four cartel soldiers stood there waiting. They aimed there AK-47 at the door and squeezed the trigger. A hail of bullets slammed into the steel metal door of the elevator, putting over three hundred holes in it as they reloaded their smoking AK-47.

"Yeah, we got them bitches for sure!" one of the Cartel soldiers named Pedro said as he walked to the elevator. The door opened and no one was there.

"What you see?" one of the cartel soldiers that stood a few feet away asked.

"Nothing. No one's there." Pedro replied.

"What you mean no one's there? You mean we wasted all those bullets for nothing?" the cartel solider that stood a few feet away asked.

"I don't know." Pedro replied, stepped into the elevator and the door closed. "Ughhh! Ughhh help!"

Gagging sounds and Pedro inside the elevator screaming could be heard, then it stopped. The other three looked at each other, pulled back the chambers to their AK-47s and aimed, waiting for the door to open only to see Pedro standing there looking spaced out and blood dripping from his mouth.

"Pedro. Homes, you okay?" one of the cartel soldiers asked as they looked at him weirdly. "Pedro, answer me Homes." he said.

As the three of the cautiously moved closer with their guns aimed. Before they could react, Layla was on the ceiling and hanging upside down looking like spider man, with one hand holding a spike that was lodged into the back skull of Pedro. It somehow didn't kill him but left him almost brain dead just standing there. In here other hand she gripped the mp5 and squeezed the trigger. Bullets tore through the first two men with ease. The third man ducked to the ground just in time. He aimed for Layla's head as she continued to hang upside down and squeeze the trigger to the AK. Layla moved Pedro's body in front of the bullets just in time. The bullets shredded his body and cracked open his skull.

"I'll kill you bitch!" the cartel soldier shouted while he continued firing.

Layla aimed and sent a bullet crashing into his forehead. He died with his eyes open and tongue sticking out. "That was easy." Layla said to herself as she let of Pedro's body and dropped to the elevator floor making a thumping sound. Layla flipped out the elevator and room doors on the right and left of the hallway began to open.

"Oh shit. What now?" Layla said to herself as ten cartel soldiers dressed in yellow filled the hall.

Layla quickly changed her magazine, and before she could aim one of the cartel soldiers grabbed her hand. She sent a hail of bullets into his stomach, but he refused to let go of her arm with the gun in it.

"Get off and die fool!" Layla screamed and kicked, but he still didn't let go even though he looked dead.

"Fuck!" Layla said, finally letting go of the mp5 and flexed her muscles in her suit.

Her spikes came out like a porcupine and cut through the flesh of five men with ease before returning. Layla squinted her eyes as she noticed a dozen short Asian men dressed in black walking toward her. She flexed her muscles and some of the spikes hit the rest of the cartel soldiers, but this gangster dodged them with ease.

"What the fuck!" Layla said as the Thai gangster ran toward her with knives. She round house kicked one, then jumped and kneed the other in the face. "Fuck! Fuck!" Layla screamed with each blow she threw as they kept coming. She felt a hard punch to the back of her head that knock her forwards as one of the Thai gangsters punched her in the jaw. She grabbed his arm, twisted it then snapped it, breaking it from the elbow as another Thai gangster spin kicked her in the face.

"Fuck! Fuck! It's too damn many! I need help. Rose! Harmony!" Layla screamed, hoping her team would hear her, but something was blocking the two-way transmitter in her ear.

She threw a left punch and a right upper cut punch, knocking one of the Thai gangsters on his ass while one tried to slice her face and another tried to chop her head off, skimming her neck with an axe. She pulled back just in time, but got side kicked in the side of her head. Her world went dark and she felt dizzy as someone kicked her feet from up under her. She curled up in a ball, praying her spikes and Teflon body suit would protect her long enough until her head stopped spinning. She could feel feet kicking her in the ribs and legs.

"Ughh!" "Ahhh!" "Ughh!" Layla could hear what sounded like fighting and men screaming as a few feet kicked her. *'Yes! My bitches came.'* she thought to herself while rubbing her head to stop the throbbing pain. It was hard for her to open her eyes at first, but when she could, she saw detached arms. and legs flying towards her in a pile.

"I love them bitches." Layla said as she eased off the floor. then her heart sunk into her stomach and she began to sweat profusely. Her eyes opened wide with fear as she watched the chain whip wrap around one of the Thai gangster's left shoulder, going under his armpit and Tess pulled. The sharp Teflon razor blades ate through his flesh like pouring hot water on ice, ripping and tearing though his bones, before coming completely off.

"You bitch!" he shouted in excruciating pain, then the whip wrapped around his neck and Tess pulled his head off before tossing it at one of the Thai hangers running toward her at full speed armed with a machete. They were no match as Tess flexed her wrists left and right, sending her chain whip cutting through their bodies as if it was nothing.

The more that ran down the hallway, the more body pieces she snatched off them until no one was left; just men on the floor pouring out blood, squirming around and crying. Tess walked down the hallway toward Layla. Layla held back her tears as her life flashed before her eyes.

"Just do it and get it over with!" she screamed.

"Do what?" Tess asked standing over her.

"Why are you still on the floor; and you could've taken them if you used your spikes right. Fight while shooting them. Get up! What's wrong with you!" Tess said, looking at her strangely with her hand stretched out.

'Wait, she doesn't know. If she did, I'd be dead.' Layla thought to herself as took Tess's hand and got up off the floor.

"Yeah, I could've taken them, but one of them get a good punch at my head. I couldn't see." Layla replied.

"No excuses. I taught you to fight through the pain. You're a woman, that's all we do." Tess replied.

"Why are you here? Me and my team can handle this." Layla stated.

Tess held down her head. "Bless has been kidnapped. I think the Cartel took him. I got to get him back; and I never attended for you to do this alone. From the look of it, you needed help just now." Tess said.

Layla got nervous when she mentioned Bless' name. Flashbacks of him thrusting inside her played in her mind. Her pussy throbbed unsuspectingly. She looked at Tess as if she knew what happens. *'She's got to know. Why else is she here? She's just waiting for the perfect time to kill me and take Bless from me.'* Layla thought to herself as she and Tess both turned around in a fighting stance when they heard a noise to see Harmony, Rose, Suyung and Jess covered in blood and looking exhausted.

"Next time we're taking the elevator, and you're taken the stairs. Fuck that! Rose stated.

"The fucking Cartel hired fake ninjas that like to chop and slice. This some bullshit." Harmony said.

"We've got Suyung. Let's go!" Jessica said.

"No, we've got to kill the head." Layla replied.

"Why? We got our team member. I say we leave." Jessica replied.

"Jess shut up. We have a score to settle." Rose said as she thought of Benjamin.

"Let's do this." Harmony said.

"Umm, why Tess here?" Rose whispered to Layla.

"Not now; but be ready for anything." Layla said as they entered room 1122.

Harmony dug inside the holster on her belt and pulled out a purple gun-like device and tossed it on the wall. They all stepped back as a small explosive went off and a large hole in the ceiling opened up. Layla tossed a gravity hook attach to a rope.

"Bitch, my hand still not healed. Y'all know I can't climb that with one hand right." Rose said.

"We'll pull you up." Harmony said as she climbed the rope first.

"You should be somewhere with a sniper rifle like I was training you. You're not ready for hand to hand combat yet." Tess stated.

"My team, not yours. Your time has passed mother. She's ready and can handle this and more." Layla replied and climb up the rope next, then Tess and Jess before they pulled Rose up.

"Does anyone have bullets left?" Layla asked.

"Everyone's out but Jessica. She's got seven left." Rose replied then casually walked out the hotel room looking up and down the hallways. Down to the right you could see large double doors leading to the master penthouse.

"Wait. We need to check this room first.' Tess said, pointing to room 1126.

"Why? I want to kill Catalina and get it over with. I told you already, this is my team." Layla replied.

"There someone in this room. I can feel it." Tess said staring at the door.

"Okay, we'll check it out. Harmony, you kick in the door. Rose and Tess, cover me." Layla said.

Harmony wasted no time and front kicked the door. Her strong massive thighs cracked the door open with ease. Layla rolled to the ground as automatic fire went off. She sent a spike into one of the cartel soldiers' eyes, and another spike into another one's throat. The third Cartel solider aimed at Layla's head. Tess grabbed her chain razor whip off her hip and snapped it. The chain whip wrapped around the man's forearm just as he squeezed the trigger, throwing off his aim. The bullets slammed into the shoulder of Layla's body suit and bounced off. Tess pulled and the razor blades on her chain tore through the soldier's forearm like a hot spoon in ice cream and ripped right off. Tess pulled her arm back, flicked it and slapped the screaming cartel solider with his own arm knocking him out; leaving him in the floor bleeding to death.

"Hmm. I gotta try that move." Harmony said, impressed at what she just witnessed.

"This isn't a trap. It looks like they were guarding something, not waiting for us." Rose said.

"You're right." Tess replied, walking to the bedroom door and cautiously opened it.

"Ahhh!" a little girl around the age 10 or 11 that was in the room jumped up swinging, punching Tess in the leg.

"Wait! Hold on, stop!" Tess said, kneeling down and grabbing her hands, noticing something in them. "Listen, I'm not the bad guy. The bad guys over there, we came to stop them."

"That's probably the crazy bitch's daughter." Harmony said.

"No, she don't have any kids." Rose reported.

"How you know?" Jess asked.

"I used to work for the Cartel." Rose stated. "That's her title cousin. She murdered her whole family. Actually, I'm kinda surprised she's alive." Rose added.

Tess looked at the little girl with tears in her eyes, ready to continue to fight. Tess pulled her close and hugged her tight. Sabrina couldn't hold back her tears anymore.

"It's okay baby. It's okay. We'll get you out of here. What's your name?" Tess asked.

"I'm Sabrina." the little girl said as she broke there embrace.

"What's that in your hand?" Harmony asked.

"It's my chicken bone." Sabrina replied.

"Chicken bone? You know what, I shouldn't have even asked." Harmony replied.

"Let's go." Layla said, wanting to get herself and team far away from New York and Tess.

Sabrina held Tess's hand as they walked out the room and down the hallway to the double doors. "You stay back with Jess okay." Tess said to Sabrina. Sabrina shook her head and walk back to where Jessica was and stood by her.

"Watch the girl and stay in the back." Layla ordered.

Jessica nodded her head and checked the clip on her gun. "Four bullets." she counted out loud.

"Let's do this." Layla said.

Harmony wasted no time kicking open the front door. They ran in and stopped, looking on wearing puzzled looks on their faces. All of them but Tess were surprised. Sitting at the desk was Catalina, drinking out a champagne glass dressed in a Teflon suit. Benjamin and Tito stood next her; but what sent fear through Layla, Harmony, Rose and Suyung's body was the red-haired woman sitting next to Catalina. Iris turned and smiled.

"It took y'all long enough. You know Teflon's are slow. Me and Tess's team would have been up here in half the time." Iris said rolling her eyes. "Oh, y'all met Habib and Gunjan already." Iris said pointing to the two Indian men dressed in black Teflon suits.

"Why y'all look so surprised?" Iris asked

"I'm not surprised at all. Where there's a betrayed and bitter bitch, there you go, not too far behind." Tess said through gritted teeth as she placed her hand on waist hostler.

"So, you were the one that told the Cartel of my last safe house and escape plans? That's how they found us. It's all clear now." Layla said.

"Umm, no that wasn't me. I would've come after you myself if I knew, and I doubt you and your new little divas would've gotten away; but hey, I guess you pissed someone else off that snitched little princess." Iris said with an evil smile on her face.

"After y'all kicked Ms. Catalina's butt that day, she smartened up and hired me to assist her. I would've done it for free, but more money can never hurt." Iris said staring at Layla then looking at Tess and blew her a kiss. "I knew you were still alive baby. I knew as long my heart beat yours did to. I miss you SOOO fucking much. You have no idea how hard it is to get a decent orgasm without you." Iris said then looked at Habib and rolled her eyes. "But I bet I know someone who's getting fucked good." Iris said and stared at Layla.

'Wait, does she know? Why'd she said that and look at me? She must know. Fuck! Fuck! She's going tell Tess!' Layla thought to herself as her mind raced, her stomach turned, and she began to panic.

'Enough of the fucking games Iris. Where's my husband? Where's Bless! I will kill every one of you! I'll rip your fucking heart out if you harm him in any way." Tess said with anger in her voice and a killer rage in her eyes.

"Umm, this one here looks a little crazy. I don't think we should test her." Catalina said as her heart raced with fear looking at Tess.

"That all for show, trust me. She's really a nice girl when you get to know her." Iris said playfully as six Thai gangsters came out from a room behind them armed with knives.

Benjamin stared at Rose while licking his lips. "I love you." he mumbled with a sick look in his eyes. Suyung stared at Benjamin and Tito.

"I don't have Bless, but I know who has him and is fucking him." Iris said with a Kool-Aid smile on her face.

"Where is he?!" Tess scream.

"He's with…" Iris began to say as Layla flexed her muscles, shooting a spike out her suit towards iris with incredible speed.

Iris' eyes opened up wide as she grabbed her twin knives out her holster and began to block them all while backpedaling. Too many were coming at her at once, so she grabbed one of the Thai gangsters by the neck that was standing behind her and pushed him in front of her, using him as a shield. Twenty razor sharp spikes filled his body, killing him painfully.

"Nice try little bitch." Iris said and release her grip on the Thai man dropping him to the ground.

Layla flexed and her spikes return. That fast the battle was on. Suyung went straight for Tito, trying to jab him in the face with the spear of her staff. He was big but moved fast, blocking it, but didn't see Harmony until it was too late. She ran up Suyung's back fast, jumped in the air and side kicked him in the face.

"Ughh!" Tito groaned as he stumbled sideways from the powerful blow.

"Damnit! I missed his temple!" Harmony shouted.

"Again!" Suyung shouted as she continued her attack. Moving with speed, shed sliced Tito's hands.

"Ughrrrh!" Tito let out a roar and charged her like a football player.

"Oh shit!" Suyung said as she took off running.

She ran towards a wall, and back flipped off it, causing Tito to run into the wall. She tried to stab him in the back, but the spear just dented the body suit he was wearing.

"I think if I keep poking or we stab hard enough our weapons can break through the amour!" Suyung shouted.

"Duh you little stupid divas." Iris said while attacking Layla.

Layla moved fast, blocking each swing Iris threw, trying to stab her; but Layla wasn't fast enough, allowing Iris to sweep her off her feet.

"Come on little diva, move faster. You're younger and better, right?" Iris teased, looking like a cat playing with its prey.

Layla hopped up and round house kicked Iris in the stomach, then upper cut her as she bent over in pain.

"Oh, I see. Little diva, you want to fight with more heart because you don't want me to tell your mommy your secret huh!" Iris said as she spit out blood and looked at Tess.

Tess snapped her chain blade whip and ripped the arm off one of the Thai gangsters before spinning around in a circle on the floor with her whip as if she was playing hot scotch. Two of the Thai gangsters jumped over the chain blade whip, but one wasn't so luckily as it wrapped around his right leg and cut through his flesh. The metal cut through his bone with ease, breaking and ripping it off his body before being tossed to his friends. Tess ran up on the last two Thai gangsters, punching one in the chest then his neck, snapping his neck when he bent over. The last one roared and swung his knife at Tess's face. She dodged it, grabbed his arm and broke it at the elbow. "Ahhhh!" he hollered at the top of his lungs as Tess slid behind him, put him in a headlock and squeezed as he struggled to break free. Tess kick him in the back of the leg, dropping him to his knees. His right arm was broken, making it impossible to use it. He tried to slap backwards to hit Tess in the face, but his efforts were in vain. Tess squeezed tighter and tighter, all while staring Catalina in the eyes, as if she was picturing it was her in her arms. instead. Catalina looked on in horror. '*This bitch is sick. I'm crazy, but there's something really wrong with her. I need to get the hell out of here.*' Catalina thought to herself.

The Thai gangster's swings became weaker and weaker, until he stopped moving and soon died in Tess arms. Tess released the head lock and watched his body hit the floor then looked up at Catalina.

"I'm going to kill you, then I'm going rip Iris' heart out with my bare fucking hands!" Tess screamed.

"Wait! Wait! Maybe we can make a deal. I have money; lots of money. You can come work for me. We can be partners." Catalina said nervously while stepping backward.

"Bitch where's my husband?! Where my fucking husband?!" Tess screamed.

Catalina reached behind her back, pulled out her blade rings and threw them. "What the fuck?" Tess said as she saw the blade rings cut through the air like a frisbee. She back flipped, then flipped to the side.

"Talk that shit now bitch!" Catalina spat as she raised her arms. and use them as a remote control for the blade rings.

Tess jumped and continued to flip as the ring blade cut through the air and followed her. "I can't keep this shit up." she said to herself as she began to feel dizzy from flipping backwards, sideways and front to evade the ring blades.

"This shit got to stop." Tess mumble as she took her chain blade whip off her holster, pressed a button, turning her whip into a sword. She stopped flipping and used the sword to block one before she quickly pulled out her second chain blade and press the button doing the same. She continued to block the rings while moving forward.

"Why won't you just die bitch! Die already! I'm so fucking tired of all you fucking Teflon Divas!" Catalina shouted as her ring blades came back to her and she threw them again.

"Oh hell no. This shit has to stop." Tess said, blocking the ring blade then press the button on her whips. They expanded and she flick the tip of the whip at Catalina's face as a distraction. Catalina dodged the strike and got out the way but didn't realize it was a set up. Tess's right whip wrapped around both Catalina's forearms. she had stretched out controlling the ring blades.

"Nice try, but my suits made of Teflon metal too bitch!" Catalina shouted. Tess grinned and pulled tighter while still dodging the ring blades. "Ahhh! Ahhh stop!

Stop, get them off! Get this thing off me!" Catalina screamed as Tess pulled even tighter.

She could now feel the chain whip razor blades eating through her suit. Her eyes opened wide as the razors finally pierced her skin. She screamed at the top of her lungs as Tess ran toward her, hopped over her desk and yank her whip hard.

"Ahhhhh!" Catalina shouted in agony as she looked down where her forearms. were supposed to be but weren't.

Blood gushed out the open wound as she moved her stubs around. She turned around to see her arms. still wrapped in Tess's chain. Tess whistle and pointed. Catalina turned back around to see what she was pointing at.

"Fucking Teflon bitches." Catalina said while crying as her ring blades spun at incredible speed toward her and she no long could control them. One slammed into her stomach and the second one slammed into her forehead, cut straight through it and hit the wall behind her. Catalina fell forward onto her desk and her brain oozed onto some of the papers strewn across her desk.

"Now you." Tess said looking at Iris as flash backs of her killing her daughter played in her head. A signal tear escaped her right eye and travel down her cheek.

Iris look at Gunjan. "Well, what your waiting for, an invite?! Kill something!" she shouted.

Gunjan took off and headed straight for Jessica. "Shit!" Jessica scream and aim the black 9mm handgun, firing two times. The first bullet crashed into his stomach and bounced off. The second one he blocked with his forearm. "Fuck!" Jessica screamed and fire two more times, aiming for Gunjan head as he ran toward her as if he was an Indian ninja. He blocked both billets and punched Jessica in the jaw.

"Sabrina, run!" Jessica said, pushing her to the side. Jessica try to punch, but Gunjan had been training with Iris for months. Fighting her was like fighting a helpless child. He around house kicked her in the stomach and sent her flying backwards onto her ass. "Ughhh! Jess groaned in pain and received a knee to the face, knocking her onto her back. Gunjan jumped on top of her and started punching Jess in the face repeatedly.

"I don't know what the big deal about y'all, but I swear I'll kill you all; and one day kill the Iris bitch!" Gunjan said, talking shit with every blow.

Jess could feel her face swelling up, then something wet dripping down her. She slowly opened her eyes, although it hurt to do so. She look up at Gunjan, who was sitting on top of her, and he was holding his neck, gasping for air as blooded leak out between his fingers. Jessica twisted her head to the side and couldn't believe her eyes as Sabrina stabbed Gunjan in the neck three times back to back with the chicken bone she was carrying.

"Ahhh!" she screamed and swung with all her little might, jamming the sharp chicken bone into his ear.

Gunjan fell to the side onto the floor and his body went into convulsions; bucking and shaking as blood poured out his neck and he try to stop it unsuccessfully until he stopped moving, looking like a fish out of water slowly dying. Sabrina looked at Jess. "I'm not gonna run from them no more. Now I'll hurt them like they hurt me. I'll take them to heaven like they took my sister." Sabrina said, wiping her tears away while smearing Gunjan

blood that had dipped onto her on her face at the same time. Jessica raise her eyebrows and look at Sabrina as if she was a mini serial killer.

Rose swung with all her might but was out of breath. Her right hand was still broke, causing her to move slower and unable to block her right side fast enough as Benjamin tried to slice her up into little pieces with his sword.

"You're still the weak bitch you always been. You think because you hang with some new women, you're strong? You're not strong. You're the same piece of shit girl I was fucking and the same now." Benjamin said as Rose blocked two of his blows but hit her with the handle of his sword in her nose, breaking it.

Harmony was fighting Habib and saw Rose's nose leaking blood out the corner of her eye. "Rose!" she shouted and try to run to her, but Habib pull her back.

"You can't go! I have a job to do. You must die so she can eat! You must die so she can eat!" Habib said repeatedly

"I don't have time for this." Harmony said to herself. "I am the weapon." she mumbled to herself before she low side kicked with all her strength. A cracking sound could be heard as Habib's leg broke and he fell straight to the ground. Harmony took off running as Benjamin hit Rose once more in the face with the handle of his sword. Rose dropped to her knees as blood rushed out her nose.

"See, you can be surrounded by people and you're still be all alone and worth nothing to anyone but me." Benjamin said as he raised his sword high over his head. "This is going to hurt you more than me." he stated.

"You're wrong." Rose mumbled.

"Wrong about what? Benjamin asked, cocking his head to the side looking down at her as if she was stupid.

"One, I have people that care for me!" Rose said as Harmony leaped in the air and drop kick him in the back with both her feet using all her body weight. Benjamin flew forward, and before he could gain his balance he hard rose say, "…And two, this is going to hurt you more than it's going to hurt me."

Rose sliced up with her sword, cutting a straight line up to his face two inches deep. Benjamin stood there frozen in shock as Rose stood up and sliced down with her whole sword before pulling it out of him. "You stupid hoe." Benjamin managed to say as his face split apart and went into different dictions, as if someone cracked him open like a walnut. Blood gushed out as he hit the floor and shook for a second.

"Who's the stupid one now; and I told you, you were wrong." Rose said down at his body.

"Ewww girl, that's just nasty! Look at his face! Eww!" Harmony said standing next to her as Tito turned around and saw Benjamin's dead body.

"Nooo!" he screamed so loud that everyone stopped fighting, He back smacked Suyung with the force of God. The blow was so hard she was knocked out the room into the hallway. "Ahhh!" Tito roared before charging toward Harmony and Rose.

"Oh shit! I think we made his hulk-like boyfriend mad." Harmony said and got in a fighting stance, but Tito ran right through her, knocking her down.

"Ahhh!" he yelled and turned towards Rose. Before Rose could attack or put up her guard, he punched her in the stomach twice then picked her up as if she weighed nothing, throwing her to the ground and a cracking sound could be heard. Before the Teflon Divas could react, he raised his boot that was made of Teflon and stomped down with all of his 320 pounds. Rose's face and skull cracked open like a squished grape.

"Nooo!" Harmony, Suyung and Layla all screamed simultaneously. Harmony pulled the razor chain whip blade Tess had given her off her hostler and flex it. It wrapped around his face and she pulled. Layla ran and jump onto the chain whip as if it was a rope, pulled two spikes out her suit and front flipped while she jammed the two spikes into Tito's eye sockets.

"Ahhhh! Aahhhh!" Tito roared in pain as he tried to pulled the chain blade whip off his face, but the razors on it cut his hands up. Suyung ran and stuck her spear into his open mouth. The tip of it came out the back of his head, dropping him to his knees as he died slowly.

Hardy pulled the whip, moved closer and placed her foot onto his back and pulled. Tito's skull and head were thick, but the chain blade whip ate right through it. Harmony yanked half his face off and he fell sideways with a loud thump dead.

"No! No!" Layla and Harmony along with Suyung ran over to check on Rose and began to cry uncontrollably. Their friend's face was unrecognizable. It was completely smashed in, and she wasn't moving or breathing.

"Rose! Rose!" Layla cried.

Suyung bent down and held her hand. "Rose!" she cried out.

"Y'all some babies, I swear." Iris said and rolled her eyes. "People die every day. Suyung, Harmony, Layla and Tess all looked at her. "Oh shit." Iris said, knowing she made a mistake. She looked over at Habib, who's leg was broken, and knew he wouldn't be no help. "Damnit. Wait. Now you don't want to do this. It's not a fair fight ladies."

"When did you ever care about fair." Tess stated as they all walked closer to her.

"Wait. Tess don't do it. It was Layla who took Bless. That's right. Your precious daughter did it." Iris said with a smile on her face.

"You fucking liar! I'm gonna kill you anyway for what you did to my child and niece you monster." Tess said through gritted teeth.

"Wait, I can prove it. Activate now." Iris said and the green contact in her left eye lit up before a hologram came out of it. "See, I been watching Damou's house as your little princess knows. I saw her go in twice and kill everyone, so I didn't kill her right away. I was cautious and followed her; and saw this." Iris said before the hologram showed Layla shooting Bless with something then talking to him. He then dropped his phone and got in a truck with her. Tess turned around.

"You took Bless; but why?" Tess ask with a confused, hurt look on her face as if she didn't want to believe what she saw.

Layla held her head down the raised it. "Fuck it, I did it. I told you this is my story. I'm tired of you always getting what you want. I wanted my own Bless, and since I couldn't find one, I took the real one." Layla said.

"But bless would never betray me. What did you do to him?" Tess replied, not understanding.

"Let's just say Ms. Wung Shu left me a few of those Chinese secrets. I'm tired of living in your shadow. In fact, I'm tired of you both. Y'all supposed to be die.

There's no room in the world for the old Divas. It's the new Teflon divas time." Layla said and looked at Suyung and Harmony. Layla pressed a button on her holster that sent out a signal. "As we planned, now. Let's kill them." Layla said.

Tess back stepped, pulled out both her chain blade whips and twirled them before looking at Iris, who stood on the right side of her.

"We can take these three young pups." Iris said holding her twin knives while smiling.

"After we kill them, I'm going kill you once and for all Iris." Tess said.

The sound of something cutting through the air caught their attention, as a chain blade whip wrapped around Iris' left leg and she fell onto her back as Harmony pulled her closer.

"Bitch, you didn't tell me you trained a baby fucking Tess. If I die you die!" Iris shouted at Tess.

Iris threw both her knives at Harmony's head. Harmony blocked one with her forearm blade, and Suyung young blocked the next one from hitting Harmony's face with her spear. Iris flexed and called her knives back to her.

"Tesssssss!" Iris screamed, dragging Tess' name out slow and long. Tess rolled her eyes, started flexing her wrist and the chain blade whips at Harmony and Suyung.

"Fuck!" Harmony said, unable to pull Iris close to block her knives and Tess' chain blade whip at the same time. She snaked her wrist and the chain whip unwrapped Iris' legs. Layla wasted no time shooting her spikes at Tess. Tess blocked them with her whip, hitting them all out the way.

"Really Layla?! I raise you! Really?!" Tess scream and ran towards Layla. Fear traveled through Layla, as she'd never seen Tess so mad. Tess retracted her whips and placed them back on her hostler belt before running straight to Layla. Layla swung a few combos punches that Tess blocked angrily before Karate chopping Layla in the throat then punched her in the face four times. She hit her in the stomach twice and jump spin kicked her in the chest, sending Layla to the ground.

"This ain't training no more my child. Where's Bless? Don't make me fucking kill you!" Tess shouted while crying, not believing that another person she had loved with all her heart had cross her.

Before Tess could reach Layla on the floor, Suyung jabbed Tess in the face with her spear. Tess block it with her forearms. and Suyung continued to fight. *'Damn this little bitch fast.'* Tess thought to herself as Suyung sent blow after blow, using her spear then kicking. She managed to side kick Tess in the face then sweep her feet from up under her. As Tess laid on the floor, she tried to stab her with the spear. Tess rolled repeatedly as Suyung chase her around the floor. Then Tess rolled toward Suyung unexpectedly and caught her with a punch to the gut, then upper cut punch her in the chain, knocking the staff spear out her hand.

"Damn fast Chinese bitch." Tess said.

Suyung wiped her mouth and sent kick after kick to Tess' face then kicked her in the ribs. "I'm Korean bitch." Suyung spat as she roundhouse kicked Tess, knocking her backwards. Tess got pissed and took a fighting stance Suyung haven't seen before.

"That's Kung fu huh? Fuck you're Kung fu." Suyung said and struck fast.

Layla recognized the fighting style and her heart raced. It was the last stance she didn't finish learning from Tess, the Bubba Palm; where all the engraved attack and strength is push into the palm of the fighter. Suyung swing, sending punch after punch, but Tess was moving out the way; moving with the punches, looking like something out the movie The Matrix.

"Why can't I hit you?!" Suyung scream frustratedly, ten Tess hit her with the palm of her hands in the rib.

The sound of Suyung's ribs cracking could be heard in the room. Suyung didn't have time to scream in pan before Tess went into a combo, hitting Suyung on the thigh, left rib and then her stomach before pulling her arms. back and hitting her with all her strength in the chest with the palm of her hand. Suyung's body lifted and flew backwards, knocking the air out of her. She hit the wall making a dent in it and lost consciousness. Layla stood up and got into the Nuba palm fighting stance. Tess charged her, sending blow after blow trying to hit Layla with the palms. of her hands but Layla block it too, moving with her elbows. It was like looking into a mirror, they moved incessantly, not missing a beat.

Layla switched it up and Karate chopped Tess in the neck, Tess gasped for air as Layla hit her with a combo in the side of her head, stomach and chest; knocking Tess back and making her cough up blood.

"You're old. I'm faster and better. It's my story now mother." Layla said as she changed her fighting stance. Tess held her chest.

Harmony and Iris were going at it. Harmony flick her wrist, trying to hit iris with the chain whip. Iris blocked it using her twin knives with ease. "You okay baby Tess, but you still got a lot to learn. I see Tess hasn't taught you enough yet." Iris said as she tossed one of her knives at Harmony's face. Harmony looked up in time but was now standing face to face with Iris. Iris smiled then punched her in the face repeatedly before flipping her to the ground and kicked her in the thigh.

"Ahhh!" Harmony scream in pain as Iris aimed for her face and came down with the knife.

Harmony flexed her muscles and her forearm blade came out, blocking it. She hopped up from the ground and swung her arms. around, trying to cut Iris with her forearm blades. Iris back flipped and harmony shot one of the firearms. blades at her. Iris smacked it away then ran up on Harmony and jumped in the air, wrapping her legs around her neck. She then twisted and leaned back, flipping harmony to the ground.

"Like I said, you got more to learn." Iris said, punching her in the face once more then placed her arm in a lock with her legs, trying to break it.

Harmony rolled out of it, punched Iris in the chest and stomach, then got into a Muay Thai fighting stance. "Muay Thai, really? You do know I'm trained in six different fight combat skills, and Kung fu; and you bust out with Muay Thai?" Iris laugh then ran up on Harmony, and soon regretted it.

Muay Thai is one of the deadliest kick boxing skills, known as the art of the eight limbs. It's a volcano style of fighting people sleep on. Harmony jumped and sent a knee to Iris' stomach then a low kick to the top of her head. She spins and hit Iris in the jaw with another elbow then a knee to her side before stepping back and mumbling, "I am the weapon." As she thought about all the bamboo sticks, she broke with her legs and kicked.

"Oh, hell no bitch! Not me!" Iris said and front jump kicked Harmony in the chin and dodged her blow, then punch her in the chest, stomach and ribs repeatedly before hitting her with a hard blow to her left eye. "You thought you'd break my shit bitch? I don't think so." Iris said and continue her attack.

Harmony could barely see. She pulled back out the chain whip and thought about the last time she trained with Tess. Iris swung to punch her in the face once more, hoping to swell shut her right eye like her left eye. Harmony caught the punch in mid-air and wrap the chain blade whip around Iris' arm before sliding down and going through Iris' legs pulling the chain blade whip; yanking iris forward and flipping her onto her back, knocking the air out her lungs and hitting the back of her head. Harmony jumped on the ground, grabbed Iris's arm, pulled and snapped it.

"Ahhh! Ahhh!" Iris screamed at the top of her lungs in agonizing pain. she rolled over as Karmony kick her in the face, knocking her out.

"Enough!" Tess screamed.

"It will be enough when you're both dead." Layla said as Harmony got up from the floor, leaving Iris unconscious and stood next to Layla.

"I can't believe this. I can't believe you'd cross this line. You burn your all your bridges there's going to be no way to get across Layla." Tess said.

"Fuck you! Enough of your fucking lectures, believe it. I've had enough of you. Layla said and sent spikes flying at Tess. Tess pulled out her whip and block them, then saw Harmony's whip coming towards her. Their whips tangled together.

"I didn't teach y'all everything." Tess said, running up on Harmony touching her chest, neck and then stomach with her fingers and twisted, touching all her pressure paints.

"Uggg! Ahhhhh!" Harmony screamed as her joints cramp up and she dropped to her knees. She tried to undo what Tess had done, but this one was different. "Ahhh!" she yelled loudly as she hugged herself.

Tess wasted no time attacking Layla, punching her in the face and touching two pressure points on her shoulder that dropped Layla to the floor. She then poked her in the chest and stomach then twisted.

"Ahhh, you bitch! You stupid bitch! This won't stop me!" Layla cried while trying to undo the move.

"Where's my husband you ungrateful little hoe? I should've left you where I found you. I can't believe you." Tess said.

"Fuck you. He's my man now. You'll never get him back." Layla said in pain and Tess punched her twice. She was getting ready to punch her for the third time, but Layla start laughing as if she was crazy.

"What's so funny?" Tess asked, looking at her as if she lost her mind.

"It's funny if you think this is going to stop me. I think I'm getting better than you and Iris. In fact, I know I am. It's just a matter of time before your trucks won't even work on me." Layla replied.

"That may be true, but I'm sorry daughter. You, you're team and Iris won't live past this day; even if you don't tell me where Bless is. I can't go through this type of pain any more. First my best friend and now my daughter? I'm done." Tess said, and Layla laughed once more as four older women walked into the hotel. One stood in the lobby, one went to the third floor and stood, and two on the twelve. Tess turned her head to see the beautiful older woman standing in the hallway.

"Hi, I'm Val." the woman said.

Layla continued to laugh as Tess studied the woman. She looked as if she wasn't fully there mentally, as is if her soul was gone. "What is this?" Tess asked, looking back down at Layla.

Layla smiled. "You taught me to always have an exit wherever I go. That's my exit." Layla said with a grin, then Ms. Val opened her blouse to reveal a bomb that was strapped onto a waist trainer. She pressed a remote button that was in her hand and the other older women that were on different floors did the same.

Boom! A loud explosion went off, shaking the whole building as the elderly women blow up theMs.elves and the foundation of the building. The hotel began to fall apart. The blast had knocked Tess back. She coughed out some grey smoke mix with dust. She looked over to see Layla and Harmony had undone the heaven touch move she did on them and was standing by the floor to ceiling glass window with Jessica and Suyung.

"What about the little girl?" Suyung asked as they all look at Sabrina standing in the doorways of the room in the halls as the building was collapsing.

"Leave her. let my fake mother try to save her."
Layla said as they broke the windows, and all jumped
out.

"What the fuck?!" Tess said, knowing no one would
survive that jump. She ran to the window to see Layla
and her team falling then spread their arms. and legs
before a parachute came out their suits. Wings were up
under their arms. and feet, helping them glide through
the air like a kite. 'I can jump on one of those bitch's
backs.' Tess thought to herself and got ready to do so
but turned around to see the scared little girl and thought
about her daughter. "I would want someone to save
Ayana if it was my child." Tess said to herself and took
off running to grab Sabrina. A hole opened up in the
floor and they fell through. Tess used her body to shield
Sabrina as the building came down and something
heavy hit her in the back of her head. She lost
consciousness still covering Sabrina.

"Get up! Get up!" Sabrina cried as the building
came completely down, killing them both.

Layla and Suyung glided to the Bronx river and fell
in, where a sports boat was waiting for them. They
swam to it and the man helped them into the boat, then
kiss Layla deeply and passionately.

"Is it over baby?" Bless asked, breaking their embrace.

"It's over. Now let's get out of New York.' Layla said.

"What about Harmony and Jessica?" Suyung asked weakly. "They must've blown in a different direction."

"They know the exit plan, we'll reconnect." Layla replied as Bless rode down the Bronx River.

Chapter Twenty-Four

Hell, on Earth

"No! Please don't! Don't do it, he's just a child!" a man could be heard screaming.

Tess slowly opened her eyes and wished she didn't. Everything on her hurt. She looked down to see that her legs were broken but held straight with a splint. Her arm and shoulder blade were broken as well. Her head spun, then she looked at her left arm to see an ivy in it and a clear bag that said moonshine on it. *'Okay, that explains why I'm light headed and dizzy; but I'm still in pain. Fuck.'* She continued to look around to see that she was chained to the floor in a brown lazy boy chair. She looked down and could see Sabrina, the little girl she tried to save, setting in the floor next to her scraping something. Tess looked out her room door. Habib held his daughter close to him along with a little boy. The boy held onto him for dear life. A Mexican woman cried and screamed "No!", and Iris hit her in the head with the butt of her gun. She fell onto the bed, then Iris pulled the little boy out of Habib's arms. Habib tried pulling him back and Iris aim the gun at his daughter.

"Look, its him or your daughter. You pick!" Iris said through gritted teeth. Habib cried uncontrollably before he stopped pulling and held his daughter tight.

"Uncle Habib! Uncle Habib!" the boy cried out as Iris grabbed him.

"Look at me! Look at me!" she shouted and bent down to the boy's height. "Your bother is dead. I'm sorry, but that means I have no more use for you." Iris said then hit him hard with the palm of her hand in his face, breaking the bridge of his nose and making it travel upwards and pierce his brain, killing him instantly.

"Nooo! No!" Tess screamed and tried to move but couldn't.

"Hey baby. I'm glad to see you're up. I'll turn up the dose of your meds up so you can go back to sleep. You need your rest love." Iris said while smiling and shut the room door.

"Now, where am I? How'd I get here?" Tess asked herself.

"The crazy red hair lady and the Indian man saved us before the building came all the way down and killed us. She brought us to a house." Sabrina said.

Tess look down and forgot she was there. "How long have we been here?" Tess asked.

"I think a week." Sabrina replied.

"Fuck! No, not this. Not this." Tess said as tears flowed down her cheeks and she cried hysterically. Sabrina stood up and use her little hands to whip her tears.

"Don't cry. We will escape her just like I got away from the other crazy woman Catalina. We just have to wait for the right time; and the crazy red hair lady messed up already, she only keeps feeding us chicken." Sabrina said and opened her hand to show Tess four jail made knives made of chicken bones. Sabrina smiled. "We just have to wait for the right time." she said, passing one of the bones to Tess before hiding the other three.

Iris came into the room and looked from Sabrina to Tess. In her hand was a box of Popeye's chicken and biscuits. she hand it to Sabrina then turned on the moonshine drip.

"No." Tess moaned as the drug made her weak and sleepy.

She looked at Iris leave the room then at Sabrina on the floor peeling the meat off a chicken bone smiling, which was the last thing she saw before losing consciousness.

Epilogue

The Pleasure of Pain 5: Harmony B's Story. Zoe life or No Life

"Girl, you're bold and beautiful." Jimmy said, talking to Tasha on the corner with his friends Raw dog and Sammy behind him rooting him on.

"Boy, you say that to all the girls; and any way Jimmy, you don't have enough money to deal with me. I like older men who give big gifts. Jewelry, nice watches. Are you gonna float some diamonds or what?" Tasha asked.

Tash was short with green eyes, a high yellow skin complexion, and a thick shape. She'd been living on the same block as Jimmy in North Miami since she and Jimmy were in kindergarten.

"What you mean, we're the same age?" Jimmy said as a red drop top Mercedes Benz with 24inch big gold rims. pulled up.

"And that's the problem. I only fuck with grown ass men." Tasha said and walked to the red Mercedes Benz. "Hey baby." Tasha said to Lynch.

"What I tell you about talking to any other man but me?" Lynch asked.

"Psst, you tripping. Them little boys. Let's go." Tasha said hopping into the passenger seat.

Lynch looked past her then stepped out his car and walk up to Jimmy and his little crew. Everyone knew who Lynch was. He was twenty-five and ran with the

Zoe Pound in Miami, who controlled most of the neighborhoods.

"What I tell y'all about standing in this corner?!" Lynch barked.

"We not selling no drugs, and we're Hattians as well." Jimmy replied.

"Fool, you're only half Haitian, you don't count; and like I said, you and your little friends can't stay on the corners." Lynch stated.

"Man, we're the Terrorist Boyz, we don't have to listen to no one." Jimmy said.

Lynch pulled out his gun and hit jimmy in the head with it, knocking him to the ground. Lynch pointed the gun at him then at his crew who raise their hands and backed up.

"Lynch, no. Please no." Tasha cried out from the passenger side of the car.

"I kill niggas for less. Your little seventeen-year-old ass don't know what power is. This is power here!" Lynch said, hitting Jimmy with the gun again. "If I see you or your friends on this corner or talking to my bitch again, there won't be no words. You punk ass nigga." Lynch said then spit on Jimmy and smiled then walked back to his car.

"I'm sorry." Tasha mouthed looking at Jimmy on the ground as the car pulled off.

Raw dog walked over to pick up Jimmy off the ground. "One day we'll get older, control everything and have the bitches like Lynch." Rawdog said.

"Fuck that, we going get ours now." Jimmy replied while getting up and wiping his eyes.

"How?" Sammy asked.

"Easy. Get some of the crew together. Lynch taught me where the power's at." Jimmy replied.

Jimmy sat in the stolen station wagon with Rawdog next to him. He kept his foot pressed hard on the break while stepping on the gas. He threw the car in reverse and the tires squealed as the car did a burn out, leaving smoke in the air. As he let go of the break, the station wagon drove backwards at high speed, crashing into the window and door of Arrowhead's Gun & Pawn shop. Once the window and door came down, five members of Jimmy's crew ran in with heavy duty garbage bags and crowbars, breaking the glass display and filling the bags with guns and bullets. The store's alarm continued to go off, sounding like a loud school bell.

"Hurry! Hurry!" jimmy said as they filled the back of the station wagon with the guns, and the stolen Honda truck in the parking lot.

"We need to go!" Rawdog shouted.

"Get two more bags!" Jimmy replied.

They filled two more, hopped in the truck and station wagon, and pulled off just before the police showed up. Ten minutes later they met up at Jimmy's small house. Jimmy looked at the thirteen members of his crew, and at all the guns they'd just stolen.

"We got two hundred handguns, one hundred machine guns and forty-nine shotguns. We're rich. Once we sell this, we'll be able to buy cars with big rims. and new Jordan's." Sammy stated.

"Fuck no. You stupid." Jimmy replied. "We keeping this and growing the Terrorist Boyz to a new level. Think bigger." Jimmy said.

"Who put you in charge? Last I heard you was crying about Lynch knocking you out. We all put in work and stole these guns. I say we sell them on the street and to the Zoe Pound. I never had shit, and a car and jewelry would be nice." a tall brown skin guy said named Ronin. Jimmy checked a chrome 45 handgun. "What, I'm supposed to be scared? We all know you're a pussy. You won't do shit…" Ronin began, but his sentence was interrupted by a loud gunshot and a bullet slamming in to his knee cap shattering it in half. Ronin fell to the floor screaming. Jimmy squeezed the trigger and a huge hole open up his stomach.

"No, stop. Please stop!" Ronin scream and put his hands up. Jimmy stopped as Ronin begged.

"My name isn't Jimmy, it's Angel of death." Jimmy said and squeeze the trigger. The bullet travel, ripping through Ronin's hand and slammed into his forehead, splitting it in two. Jimmy look around. "Now, does anyone else have a problem with what I'm saying?" Jimmy asked as he looked at the rest of his crew.

Everyone shook their heads no. "Okay. Let's dump Ronin's body on the south side. Everyone takes one gun, and let's get started on to the next plan."

"Jimmy, what the next plan?" Sammy asked.

"My name is Angel now." Jimmy replied.

Lynch stopped at a corner and one of the Zoe crew walked up to the car, dropping a brown paper bag of money on Tasha's lap. "It better be all there." Lynch said.

"It is." the Zoe Pound gangster replied and walked back to the corner, selling a dime bag of crack to a crackhead.

Lynch's phone ring. "Answer it, and it better not be one of your hoes Lynch or I'll fuck you up." Tasha said.

"Bitch shut up. It's my mother." Lynch said looking at his iPhone screen. "Hey momma, what's happening'? I just gave you five stacks the other day, you can't be out that fast. I told you about buying things from Amazon all day.' Lynch said.

"No baby, it's not that. My chest hurts and I can't breathe. Please come fast." Lynch's mother said.

"Did you call the ambulance?" Lynch ask but heard the dial tone.

Lynch's heart raced as he thought of his father, he lost three years ago to a heart attack. His mother was in her early fifties, and his worse fear was losing her. Lynch stepped on the gas and sped through the back streets.

"Baby what's wrong? What's wrong?" Tasha ask once more.

"It's my mother. I think she's having a heart attack."

Lynch pulled up on the North side of Miami and shook his head. He tried to get his mother to move the nicer side of Miami, but she refuse to leave the home that she got with his father. Lynch hopped out the car, ran to the front door and took the keys out his pocket. He unlocked the door, and as soon as he stepped in something hit him in the back of the head knocking him to the ground as the door shut behind him. Lynch reached for his gun in his waist and felt the barrel of a gun to the back of his skull.

"Don't move." he heard a familiar voice say.

Lynch looked up to see six men in his mother's house not counting the one that was behind him. His hands was pulled behind him and zip tied tightly. One of the men rolled him over and took his gun off his waist.

"Are y'all stupid? Do y'all know who y'all playing with? I'm a Zoe Pound lieutenant. You all will die." Lynch said as one of them helped him up to his feet. "Where's my mother?!" Lynch shouted then began studying their faces and realize he recognized a lot of them from being the younger boys in the neighborhood that were between the ages of 15-18 years old.

"Jimmy that you? What the fuck are you doing? I'll fucking kill you. Zoe Pound don't play boy."

"Shut the fuck up." Jimmy said and hit him in the head with the gun, bursting open his forehead and blood start to gush out. "Take him to the bathroom." Jimmy order, and two of the armed men led him to the bathroom.

"When my sister find out about this y'all all dead!" Lynch shouted then stop talking once he made it to his mother's bathroom.

His eyes opened up wide. Blood was everywhere and his mother was in her favorite blue grown with her feet, hands and mouth duct taped. Her forehead had speed knots on it, and blood dripped from her mouth. She looked up at lynch while crying.

"What's wrong with y'all, that my mother? That's an elderly woman. That's not part of the streets rules." lynch said as tears streamed down his cheeks.

"Where you keep your drugs and money. If you tell me I won't kill your mother." Jimmy said.

"Fuck you!" Lynch shouted.

Jimmy smirk then aim at Lynch's mother's foot and blew a large hole in it. "Ahhhhh!" Lynch's mother try to scream but it was muffle by the duct tape over her mouth. Lynch went crazy trying to break the zip tie, hitting one of Jimmy's crew with his shoulder. Jimmy kick him and he fell onto his jaw with his hands still zip tied behind him, so there was no way to catch himself.

"Now let's try this again." Jimmy said.

"Okay Jimmy. Okay. Just don't hurt my mother. I don't keep nothing at my condo. That's stupid if cops rush me. I have my guns, money and drugs in storage unit. Number 232, down by Home Depot; and I stashed $50,000 in the pantry closet floor in this house. Now let my mother go Jimmy." Lynch said as Jimmy took the keys out of his pocket and throw them to Rawdog.

"You and Sammy go check the storage and text back if it's clear."

Rawdog shook his head and left follow by Sammy. Sammy returned pulling Tasha in the house and toward the bathroom. "I'm out." she was in his car." Sammy said and left Tasha standing next to two member of the Terrorizer Boyz crew. Jimmy turned around and looked at her. Tasha studied the whole situation. 'If I don't play this right, these nigga gonna kill me.' she thought to herself while looking at Lynch's mother in the bathtub crying and bleeding.

"What should we do with her?" one of Jimmy's boys asked.

"Zip tie her." Jimmy ordered.

"Wait! Wait Jimmy, don't. Please don't hurt me." Tasha cried.

"Why shouldn't I? Haven't I always been just a little boy to you? You've shown me no respect, so why should I respect your wishes?" Jimmy replied.

"Please don't hurt me." Tasha begged.

"Shut up." Jimmy ordered as his phone ring. He answered it, "Yes."

"It's all here." Rawdog replied.

"See, I told I keep my word Jimmy. Let my mother go." Lynch said from the floor.

"Hold him down." Jimmy order then walked over to the bathtubs and wrapped the shower curtain around Lynch's mother's face. She gasped for air and struggled as Jimmy choked her.

"No! No!" Lynch screamed and wiggle on the floor as two men held him down by his shoulders and he looked on in horror as his mother stop kicking and moving, dying with her mouth open and eyes. "Momma! Momma no!" Lynch screamed. "Jimmy I'm gonna kill you! I'm going fucking kill you and everything you love!" Lynch screamed like a crazy person and tried to break free of his zip ties but couldn't. Jimmy lift him up and stuff his head in the toilet.

"Fuck you!" Jimmy yelled. Lynch tried to breathe but couldn't and ended up swallowing pee water. He stopped moving and Jimmy spit on the back of his head. "Burn everything and let's go." Jimmy said, and his crew went to work pouring gasoline everywhere in the small house.

"What about her? one of the men asked pointing to Tasha, who was laying on her stomach on the floor.

Jimmy pointed his gun at her head. "Jimmy no. Please no." she cried.

"My name isn't Jimmy, it's Angel of death." Jimmy said and squeezed the trigger.

Chapter Two

Three weeks later…

Harmony sat in a truck with Jessica by her side. "I can't believe we survived that jump. I never thought we'd make it, but Layla's plan worked; but how do we find her and Suyung?" Jessica asked, but Harmony had tuned her out, all she could think about was Rose.

She tried to fight back the tears as images of her and Rose training together, cooking together and Rose telling jokes flooded her mind. Harmony pulled over to the side of the road and cried hysterically. "You drive." she said and got out the truck to walk to the passenger side as Jessica went to the driver's side. "But yes, we'll met up with Layla in Boston, that's the plan. Until then we don't need to contact each other. We just blew up a whole fucking building, that's going bring the FBI in to investigate. We gotta stay low for a while." Harmony said while trying to hold back tears, then her burner phone ring. She looked at it strange because only two people had that number, her mother and Blue Banger. She looked at the number to see it was her mother, so she answered.

"Hello mom. Is everything alright?"

"No, it's me Cha." the male voice said, and Harmony knew it was her gay cousin.

"What's going on? Where's my mother, is she okay?" Harmony asked as her heart raced.

"Harmony, you need to come home now." Cha said.

"Are my mother and brother okay?!" Harmony shouted.

"I can't say much on the phone right now, my life's in danger; but come home to Miami and find me." Cha said and the phone went dead.

Harmony called the number back, but it just rang and ring as a bubbly feeling was in her stomach. All she could think about was her mother and brother. "Fuck that, switch back over." Harmony said and crawled back into the driver seat as Jessica got back in the passenger seat.

"What happened? What's going on?" Jessica asked as Harmony got of an exit and got on the highway in the opposite direction. "Where we going? Boston's the other way."

"We're going to North Miami." Harmony said as she focused on driving.

Chapter Three

Death to The Teflon Divas

Dewan Jackson, also known as Bulldog was handcuff to the bed at Brooklyn Hospital, in a private room. Outside his room sat two police officers that both look to be sleeping, but no one notice the foam dripping out of there mouth and that they weren't breathing.

"That damn bitch." Bulldog said as flashbacks of Harmony killing his cousin played in his mind. He looked up to see a heavy-set nurse dressed in all grey scrubs. Bulldog looked at her strangely. She kinda looked like the fat woman from the movie Precious, and she was eating ice cream out of a small pint. She sucked on the spoon and Bulldog's facial twisted up in disgust.

"Boy, don't you look at me like that. I'm here to help you get what you really want." she stated.

"I don't think I want that." Bulldog replied while trying not to imagine having sex with her.

"You couldn't hit this if you wanted to. Your dick probably couldn't reach. I'm taking about revenge for your cousin and killing the bitch that put you here." the woman said, and her words caught Bulldog's attention.

"Here, take these keys. Uncuff yourself and put on this nurse's uniform. Let's go." the woman said.

"Who are you?" Bulldog askes as he uncuff himself and quickly put on the uniform.

"I'm Red Velvet, but you can call me Red for short. Now let's go kill that bitch that hurt us both." Red said as they made their way out the room and then the hospital.

True Glory Publications

IF YOU WOULD LIKE TO BE A PART OF
OUR TEAM AS AN AUTHOR, PLEASE SEND
YOUR SUBMISSIONS BY EMAILTO
TRUEGLORYPUBLICATIONS@GMAIL.COM.
PLEASE INCLUDE A BRIEF BIO, A SYNOPSIS OF
THE BOOK, AND THE FIRST THREE CHAPTERS.
SUBMIT USING MICROSOFT WORD WITH FONT
IN 11 TIMES NEW ROMAN.

Check out these other great books from the desk of National Best-Selling Author Shameek Speight

Hush

SHAMEEK A. SPEIGHT

AUTHOR OF A CHILD OF A CRACKHEAD SERIES

HUSH

She's Only 15

You're A Part of Me

YOU'RE A
PART OF ME

NATIONAL BESTSELLING AUTHOR
SHAMEEK A SPEIGHT
AUTOR OF A CHILD OF A CRACKHEAD SERIES

Made in the USA
Columbia, SC
28 April 2022

59575449R00347